Praise for *Hidden Moon*

"*Hidden Moon* reads more like a spy novel by a Korean Kafka. Final word: Fascinating."

—*Rocky Mountain News*

"Church's spartan prose is a perfect match for the sparseness of the North Korean landscape."

—*The Charleston Gazette*

"With wit and efficiency, Church masterfully evokes the challenges of enforcing the law in an authoritarian society and weds the intriguing atmosphere to a fast-moving and engaging plot."

—*Publishers Weekly*

"Nothing short of brilliant."

—*Library Journal*

"While [*A Corpse in the Koryo*] invited comparisons to Martin Cruz Smith and Robert Janes, this second in the series makes it clear no comparisons are necessary: this series stands on its own."

—*Booklist*

Critical Acclaim for *A Corpse in the Koryo*

"*A Corpse in the Koryo* is a crackling good mystery novel, filled with unusual characters involved in a complex plot that keeps you guessing to the end."

—Glenn Kessler, *The Washington Post*

"The best unclassified account of how North Korea works and why it has survived. . . . This novel should be required bedtime reading for President Bush and his national security team."

—Peter Hayes, Executive Director of the Nautilus Institute for Security and Sustainable Development

HIDDEN MOON

Also by James Church

A Corpse in the Koryo

HIDDEN MOON

An Inspector O Novel

JAMES CHURCH

Thomas Dunne Books
St. Martin's Minotaur ♊ New York

This is a work of fiction. All of the characters, organizations, and events portrayed in this novel are either products of the author's imagination or are used fictitiously.

THOMAS DUNNE BOOKS.
An imprint of St. Martin's Press.

HIDDEN MOON. Copyright © 2007 by James Church. All rights reserved. Printed in the United States of America. For information, address St. Martin's Press, 175 Fifth Avenue, New York, N.Y. 10010.

www.thomasdunnebooks.com
www.stmartins.com

Map by Paul J. Pugliese

Library of Congress Cataloging-in-Publication Data

Church, James.
    Hidden moon : an Inspector O novel / James Church.—1st St.
Martin's Minotaur pbk. ed.
        p. cm.
    ISBN-13: 978-0-312-38766-2
    ISBN-10: 0-312-38766-0
    1. Korea (North)—Officials and employees—Fiction. 2. Pyongyang (Korea)—Fiction.
3. Bank robberies—Fiction. I. Title.
PS3603.H88H53 2007
813'.6—dc22

                                                                                2007024593

First St. Martin's Minotaur Paperback Edition: November 2008

10 9 8 7 6 5 4 3 2 1

For Mr. Kaufman
With thanks

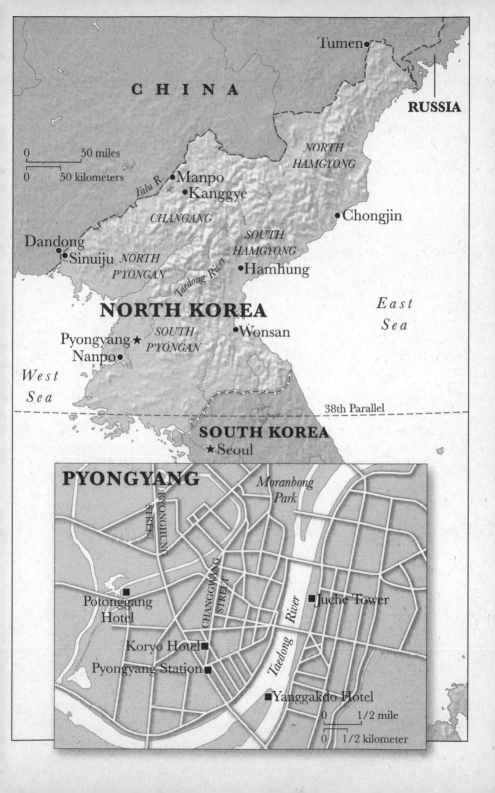

PART I

Chapter One

The afternoon lay strangled in a gloom of Chinese dust. Brown light, brown shadows twisted slowly over a naked riverbed. A kilometer or so beyond—distances were hard to judge against the dim, muddied horizon—a dirt path struggled up a hillside, pulling a reluctant village of broken, brown-roofed houses. A crumbling embankment crept by. A man's head appeared. His blank eyes stared into the passing windows, then looked away, his face dusty, lungs and mouth and teeth and thoughts all gone to brown dust.

Suddenly, laughter broke out in the coach; a few passengers moved to get a better view. One woman, her voice too loud, shouted, "There!" From nowhere, a flash of color became the shiny red boots of a small girl, her hair flying behind, arms pumping, breathlessly leaping, soaring across a single patch of newly turned, black-furrowed earth. The girl waved, both hands above her head; the passengers clapped and knocked on the windows. The whistle sounded. For a moment, it pierced the shroud, and then, suddenly, it was gone. People returned to their reading, sleeping, drinking tea, anything to make the time pass. The train creaked around a bend; the red boots disappeared from view. One or two watched for another sign of spring, a forsythia bud or the faint feathered green of a distant willow. But there was nothing to see besides the wind, wandering through fields of rotting brown stubble. It was too soon. Even late March was too soon. And there was still too much damned dust in the air.

2

Turning from the window, I realized a man in the aisle was standing quite still, staring at me. He smiled absently when he caught my eye and nodded as if we were acquainted. For a moment, I thought he might sit down and begin a conversation, but he walked past and into the next car without a word. It was hard to tell if he had a limp or if it was just the coach swaying. I settled back to try to sleep, but the image of the riverbed stared from the edge of consciousness. Rivulets of stone fed pebbled ponds; great rivers of rock flowed to a bouldered ocean that never knew the moon. A man was walking along the gravel shore. As he passed he glanced at me, and his sallow face became a sallow sky; the image was unnerving, and worse, it would not go away. I sat up again and looked around, but the man who had been staring at me was nowhere in sight. He had been wearing a brown cloth cap, a workman's cap, though he didn't carry himself like a workman. There was something self-assured about him; his smile never broke even when our eyes met. I had felt off guard for an instant, but he didn't waver; it was as if he had been waiting for me to turn to around, to measure my reaction at being observed.

The more I thought about it, the more I realized that the idle smile on the man's lips reminded me of a boyhood friend who wore a similar look when listening to the wind in the line of trees that marked the edge of our village. Often I had watched from a distance, wondering why he was smiling. Then one day I realized it wasn't happiness but despair, a vacant smile attached to nothing, leading nowhere.

My friend, let's call him Chung, was a year older than I, a head taller, with long legs that gave him a gait I could match only by taking a small hop every few steps. He ran faster, jumped higher, than anyone else in the village. We were neighbors, his house close to my grandfather's. Chung's father had been killed in the war, somewhere in the mountains on the east coast in the brutal winter of 1950. His mother never remarried. She was small and maybe a little crazy, a woman who kept to herself and rarely talked to other people except to worry aloud about her son's health. She need not have bothered; he was never sick.

The summer before Chung and I joined the army together, we were both sent to a large cooperative farm about a hundred kilometers away to help tend the fields. Twice a month, when propaganda teams came by, we could sit on rough benches after dinner to watch a silent film playing shadows on the cracked wall of a whitewashed shed. The crickets sang but then grew still, listening to the click-click-click of the sprockets being torn, one after another, by the old projector. That was how Chung's eyes flickered when he looked at you, a broken film playing on a hot summer night.

I turned back to gaze out the window. No, I decided, the man in the aisle was a stranger; we didn't know each other. His smile meant nothing. At last I dozed, until with a groan and hiss of brakes the coaches bumped each other in protest, then came to rest. Stepping down to the platform, I shouldered my bag and made my way to the square in front of the station, wondering where to go to escape the windy gloom that swept the city. I set off toward a small restaurant a few blocks away, near the Koryo Hotel, where they served plain food, simple and cheap, a bowl of soup and, if they had any, a piece of fish. I needed something to wash the dust out of my throat. I needed to sit where the diners ate quietly, a place where, unlike in Beijing, people didn't chatter loudly to no purpose. The street was deserted; no neon signs assaulted the dark. Two cars passed slowly, their lights off. It felt good to be home.

3

Min stood in the doorway of my office, watching me sand a scrap of oak. It was from the side of a blanket chest we'd found in an apartment abandoned by a smuggling ring. They might have been Ukrainian; we never knew for sure. The place had been empty for weeks. The smugglers knew we were on their trail almost before we realized they existed. It hadn't bothered me, missing a band of foreign crooks, but the Ministry wasn't pleased. Everyone who worked on the case eventually found an unflattering note in his file. The gang had used an axe on the blanket chest and on the few other pieces of furniture in the apartment as well. It was their way of telling us to keep our distance. The chest deserved better. I salvaged what I could; no sense wasting completely good oak.

I could tell from the way he fidgeted that Min had something to say. He was waiting for me to acknowledge his presence. After a minute or two, he coughed, a sign of surrender. "Pardon me, Professor." Min sometimes used mild sarcasm to cover a retreat. "If we're not too busy, if we're settled again in the office after our vacation, perhaps we could discuss police business." He paused for dramatic effect, one last effort to recapture the offensive. "There's been a bank robbery."

For a moment the sound of the sandpaper scratched at the quiet afternoon. " 'We' weren't on a vacation," I said at last. " 'We' were on a delegation." I turned the oak over a few times in my hand to check for rough spots before looking up to acknowledge his main point. "A bank what, did you say?"

"The central file must still have you listed as liaison. Why would they send an inspector on a delegation like that?"

"I just go where they tell me, Min."

"Right. Remind me to check next time I'm near the file room." He gave me a sly look. "Did you go out to any of those bars? Supposed to be some good places in Beijing."

I nodded. "Supposed to be. Get yourself on a delegation sometime."

Min shrugged. "The furthest I ever go is Nampo to deal with drunken sailors. Did I tell you about the one that got left by his captain, off one of those foreign ships?"

"Once or twice."

"Out of curiosity, what is it you do on those trips? Your reports don't say."

"I sit a lot. Give advice."

"You?"

"People always want to know where other people are. Sometimes they don't even ask. They walk in, I point."

"That's it?"

"No. Occasionally it gets exciting. Someone needs something. I go and get it."

"Fine." Min walked over to my window, which looks onto the front gate and the street. "Don't tell me what you do." He turned and stared outside. "Nice view," he said. He was gathering his thoughts, and I wasn't expected to say anything. Finally, he turned back to me. "Someone robbed the bank. I think it's called a 'heist.'" He used an English term, something he rarely did, and then rubbed his broad forehead as he considered whether this was the right word. "Or maybe 'feist.' You don't watch the movies? I thought they had them on all the damn TVs in those fancy hotels in Beijing."

"I was hardly in the room. The delegation was always in meetings."

"So it said in your report."

I let that pass. "To tell the truth, I don't know what you're talking about. Have we ever had a bank robbery here? None that I can recall, at least, not since I've been in the Ministry."

"A long time."

"Too long." I blew the sawdust off the oak and held it up to the light. Oak takes time getting smooth, especially a piece that has been axed into splinters. Even under the best circumstances, you have to be relaxed to tackle oak. If you also have to restore a sense of dignity to the wood, to coax it back to life, that takes even more concentration. If you're not feeling patient, my grandfather would say, leave oak alone. I looked up again at Min. He didn't look patient.

"There's nothing in the training manual about bank robberies." I pointed at the green-covered book on the floor behind me. It had been there when I came into the office years ago, and there had never been a reason to disturb it. "That means no standard procedures, no approved plan of operations. I wouldn't know where to start." I turned the piece of wood around a couple of more times in my hand and then tossed it into the out-box. "In fact"—I smiled because it was almost true—"I'm not even sure where the bank is."

Some people might have frowned. Min's expression didn't change. Instead, he clasped his hands behind his back and began a familiar ritual, pacing in front of my desk. Since he became chief inspector two years ago, the rhythm never varied, spring or winter, sunshine or rain. Four steps up, a slow turn, a glance out my door into the empty hall, then four steps back. Two revolutions, never three, then he would speak. "Don't play dumb, Inspector. The bank is in your district. You drive by every day, and you know it. The Ministry says this needs to be solved quickly or it will scare away foreign investors. Our job is to keep them safe and happy. If we become known as a country where bank robberies go unpunished, investment will dry up, the flow of good things to those for whom good things are required will slow, and the Ministry of People's Security will be blamed." He stopped pacing and gave me a meaningful look. "Obviously, the Minister's head is on the line."

"Aha, the main point."

"No, Inspector. Not the main point." He started moving again, but more slowly, more deliberately. If he resumed pacing, it usually meant the conversation would be extended. "The main point is . . ."

"Why don't you sit down, Min?" I pointed to a chair.

This time he did frown, slightly. He didn't like to sit in my office; he thought it broke the sense of hierarchy, what little we had. Frowning or not, at least he was standing still. "The main point," he said, "is that I want the crime solved. Yes, I've been away on other business for the past week, but I've not been idle. I've been in meetings." The silence was heavy. I let it sink, content to wait for Min to turn, look out the door, and then finish his thought. "Important meetings."

"Bank robberies," I said, "are rarely solved. Certainly not in meetings, however important." The phrasing was delicate because there was no sense antagonizing Min over this point. He thought meetings were a key to the well-being of the office. To me they were a waste of time. We chalked it up to personal style, though I suspected it was something more, a character defect on his part.

"So! You are familiar with bank robberies. I thought you didn't know what I was talking about. No movies, you said."

"Not from movies, from television, which I watch at the Foreign Ministry to keep up on the foreign news. We have to go there since— just to remind you—all we have in this office is a radio. A radio with bad reception, to say nothing about the choice of programs." I watched the complaint walk out the door, without Min even nodding in its direction. "From what I've seen, every civilized country has bank robberies. It helps the circulation of money, one theory goes. You never heard of Robin Hood? Or John Dillinger?"

"Why are you hanging around the Foreign Ministry? You have no business there these days." Min sniffed the air suspiciously. "Do you?"

"Liaison." It was the right response. The chief inspector likes to hear we are being modern, keeping up contacts with other departments, studying the latest international police techniques, learning the jargon. He grunted, so I continued. "The liaison officer has a TV in his office. Some ministries do actually supply equipment to their people." I looked around my office to indicate where there was space for a television. "I don't know what he watches most of the time, but you can hear him switching to the news when he thinks someone is coming down the hall."

Min looked at me, then at my out-box, then turned without a word and walked back to his office. I closed my eyes. It was a wonderful spring day, the first Friday in an April of peace and calm; the air was fresh, the trees were budding, and I had nothing to do. My phone rang. It was Min. "Wake up and get in here. We need to talk." He lowered his voice. "Who is this Di Lin Ger character?"

4

Min was leaning back in his chair, fingers laced behind his round head, his eyes half closed. With anyone else, this posture might have been a show of dominance, a touch of boredom to signal supreme disinterest in any conversation we were about to have. That wasn't Min's style. In all the time we'd worked together, he had never been overweening. Twenty years ago, when he was promoted to senior inspector, he pretended it didn't mean anything and was careful never to let his old friends think his nose was in the air. When the Ministry was reorganized and he was handed the job of my unit's chief inspector, he waded in carefully. For several months, he didn't rearrange the pictures on the walls of his office; he even left the old calendar up well into the new year, just to make the point he was not trying to clean house. Min was not a man impressed with his own authority. This is why I liked him, for all our differences. His heart was in the right place, and that counted for something.

Though he never said so, I knew that Min had not expected to rise this far in the chain of command. He never would have but for the death of my former chief, Pak Su In, shot four times in a short, deadly gun battle with a Military Security squad that didn't know he was armed and suffered its own casualties as a result. The incident, which officially never happened, led to the dismissal of the elderly Minister of People's Security. The Minister's replacement, a much younger man who never offended anyone in his life, was ordered to find someone to fill Pak's vacant post, and to make sure—very, very sure—it was someone with no hidden strengths. Min was a realist. He knew why he had been picked, and he never pretended otherwise.

On one thing, though, Min did place modest emphasis, the prerogatives of his title, and here I did not fault him. Deference to a title was important, he said, because if we in the frontline Ministry offices did not observe a clear hierarchy and sense of order, how the hell could the people on the streets be expected to do so? Ritual, he liked to say, was the basis of civilization; a system of beliefs was what separated man from other animals. The phrase "other animals" came out with a certain grim satisfaction.

One of Min's central beliefs—where it came from, he probably did not know—was that it was proper and necessary for "power" to be seated. He never paced around his own desk. Whatever people might think of him personally, he used to remind me, he was a chief inspector, and chief inspector bottoms belonged on chairs when the job called for addressing subordinates. Min was a smart man, he was cautious, and he preferred to sit.

There was a moment of serenity while I waited at the edge of his office. It was pleasant to lounge against the door frame, looking beyond Min and out the window that overlooked the courtyard separating our offices from the Operations Building. The two tall gingko trees in the corner had no leaves yet, but the tips of their branches were supple with promise. Pak had loved those trees. He had waited eagerly through each dreary winter to see them come alive in spring. Every October, he would stare out the window for long, quiet minutes. It was sweet mourning, he said, the way the leaves turned gold in the dying sun. One summer, the Ministry had sent two workmen over to cut the trees down. Pak demanded to see the orders, which said something about how the branches were scraping the sides of the building and the roots would make it difficult to lay pipes between the buildings—as if any pipes would ever be laid. Pak gave the workmen five US dollars each, signed the work order on the "completed as instructed" line, and told them not to come around anymore. Min, by contrast, paid no attention to the courtyard trees; he said he'd seen enough wood during his army days to last a lifetime.

When he realized I was standing at his door, Min sat up and looked at me uneasily, as if surprised to find me there. "Eh, Inspector," he said at last, "thank you for coming."

No matter we had seen each other less than two minutes before, or that he had just called me to his office. He liked to begin these sessions this way, with a certain practiced formality. I nodded. It did no harm to play along with these rituals, because in truth, Min had no hold over me. On paper, even on the creased, outdated organization chart that hung on the wall beside his desk, he was my superior. But we both realized that on what really counted, the advantage was mine. I had longer service in the Ministry and understood things about its scuffed corridors that he did not. He needed me; I didn't need him. Reduced to brutally simple terms, if I retired, he would be assigned one of the new breed of police inspectors—total recall of new regulations, very concerned with promotion, little experience, and no sense. This, Chief Inspector Min did not want.

"I was serious about the robbery." Min opened a folder and pretended to read. "It happened Wednesday before last, about noon. Why the duty officer didn't bother to look in the daily file and alert you, I'll never know." From the way he squinted, it was clear he was skipping over details he didn't want to tell me. It was equally clear he was not telling me the truth. There had been nothing in the duty file about a bank robbery. But he knew that I knew he was lying, so it didn't bother me. He was trying to get to the point, and the best way there happened to be through a minor bending of fact. "The Gold Star Bank. They used to deal in foreign investment, illegal currency swaps, funding overseas operations." He looked up to make sure I was listening. "Last year, they saw which way the wind was blowing with all of this talk about new economic realities, so they set up a section for domestic customers—savings accounts for merchants who will stand in line for hours to deposit the week's profits. Some of the local foreign businessmen opened euro accounts rather than keep stacks of cash in their hotel rooms. Nothing was insured. Why bother? Who ever thought a bank would be robbed in safe, gray Pyongyang."

In a heartbeat, I knew we didn't want to get saddled with this case. The lack of entry in the duty log could have been an oversight. But if everything else Min had said so far was true, the Ministry wasn't remotely interested in a solution as such; they wanted a political problem solved for political reasons, having to do with the current tides in the capital. Ocean tides were reliable and predictable, pretty much a function of the moon. Political tides were more complicated, and usually more dangerous.

Convincing Min to throw the case in the bottom drawer and forget about it would be difficult, but nothing was impossible; well, not this, anyway. The Ministry could be pacified eventually, and all would be well in our little sector of the world. "Yes, good question," I said. "Who would have thought there would be a bank robbery in the capital?"

"Someone obviously did, Inspector." Min closed the folder as if it were a precious old book and laid his hand atop it, to keep the facts from flying out. "Somebody thought about it, they planned it, and then they executed it. In broad daylight. In your district, I might add, with silk stockings over their faces. That must have been a sight. Witnesses say they sounded like Koreans but not from Pyongyang. Some in the Ministry apparently think they might have been Chagang people. It's possible, I suppose, though I don't think there is anyone in Chagang smart enough to conceive something like this. You haven't heard a peep from your contacts?"

Min was Pyongyang born and bred. He thought this one of the luckiest things in his life, being born in Pyongyang, and seemed prouder of that than of being a chief inspector. Not surprisingly, he had a low opinion of anyone from the provinces, even if they outranked him. If he had to, he could leash his contempt. I'd seen him do it more than once with the Ministry's senior party secretary, a wiry, bad-tempered man from North Hamgyong—the only place

Min considered even more backward than Chagang. During army service, Min had been stationed in the mountains of Chagang. He was tight-lipped about what he did, but he made it plain the place hadn't rubbed him the right way. He never had a good thing to say about it, or anyone he met there. Whenever we had a few drinks, he made especially unflattering comments about Chagang women.

I didn't care where people thought the robbers were from; in fact, the last thing I wanted was a discussion of the suspects. "My contacts are relaxing in the sweetness of the season, those able to buy their way out of going down to help the farmers for a few weeks." This was where I needed to plant a seed of doubt in Min's mind. "I have to say, already something about this case smells funny to me. This robbery—if that is what it was—happened over a week ago. There was nothing in the duty file"—I watched, but Min's face didn't change expression—"so why is the Ministry only getting around today to asking us to begin an investigation? By now, the people in those stockings could be anywhere. It seems to me that this isn't going to get solved, not at our level, and we would be doing ourselves a big favor to let it expire from inattention."

"Could be; the suspects could be anywhere, as you say." I had a momentary surge of optimism that we were about to drop the whole thing. "But in fact"—Min's eyes darted into the hallway, then slid back to me tinged with conspiracy—"one of them isn't. Keep this to yourself, Inspector. He's not just anywhere, he's somewhere specific, by which I mean, specifically in the morgue."

"This is a secret?" It was painfully clear that Min was not going to let go of this as easily as I'd hoped. There was more to it than he'd first let on. If the bastards had all vanished without a trace, skipped back to wherever they were from, it would have been one thing. But now it appeared we had a body, and that would complicate matters. When there was a body, there was liable to be paperwork, and if there was paperwork, boxes would have to be checked.

"No, Inspector, it is not exactly a secret, but we want to be discreet about this case. The fellow was hit by a bus, one of those new red double-deckers someone is shipping in from overseas." He paused to consider this fact. "I doubt if the import approvals are in order, but that's not our problem, bus imports."

I nodded but said nothing. If I waited, Min would find his way back to the main point.

"The bank robber had run out of the bank and was in the middle of the street when someone—perhaps one of the foreign businessmen lolling around—pointed out he hadn't taken the silk stocking off his face." Min gestured at an imaginary mask. "So he stopped to remove it. That was the wrong thing to do, in the middle of the street, in front of a new red double-decker bus traveling, I'm reliably informed, at a high rate of speed. Where did a gang of bank robbers get silk stockings, do you suppose?"

"Was the gang from Chagang? Maybe they got the stockings there."

Min snorted. "They don't have silk stockings in Chagang, Inspector. The women all wear baggy pants and have sunburned faces. Besides, we don't know where they were from." He made an odd noise with his lips, an expression of annoyance at my attempt to goad him. "No one knows, but I can tell you, this one fellow won't be going back there, wherever it is. He didn't do well against the bus." Min looked down at his desk and shifted uncomfortably in his chair. "I was called to the morgue this morning before you came in." The chief inspector did not like corpses and hated the morgue. He only went there under extraordinary circumstances. I mentally filed away the bad news that someone had convinced him that this case was extraordinary. "I didn't actually see the body, of course, they wouldn't let me, but they showed me a photo, several photos, actually."

A warning flag went up. Where was the body? "And you didn't press the point, I suppose."

"What point?" Min looked at me with a hint of concern, a minute lifting of the eyebrows that no more disturbed his placid exterior than a wispy cloud might mar the sky at dusk.

"Let me review, just so I have it straight." My presentation had to be subtle; it was important that the chief inspector never know what hit him. I repeated a few points; sometimes it helps to say things to Min more than once. "This feist, assuming that is what it was, happened several days ago. Nothing was reported to us." The passive was the safest route here. Min didn't twitch. "It happened in our sector, but we were not informed. We might even say that the news was withheld." Again the passive; again I paused. Min offered no protest, though his brow suggested a notch more concern. "You were brought into the case this morning and called to the morgue—a place you hate to go." Min rocked slightly from side to side in confirmation. "When you got there, they wouldn't let you see the body. Maybe they don't even have it anymore. They showed you pictures, all no doubt taken in poor light with an old camera." Again, no protest. "All of this you are instructed to mention to me only now, at lunchtime." I looked at my watch, and Min glanced at his. "After lunch, actually. I'm telling you, it doesn't sound like there is much urgency to this thing. And if I were suspicious, I'd say there are already signs it belongs in category three."

When he heard the term "category three," Min pursed his lips and closed his eyes, his brow still minutely troubled. Over the years, completely out of channels, a classification system for cases had grown up among the sector-level inspectors. The Ministry often sent down memos warning against the use of this unsanctioned system, only reinforcing suspicions that it was pretty close to accurate. Category one cases were simple enough—those we were expected to investigate and, where possible, solve. Category two cases were those we were expected to be seen as investigating but not to solve. Category three cases were those we were to avoid—leave every stone unturned. In fact, for a category three case, it was best not even to record that there were any stones. No records, no files, no nothing.

A moment later, Min's brow cleared of concern when he realized I was not questioning his judgment but something larger, beyond his control. What was beyond his control—like bus imports—did not worry him. Category three cases never worried him. "Leave it in the compost heap, Inspector," he'd say when we were faced with a case that screamed at us to steer clear. "Let nature take its course."

I waited for Min to mention the compost heap. Instead, I heard, "But what if this is not category three, Inspector?" There was an undertone of petulance in his voice I didn't like. "The Ministry has made it plain to me there is plenty of urgency to this one. Plenty of it. This file here"—he picked up the file and waved it like a cardboard battle flag—"is marked 'Urgent.' But there is also, shall we say, caution at the upper levels."

"Caution." The word hung in the air between us. "First discretion. Then caution. In equal measure, I suppose?"

Min rocked slightly in his chair, another small sign of annoyance. The chief inspector was not a man of grand gestures. Especially when he was seated, you had to pay attention to know what was going on in his nervous system. "I was told," he said, "and this is all informal and just between us, that at first some thought . . ." He paused and regrouped for a moment. "Careful consideration, let us call it, was given to pretending the entire episode never happened." He looked to make sure I was following his train of thought. "But there were seen to be a number of problems with that course, especially in this enlightened age of fresh ideas and new realities." If Min was hoping I would nod in agreement, he was disappointed. He continued, "In the old days, this episode at the bank would have been declared a nonevent, nothing more said. We would have been instructed, quietly and discreetly, to keep our ears open for rumors of anyone with extra spending money. Either we would have found them, or we wouldn't. But that was then, this is now."

"Maybe so, but I'd say that having someone with a silk stocking over his head riding on the front of a double-decker bus . . ."

"Red."

". . . a red double-decker bus in the middle of the day would get noticed. Rumors would start going around."

"Oh, yes. It is worse than that, let me tell you, Inspector. An English businessman about to enter the bank stopped at the front door for some unknown reason and saw the whole thing. Maybe he's the one who made the fatal suggestion that the robber remove the stocking from his face. By now, the whole damned foreign community has heard the story from this Englishman, and they have heard it in detail. More detail than, in fact, actually exists. They're spinning tales about it, laughing over drinks in their snobby bars. This is what comes of opening to the outside. Too many eyes that don't know when to look the other way. Too many eyes, too many round eyes." He shook his head. "And then what? Options fade, exits close, impossible orders come down to the Ministry from above, and before you know it, they pass through the Ministry like a dinner of bad fish and land, at last, on us."

Min pinched the bridge of his broad nose. "Us," he said in a resigned tone. His eyelids fluttered delicately. They did that sometimes. I often wondered if it was a practiced gesture. It had to be done just right; otherwise it would look like a nervous tic. "The whole damned foreign community knows," he said, "and you, the inspector whose district includes the bank, have heard nothing?" He was suddenly silent, and then he made that noise again with his lips. I had a feeling I knew where we were heading. "I have on this badge, as you can easily see, Inspector." He pointed at his chest. "It is said to signify our allegiance and great respect for those to whom we offer such things without question."

I had to admit, this was another mark in Min's favor—irony. He was good at it, almost masterful. Anyone looking at a transcript of his remarks could never accuse him of anything. But anyone who heard him could not mistake what he felt.

"You, on the other hand"—his eyes settled on my shirt—"are naked in that regard. Well, I usually don't give a damn what you do once you leave this building, but before you go out the front door on this investigation, especially this investigation, you will find your own badge somewhere in your desk amidst all the wood shavings and you will put it on. Am I clear?"

There was a silence that seemed best unbroken. Min rarely pressed anymore on the badge, a small portrait of one or the other of the Leaders. I never wore it when I was on duty. I rarely had it with me off duty, either. The failure to wear it on a regular basis went into my file every once in a while, but no one followed up. I was the grandson of a Hero of the Republic, the flesh and blood of a revolutionary from the glorious struggle against the Japanese. In the years I grew up in his house, this national hero, my grandfather, told me stories about the early days, about events and people. He had a great store of rumors. I learned plenty, and I remembered details. Even now, half a century later, a number of still-important individuals didn't care to have those details repeated.

Displaying the pin was not so much the problem; it had nothing to do with politics. The problem, frankly, was putting it on every morning. I didn't like the little holes it left in my shirt or the way it pricked my finger. So it stayed in my desk drawer in a relatively honorable location near the front. I made a show of considering Min's request, put my hands in my pockets and rocked back on my heels.

"Anything else I should know?" I probably should have rephrased what came next. "Like, for instance, what you aren't telling me?"

Min massaged his temples. The battle of the badge had been fought again, to no avail. He cut his losses, as he always did, by letting it drop. "You know what I know, Inspector." This was another lie, but it was only of a bureaucratic sort, nothing malicious or personal. The file Min had been waving over his head was practically empty. If it had three pieces of paper in it, I would have been surprised. The Ministry didn't know much more, or they wouldn't have assigned us the case. If it was really so sensitive, they would have handled it themselves, putting together a special squad under the Minister's direct supervision in a concerted attempt to keep the State Security Department from moving in and taking the case away from us.

"One last thing, Inspector." Min adopted a tone that meant he hoped I would accept what he said without comment and go off to do as he instructed. It was a forlorn hope, but he clung to it. "The Minister wants a solution by the end of the month."

"That's not so far away." I looked around for a calendar. There was none. The chief inspector thought the photographs were too posed and the colors unreal. "You ever seen cheeks that red?" he would ask. We soon learned it was a rhetorical question.

Min sat back and closed his eyes. He knew I didn't work well with deadlines. "Just be glad this didn't happen in February. We'd have even fewer days to solve it."

"Are we done?"

"I am." Min smiled, a little grimly, the sort of thing a man with his eyes closed will do. "I'm done. You are just getting started. I want daily reports." There was no sense giving orders if he couldn't see their effect; his eyes opened, reluctantly. "Daily means every day, incidentally. We'll finally get to use those new forms the Ministry distributed in January. They have to be filed in multiple copies, so press hard when you fill them out. But not too hard, or the paper will tear."

"What if I fill out a batch for you right now: 'Nothing to report.' It could save time. This is category three, trust me."

"Solve this, Inspector, all will be merry, they will sing your praises. The Ministry wants it solved. Screw it up, and I will be instructed to write your transfer order, in multiple copies, to someplace cold and lonely."

This wasn't much of a threat. He would sooner slit his wrists than transfer me. But it was all he could think of at the moment, I could tell. "Is this the new management style we keep hearing about? Very effective." I grinned at him, but he wasn't about to let me break the mood. He looked somber, almost painfully so. "Alright," I said, after deciding there was no way around it for the moment. "Only one thing I need."

"What's that?" Though he long ago accepted his limitations, at heart, Min is not really a placid man. He usually hides behind a bland mask; except for a wrinkled brow or fluttering eyelids, his face rarely shows what he is thinking. Money is the exception. When the subject comes up, almost imperceptibly, his eyes narrow until they are slits. It is animal-like, something a tiger might do while watching a deer walk across an open meadow. You imagine evil things, watching his eyes disappear.

"Inspector, you were about to say something?" The eyes were practically gone.

"Me? Yes. And it was this." I blinked to gain enough time to remember. "I know we are in straitened circumstances . . ."

"Get where you're going, O."

"Money; I'll need some."

"Why?" Ever so slowly could the chief inspector speak, so that even a single word consumed a large amount of time and space.

"You asked the key question yourself, don't you remember?"

"What?" More time, more space.

"Where did a bunch of crooks get silk stockings?" It seemed harmless enough for me to walk through the markets, looking for stockings. "If we can answer that, we'll have a good place to start. Somewhere, a twinkling star is warning me not to touch this case, but you say the Ministry wants it solved. Alright, we have to start somewhere, and a good place to start is the stockings the bank robbers—if that is what they were—had over their faces. I'll need to do research on stockings, who sells them, what types there are, I mean, quality, place of origin, size, maybe color for all I know, whether they had split up a pair or two pair between them or were working from odd lots. I'll have to buy some, once I figure out where they're available. You can't expect me to afford shopping for silk stockings on an inspector's salary."

"Out."

5

On a breezy early April day, just after the last of the Chinese dust has blown off toward Japan and the skies have cleared to a newly scoured blue, the prettiest place in Pyongyang is along the banks of the Taedong River. Some people might argue and say it is prettier in the small hills behind the Moranbong Theater, where the dogwoods bloom against the stones of the old fortress walls. Nice enough, but there are usually too many schoolchildren there learning to draw. The girls chatter and laugh; the boys run after each other. A few sit seriously, holding their brushes over the paper, observing the scene. Some actually paint something, and smile shyly if you nod in encouragement. If you're in the mood, watching the children is fine. But to me, the riverside is better, quieter, more serene. There aren't many benches, so I am always glad to find one unoccupied. I don't like to sit with strangers.

The lack of seating—other than on the grass, which grows in patches this time of year—is the result of too many bureaucrats with too little to do. Almost forgotten in the General Bureau of Urban Planning was a small unit of landscape architects looking for ways to justify their existence. Out for a morning stroll, one of the architects stumbled over the benches along the river. Several memos were dispatched claiming that riverside benches made for clutter, interfered with the natural beauty of the spot, and so forth. One of the memos landed on the desk of the People's Culture Commission director, the man who had authorized, at some cost to his small budget, the benches along the river to begin with. He had justified the decision on the grounds that without benches no one would walk on the riverside path. I knew this, because I had to go back and look at the memos when everything landed on my desk.

I discovered that what the commission director didn't say was that if no one used the path, the snack vendors who had paid him monthly bribes for occupancy rights near the river would be out of business. The director impressed me as a thoughtful man and kind in his own way, but not to the extent of overly worrying about the fate of the vendors. However, he knew that, bribes having been paid punctually on the fifth of every month by all concerned, if customers stopped coming because the benches had been removed, letters of complaint would appear. Such letters inevitably ended up in a file, and in this case, he was certain, they would make their way to his.

The dispute should have been solved in a dreary meeting with a political cadre, possibly a short woman speaking in hard-edged tones. Unexpectedly, it became a police matter. The commission director had no faith in political cadre, male or female, and the more he thought about it, the more he did not like the idea of letters of complaint in his file. One day, a Friday, he brought a few more wooden benches to the riverside, slopped on green paint he "found" along the road near his apartment, and went away. That night, the benches disappeared, every one of them. The director filed a complaint the next morning. He sat, vexed, in my office and said in a loud voice that he knew exactly who was responsible. I told him suspicions weren't proof. That might have ended the matter because there was not much else to be done, and I was not inclined to do it, certainly not on a Saturday. We were shorthanded at the time, and chasing architects— which I had done early in my career—was not high on my list. But a few days later, a report came in from one of the security patrols. Around midnight on the night the benches vanished, a patrolman sitting under a bridge for a smoke had heard someone walk by speaking Chinese. He didn't know if it meant anything, but he said it was rare.

Pyongyang has a small Chinese population. Over the years, I've made it my business to stay friends with a young Chinese woman, fairly pretty and quite observant, who does a good job keeping track of who spits and who doesn't among her countrymen. After a quiet dinner with her, and a phone call or two, it became clear that the landscape architects had hired Chinese thugs to get rid of the benches. They hadn't planned for the cheap green paint, which never completely dried. When the bench robbers got back to the hotel on Yanggak Island where they sit around the lobby and bother the prostitutes, the paint moved from their clothing to the chairs. The manager told them to go to hell and not come back. They broke his revolving glass doors on the way out.

It wasn't much of a challenge to solve the case after that, though we never found all the benches—not even most of them. Apart from the green paint in the lobby of the hotel, they disappeared without a trace. The People's Culture Commission was denied extra funds to buy new ones, so the few that were recovered had to be spread out. They sat like lonely outposts, which was fine for the young couples who used them as often as they could, on all except the coldest nights. The case file came back from the Ministry Review Board without any words of praise, without any comment at all, other than a note attached with a broken staple: "Pending."

At least now, in the sunshine, it was pleasant to sit on one of the benches, repainted a dull white, and let my thoughts roam. They kept roaming to the bank robbery and to a persistent sense I had that, whatever Min thought the Ministry wanted, we should keep away from this case. I checked my pockets for a scrap of wood. On a spring day, a piece of mulberry is soothing, uncomplicated. Mulberry is friendly. Maybe that's why silkworms like mulberry leaves so much; maybe the Chinese princess who first fed such leaves to them was smarter than her father, the Emperor, realized. I didn't have any mulberry with me. There was nothing but a few pieces of paper for taking notes; no wood, no sandpaper. In my shirt pocket, I found a cigarette that was slightly bent in the middle. I smoothed it into shape, rummaged around for a match, then lit the tobacco. It was a local brand, out of a half-crushed package that sometimes sat in my desk drawer covering the badge I never wore. I took a few puffs and balanced the cigarette on the edge of the bench.

A young couple sat on the grass in front of me, leaning against each other. The man kept looking over his shoulder, but I didn't take the hint. I had rescued this bench; I could park on it as long as I wanted. A two-man patrol walked by, and the couple moved apart; the older patrolman gave me a halfhearted salute and a tight smile, then returned to a conversation with his partner. The couple leaned back against each other. The man turned to give me another look, but I was already thinking about getting up.

There was no sense getting too comfortable—my next stop would have to be the city morgue. I couldn't be sure how long they would keep the bank robber's body. They might have already dumped it, which would explain why Min was only shown photographs. If they had already dumped it, I needed to know why. Incompetence was high on the list of possibilities, but there might be another explanation, a category three explanation that I could use to convince Min to let us drop the whole thing.

The morgue is not part of the Ministry. It's not even really connected to the security services anymore. It works according to its own needs, and strictly on a space-available basis. It was never big to begin with, just a small addition at the back of the central hospital. Under the new economic program, with everyone urged to make a profit, the hospital decided to partition the morgue, move in some beds, and fashion two or three private rooms for paying, foreign patients. Patients pay their bills. Stiffs do not. I finished the cigarette, tossed the stub in the river, and climbed the steps back to my car. As I started the engine, it somersaulted across my mind that cigarettes made me jumpy. I wondered if it was possible to smoke mulberry leaves. I wondered if the Chinese princess had tried.

6

The door to the morgue was locked. I knocked, but no one answered. I knocked again, listened for movement from inside, then decided to let myself in. The morgue could be considered an official location, even if it isn't part of the Ministry. Death was an official act, more or less. Anything that permanent had to be considered official. I was on official business, I told myself, and that meant I was allowed into official locations. The logic was weak; the lock on the morgue's door, on the other hand, was not. It looked old, but it defeated every trick I tried with the cheap lock-picking set I carried around.

This job of picking locks was newly assigned to the local sector offices, and we had no standard-issue equipment. Once, there was a specialist who did nothing but pick locks. It was said that he learned his trade in Moscow during the years when the Russians pretended we were brothers and worth training. He was a very quiet man. Picking locks was a quiet profession, I always thought, so it didn't surprise me that he never responded when I greeted him in Russian. If we needed to get into a building, we'd wait outside for him to arrive. He'd walk in past us without looking up, and emerge a few minutes later. In those days, most doors weren't locked anyway, so it was rarely a problem.

After cuts in the Ministry's budget—part of a larger move, we were told, to embrace "new realities"—the lock man moved on to other things. He opened his own shop, exactly when more people were installing locks to keep out the reality of an increase in the number of crooks. So, no more designated lock expert, no assigned equipment, and no approved procedures for entering all of the suddenly locked buildings. There was nothing to do but follow the old practice, sitting around outside, figuring whoever was inside would have to come out, or, if they'd already left, would eventually return to open the door and go back in.

One drizzling afternoon last autumn, when Chief Inspector Min was at the local market, he fell into conversation with a merchant, a Chinese-Korean who showed up a few times a year with a suitcase full of goods. Min came back to the office with two small bags, one of which he laid on my desk, like a cat bringing a wet, dead bird into the house.

"What is it?" I nodded at the bag.

"Exactly what we've been looking for, Inspector, a lock-picking set. I used what was left of our office funds, since we'll never get anything from Central Supply."

"Other office chiefs come back with rice cookers, or even a small icebox. What good is this?" I opened the bag and held up two narrow metal blades, one slightly thicker than the other, each attached to a wooden handle—some sort of junk wood, though I couldn't tell for sure what it was because it was painted black. "Made in Romania." I read the small stamp on the handle of one of them. "Good for breaking and entering in Bucharest maybe, but probably worthless in Pyongyang. Have you ever seen the bookcases they make there? Nothing fits with anything else."

I was right, the lock-picking tool was worthless even for getting into a morgue. I went around the side to a window set high on the wall and tried to see in, but the window was curtained. Just as I got on the sidewalk leading back to my car, a harried-looking man in a blue coat walked past, opened the door with a key, then slammed it so hard a puff of dust rose from the top of the door frame.

Another knock on the door, answered this time; the peephole opened, and I could see an eye looking out at me. "What do you want? We're closed for lunch."

"I don't want lunch. Inspector O." I flashed my ID toward the peephole. "On a case. Open up."

"How do I know you are legitimate? You aren't even wearing a pin."

This was no time for a discussion of political symbolism. "It fell off. Open the door. You know who I am, I just told you."

The door opened. The man in the blue coat peered around the edge. Now that I got a good look at his face, he looked familiar. "Sorry, Inspector, I'm not trying to be difficult. My orders are not to let anyone in until we finish the autopsy. Believe me, it's not my idea, I'm not looking for trouble. I don't even want this job. I studied bridge engineering in college. Someday maybe I'll show you my de-signs, very well received in their day. Cables, vaulted whatnots soaring above river gorges. Meanwhile, can you do me a favor? Go away."

At least I knew that the body was still there. "Who gave you the order for the autopsy?" At that moment, my cell phone rang. No one had any reason to call me, and no one but Min was supposed to know my number. It was very loud. I'd wrapped it in a glove, but that did no good. Worse than the volume was the tune. Birds stopped singing, stunned, when they heard it. As soon as it rang, I knew I could never get to it in time to turn it off. I probably couldn't find the switch, or the button, or whatever it took to kill the thing. The longer the tune played, the wider the little man's eyes became. He stifled a laugh. He fluttered his hands delicately and put them to his brow. He stifled an-other laugh, this second one only barely. Still the phone wouldn't quit; if anything, it got louder. From now on, the damned thing stayed in the car, under a blanket. Maybe I could even lose it; possibly it could slip from my hand into the river. No one in the Ministry knew how to change the ringer, or so they claimed. "Crazy, you're the only one with that problem, O," they said. "Must be preprogrammed or something. Try and find an instruction manual."

Finally the phone fell silent. The little man coughed and looked away. I knew it was probably hopeless to try to regain a sense of control, but I was aggravated enough to make the effort. "The order for the autopsy, who gave it to you?"

The little man opened the door a crack wider. "I don't know, it's not signed, but it has a big party chop on it, and a number, in red ink. We get them maybe once a year. The courier quakes in his boots when he hands one of these over. The doctor reads them, shakes her head, then locks them in a little safe under her desk. I don't know what they say exactly, I only get a quick glimpse. But I know what they mean. Do the body, then get rid of it, forget you saw it, tidy up. Does it look like poison? No, can't be! Must have been natural causes. That look of agony on the stiff's face was just a result of muscular resonance, happens all the time, check the box that says, 'No further investigation necessary.' Have a cup of tea, clear your mind, look to the future." It was more than he meant to say, and he looked nervous when he had said it.

"What is muscular resonance? I've never heard of it."

"It's a made-up term." This was said in a surprisingly matter-of-fact tone, as if morgues get to make up vocabulary as a law of nature. "Someone here invented it a while ago to satisfy the paperwork, and we've never had a question. By now, there must be a thick folder somewhere up top, marked 'Muscular Resonance.'"

"What about the stiff in there that got hit by a bus?"

He paled. "No such animal, Inspector. Now, go away, would you?"

"You said you were doing an autopsy. How many bodies do you have in there?"

"We don't deal in numbers, we deal in quality. Whatever we have, we have. I wouldn't know about buses."

Clearly, they still had the body of the bank robber in there. So why wouldn't they show it to Min? And why didn't they want to let me in? If this wasn't category three, I didn't know what was.

Curiosity is fine, but sometimes it impairs judgment. If they didn't want anyone to see the body, it was because they didn't want anyone to see the body, or to ask any questions about it, or even inquire about articles of clothing. Normally, I would have figured it was the morgue's business and walked away. But not this time. This time I said, "You have any silk stockings lying around?" The little man responded with a blank look. I had been curious; now I was mad. It wasn't an innocent blank look, not one tinged with puzzlement or edging toward incomprehension. It was defiantly blank, and I didn't plan to spend the afternoon on the doorstep of the morgue held at bay by such a look. Then I remembered the face. "You may not know me, but I know you. Your aunt lives in my building, on the ground floor. She needed medicine last year. I got some for her."

I could tell this registered. It was true, I did recognize him, and I did get some aspirin for his aunt. She had repaid me with a promise to be a matchmaker. She knew some girls in the countryside who would be good for me, she said. Hard workers. Simple needs. Knew how to boil water.

The door shut in my face, but there was no click of the lock. I decided to wait. A minute later it opened a crack; a hand stuck out, with a stocking dangling on the end of it. "You didn't get this from me."

"Only one?"

"That's right." The stocking was torn and had a considerable amount of blood on it. Still visible along the top and up one side were small designs. At first they were hard to read, but when I examined them more closely, I saw they were monograms, Western letters, CB.

"You'd look pretty silly with this over your face, wouldn't you?" I held up the stocking.

He opened the door wider and peered around the corner. "No, because I wouldn't put that thing over my face."

"What do you think the CB means? I've never seen stockings like that."

"You're the inspector, not me."

"There's a place in my sector, Club Blue."

"I wouldn't know."

"No, I'll bet you wouldn't. You always have spare stockings lying around? Or only when they come in with corpses that were never here?"

He began to look like he was thinking of closing the door.

"You must have autopsy equipment in there, right?"

"Of course."

"Little scalpels, tiny picks."

"Something like that."

"You can do fine work, delicate work?"

He shook his head. "Forget it, Inspector, I can't dissect a cell phone."

I patted my pocket. "Don't jump to conclusions, it's bad for your ankles. Just one thing more."

He waited.

"You wouldn't have any other suspicious deaths that you've been keeping to yourselves, would you?"

"Meaning what?"

"Meaning I'll be seeing you around."

7

Two flights down, the door opened into a dark room. It wasn't locked, or at least not very. This lock was cheaper than the one on the morgue, so it gave way after a little twist and a nudge. I stepped inside; the entryway was dark, and so was the hall, but at the end there was a faint light and the sound of music. I walked toward the music, feeling my way along the walls. A flashlight would have been good; mine was in the back of my desk drawer, with only one battery. There were none in the Ministry storeroom, and the supply clerk said none would show up until next year. He always said this with some satisfaction, as if informing us what we couldn't have was part of his job description.

The room at the end of the hall turned out to be a drinking club, with high stools along the bar, and on the back wall a long mirror and rows of classy bottles of champagne and whiskey and expensive-looking glasses. Against the other walls were tables, some of them surrounded by velvet curtains, the rest just empty. I sat on a stool and looked down the bar. The music got a little louder, by degrees. Not like anything they played in the karaoke bars for the foreigners; it sounded deeper, maybe African. This was a bad idea, following up. It broke all of my rules about staying out of swamps. But the stocking with the monograms made me curious. I pretty much kept away from these clubs. Some inspectors liked to keep close track of the ones in their sectors. They said it was important to follow the activity; it was also a good way to get free drinks. I was more inclined to noodle restaurants, but the girls in the noodle restaurants didn't wear monogrammed stockings, I had to admit.

"We're not open, but what's that to you?" From somewhere behind the bar, a voice emerged.

"The door wasn't exactly locked. I figured it meant you were serving."

"This is a night place, friend. We don't serve drinks until the sun goes down. You got business here, breaking in?"

I finally located the bartender in the dark, a short man with no neck wearing a black shirt. He had a broom, but he wasn't sweeping.

"What's that music?" I always start with an easy question.

"It's from the Caribbean somewhere. Any creep would recognize it. You didn't come to listen to records, that's for sure, and you have no cause to break into an honest establishment." He had a funny, high voice.

"We'll see about honest. Where's your license? It's supposed to be on the wall where I can see it." I looked around for the pictures that should have been there, two of them, father and son looking down. "You also are missing some fine portraits."

"Careful, Inspector, don't get carried away." Another voice from behind me, a polished voice, probably coming from a tailored cotton suit, or a herringbone sports coat and trousers with a sharp crease. I turned around slowly. None of the tables had been occupied when I came in. Now the one closest to the end had a man sitting with his back to me. He was facing a mirror that was attached to a door, maybe an office behind it. From the reflection, I knew he was smiling—his teeth were shining—but I couldn't see his coat.

"The license must have been lost in the mail, Inspector. I arranged for it myself, went over to Changkwang the other day to make sure. They said the piece of paper was on the way. But you know, they always say that."

The central party offices are on Changkwang Street. Heavy-weight; not everyone can get past the guards. This man could do it, if anyone could. He had something unusual, a golden aura of self-confidence that surrounded him. It went beyond his trying to impress me, talking as if he went to Changkwang Street just to blow his nose. That part was just an act, I felt sure. Humble he wasn't, but there was something judicious about him, as if he knew how far to play out his leash, a little at a time. "The mail doesn't concern me," I said. "My concern is making sure people follow the law, keep our city a nice place to live and a good place for foreigners to visit, so they make friends with the locals and spend money."

"Well, what do you know, that's exactly my concern, too, Inspector. You are an inspector, aren't you? I hope they wouldn't send someone of lesser rank to shake me down." He gave a low chuckle, the way people who find themselves amusing sometimes do, though I had the feeling even that was part of his act. "Foreigners come in here to get away from politics, you understand?" He looked around the walls as if to indicate all was in order. "What's important is not what we show but what's in our hearts, am I right? It makes the foreigners feel more comfortable if there aren't too many symbols around, staring them in the face. Foreigners don't like politics. They like the music, they like the drinks and the atmosphere, they like the company. They love the company. They really love the company.

And so they spend money. I make a profit, I pay my fees, I look after my friends, and they look after me. No fuss, no muss. You understand, Inspector, no fuss, no muss. We really are closed; I must ask you to leave."

"I'd like to, but I can't."

The bartender started sliding toward the far end of the bar. I reached over, grabbed his wrist, and gave it a twist, hard, so he yelped in pain and dropped the broom. "Stand still, friend. I don't like people slipping away while I'm talking."

The man at the table got up and turned around. For a couple of seconds the crazy thought went through my mind that he might have a gun, but he only pulled a wallet from his jacket. The jacket fit him like a glove, made his shoulders look big and his chest full. The jacket was a brown herringbone; his trousers were a darker brown, the crease was so sharp he probably used it to open his mail. "Here, Inspector." He was holding several big bills, euros. "This is for you. Just a token of my appreciation for your coming down here to see if everything was alright. You're right, we do need a new lock. I'll see to it. Come back tonight. The drinks will be on me, and the company will be, too." He looked at my shirt and grinned. "Like I said, it's what's in our hearts that counts."

"Kind of you"—I nodded at the bills in his hand—"but not today. You could do me a favor, though." I reached into my back pocket and pulled out the silk stocking. "Would this belong to your club? It has monograms on it, CB, even one along the top edge, very sexy; not where anyone would normally look."

"Not normally, Inspector. But it happens. People sometimes look in funny places." He took the stocking and held it gently in the air.

"Yours?" I asked.

"I'm partial to socks, but who knows what the girls wear, or where they leave their clothing once they walk out of here in the dark of the morning. This is torn pretty bad." He looked at the blood and then at me, a careful look, very measured, as if he were considering how much of his leash he had left. "CB, that could be us, Club Blue." He smiled at me and handed back the stocking. "I don't want to have to make a phone call, Inspector. Please leave."

I looked around the room. "Nice place. Wouldn't be so nice if it were covered with broken glass. There are some Chinese boys on Yanggak Island who love to break glass, for fun."

As the bartender turned to look at the champagne bottles and the expensive glasses, I saw he had a long scar down the left side of his face, a scar from a knife or maybe a broken bottle. Most of the bartenders in these drinking clubs are pretty boys, white jackets on pinched waists, high cheeks and soft hands. This one was ugly. Ugly isn't always mean, but in this case, I had a feeling it was.

"I'll be back after I'm off duty, to collect on that drink. No doubt that license will have arrived and be on the wall by then."

The man in the herringbone jacket nodded slightly to the bartender before he smiled at me, though it wasn't the sort of smile that leads to long friendships. "We'll look forward to that, Inspector."

8

As long as I was out and about, enjoying the spring air, there was no harm going to the bank. For one thing, it would give me ammunition to use when Min complained I wasn't doing anything. "Been to the bank," I could say, giving him a level gaze. "This is category three, Min. Why don't we cut it loose? Let SSD kill themselves over it." Then I'd nod, gravely if the moment seemed right.

The bank was in a three-story building with a gold star on a signboard. There was nothing else to show it was a bank; the guard post at the base of the uneven steps leading up to the entrance was empty. The front windows on the first floor had been bricked up, except for slits along the top to let in some light. The original door had been replaced with something a little sturdier, metal with designs to make it look like a brass gate in a palace. There was even a fake iron grate in front of it. A bright metal plate surrounded the double locks, and the handle felt solid. Inside, the place was dark and musty. The light slits on the front wall were stingy, and the overhead fixtures were short on bulbs. The floor was carpeted, something flowered under the dirt; off to the side a series of desks sat behind a low wooden railing. Along the back wall was a counter with three teller windows. One of them was broken and had a piece of plywood filling the gap; the other two were shut. The plywood caught my attention, and I started over to look at it more closely.

"Can we help you? Would you like to open an account?" At a desk off by itself, in the corner, a middle-aged woman in a pale yellow dress looked at me. She brushed a wisp of hair from her face and stood up. I took my ID from my pocket. "I'm from the Ministry of Public Security. We have some questions for you, or maybe your manager."

The woman leaned back against the desk. "I thought you had changed your name to People's Security. Or are you still Public?"

I looked quickly at my ID. "People's, Public, it doesn't concern you."

"Questions from police of all descriptions belong behind there, in the offices. We don't want to scare the customers, especially the foreigners."

There was no one else in the room, so I assumed she was speaking metaphorically. "Were you here the other day, during the robbery?"

She walked over to me, on high heels that accentuated her height. She was tall and slender, maybe younger than I first thought. "I told you, we don't want to scare the customers, or don't you get it?"

There was nothing wispy or slender about her manner. She was rude like a hammer before it comes down on a nail. "The office is in the back. If you want to talk, that's where it's done. Out here, we do business. Okay with you?"

"Fine," I said. I pointed to the windows along the back. "That plywood in the teller window is a nice touch, gives an impersonal place like this a more natural feel. Where'd you get it? Plywood isn't easy to find."

She looked at me in disbelief, then shook her head. "How the hell should I know? It isn't part of the decorating scheme. The window broke, and the janitor put it up."

"So, you do answer questions out here. There aren't any customers. There isn't even a guard out front. Isn't he posted all the time?"

"We didn't have enough operating capital to pay him. Everyone told us it was safe in this city, anyway, so we let him go."

"He was a private guard?" I never heard of such a thing.

"No, he was from one of your security departments, I don't remember which one. But the agreement was we were to pay his salary. They insisted that they weren't going to spend their budget for a guard to look after our money. Can you believe it?"

"When did he leave?"

"About ten days ago." She watched me steadily. "Yes, that is just before the robbery. We don't think there is any connection."

"Good, always good when the victim analyzes the situation. That saves us a lot of time. How about you lock the front door and sit over there with me while we review what went on. By the way"—I looked down at her legs—"you don't wear silk stockings, do you?"

"I can't lock the front door during business hours, it's against bank regulations. And if you start harassing me I'll file a complaint that will dump you in a pig farm so far away you'll have to check a map each time you take a crap." She paused and brushed the hair out of her eyes again. "I need to see your ID up close. You can't just come in here and flash a piece of cardboard across the room." A lock clicked on the back door, the one she said led to the offices. Suddenly, the whole city was nothing but locks.

"What a shame." I shook my head. "Don't tell me, everyone just went out to lunch and I should come back later." At some point, I'd want to get into that room, if for no other reason than they didn't want me to see it. Though she had said if I wanted to talk about the robbery, I should go back there. And then they had locked it. If there had ever been anything of interest in there, it must be gone, but maybe not everything. There was no reason to push my way in just now; I'd only end up looking around at blank walls and a swept floor. I couldn't do a thorough search by myself. Better to wait; maybe someone would put something back, get careless, if they thought the coast was clear.

"Wrong, not later, never. The bank has an internal investigation under way. We don't need you, and we don't need your ministry nosing around." I may not have been listening closely. She had a face that was unusually pretty. Her skin was the color of copper, her cheekbones were high, and I realized she spoke with a slight accent. "There are ways of making that point stick, if you choose not to pay attention to me. Do I make myself clear, Inspector"—she looked again at my ID—"O, is it?"

"Don't worry," I said. "You get high marks for clarity. If I could go out that door and not come back, it would be fine with me. But that's not possible. I have my orders, and until I get new ones, you are on my list." I took a scrap of paper from my shirt pocket and held it up. "You'll find I'm persistent. Polite, mostly, but persistent. I don't know your name, by the way."

"You don't need to know it, but if you must, it's Chon. Good day, Inspector." She stood in a solid enough way, more solid than you'd think someone with her waist could stand. In the howling wind of a winter storm she might sway, but not here. I hadn't eaten since early morning, and it was a good time to find a bowl of noodles. I nodded, looked at the plywood again, and went back outside into the sunshine.

Chapter Two

So far, anyone looking casually at the whole thing would say there was nothing interesting about the case itself, other than that it was the first bank robbery we had ever had in Pyongyang, perhaps in the whole country. Maybe there'd been one over on the east coast, or maybe up in the special zone with the casinos, and they hadn't told us. But I doubted it. I also wasn't looking casually. Admittedly, there were interesting angles to it. The stockings were interesting. The lady with the waist was interesting. The real problem was that even at this early stage, I knew, knew absolutely, beyond any doubt, that somebody didn't want the case solved. There wasn't anything big or obvious I could point to, just little warning flags. Over time I'd learned that the size of the flags was not important, the real question was the number. Already there had been plenty, and they had STAY AWAY written all over.

I knew it. I had a feeling Min knew it. But there was a certain dance we had to perform first. Until Min actually ordered me off, formally, I had to keep following footprints leading nowhere. At least

I had to hope they led nowhere. If by accident I stumbled on a real clue, it would be nothing but trouble. Looking into the stockings seemed safe enough for the moment.

Min was staring out his window when I climbed the stairs and knocked on his door after lunch. He didn't turn around, but from the way his back was tensed, you had the sense he didn't feel he was on solid ground and he didn't know when he'd find some again soon. There were only two reasons Min stared out his window like this, looking at trees he did not like. Either he was deeply worried, or he was miffed.

"You took the office car." His voice sounded miffed, but his back told me he was worried. "You know perfectly well you are supposed to use the duty car. It may not be quite so pretty, but that's what you're assigned, it's on our books for daily use, and more to the point, it has the plates you need to get around. No one has driven it in weeks. What if the battery goes dead? I know, I know, following the rules is sometimes difficult, irksome." I could see his reflection in the window; his lips moved slightly as he groped for another word. "Burdensome. I hope we're not putting too much stress on you, Inspector. If we are, please note it in the daily log—the same log that doesn't even have an entry in it for your using the car, either car. Maybe we can find a more tranquil place, out in the countryside. Working in a rice field, they say, is quiet."

"I've been thinking." Ignoring the chief inspector is sometimes the wiser course, especially when he begins speaking in threes. It means he is feeling pressure from above, and provoking him only makes matters worse. I turned to the subject at hand. "You say the Ministry wants this solved. According to you, the upper levels are hell-bent on a solution. The funny thing is, no one I've talked to today will tell me anything. Everything they say points toward unknown figures at higher levels that want me to go away. Why is that, I wonder."

Min laughed, though he didn't bother putting any mirth into it. It was a very tense laugh. "You wonder. Just take my word for it, will you?" He finally turned and gave me a smile that looked like he had bought it in the state store; maybe it came from one of those cans that had sat on the shelf a long time. "I already told you, this is sensitive. The Ministry thinks it might scare the damned foreigners, and if they go, where do we get investment?" He said the last word as if even speaking it cost a lot.

"Investment? Since when is the Ministry in charge of economics?"

"You and I are frogs in the mud, Inspector, but there are those with the means all around us. We have a lot of enlightened people in this Ministry, believe it or not. They know what is going on."

"People with means are enlightened. Frogs are not, I take it."

"Foreign money fuels growth, there are no two ways around it. The Ministry understands that, and it understands that keeping the foreign pocketbooks happy has benefits all around." He looked at me, and I looked at him. "Well," he said, "almost all around."

A small warning flag popped up. "Yes and no. I can see that it's obviously sensitive, which is why I'm inclined to go back to my office and forget the whole thing. But this isn't about scaring foreign money away. That's what the woman at the bank wanted me to think, only she wasn't very convincing. She really wasn't even trying that hard. Nice waist, by the way."

"Inspector, I warn you." Min sat down, and his eyelids fluttered once or twice. "I know you have a hard time getting the central point sometimes, but please try. This . . . case . . . is . . . important. That means we have to concentrate, not go off on wild goose chases, and not stop to admire waists. You went downtown to one of those drinking clubs. Why?"

I indicated I'd be back, quickly crossed the hall to my office, and dug around in the top drawer of my file cabinet for a piece of pine. Good, dependable pine. It was the best thing to have at the beginning of an ugly case. Nothing fancy or elaborate, nothing with any quirks or special needs. Pine was uncomplaining, not proud, lazy as a summer day, and just as complacent. That's why pine trees take so long to grow, sheer laziness. I found what I was looking for, a small oblong piece with one edge smoothed and the other still with that prickly feel where a rough saw bit the wood. As soon as it fit into my palm, I took a deep breath and stepped back into Min's room.

"Don't tell me you want me to stay away from that drinking place. For one thing, it's in my sector." Conversations with Min get picked up easily enough. We were both used to interruptions. "Between the ugly bartender and the slick owner, the two of them know something about this robbery, though I wouldn't say they were directly involved. At least not the owner; his bartender might be a different story. For sure, even if they're not involved, and even if they don't know exactly who was involved, they must know someone who does. That sort of place attracts bad types." I looked down at the piece of wood in my hand. I was supposed to tell Min to drop the case, and here I was arguing in favor of following up at the club.

"Where did you get that silk stocking?"

"If you know everything I've done today, why don't you just write the report yourself?"

"I only know what I'm told, Inspector, and I got a phone call telling me to assign you to something else."

We stared at each other. I could hear a whole line of warning flags snapping in the wind. Min shrugged, finally. "I don't know who it was, and so I'm not giving you any orders one way or the other. As far as I'm concerned, the Ministry still wants this solved, and I've put you in charge. So solve it. Go away. And get rid of that damned piece of wood."

"I'm more than liable to get someone important annoyed with us if I proceed with the investigation, you realize that." The level gaze I was going to use to drive the stake through the heart of the investigation was out of reach.

"Inspector, you annoy me on occasion, that wood annoys me, but it doesn't stop you. I'll back you up, and as far as I can tell, the Minister will, too." He paused to consider whether his note of uncertainty about how far the Minister would go to support us was clear enough. It was. "If there is a change in that, something more than an anonymous caller, I'll be the first to let you know."

"What about the lady with the waist?"

"What about her?"

"She's a potential source of information. I may have to sweeten her up. Bowl of noodles, an evening at a karaoke bar. Talk doesn't come as cheap as it used to. People don't just jump when I tell them to."

"The answer is *nyet*, to quote a Russian I once played cards with all the way from Moscow to Khabarovsk on the train. My only trip outside." His eyes got a faraway look. "Have you taken that train, Inspector? Trees passing outside the window endlessly, even you would go crazy." Then he shook his head. "I'm not paying for information. You'll have to weasel it out of this lady some other way. Try turning on the charm. Dress up for her, why don't you? Put a handkerchief in your breast pocket or something." He pretended to study a file on his desk. It had been there for months.

"Don't ask me why, but I don't think this thing was planned by Chagang people."

Min looked up and frowned.

2

I did some paperwork, stared at the shadows as they crept across the cracks in the ceiling for a while, then got in the office car and drove toward the Gold Star Bank the long way around, across one of the newer bridges over the Taedong, through old blocks of apartments, past the diplomatic compound, over to the university, and finally back over the river. Traffic on the street in front of the bank was sparse, no buses. There was plenty of space to park, but I didn't want to get too close. I found a deserted cross street from which I could watch the back of the building and pulled over to wait. It was getting to be night, and it didn't take long for night to arrive.

After fifteen minutes, the back door opened, and a man hurried down a path that cut across an empty lot. He had on a cloth cap and was hunched over. It was too dark to see his face; there was only a slice of moon and no lights this far away from the main road. A minute later, the door opened again, and the woman in the yellow dress stepped out. She looked up and down the street, started to walk in my direction, then turned and strolled the other way. It wasn't the sort of move she would have made if she'd seen my car, nothing abrupt. It was more like she'd changed her mind, remembered she had to be somewhere else, but not urgently. I was about to get out of my car to follow her when the door opened a third time, and a man with broad shoulders appeared. He walked with a confident step you could distinguish a kilometer away. I was willing to bet the crease in his trousers was sharp. If it wasn't my new best friend from the Club Blue, it had to be his twin brother, golden aura and all.

3

I thought for sure he would have a car and driver. Instead, he walked across the street and into the opening that led to a group of old two-story buildings. The whole block had been designated for replacement a few years ago, but as usual there was a delay between designation and implementation. As a result, the people who lived there were never sure when they would be told to move out. In fact, those with any connections had already left and been assigned new apartments on the other side of the city. The remainder sat around and fretted; a few complained to me whenever I walked by. This was part of my district, and they thought I should listen. It wasn't the sort of place a man with creases on his trousers would live. If he could talk his way into the party offices for a business permit, he could easily get himself a four-room apartment in one of the new buildings in the western section. So what brought him here? It might be home to his ugly bartender, though I'd have heard about it if someone new moved into the neighborhood. It was already too late to try to follow the trousers. Anyway, even with this little snapshot I'd seen enough. There was now a line connecting the bank to the drinking club to these old apartments. I didn't know if it was a straight line, a dotted line, or a chorus line, but it gave me somewhere to start.

I stopped myself. Start what? This case wasn't going anywhere, not anywhere good, anyway, no matter what Min said. And I still wasn't convinced he believed the argument he had fed me about making foreign investors happy. Maybe for the time being he wanted me to be seen poking around in a few places, enough to keep the Ministry off our necks, though he would never admit it. In about a week they'd tell him to reel me in and forget the whole thing. That anonymous call had been a straw in the wind. It let them say they'd warned us if something went wrong, but it gave them time to say they hadn't shut down the investigation if they discovered at the last minute that this was really a category one case after all. Even the Ministry wasn't sure which way to jump on this one, I'd bet on it.

What it all added up to was a slow roll, everything done in order, nothing rushed. Just take out the training manual and follow recommended procedure for general investigations, page by page, paragraph by paragraph. In a day or two, the lady with the waist could be questioned more closely. The back room at the bank could wait a little longer, too. I'd even put the stockings aside for the moment. Working on the bus angle was probably a wise step, especially because it was unlikely to lead anywhere. The Traffic Bureau would have a report on the accident; they might even have impounded the bus, though fortunately they probably wouldn't be able to keep it very long. The tour company—which was undoubtedly not run by one of Min's frogs in the mud—would want it back in service quickly. Most likely, no one would have bothered to ask the driver why he was so far off the normal traffic route. No one wanted to know. I probably didn't want to know, either. Luckily, the Traffic Bureau was closed for the day. If I got to their offices not too early in the morning, I might have some nonanswers by afternoon.

My cell phone rang. It was still in a glove in my coat pocket, and my coat was in the backseat of the car. I reached over to retrieve it, hoping this was anyone but Min. Not that anyone else had the number.

I pushed every button until a voice emerged. "Min here. That you, O? Why does it take you so long to answer?"

"Sorry, but I can't figure out how to use this damned thing. Why do we need them? The radio worked fine."

"Mobility, O. It makes us mobile and in touch." A slight pause to complete the triad. "And modern. Three hallmarks of a successful police force. If you didn't have that fairy music for a ring, you wouldn't be so embarrassed when someone contacts you."

"So pick something muscular for me next time I'm in the office with nothing to do. And program it in. I can't. Why did you call?"

There was a silence.

"Hello? You there?" What good were these things, always fading out. At least the old radios spit and crackled when no one was talking.

"I'm here. I'm rereading a message we just got from the Ministry. There is something I needed to pass on . . . ah . . . here it is. Listen to this. 'Under no circumstances is the investigation to proceed beyond the information-gathering stage without direct orders from the Minister.' Got that, Inspector?"

"See?" I pushed a warning flag out of my face. "It's exactly what I said. They told you they wanted the case solved, now they don't want us to do anything to solve it. Okay, I'm sitting here gathering information. Maybe I'll gather information at home after dinner."

"Negative."

"Speak in full sentences, Min, this isn't the army. Am I not to go home, or am I not to have dinner?"

"Go home, get an hour's sleep, then go out. Go drinking at that club if it suits you. Get a bowl of noodles somewhere. Keep your eyes open. But don't call me. In fact, turn off your phone and keep it off."

"Good." I searched for anything that might be an off switch.

"In fact, leave it in your room. I don't want it ringing and giving you away. Leave your ID in your room, too, for that matter. Don't make it obvious we are on this case."

"On what case? They want us to close it down."

"It's messy, I admit, Inspector. We have a complicating factor

I didn't tell you about before. There is a rumor that the State Security Department wants to grab this away from us. You think the Ministry wants us to close it down, but I think they are just trying to keep their balance until they figure out our next move. If we take one wrong step, SSD will grab it, and that would look bad, very bad. The last time they took over one of our investigations, I had to stand up and explain things at three Saturday sessions in a row. The Minister attended all of them, and he took notes. Believe me, it was painful. A lot of talk about how this was another blow to the Ministry's pride, and a lot of nasty glances my way."

"Budget."

"Of course it's budget, you think I don't know it's budget?" Min's voice faded, and I knew he was looking out in the hall to see if anyone was standing there. "If we let SSD take this case, this sector will be cut to the bone, past the bone. The Minister will personally tear up every request for supplies. He'll make sure I attend every Saturday meeting for the next year, no exceptions. You know I hate those sessions."

"I thought you liked meetings."

"Not Saturday meetings. All of this picking at ideological scabs; I find it unseemly, belittling."

I waited. There was nothing. It was clear things couldn't proceed merely on a duo. "Tasteless." I threw it in the pot just to keep the conversation bubbling.

It was quiet, Min probably pulling thoughtfully at his ear. "I was thinking more along the lines of indecorous," he said finally.

A little soft, but I wasn't going to argue. "How late do I stay out, all night? Do I come into the office tomorrow morning without shaving? Or do I get to sleep until lunch?"

"I'll be at work at 7:00 A.M., Inspector, and you'll be here to greet me."

Not likely, I thought. "Static on the line, talk to you soon." I pushed what looked like the off button on the phone and threw it in the backseat. "Mobility my ass."

When I arrived at my apartment, there was a block committee

meeting going on in the downstairs hall right at the entrance. They were discussing people who hadn't done their fair share of work in the apartment's vegetable garden. I backed out the front door and went around to the one on the side, quickstepped to the stairs, and went up four dark flights to my room.

4

There was a knock on the door. One of the old women from downstairs stuck her head into my apartment. "A phone call for you, Inspector." She grinned. "It's a woman. Sounds like she needs you. Sort of breathless."

"You want to listen in on the other line, or can I just file a report when I'm done, Mrs. Chang?" I was lying down, thinking about dinner.

The old woman laughed and opened the door wider. "You better hurry along, she might hang up and call someone else."

The phone sits on a wooden box in the hall just inside the front entrance to the apartment house. It was off the hook when I got there, and a young man was pacing impatiently nearby. "Can you speed it up? Someone is going to call me any minute."

"They might be calling right now, for all you know. Relax, they'll call back." I picked up the phone. "O here."

"Inspector, this is Miss Pyon, remember me?"

"Yes, the delightful Miss Pyon, of the beautiful golden noodles. Or perhaps it should be the other way around. What can I do for you?" I didn't know Miss Pyon well, but I owed her money. Salary was episodic, expenses were uninterrupted. Some restaurants were getting very strict about being paid. Miss Pyon had agreed I could have a bowl of noodles whenever I showed up if, in turn, I would establish a protective bubble around her place. There were only seven or eight tables, so it didn't have to be much of a bubble. She said she'd been having troubles—of a sort she wouldn't specify—and thought regular presence on my part would help. Exactly how, she wouldn't say and I didn't inquire. Probably she was prone to hysteria. As far as I could see, it was a quiet place, and the noodles were alright, dependable. How she got my number was a question I might want to have answered. I had never told her where I lived. Maybe some customer had recognized me, or maybe she had made some inquiries.

"Could you come over and sit in my shop for a while? Just have some noodles and radiate your calming presence." She didn't sound hysterical, but there was a note of unease in her voice.

"Problems again?" I smiled at the impatient young man.

"Maybe we can avoid that if you are here." In an instant she was past unease, edging toward anxiety. "A couple of drunks."

"Surely not." I tried to sound reassuring.

"They've been around before, and the last time they did a lot of damage."

"It's probably nothing."

"It's not nothing! It's something. This isn't the normal drunken shuffle." Anxiety was in the rearview mirror, and we were heading toward hysteria.

"I'll be there."

5

The two men at the next table were loud, laughing at jokes that were not funny. Even they didn't think they were funny, but they were drinking and getting into the mood where every third word gets a laugh, no matter what it is. One of them belched, they both laughed. It didn't seem anything out of the ordinary to me. I got up to leave, but Miss Pyon came up behind me and put her hand on my shoulder. "Stay, Inspector. Things are already calmer, believe me."

"Actually, I don't think you have much to worry about." I nodded at the two men. "Who are they?"

"I don't know. They don't come here regular, and I'm not looking for them to start. That bad, I don't need the money. The short one is a pig, and if he grabs for me one more time, I'll cut off his—"

"Never mind that. I'll just sit awhile. How about noodles and some tea, if it's not too late."

"Late? We stay open past midnight. And if we need more noodles, we send the boy down."

"Don't tell me, I don't want to know where the noodles come from. It will spoil the mystery. All these years I imagined they sprang from somewhere magical."

The men at the next table started laughing again, until the taller one had a coughing fit and knocked his glass off the table. "Hey, girlie, get us another, and one for your friend, too." The short one pointed at me in a way that told me he was not drunk, not even close.

I pushed back my chair and moved to their table. "Wonderful, this restaurant. Stays open late, you know that?"

The one who had been coughing looked up at me with angry eyes. "Go away. No one likes you. Your type is a cloud covering the sun, there's always one of you around."

He struggled to his feet, but his friend grabbed his arm. "No clouds but it rains, eh, Kim? Let it go. Sit down, let's have another drink." Kim took a sip, sat back with an expression of surprise on his face, then fell off his chair. I knew he was dead before he hit the ground.

The other customers looked startled at the sound. A few put down their chopsticks right away and drifted out; the rest waited a moment longer before deciding not to stay. None of them said a word. They moved quietly across the room, not even glancing at the body on the floor. When they had all left, I searched my pockets, looking for my mobile. It was in the backseat of the car. I turned to Miss Pyon. "You must have a phone in this place, you called me."

"Not up here." She was staring at the body. "It's on the ground level. We only use it sometimes."

"Time to use it." I spoke carefully, because she looked like she was getting hysterical, and when women like her get that way, they freeze up, or they start screaming. "Why don't you walk down the stairs one at a time, no need to run, find the phone, and dial this number." I handed her a card that had my office number on it. "Tell whoever answers that Inspector O needs a couple of friends to visit him. They know where I am. Can you do that for me?" I smiled a slow, comfortable smile, but it was too late. She was already screaming.

6

The two duty officers that night were Sad Man and Little Li. They were on duty most nights. No one else wanted the night shift, and they both hated working days. The Sad Man's real name was Yang Tu Man. He had lost his family in a fire nearly ten years ago, two sons, his father, and his wife. The flames didn't do much damage, but the smoke was toxic. For a long time afterward, he didn't speak to anyone; he didn't even show up at work for several months. Eventually, he started coming in nights so he wouldn't have to deal with other people. Mostly, he worked on the files. After a while, they told him he'd have to answer the phone, too, but not to worry because no one who called at that hour was looking for conversation. When the phone rang, Yang would listen, then say, "Yeah, yeah. Okay." And hang up. The central personnel section recommended transferring him out into the countryside, somewhere he could be alone. But when his case came up for review, the recommendation was reversed, no one could figure out why. So he stayed in the capital, in the same apartment where his family died. Some of his neighbors washed down the walls, but the place smelled of smoke for a long time.

Little Li—his name was Li Po Jin—was tall, maybe the tallest man in the Ministry, with a long face and a big chin. The Ministry's construction sections tried every way they could short of kidnapping to get him into one of their battalions. He laughed at them. "My mother didn't raise me to build dams," he'd say whenever they called, and then he'd wander out to Personnel to make sure that no request for his transfer ever made it to the right desk.

Li and Yang got along better than any two people I knew. Whenever someone told the Sad Man to cheer up, Li would say, "Aw, let him alone, would you?" He'd put his big hand on the Sad Man's shoulder. "How about a beer or something? Now's the time." And he'd bend down slightly to look into the Sad Man's face.

The Sad Man had a good sense of a place as soon as he walked into a room. He picked up little clues that most people overlooked, things that were there and things that should have been but weren't. Once when I asked him how he did it, he shrugged his shoulders and stared at me with melancholy eyes. "Being sad means you see the world as it is."

Other than routing paper, Little Li wasn't gifted in any way. Despite his height, he added nothing to the Ministry's basketball team, which rarely won a game in the interagency tournaments. He was a mediocre inspector; his best point was his bulk. He wasn't actually strong, but he looked like he could pick up a truck, and that was enough to keep most people from getting ideas about running away when I needed them to stay put. The two of them—Yang and Li—weren't much good during normal working hours. Li had headaches in the sunshine, and Yang slipped into unbearable melancholy whenever he was in a room with more than three people. He couldn't question suspects, even at night. They complained it was too depressing to be with him, and they clammed up.

Yang stood at the entrance looking into the dining room. His eyes swept over the tables, then he walked over to the body on the floor. "What's with him?" He gave me a gloomy look.

"Dead," I replied. "You here to help or to ask moronic questions?"

"Aw, leave him alone." Little Li stepped beside me, frowning. "This one giving you trouble?" He pointed toward the short man still at the table, who was picking his teeth in a mean way. He had on a dirty red shirt with no collar, like a Russian waiter in a cheap restaurant. Li looked down at him. "Name."

The short man examined the toothpick, then put it back in his mouth. "You plan to stand around jib-jabbing all night? I got places to be, people to meet." He pointed at the body. "I think he had a heart attack or something. Damned shame, but what can you do?" He pushed back his chair and started to get up.

"You're not going anywhere," I said. "Be friends with the chair, and the chair will be friends with you. Make a mental note to sit still while we get some answers. In other words, relax."

Little Li smiled. I could see him mouthing the phrase to himself, "Be friends with the chair." Yang knelt by the body and started going through the pockets. He pulled a wallet from the jacket, a thick brown wallet filled with euro notes. "Hey, O." He looked up at me. The man really did have awfully sad eyes. They made me think of cold, dark afternoons in November. Rainy afternoons, with the wind just starting to come down the street and nowhere to be but alone. "This guy was rich. Only I don't think he'd been rich very long."

"I'm listening." I pulled the toothpick from the mouth of the man in red. "Show a little respect, pal. Your friend there just keeled over, picking your teeth is not polite." I broke the toothpick in two and handed the pieces back to him. Little Li laughed.

"The bills are in perfect order, all facing the right direction, smaller ones in front, larger denominations in back." Yang held up a wad of bills. "No one keeps money in a wallet in that sort of order. Maybe in a money clip, not a wallet."

The man in red craned his neck to look at the bills in Yang's hand. His face flushed before he turned to Little Li. "How about you and me go out for some fresh air, Inspector? It's unhealthy in here, bodies on the floor and all. Anyway, the bathroom is on the first floor, and I got the urge."

Li looked at me, then at Yang. "You okay?" he asked. Yang nodded.

"Go on, and put in a call for a wagon to take this body out of here while you're downstairs." I turned to Yang. "Here, give me the wallet."

Yang looked at it intently; the sadness left his eyes for a moment but then returned. "All yours, O."

The man at the table nudged Li. "You'll never see that money again. He'll take it all for hisself."

Li put his big hand on the back of the man's neck and lifted him out of his chair. "That was your money, was it, in your friend's pocket?" The man gasped for breath until Li put him down and loosened his grip. "I still don't know your name. Say, you're breathing funny, you have asthma or something that interferes with your airways?" Li clapped his hand on the man's shoulder, so he sagged slightly. "You want to walk by yourself, or you want me to carry you downstairs like a rabbit?"

"Don't strangle him here," I said to Li. "Wait till you get him back to the office."

Yang scrambled to his feet. "You still need me?"

"Stay until the body gets moved, will you? Maybe we can talk a little." I nodded to Li, and he took the man by the arm. I could hear him going down the stairs, saying, "Careful, stairs are bad for people with asthma."

Yang pulled a handkerchief out of his pocket and picked up the glass the man on the floor had held before he tumbled off his chair. He sniffed it. "We should take this in. Doesn't smell like anything but *soju,* but you never know." He turned to Miss Pyon, who was leaning against the wall, still pale, and then looked at me.

"She didn't do anything," I said.

"If you say so. I wasn't here." Yang looked down at the body.

"But something happened to him," I said, "and it wasn't his heart."

Chapter Three

It was his heart." The pathologist took off her gloves and her mask. I kept my mask on until we walked into the better air of her office and closed the door to the autopsy room. "It was diseased. Could have occurred at any moment. Could have gone when he was crossing the street, when he was making love, when he was sitting in a chair watching TV. He happened to be in a restaurant drinking, that's all."

I couldn't believe that someone sitting next to the character with the red shirt just fell over dead. "You're sure nothing pushed it over the edge?"

"Like what, Inspector?"

"I don't know."

"Neither do I. Don't speculate, it's a sign of insecurity. We can wait for the reports on what was in his blood and his stomach, but I don't think they'll tell us anything. Anyway, it might be a month before we see them. The testing laboratory is very low on chemicals, and their equipment has been sent out for repair. According to his identification, he was thirty-five. I'd say he lived five years beyond his appointed day, that's all. Just a matter of time."

"What about the body that was brought in here the other day, the one hit by the bus, was that also a matter of time?"

"Tell me, Inspector, did you see any other bodies in there? The one you just brought with you is all I have. I've got vacancies, if you're interested."

"I asked you a question."

"You got an answer." The pathologist dropped the gloves on her desk. "I use these a week at a time. They're only meant to be used once, then thrown away. If I wear them again, they contaminate the evidence. If I throw them away, I won't have enough to last the month."

I looked at the mask in my hand. The pathologist laughed. "I opened a new one for you, but the next person here gets a dose of whatever you are carrying around."

"When you receive the reports on the blood and stomach, even if they're delayed, let me know. You have my number. Maybe it's simple, like you said, his heart just gave out, but if there is anything in his system out of the ordinary, call me."

"I will."

"Unless you get another set of orders with red numbers." I looked around the office. "I need to see your file with those orders."

She stiffened. "I don't give the orders, Inspector, I follow them. And you don't have authorization to see that file. You know you don't, so why did you even ask?"

I smiled. "It never hurts to try."

She opened the desk drawer and held something out for me. "I can't give you those orders, but this business card was inside his jacket, in the lining, actually. You can have it. Strange, wouldn't you say? It's from somewhere called Club Blue. Mean anything?"

"It might. You always check the lining?" I put the card in my pocket and then stuffed the mask in as well.

"No, but there was a hole in his pocket and it slipped through. There was also a piece of gum."

"I'll just keep the mask with me in case I have to come back."

"Welcome anytime, Inspector, anytime at all." She sat down at her desk. "You know the way out."

2

"Where's that wallet full of money?" Min dropped the normal "where have you been" when I walked in the next morning. I could tell he was angry. There was nothing on his face, and barely anything different in his voice, but he rarely went straight to the point.

"It's safe and sound, don't worry." Trouble this early in the day wasn't good. We should have gotten rid of the bank robbery case by now, but it was still hanging around my neck.

"I want it on my desk, immediately."

"Can't, I don't have it on me. It's at home."

"In your apartment house, the one with no locks on the doors?"

"What's the problem? No one goes into anyone else's apartment. We have a code of honor."

"A code of honor, in an apartment house filled with people who don't have a pot to pee in? Why do you insist on living in that place? We could get you into somewhere nice, nicer than that, anyway."

"It's home, I like it." Where I lived was my business. Min knew better than to tangle with me on that.

"Fine, that's your affair, though it keeps triggering questions in the quarterly reviews. Somebody in the Ministry has started voicing suspicions that it isn't normal for you to refuse multiple offers for a better place with more room. They think it must be a ruse."

"Pardon me, but bullshit. What am I going to do with more room? Anyway, they're good people in those apartments, no pretensions."

"I know you are fond of the idea of the perfectibility of mankind, Inspector, but not at the expense of the Ministry's procedures, please. How do you even hold on to such a notion? Every day we have examples right in front of our eyes telling us it isn't true."

"I don't believe such a thing. I never said I did."

"You don't believe in the perfectibility of man?"

"Careful."

"We're not talking about me, Inspector, we're talking about you. What I believe, I keep to myself."

"So do I."

"Ah, how I wish that were so. Do you know how much trouble I have every month, juggling the figures so it doesn't come out that we are the office with the lowest arrest rate in the city?"

"We happen to work in a refined part of town, is all."

"So, now you are suggesting that crime has a socioeconomic dimension, and that poorer people are more prone to crime than those who are better off?"

I laughed. "Rich people just commit different sorts of crimes. I see it every day at the markets."

Min shook his head. "That's not what we are discussing at the moment. We are dealing with something more philosophical than the price of shoes. We are discussing your view of mankind. Tell me, do you believe that man is already perfect? That there is no need for, shall we say, the gentle guidance of our leaders, who know, shall we say, the truth?"

Min's mastery of the ironic was suddenly a little thin. "This conversation is going to get one of us in trouble," I said.

"No, it won't. I'm certainly not going to remember it five minutes from now. But you have my interest piqued. As long as we are on the subject, why *are* our arrest figures so low?"

"People make mistakes; they are not always crimes."

"That isn't for us to judge."

"Not in a formal sense, no. But you'll admit there is a difference."

"I admit nothing, Inspector. You haven't answered me. Do you believe man is already perfect?"

"What difference does it make what I think about mankind?"

"You are squirming like a fish on a hook. You have a guilty look in your eye. I've caught you, haven't I? You basically think people are good, that they might commit bad acts, mistakes as you put it, but if we were to tote everything up, take the sum total of their lives, on balance mankind is more good than bad. How could I have landed the only policeman on the continent, maybe even on the planet, who believes such a fantasy?"

Neither of us said anything. I looked out at the gingko trees. Min examined his nails.

Finally, he cleared his throat. "You realize, Inspector, by extension, if you believe humans are perfect, you are saying the same about yourself. That's what the lady with the grating voice will conclude, before she pronounces sentence on us, and trust me, it will be both of us. I'm your supervisor; if your thoughts have gone astray, they'll say it was because I didn't give you proper oversight."

"I haven't said anything, Min. You've been doing all the talking, and all the inferring, and all the surmising."

"How did we get into this, anyway?"

"You said I shouldn't trust the people in my apartment house."

"For now, for the sake of argument, we'll grant the perfectibility of the people in your humble dwelling, Inspector. But there are other people, many other people wandering around, from all sorts of places."

"Chagang."

"Yes, Chagang."

"Maybe even worse."

"Leave the Chinese out of this. My only point is, you don't know who might be padding down the dark halls of your apartment house at this moment."

"Well, I think I might. More to the point, I know who isn't, and anyone who doesn't belong there isn't. Maybe the doors of your building are open for one and all. At my building, there is an old woman who guards the entrance. She has nothing better to do than stop people she doesn't recognize, and if she says they can't pass, they don't."

"What about Yang? Could he get into your building, with a Ministry ID?"

"I doubt it."

"Well, he did."

A warning flag hoisted itself up the flagpole. "How do you know?"

"Because he was at your apartment this morning after you left, and he says he couldn't find the wallet."

"He went into my apartment? My apartment? Without asking my permission?"

"I told him to." Min had his head down so he didn't have to look at me.

"Well, that's that, then." I was determined to keep an atom of nonchalance in my voice, and nearly did. "If you don't need me, I'll be going."

When Min picked up his head, he had a doleful look on his face. Having the apartment of one of our own staff searched was wildly beyond anything we'd ever done in our office. No chief inspector could expect to pull something like this and hope to keep his people with him. All I could figure was that Min was under so much pressure on this case it had undermined his judgment.

"Now, Inspector, this minute. I want that wallet, and I want it to be full of nice, crisp euro notes, all in order." He was trying to sound resolute, but I could tell he felt bad.

"I thought Yang brought it back."

"I told you, he said he couldn't find it." Min thought a moment. "Would you describe Yang as one of your perfect people?"

"Go to hell. You can go straight to hell." My voice was unnaturally strained, it had taken on the timbre of a fighter plane off in the distance, lining up to strafe a truck convoy at dawn. I shook off the image. My parents had been killed in a strafing attack during the war, a lone jet in a barely light sky. I rarely thought about it, but when I was mad, it bobbed to the surface sometimes.

"Well, is he?" Min caught the ominous rumble and pushed back slightly from his desk.

"Yang is fine. Still a little shaken, but he's coming out of it, slowly.

The man just needs some more time. It was a shock, losing his family like that." Min had crossed another line, this one worse than the first. It was galling enough that he had ordered a search of my apartment, but I was even angrier at what he was insinuating about Yang. The only thing to do was to change the subject, or walk out. "So, you and Yang discussed the death of that fellow in the noodle shop?"

Min was glad to follow my lead. "Yes, we talked about that. And if it was only that, it would be dandy. But the guy that Little Li dragged over here last night was out again in an hour, and he was spitting mad about how he was treated."

"He was treated fine. No one roughed him up. Neither Yang nor Li would do that. He had a nasty disposition, that's all, and he was extra interested in the money. In case anyone has forgotten, he was sitting next to a man who fell off his chair into the great void under suspicious circumstances. We needed him to answer a few questions. Yang would have made a few mournful queries, Li would have taken a couple of hours typing up the report, the guy would have signed it, and he could have walked into the night."

"Except for one thing. He's somebody's son."

"Oh, excuse me. I'm somebody's son." I hesitated. Well, I was, even though I'd barely known my father. "You're somebody's son. We're all somebody's son, unless we're somebody's daughter."

"Good, thank you, Inspector. Further lessons on lineage will be especially useful when we are on our way to a fucking coal mine in the fucking mountains."

"It's that bad?" Pressure apparently didn't even begin to explain what Min was feeling.

"No, worse, much worse. He is not only someone's son, he is someone's husband . . . stop . . . don't say anything, Inspector." Min raised his voice and started speaking faster. "I don't doubt that he is also someone's cousin, and someone's nephew, as well. Let me put it in words that will be plain, even to you. He is well connected. He moves in important circles." He took a deep breath. "And he is now our enemy."

"Why was he in that little noodle restaurant if he is such a big shot?" It was unsettling to see Min so rattled. We had lots of enemies. One more wouldn't kill us—unless it was someone close to the center.

"I don't care. I don't care at all where he dines. He can come in here and dance on my desk if he wants to."

"What about his dead friend?"

"Case closed. Episode never happened. Our prime witness is untouchable."

"No, not yet, there is blood work and—"

"Closed. Locked. Sealed. I don't care about his dead friend, not for one single, solitary second. Got it? The pathologist called to say the chances of getting anything back from the lab this century are zero; she said she's sure it was his heart, and if she's sure, that's good enough for me. Now, bring me that wallet, and there better not be one bill missing."

"The dead man, the owner of the wallet, had a business card from Club Blue in his jacket."

"Anything else?"

"Some gum."

Min threw up his hands.

"And"—I didn't think this would weigh very heavily with Min, but I might as well throw it on the scale—"I saw the manager of that same club coming out of the Gold Star Bank last night."

"So what? He was probably putting his money in the bank. That's what people do these days, don't ask me why. I wouldn't trust a bank with my money. And our dead friend might have liked drinking clubs. It means nothing to me. All I care about at this moment is that wallet, not gum, not business cards—the wallet."

"It wasn't his wallet, I told you. We didn't touch his wallet."

"He says it is his. He says you stole it."

"A lie."

"A well-connected lie, Inspector." He stopped for a moment and seemed to regain some composure. "Alright, of course I know you didn't steal the wallet, but how are we going to explain it when we send in a report that claims your apartment now doubles as our evidence custody room?"

"Where do you suppose he got all those big euro bills?"

"Not from the bank robbery."

"How do you know?" Min was developing a bad habit of telling me things I did not know.

"Listen, the robbers got away with three bags of small bills, nothing bigger than a fifty. From what Yang says, the wallet had mostly one-, two-, and five-hundred-euro bills."

Fine. Good. You have so many facts, why don't you take over the investigation? Here." I pulled the few notes I had on the case out of my pocket. "You can have these. Best of luck."

"Inspector." Min's voice dropped to a soothing register. "It's your case, you have the lead. Keep your notes. You do as you see fit. I'm just telling you a few tidbits that I happen to know." He folded his hands on the desk and leaned toward me. "Look, it is painfully obvious every day that I'm not as good a chief inspector as Pak was, but what can I do?"

This came out of nowhere, though I knew it wasn't nowhere or he never would have said it. It must have been eating at him for a long time. I'd have to do something, suggest we sit and talk to clear the air. It was past time for that, anyway. But not now. Right now we had a big problem—an accusation that we had stolen some money. It had to be fixed in a hurry. "Anything else you happen to know?"

"Not at the moment. If anything pops up, we'll chat."

It was irritating, that phrase. "Thank you. I'm interested in things that pop up, always have been. Sometimes I say to myself, 'O, try to pay more attention to things that pop up, can't you?' "

Min frowned before looking down at his desk. He moved a file folder from right to left, straightened it, then moved it back where it had been. "Don't let's be at each other's throats, Inspector. It won't do either of us any good."

"There are some times, Min, I have the feeling there is nothing that will do any good." That came out harsher than I meant it, but it was out and there wasn't any way to make it softer. Better just to let things cool off. I left without saying anything else; Min's sigh was audible all the way down the hall.

3

I was ready to waste a few hours at the Traffic Bureau trying to locate the file on the accident. The accusation about the wallet and the search of my apartment told me that the pressure on Min was at a danger point; the case had sharp edges, and anyone handling it was going to get sliced. The sooner we dropped it, the better. But I had to admit, there was something odd about it, something that made me want to hold it up to the light one more time before dumping it in the trash. For one thing, it wasn't usual for a bus to hit a man wearing a silk stocking over his face. It would be interesting to see what the Traffic Bureau file said, and I figured the case would have been discussed enough in the halls that it would be easy to find what I needed. I just had to make sure I didn't find out too much.

When I got to the Traffic Bureau, a sign on the front window said they were all in a political meeting and wouldn't be open for business until after lunch. I walked in anyway. Sure enough, the front desk was deserted, but there was more laughter from a room in back than I normally associate with political meetings. Finally, the door opened, and a line of traffic officers in white uniforms came out. Most of them had deeply tanned faces, from being outside in the weather all the time. I recognized a couple of them. They nodded as they walked past but didn't say anything.

I went up to the front desk as the officer on duty sat down and told him what I wanted. "Who needs to know?" He stared at my identification card. He was a little man, very fine bone structure. He moved like a bird.

"I do."

"And who are you?"

"What do you mean, who are you? It says so right here, on this card. Got my picture, my name, the signature of the Minister of People's Security. That is usually enough. You have special requirements around here these days?"

"What's your problem? I asked a simple question, who needs to know. It has to go on the release form."

"I told you—I need to know. And I told you who I am. That's who goes on the release form. Me. We finished with the formalities?"

He took my ID, looked at it for a long time. "Sorry. No such incident."

"What do you mean, no such incident? There's a body in the morgue that says there was."

"Really? You talked to him, did you, the body?"

"No, but I talked to the person who did the autopsy."

"Really? Someone told you they did an autopsy?"

"Not exactly."

"No, not exactly. Not at all, from what I hear. If there is nothing else, Inspector, we're busy." He picked up the phone. I put my hand on his little wrist, gently. Even so, it wasn't the smartest thing I've ever done.

He put the phone down, stared at my hand for a moment, then looked up at me. He was trembling with rage. "Never do that, Inspector. Never, ever do that."

I patted his wrist. "That didn't hurt, did it? But we weren't done with our conversation. I showed you a valid identification card. You are blocking my investigation. That is against regulations."

He stopped trembling long enough to sneer. "There is nothing to block, Inspector. That's what I told you. We have no file; there was never any accident like you described. Go away. And I mean now." The sneer was replaced by a grin. "I hear SSD is moving into the case. That's bad news for you inspector-boys, makes you look like a bunch of ducks."

This was sometimes called "healthy tension" between different parts of the Ministry. Actually, the Traffic Bureau hated us, the construction troops despised the traffic cops, and nobody could stand the guards at the camps. I could stay and make a nuisance of myself, but it would tie me up for an hour, and even then I knew I wouldn't see the whole file—which, if I stopped to think about it, I had to admit I didn't want to see. But I also didn't want some runt of a Traffic Bureau clerk telling me what I could see and what I couldn't. His superior would be more amenable, even offer me tea, but claim to have no information. He would make phone calls, he would tell me: You can rest assured, Inspector, I'll call all the way up the line if that is what it takes. He would promise to make inquiries: Most certainly, Inspector, we will continue to search the records. He would get back to me: As soon as I hear anything, absolutely as soon as I hear, I'll call you. None of it remotely true. Better to leave now and cut my losses.

On the walk back to the office, I decided enough was enough. I'd put the case file in the bottom drawer and forget about it. Min wouldn't like it if SSD took over, but that was the least of my concerns. If he had to deal with it in the Saturday meeting, that was his problem.

When I got back to my office, I heard voices coming from Min's room. A minute later, my phone rang.

"O here."

"Inspector, come into my office, please."

"I need to write up one of those daily reports for yesterday."

"No, you don't, and you didn't get anything done at the Traffic Bureau, just like at the bank and that bar. We need to talk."

Min was behind his desk, and in a chair against the wall was a lanky man, probably in his late thirties, wearing an open white shirt with cuffs that could knock your eyes out, a blue blazer, and tan slacks. His hair was short and neat. He had a dark complexion, made darker by the large, square sunglasses that hid his eyes and a good deal of territory around them.

Min stood up as I walked in, which put me on my guard. "In-spector, I want you to meet someone." The other man nodded but didn't get out of his chair. "This is Lieutenant Han, from SSD. He'll be working with you on the bank robbery."

So, the boom had been lowered, even faster than I'd expected. Maybe too fast. I eyed the man from SSD, a long, thoughtful look, nothing to suggest I was surprised, or concerned, or already felt quick-sand up to my waist. The man from SSD returned my gaze, or maybe he didn't. He might have been sleeping, for all I knew; you couldn't be sure what was going on behind those big dark glasses. I turned back to Min. "Good of SSD to make the offer to work with us, but unneces-sary. This is an important case." I paused to make sure I had the next sentence phrased just right, with the sarcasm decently buried. "They should handle it, and we wouldn't want to weigh them down." Lieu-tenant Han didn't respond, but Min did, before anything like an awk-ward silence had a chance to establish itself.

"The State Security Department has been assigned to this case, Inspector, in conjunction with us." Min was talking fast, clipping words like hedges; that usually happened when he was nervous or in the presence of people who clearly were—or might conceivably be—a threat. "You can imagine how the Center wants all resources working together. The Minister has personally approved." This I doubted, unless the word "approved" was taken in the strictly literal sense of signing one's name to a piece of paper. Min must have read my mind. "The signed order is coming down later today. You and Han here can start before it arrives. Take some time to get ac-quainted, get used to each other's mode of operations, that sort of thing. You'll need to give him a full briefing on where things stand. Teamwork, Inspector." Min's voice was looking for a false bravado it couldn't find. "That's the new way. No more lone-wolf policing. Teamwork." The word seemed to give him a certain ballast. I was afraid he might repeat it again, but he only looked at us in turn and fiddled with a pencil.

Now there was an awkward silence. Han finally stood up. I thought maybe the reference to wolves had stirred him. "All we have to do is solve this, Inspector. After that, we can go back to normal." He spoke with his mouth mostly closed, in a voice that sounded like he was borrowing it from someone else. This kid was not going to be much help, already I knew that. I'd trailed along with SSD many times before, and it was never pleasant. At our level, they were a threat, alright, but not the usual type. When they weren't lazy, they were stupid. The combination was inevitably lethal for someone; I always tried to make sure it wasn't me. The only time it was really serious was when SSD headquarters became personally involved. Those people had heft, that we knew, and you didn't want to get in their way.

"Fine, good to have you with us, Lieutenant." I took the silk stocking out of my back pocket. "You wouldn't have the match to this, would you?"

Min sat down. The chair creaked, but he said nothing as he covered his eyes.

Han followed me back to my office. He looked around the room. "Where's your computer?"

"We don't have computers." This was the first sign of trouble. SSD had a bigger budget and was better equipped. Even more galling, it liked to rub our noses in the fact that it was operating from a higher plane than the rest of us. What SSD wanted, SSD got. "We don't need them, actually." I gestured around the room to suggest the office was more than sufficiently equipped.

"Is that so?" Han went over to my file cabinet. "You have everything in here?" He opened the top drawer, where I keep my wood scraps and my sandpaper. "What's this?"

"I keep that mostly empty for evidence." He didn't say anything. I pushed the drawer shut. "You like wood?"

"I use it to pick my teeth. Where's the paper on this case?"

"Wasn't it in your computer?"

Han slowly took off his glasses and put them in his shirt pocket before he fixed me with a cold look. He did have eyes, after all. They were way too gentle for SSD, almost a girl's eyes, but he had perfected the cold look pretty well. "It doesn't matter to me how we get this done this, Inspector. Because when everything is over, I have someplace useful to go back to. You, on the other hand, will still be here." He dusted off the chair with a handkerchief before he sat down. "You see what I mean?"

"Tell me, Han, harassed anyone interesting lately?"

"What?"

"That's SSD's main job, isn't it? I mean, harassing people."

"You want to be real careful, Inspector, from here on out. Real careful in what you say."

"No, seriously, I'm interested, Lieutenant. You must have techniques, am I right? A phone call comes in; it's anonymous and for some reason untraceable; someone tells you that someone else just said something questionable about—"

"Like I said, Inspector, be real careful."

"Well, you know what I mean. So you start up a file or something. It must be hard to keep track of all those phone calls, all those people who say things in such soft voices. Hard to hear people talking that soft, sometimes. You never said 'something' yourself? I mean, you can tell me, Lieutenant, just the two of us here."

"Inspector, I'm going to do you a favor and pretend my hearing has gone bad. We have a lot of work to do, let's do it."

"Good, let's go harass someone, Lieutenant. You can show me how it's done."

Min stopped me on the way out. "Inspector, could I see you a moment?" He shut the door when I stepped into his office. "Lay off the kid, would you? He's smart, he has a good reputation. Maybe if we stay on his good side, he'll go away happy."

"You forgot one thing. He works for SSD. The last thing in the world he wants to do is help the Ministry."

Min went over to his desk and sat down. If his chief inspector bottom was on the chair, it meant he was going to say something important. "I'm going to tell you this once, Inspector. One time, a single, solitary time. Listen carefully, please. We cooperate with SSD on this, or they eat us alive." He closed his eyes. "Don't argue, just do it and let's get back to normal, like the man said."

4

The two of us were in Han's car, heading toward the Gold Star Bank. Han was driving with one hand, holding a cigarette in the other. It didn't take much to convince him that his car was better than mine, and that if we were taking his car, he should drive. The driver always thinks he is in control, exactly what I wanted. Things would go smoother if Han thought that he had the lead and that I recognized his position. I looked out the window and wondered why no one from SSD ever knew anything about investigations. Or why they wouldn't listen to anyone who did. Maybe it was the gene pool they pulled from. Han was driving too fast. That was another SSD trait.

"We in a big hurry?" I put my hand on the dashboard to brace myself as we pulled around a truck.

"I'm driving, Inspector. When you drive, you pick the speed. Let's agree on that, shall we?" In that borrowed voice again.

I took a piece of poplar wood out of my pocket and began sanding it with an old scrap of sandpaper. There wasn't much left of the sandpaper, and poplar isn't all that interesting. I was just going through the motions. The car swerved as Han reached for my hand and yelled, "Hey! You're messing up my upholstery."

"You're driving," I said. "I'm sanding. Let's agree on that." I brushed the front of my shirt. It always amazed me how much sawdust came out of a little piece of poplar; sawdust and matchsticks. Trash wood, my grandfather would say.

Han pulled over and braked sharply in front of the train station. "Put it away, Inspector. I heard about you and wood. You can mess up that dump you call an office with sawdust if you want, but not here. In fact, don't do it in my presence, not on this case." When he was angry, I noticed, he fell into using his real voice. It was younger, not so tough.

I blew some sawdust against the front windshield and watched it settle on the dashboard. "I'm not here because I volunteered, Han. As I recall, the sequence was this: You showed up in my chief inspector's office, and he told me to cooperate with you. It was a Ministry order. We were to work as a team. I'm doing my part; I'm doing what I do. If you want to make changes to that, be my guest. Get your headquarters to call you back home. Otherwise, we have work to do. Sawdust bothers you? File a complaint. Trust me, it's a lot easier to clean up sawdust than it is to repair cigarette burns in upholstery." I waited, but he didn't have a smart answer ready, so I continued. "Tell me something, if you don't mind."

"What?" Kind of sullen but also, I thought, preoccupied.

"You wear those sunglasses when you sleep?"

Han threw his cigarette out the window and stepped on the gas. A traffic policeman was crossing the street to see why we were stopped. Han sped past him. "Okay," he said. "Good. We're beyond the getting-to-know-you stage. The textbooks refer to it as 'initial posturing.' It has been established beyond a reasonable doubt that you don't like SSD. That's your problem. Can we move on to something else?" This was still his regular voice, but I could tell he didn't have a chance to use it much, except maybe when he was talking to himself.

"Move on to something else," I said, "such as?"

"Such as the bank robbery we're supposed to be investigating."

"Is that the next stage in the textbook?"

"Inspector"—Han turned into a side street that took us two short blocks from the bank—"I'm not interested in our becoming fast friends. All I want is to see this case file in the out-basket." He switched off the engine, took off his sunglasses, and pulled a notebook from a side pocket on his door. "Your out-basket had a piece of wood in it, oak I think it was."

"What sort of oak?" I wasn't going to give in that easily. Maybe oak was the only tree he knew.

Han leaned back and smiled. "Oak, that's enough."

"Fine, we're back to stage one, getting acquainted." Han didn't fit with the normal SSD character. I'd never heard one of them refer to a textbook, or to any book, actually. "If I had to guess"—I stared out the windshield—"I'd guess you aren't from SSD. The blazer had me fooled, but no one from SSD is so smooth, and none of them know oak from abalone. Who are you really?"

Han didn't break stride. "Just who your boss said I was. We have been put together to focus resources on a crime the Center wants solved. You have a reputation as a competent investigator." Curiously, it sounded like a compliment. "I have access to files and equipment you lack. I've worked in SSD for almost eight years. Satisfied?"

"No. It's a sad day, when one ox can't pull the cart."

"Let's leave farm implements out of it for now." He started thumbing through the notebook. "This woman, Chon, at the bank. Have you seen her file?"

"She doesn't have a file."

"Inspector, everyone has a file. I have a file. You have a file." A faraway look came over his face. "And it's some file." He closed his eyes briefly, in a kind of ecstasy I didn't like. "Anyway, I can have her searched in our records." He checked his cuffs. "At least we can see if she exists on the computer. She works with foreign currency; most of those people have to fill out special paperwork."

"Only one problem, we don't have her full name yet. She hasn't been formally interviewed."

"What does that matter? Her name should be cross-filed under the bank's employees."

"So, why are we sitting here? Drop me off, and you can go back to your office to check."

"Go back? I'm going to call in her name from here. It will only take a couple of minutes for the computer run. That way, when we go in, we'll have something to talk about." Han took a cell phone from his coat pocket, dialed a number, said a few words, then put the phone on the dashboard and slumped down in his seat. "Now we wait."

A few minutes later, the phone buzzed like a bee. Han pulled it to his ear, nodded his head, then turned it off.

"Impressive," I said.

"Yes, they move fast."

"No, I mean that buzzing. How do you get it to do that, instead of playing music?"

Han snorted. "Give me your cell number. I'll call you so we can see what you have."

"Not a chance." I climbed out of the car. Whatever tune was programmed on my phone, Han didn't need to hear it. "It's time to go to work."

"Don't you want to know what they have on her in the files?"

"Nope."

"Why not?"

"Because they don't have anything. I already told you, she doesn't have a file."

"How did you know that?" Han looked in the rearview mirror, frowned, and smoothed his hair.

"I checked. Women like her don't have files. Women like her know a certain level of people, and people at that level don't want to be in the files of women like her. It's too hard to do, staying out of her file. The easier route is just to get rid of it, pay someone to lose it. Maybe we can go through the foreign visitors' roster that the immigration people have, but I don't think she'll be there, either."

Han shook his head. "Don't worry; someone has a file on her, someplace. Let's find out who she knows." He smiled at the mirror, ran his finger over his teeth, and then frowned again. "I hate dealing with people who don't have files. There is something abnormal about it."

Just as we reached the bank's front door, Han took a pair of latex gloves from his pocket. "You have a pair of these, Inspector?"

"No, but I have this." I put on the mask from the morgue. "Do

I really need it? We're not going to do an autopsy, Han, we're just going to ask the lady some questions."

"This is a crime scene, Inspector, and there may be evidence. Without these gloves, you'll contaminate the place, leave fingerprints. Take off the mask. They'll think it's another robbery."

"The crime took place days ago. By now hundreds of fingers have visited. There's no physical evidence left. But who knows, you can always get the flu."

"Are you really going to leave that mask on?" He was sounding nettled.

I opened the door and walked in. "Don't worry, it's just us." One of the desks was missing, and no one was sitting at the other two. The three teller windows along the rear wall were open; the broken one had been fixed. "Good security practice." I turned back to Han. "Front door open, and the place is empty. No wonder they got robbed. If you need some cash, Han, it's there in the back. Help yourself."

Han pulled off his gloves and stuffed them in his back pocket. "Something isn't right here, Inspector."

"You're telling me. Overnight, they've cleaned the place up, rearranged the furniture, and left for Switzerland. A good piece of plywood has disappeared, as well. It was exterior plywood, but they were using it inside, which wasn't very smart. You could get splinters."

"No one's gone to Switzerland, trust me on that. Keep your eyes open while I go to check the back. Whistle if you see anyone coming."

"Don't bother. They're in the back waiting, watching us on the security camera right now." I pointed at the small camera bolted on the wall close to the ceiling in a back corner, over one of the desks. "I wonder if it taped the robbery. Wouldn't that be a lucky break?"

"You're out of luck, Inspector." Miss Chon came in behind us through the front door. "We don't tape. We just monitor from the back, mostly to make sure the clerks stay honest." She frowned as I turned around. "I don't have any communicable diseases, nothing that is airborne, anyway. You can take off your mask." She looked at Han, then back to me. "I see you felt the need for reinforcements. I already told you, we don't require an investigation."

"And I told you, I am polite but persistent. This young fellow is not from my ministry, but he is more persistent than I am, and probably not as agreeable."

Miss Chon didn't bother to look at Han again. "I don't care who he is. You'll both have to leave, unless you have financial business to transact with the bank. Since the robbery, we aren't letting people loiter. No one even comes in if we don't recognize them as a customer." She walked over to her desk and sat down. "I don't recognize either of you."

"Do you have any idea who you're talking to?" Han was back to his tough voice, though the overall effect wasn't helped by the buzzing coming from his coat pocket. "This is an SSD investigation, and the inspector and I will stand here until the mountains fall into the sea if we feel like it."

Miss Chon was wearing a red dress with a white belt that made her waist look even smaller. It was a wonder she could breathe. "You'd better answer your phone before then. It might be your mother." She smiled at me, I smiled back.

Han swore under his breath. "Get your manager out here. And where are the records?" He fumbled in his pocket for the phone; the buzzing stopped.

"Before we see the manager, we need to ask you a few questions." I smiled again at Miss Chon. "Nothing too probing. Were you sitting out here when the robbery occurred?"

"This is my desk, isn't it?"

"I don't know whose it is. You weren't sitting here yesterday. You were sitting at the desk that isn't around anymore. You got tired of it? Needed a newer model?" I looked at the indentations in the rug where the other desk had been. It must have been heavy; the marks it left went deep into the carpet.

"It isn't a crime to move furniture, Inspector, unless your ministry has discovered regulations from the old days, when things were tidy and dull. We needed a new interior scheme, that's all, something that would attract more foreign customers. We hired a decorator, an Italian man who favors silk shirts that open to here." Wherever "to here" was would look good on her, but I pretended not to notice. "He told us the colors were too plain and the furniture was too heavy. So, we're lightening things up. Yesterday seemed like a good day to start."

"This may come as a surprise, Miss Chon, but a bank robbery is considered a serious crime, and altering a crime scene is a bad thing to do. It's actually hampering an investigation. That's not from the old days; in the old days there weren't investigations." The look on her face told me she wasn't going to chew her nails over the news that she had altered a crime scene. I moved along to something else. "What about that teller window? How did you get it repaired so quickly?"

Miss Chon crossed her legs and began to dangle one shoe off her foot. She looked very comfortable. "Quickly? What do you mean, Inspector? We've been waiting to get that fixed since February. The glass only came in this morning. The janitor put it in himself. He said we're not to touch it for a couple of days, something about letting the glue dry." Miss Chon reached over and massaged her ankle. I could hear Han's labored breathing behind me.

"Maybe we should see the manager now," I said.

"You already have, Inspector. Who did you think I am, a clerk, a pretty face to greet the men with bags of money? I'm the manager. And if you have no more questions, I'm very busy." She looked up at the security camera for an instant, then turned back to me. "We're closed today to customers. Tomorrow, to mark a fresh start, to help clear away the memory of the robbery and the unpleasantness outside, we're holding a small party in the afternoon, at five o'clock. I know it's a Sunday, but perhaps if you're not busy you'd like to come, you and the bumblebee from SSD."

As we walked back to the car, Han was silent. Just before he got in, he gave a little skip. "I knew it." He opened the door and then slammed it shut. "I knew it."

"Something I missed?"

"She's in on it, Inspector. Did you see the way she was sitting?"

"I did. But you seemed to be paying more attention than I was."

"What did it tell you—I mean, her posture, her demeanor?"

I opened the door and slid into the passenger seat. "She sits like a lady who knows how to cross her legs."

Han climbed in on his side. "No, she doesn't. She doesn't sit like a lady at all. Her bearing was all wrong. She's nervous, shifty. She didn't make eye contact with me once."

"I think she doesn't like you."

"Of course she doesn't, I'm from SSD, and I'm a threat. She has a guilty conscience."

"So why did she make eye contact with me?"

"Because she knows you're not a threat, Inspector. She thinks you're a clown."

"Really, is that so?" I took some paper from my pocket and jotted a few notes. "Who do you think was in the back room?"

"No one."

"I'd say you're wrong, I'd say there was someone. She was nervous, I'll grant you that, and she needed to get us out of there before we went into the back to take a look. She glanced at the security camera, not very long, but long enough to tell whoever was back there to leave. What did you think of the glass?"

"What glass?"

"The new glass in the teller window. She said the janitor did it himself and then told her not to touch it for a few days until it dried."

"So?"

"It wasn't glued. You don't glue glass into place. You use putty. But this was just sitting in a slot in the frame. It could fall out if someone slammed the front door."

"Who cares?"

"Why would she make up a story about something like that? More to the point, why would anyone who knows about being a janitor talk about gluing in the window?"

Han rubbed his nose. "You said there was a desk missing."

"A heavy desk."

"What was in it?"

"At last, a good question, Lieutenant Han. Now I have one for you. Shall we get something to eat?"

Chapter Four

It was Sunday, but I went to the office anyway. Now that SSD had moved in on the case, it would be harder for us to drop. But there is always a hole in the clouds. If the case was actually supposed to be solved—which I still doubted—then SSD would fumble around and trip over evidence, but we might eventually pull some facts together. If it wasn't supposed to be solved, I knew SSD would make sure we didn't get ourselves in trouble by finding anything remotely like a concrete lead. It was unlikely we'd discover anything at the party Miss Chon had mentioned, and that was fine. A party is, after all, a party. No harm in standing around.

Meanwhile, I decided to drive over and nose around the neighborhood near the bank. There were a few residents in the old apartments who spent the whole day doing nothing but sitting around with their eyes open. Imagine my surprise when it turned out, on the day of the robbery, they had all been somewhere else. None of them knew a bartender with a high-pitched voice and a scar on his face, either, though a couple of them flinched when I told them they'd better believe I'd remember how they helped me out on this.

I went back to the office and made a few phone calls to my friends to see if anyone had heard anything out of the ordinary. None of them had. Han picked me up around five o'clock; he didn't have much to say on the drive over. I'd never been to a party at a bank, but the festivities at the Gold Star were not what I had expected. There were several foreigners, mostly Europeans, mostly male, mostly sipping Scotch. A few of them stood talking to young Korean women whom the bank had rounded up to serve as hostesses. They were in traditional Korean dress, pale colors that made them look like the sky at dawn, quiet and calmly innocent. They laughed among themselves, smiled at the foreigners, and moved away when Han and I walked in the door. I didn't recognize any of them.

Miss Chon acknowledged our presence with a nod but didn't come over to greet us. Han felt put out immediately. "We shouldn't have come. I knew we shouldn't have come. There is nothing to learn at this sort of event."

"Relax, have a drink, talk to one of the girls."

"That may be your ministry's style, Inspector, but SSD still has high standards. These people are all suspects, every single one of them. I don't mingle with suspects."

"Why are they all suspects?"

"Because they are all at the scene of a crime."

"Good thinking, Han. My orders, on the other hand, are never to pass up a glass of good Scotch. One of these foreigners may have observed the robbery; so much the better. You pretend they're suspects, I'll pretend they're witnesses, and we'll see who gets to talk to the prettiest girl."

Han scowled. "Don't tell them who I am."

"Don't worry, I'll pretend you're not even here." I picked up a drink and waved a girl over. "You may ignore him," I said to her. "But you must not ignore me."

"Why would I ignore you, Inspector?"

"Have we met?"

"Yes, but you seem not to remember."

"Forgive me, truly. If we had met, surely I would remember your smile."

She gagged but recovered nicely. "I used to supervise the Ministry's guesthouse," she said. "Your chief inspector, Pak, got me the job." There was a pause, just a heartbeat, as she watched me. Speaking of a nonperson who had died in a nonevent wasn't wise. "You were there for a lunch with a German delegation some years ago. Or perhaps it was Austrian. They were unhappy with their schedule. They kept saying they had requested a meeting with the Minister but that no one was paying any attention to them and all they were doing was sightseeing. My waitresses said they hardly ate a bite and talked the whole time about lodging a protest."

"Your waitresses said that? They knew German? No one told me."

"So, you remember the lunch, but you have forgotten me." She took my arm and led me under the security camera. "This is better. The camera can't find us here."

"Some reason it shouldn't?"

"What do you know about the manager?" She glanced at Miss Chon.

"She's tough."

"She has to be. She's a woman. And she's a foreigner."

"I was positive about the first, and pretty sure about the second. But she looks Korean."

"She isn't. She's Scottish."

"Are you kidding?"

"Well, that's what her passport says. I'm supposed to be watching her, but she is good at slipping away."

"I thought you were in charge of waitresses."

"A man can't follow a woman, Inspector." She laughed at nothing and put her hand on my arm. "The Ministry finally figured that out. Isn't that wise?"

"If you were going to buy some silk stockings, where would you go?" I made a point of not looking at her legs. I can stand around at parties alright, but small talk is not my forte. The first thing that came into my head was stockings. The wisdom of Ministry personnel matters could wait for another time.

"Aren't you going to ask me what size I wear?"

"No, I am not. I'm sure it's something very petite, and not my business. But I do need to know, do they sell them in the city? Or would you have to put in an order with someone going outside to bring them back?"

"It depends, Inspector. On the side of the train station, there is a Russian who is said to sell such things from a suitcase he is said to carry."

"Okay, now I'll ask. What size do you wear?"

"Smile, act like I'm a good hostess." But after I smiled she said, "No, never mind. Just look interested."

2

Han dropped me at my apartment around dinnertime. "I'm going to follow up some leads, Inspector. Question some sources that we have; just leave that all to me. Call me tomorrow and we'll figure out our next move. I'll even fix your cell phone, if we have time."

"Wait a second, Han. You told me the Center wants this solved. What did you mean?"

Han took off his sunglasses so I could see he was scowling. "I never said such a thing."

"My mistake, I apologize. I suppose you also didn't say that SSD has the lead in this investigation."

"That I did say."

"Do you have orders or something showing you are supposed to take the lead? Forget protocol; I mean orders. If you do, I'll just go back to my office and type a final report. SSD can have it."

"I wasn't speaking formally, Inspector. But one of us has to take the lead, wouldn't you agree, and it might as well be the one with the equipment and the resources to solve the case. That's no reason for you to drop out. It's just the way things are." This was not normal SSD gloating. At this point, he should have been suggesting I was barely good enough to shine his shoes.

"Why should I stay working on a case the Center doesn't want solved?" It wasn't an idle question. I was passing him a knife, handle first, and pointing out my vitals.

"No one said the Center doesn't want it solved."

"But no one said they did." He didn't want the knife, which worried me more than if he had. I was going to be his trussed pig, not ready for the slaughter.

3

The woman in the next apartment had left a bowl of rice and a small glass filled with old kimchi on the wooden chest inside my front door. I gave her money every week, and she would go to the market for me. She didn't prepare anything elaborate, but there was always something waiting, no matter when I came home. The food sat by itself on the chest; there was no wallet—with or without euro notes. It hadn't been knocked onto the floor by mistake, and she hadn't tried to be helpful by putting it in the drawer. I opened the window and lay down. Han occupied my thoughts for a couple of minutes, then I thought about stockings and Miss Chon's waist, and then I did what I sometimes do when I lie down. I fell asleep.

By the time I got back to the office, it was already dark, but I could see from the street that the lights were on. That meant Min was there; he always turned the lights on in every office when he worked at night. He said it was good if people on the street thought the Ministry never slept. It was the right moment to walk into his office and tell him to either give me everything he knew about this case or take me off of it. The Ministry had assigned someone, a former waitress for crying out loud, to follow the manager of the Gold Star Bank. No one informed me. Min had sent Yang to my apartment and then told me Yang had not seen the wallet, which had been in plain sight on the chest next to the door. How could he not see it? It certainly wasn't there now. My neighbor wouldn't take it; no one in the apartment house would.

Min was on the phone. He was seated at attention, which meant it was an important conversation. The way he waved me to a chair told me he was being chewed out. By the time he hung up, he was sweating slightly. "Inspector, this is not going well."

"Complaints? More threats to drop the case?"

"Worse, orders from the Ministry to solve it immediately. How can we do that? We're bogged down with SSD, you say no one will open their files, that fellow from the other night—"

"The well-connected one?"

"Yes, him. He has connections with the Central Committee."

"What about the bank manager?"

"What about her?"

"She's being followed."

Min began to doodle on a file folder. I didn't say anything, leaving the only sound in the room the moths fluttering around the light. "That's it?" he finally asked. "Okay, I knew she was being followed. Well, no, I didn't actually know that. I just knew she was already high on the Ministry's list of suspects."

"And you didn't tell me."

"I don't trust Ministry lists. I had to see if you came to the same conclusion. I think the real reason they have their eye on her is that she's a foreigner."

"Yes, I got that. She's Scottish."

"Scottish? Are you crazy, Inspector? She's Kazakh."

I shrugged. "She could be anything, for all I care. But her tail told me she has a Scottish passport."

"You talked to the guy who is tailing her?"

"Not a guy. A woman, a waitress actually, as if you didn't know. Maybe I should retire." Panic flashed in Min's eyes, raw panic, the same emotion passengers on boats convey when the water is up to their knees and waves are breaking through the windows. Time to put another hole in the hull. "I thought after all these years I was respected for my ability. I do at least know how to tail people. But I take it I am wrong, my abilities in that regard are no longer respected, and perhaps the Ministry thinks I am no longer needed. Very well, my request for retirement will be on your desk by tomorrow. Good luck working with Han."

Min quickly picked up the phone. "Go away," he said to me before he started dialing. "It's late. Go sit in your office and work on your bookshelves. Let me check a few things. I'll be down in a few minutes. Don't fill out anything."

An hour later, around 10:00 P.M., Min was at my door. I was studying the plans for the bookshelf that would fit on the far wall in my office. The office was small enough so that there was little to distinguish the far wall from the near one. The ceilings were very high, which made for a lot of space, but all of it on the vertical. It was like being a farmer on a mountaintop. The bookshelf wasn't anything I'd ever get done, I knew that. I had found some lumber, but never exactly what I needed. When I could get any wood screws, they were the wrong size. But I enjoyed studying the plans.

"Inspector, I've got my footing back. I apologize for not being overly forthcoming these past few days, but I had the feeling a typhoon was coming. The problem was, I didn't know from which direction. Now I do. No need for you to retire."

"If you didn't know whether or not a typhoon was coming, why did you put me in its path with a silk stocking in my pocket?"

"I would have told you when to jump for safety, don't worry. But I needed some clarity first. I had to have a better focus."

"And now you have it?"

"I have focus. And you, you have that wallet? I thought I told you to bring it in."

I opened my desk drawer. "Right here." Actually it wasn't; I didn't know where it was. It had disappeared, but I couldn't tell that to Min. He would demand a search of each apartment on each floor, and not a light dusting, either. These would be thorough searches, everything turned upside down. The neighbors wouldn't talk to me for months. I closed the drawer. "We're not going to give it back to Mr. Well-connected, are we?"

"No, he won't bother us."

"And why not?" I could see from Min's expression that we were off the wallet onto something more troubling.

"He was found dead, with a knife in his back, in a dark alley near a certain drinking establishment."

"Ah, I love it when the plot thickens."

Chapter Five

Some people might have said a walk to the train station the next morning wasn't the best use of my time, but efficiency was taking second place to survival. The investigation was becoming more complicated by the day. Murder does that. First the Ministry wanted the case solved, then they didn't. And then they did. SSD was thrown in, so quickly it almost seemed to me that someone had planned their involvement all along—either to put pressure on us to get the matter solved, or to make sure it wasn't solved at all. I was used to opaqueness in these things, but this exceeded what was normal. And now there were warning streamers attached to the normal little warning flags, all telling me that guessing wrong on this case would not be minor. Realizing I needed to stay on safe ground for the time being wasn't much comfort; it just meant I had to worry about how to tell safe ground from a cesspool. I didn't sleep much that night, until finally, about dawn, I decided that maybe the best course was still just plodding through the preliminary steps in a way that would make everybody happy. I would do enough to keep the Ministry off our necks if they really were panting for a solution. I would not do nearly enough to scare whoever might be watching from one of the darker corners of the city, if someone above the Minister was determined to keep us going through the motions without getting anywhere near the truth. Besides, I was still curious about the stockings.

One thing that had me more than a little worried was SSD's involvement. I didn't care if it smudged the Ministry's image; that could be repaired. Something about Han's approach suggested that somewhere at the core of this case were security concerns beyond what a simple bank robbery—even the first one on record—would warrant. As long as he was assigned to the case, I was supposed to check everything with Han first. Protocol gave SSD pride of place in a joint investigation. It was the main reason we made a point of leaving unopened any orders that had the word "joint" in the subject line. Apart from that, I was unsure about Han himself. He was smoother than he ought to be. His awkwardness was off; it was almost too practiced. It could be that he was from a new SSD breed trained to hide a level of competence that no one suspected they had. A new little warning flag, waving from its own rampart, didn't think so. I had to admit, the SSD officers I knew didn't spend a lot of time investigating. To them, everything was just bending thumbs. Han didn't fit that mold. Anyone who could recognize a piece of oak was capable of learning; most of the people I'd met in SSD weren't.

I got a little sleep and arrived at the office somewhat past the start of my shift. Min was gone, probably to a staff meeting at the Ministry. I had a few things left to do at my desk, some old paperwork to initial and send on, questions from an inspector in a sector at the other end of town to answer, a name trace file that had been on my chair for weeks. It was midmorning before I got out of the office and onto the street. Min was still stuck in his meeting, which was fine. My mobile phone was off, stuffed in the back of my desk drawer. When he complained later he couldn't find me, I could say that I needed to go out and think, that the area around the station was nice this time of year, lots of people walking around, most of them in a good mood because of the weather. What I didn't have to say was that the reason I went over there was to find a Russian with a suitcase full of silk stockings.

Right away, there was a detour I hadn't expected, because the sidewalks on the main route were torn up and new paving stones were being put down. There hadn't been anything wrong with the old ones from what I could tell, but the city was being "beautified," and that meant new sidewalks, new paint on the front of the buildings, even new windows for some of them. The work gangs didn't mind being outside in this weather; only a few of them were actually working, anyway. The rest of them sat on the new curbs and watched. The detour took me onto a street with two or three new restaurants and a barber. The restaurants were still closed with the curtains shut, but the barber was in good spirits and waved me in. He thought he had found a "supplier" for new scissors and maybe even a hair dryer, at what he said was a "good price." That meant it wasn't legal, but I figured there were a few things higher on my list than stolen scissors.

The barber said the detour had increased his business and he hoped they would never get the new sidewalk finished. By the time he was through talking and started to cut my hair, one of the restaurants was open. It was too beautiful a day to eat near the station, so I hung around for another thirty minutes while they rearranged the tables to fit in more customers.

When I finally arrived at the station, it was early afternoon. The station and its neighborhood aren't really in my area, and I had to make sure that the inspector with formal responsibility—an older man named Hyon, who had a keen sense for knowing when anyone crossed into his sector—didn't get suspicious. If he did, he might file a complaint, and that could mean an exchange of angry memos followed by a meeting or two presided over by the lady with the shrill voice. The street patrols don't give a damn, sometimes they don't even know, when out-of-sector inspectors tiptoe through. But inspectors in charge keep careful track. They have to; otherwise, something funny might happen when they aren't looking, and they could get blamed.

Most people can be very territorial when their backsides are at stake. As it turned out, Hyon had been unable to come up with a good excuse why he shouldn't "volunteer" for farm work and so had been sent out to the countryside for a week. His fill-in didn't care what I did, as long as I was quiet about it.

2

"I thought you might come by, Inspector." The man sat on the ground leaning against a gingko tree twice the size of the ones in the courtyard outside Min's window. A jacket folded up behind his head served as a pillow. He had taken off his glasses, and he looked up at me with a squint. "It took you longer than I expected." He hadn't shaved for several days.

"Is that so? Who might have told you that I was interested?"

"I have friends, you have friends; sometimes friends talk to friends. Sometimes they are even the same person." He searched around on the ground for his glasses. A little anxious, it seemed to me; the sort of person who feels off balance if he can't physically see what he's confronting. The sort of person who doesn't like to be interrogated in a dark room.

"We could speak Russian, if you'd be more comfortable."

"No, Russian is the one language that doesn't make me comfortable. Korean is fine. Not especially melodic to my ears. But good enough; just ignore my grammar."

"You mind if I sit?"

"Inspector, please, it's your country, for thousands of years, all yours. Maybe you had the same problem for a while with the Mongols that we did, a slight break in the chain of national custody. But that was temporary, wasn't it, thanks God." He finally found his glasses. He studied me closely, taking in the details that the squint had missed, and as he did, he became less anxious.

"So, you don't mind if I sit?"

He smiled and indicated a place beside him. "Please, do me the honor."

I didn't move, but stayed where I was, looking down at him. "You seem a little pale. Are you feeling alright?"

"Me? Kind of you to express concern. Not many people do. I'm fine. Sometimes the food here doesn't agree with me. This is not a criticism, just a reality. I have what you might call a nervous stomach. And I wouldn't mind a bath. Sit, please, sit. Sit, Inspector, my neck is cramping, having to look up at you."

I sat. "Your hotel doesn't have a bath?"

"I'm not in a hotel, I can't afford it. I'm staying with friends."

"Friends." I paused. "Your friends made sure you registered, as they should?"

"When in Rome, Inspector."

"I've only made it as far south as Switzerland." Which was true, in a manner of speaking. "Italy intrigues me, though."

"Perhaps you should read Goethe. He was intrigued, as well."

"Thank you, there's probably a copy in the office." To his credit, he did not laugh out loud. I got down to business. "Where are your papers, if I might ask? The hotel would normally keep them, but in this case . . ."

"Ah! Fortunately, I happen to have them with me."

He extracted his passport from a pocket in the jacket and handed it to me. His name was Yakob Logonov, born in Odessa in 1942. The three most recent stamps in his passport were forged, I could see that immediately. For six months, soon after I got out of the military, I had worked in the office that forges stamps for Ministry travelers. It was not the sort of work I would choose for a career. Too meticulous, too fine grained for me. Very fussy, like those miniature trees people sometimes grow in tiny pots. I had transferred to another office— foreign liaison—as soon as there was an opening.

I glanced at his passport again, casually. These were good forgeries, too good to be Russian, unless he paid more money for them than his clothes suggested he was worth. Then again, it was possible he was here working for the Russian service. In that case, I probably wouldn't have been able to tell the stamps were fake. But, to keep us guessing, sometimes they wanted us to notice the forgeries, so we wouldn't think they were theirs. It was a complicated game. Foreign liaison was simpler, although dealing with foreigners could be painful.

"Now that I know who you are, or rather, who your passport says you are, let me introduce myself. Inspector O, Ministry of People's Security—but it seems you already knew this, from a mutual friend." He nodded solemnly. I continued. "About three weeks ago, you entered, is that right?" I took one last look, then handed back the passport; he put it in a different pocket. That was a little unusual. People tend to carry things like passports in the same pocket, all the time. When they get into the passport line, they sometimes move their documents to a more convenient place, but after they are past the immigration booth, they move them back again. You can stand at the airport and watch the line for hours; the only people who don't follow that pattern are people who are going to forget where they put things. You see them off to one side, frantically going through their belongings. So, I could assume he had been waiting for me, just like he said, with his passport ready to offer. And now he figured he had passed through the line and could put it back in the accustomed place.

Alright, he wanted to make sure I saw his entry stamps. I had seen them. Whether he wanted me to react I wasn't sure. In any case, my main interest at the moment was in stockings, not passport forgeries. If the stamps had been sloppy and obvious, I would have been forced to say something. But good work like that had a purpose, and there wouldn't be any way to find out what it was if we took him into custody and packed him off back across the border. For sure, if I got bogged down in forged stamps, we would never get around to stockings.

"Not quite three weeks ago, that's when I entered." He spoke Korean well enough, though heavily accented. "It was still dusty then, millions of small grains of China swirling in the sky, blotting out the sun, reminding everyone that the central kingdom is a land not to be

ignored. Russian soil tends to stay put, even that which is not perma-
nently frozen."

"Train?"

"Yes, I came through Dandong, via Beijing."

"Big city. Beijing."

"Too big. It has no idea where it is going or what it is becoming. Too
many upscale stores, barely enough room anymore for vendors like me."

"You came here to sell stockings?"

"Yes."

"What made you decide to do that?"

"Let me put it in nontechnical terms, Inspector. Korean legs have
reached the point where they need stockings. There is pent-up demand.
I recognized it as soon as I arrived here for the first time a couple of
years ago. But I didn't just act blindly. No, I studied the situation. I
looked at a lot of legs, believe me, and there was no other conclusion to
be drawn. Young women wearing baggy trousers, a great waste. So now
I come twice a year, sell out a suitcase or two of stockings, then go
home and reinvest the profits. Capitalism, I hope you don't mind my
saying so, is wonderful on this small scale."

"Where's the suitcase with the goods?" I glanced around the tree,
though I already knew there wasn't a suitcase nearby.

"All sold, completely gone, even the ones with runs up the sides.
For good measure, I sell the suitcases, too, when I'm done. That way,
I don't take a lot of time with customs officials when I get home."

"You're a good salesman."

"I do my best."

"Regular customers?"

"Some."

"Women?"

He smiled. "Mostly."

"Your grammar is impeccable, but we seem to have hit a low point
in your vocabulary. Or have you become unnaturally guarded in your
answers?"

"What a coincidence, Inspector, I was going to ask the same thing about your questions. They're somewhat curt. That makes it difficult for me to figure out what you want to know."

"When I want you to figure out what I want to know, I'll give you written notice. Meantime, what I want right now is enlightenment. If you had any merchandise left and I had a pressing need to buy some stockings, what would I look for?"

"Depends on why you want them. Pressing needs come in all shapes and sizes."

I lay back and looked at the very top of the tree. "You ever notice, Logonov, my friend, that trees know when to stop growing? A tree line tends to be pretty even. None wants to stand above the others."

"Maybe the really tall ones get chopped down, so the others try to keep unobtrusive."

"Yes, I suppose you have a point. That would be something a good salesman would notice."

"What's that, Inspector?"

"Behavioral norms, the flow of the ordinary."

He was silent and took off his glasses again. For the moment, he had decided I wasn't a threat. He didn't have to watch me so closely. Slowly, he smiled to himself, and when he spoke, it was with a lighter tone. "A good salesman has a feel for many things, Inspector. We can sense desire, obviously. When someone has an unfulfilled need, it speaks to us."

"Like stockings."

"Like many things. Please understand, I'm not talking about some minor cultural bauble, Inspector. Material needs are not simply extraneous. Most people don't realize that acquisitiveness is not a cultural trait; it is not imposed by society. It cannot be squashed by government fiat, you realize what I'm saying? Not a criticism, please understand. Purchasing, buying, bartering, trading—this satisfies a need, somehow, that has been carried over from before we were human."

"Very philosophical, very deep; not to mention very convenient, for a salesman, to have identified such a universal basic human need. It must be a comfort, professionally, I mean."

"You wanted to know about stockings?" His tone was a shade less light.

I sat up. "Not really. I thought I did. But you are a most observant man. I think you will save me a lot of time by answering just a few simple questions. Because you realize by now that I am also an observant man."

"You want to know about my customers."

I nodded.

"Mostly women, mostly young. They can't afford much, but it gives them great pleasure when they buy even a single pair. A few people want to buy in bulk, twenty or thirty pair, but I don't do that. They only want to resell them at a profit, and I do not consider myself a wholesaler."

"What about the midrange?"

"You mean, between one pair and thirty." He paused. "You mean, perhaps, five."

"Five, or seven."

"You want to know who bought singles, not pairs?"

I shrugged. "Man or woman?"

"Man. Unfriendly fellow, not very well mannered, and he seemed in a hurry."

"Ugly."

"You might say that."

"A scar." I drew a scar down the right side of my face.

He smiled. "Other side. It's not nice to play games, Inspector."

"Anything that stood out about the stockings he bought? Color? Style? Size? Very sheer?"

"They had club monograms. Bars have taken to ordering them for their girls. I might get the order on one visit, and by the time I return with the goods, the place that ordered them has gone out of business. Or they have decided they don't want the whole order."

"CB."

"Club Blue. They ordered ten pair last fall when I was here. But they ended up only taking eight pair. And the way they had them monogrammed, sort of randomly on the ankle and up the inside of the thigh, a lot of girls don't like them. So I had these two pair."

"But the man in a hurry?"

"He took three."

"You couldn't sell him two pair?"

"He was adamant, said he was accountable for the funds, and that he was told only to buy three. That's all he would take."

"Why didn't you just throw in the fourth for free?"

"Inspector, please, we are talking about universal forces, something like gravity. You think I'm a rug merchant?"

"The man was in a hurry, he was unfriendly, you said. You noticed a lot more. He paid in dollars?"

"Euros. Big bills. I couldn't make change, and he absolutely refused to go to a bank to do so. Finally, we went over to another vendor, a seller of undergarments, a fine gentleman, who could get his hands on some change."

"You remember when this was?"

"The last week in March, a few days after I arrived and made the deliveries of the orders from last year. I do that first, make the deliveries, renew acquaintances, that sort of thing. Then I set up shop and sell the remainder of my inventory. Then it's time to go home."

"I'm happy to say this time you don't need to hurry home."

"It's not a problem. I can be on the train tomorrow."

"No, you're welcome to stay another week, maybe even two."

"Stay? Here? Inspector, I appreciate the offer but cannot possibly accept."

"You cannot possibly refuse. I'm forbidding you from leaving. I may have more questions, and I can't wait until you return six months from now."

"I'm happy to give you my phone number in Russia."

"If you try to leave, you will be apprehended. You may think the border controls are lax and a little money will make them even more so. Don't make that mistake."

"What will I do for the next few weeks? I can't just loiter in the streets."

"You can sit and watch for signs of more pent-up demand."

"What about a bath?"

"I don't think I can help you there. I'd advise you try checking into a hotel for a few days. Give the front desk my name if they make any trouble, but I don't think they will."

"That will take all of my profits." He leaned back against the tree again. "Will you have me followed every day?"

"If you want."

"How can I get in touch with you?"

"Just tell our mutual friend. If you don't mind my asking, what did you do with that single, last stocking?"

Logonov looked surprised. "What else could I do? I sold it to a woman with one leg."

3

When I got back to the office, my phone was ringing.

"O here."

"I've been calling all afternoon. Your mobile phone is switched off, and no one knew where you were. Is that how your ministry operates?"

It was Han, and he didn't sound happy. "This isn't the complaint line, Han. What do you want?"

"You were talking to a Russian near the train station. I want to know why and, more important, why you didn't tell me you were going there."

"I was out for a stroll, that's all. There are some big gingko trees near the station, have you noticed?"

"You weren't talking to trees. You were talking to a Russian. He sells stockings. We have our eye on him, and I don't want you sticking your nose in the middle of it."

"Eyes, noses, that's a lot of body parts, Han. Easy to get them confused, if you're not careful." So, apparently someone else had seen the fake stamps, too. It could be Yakob wasn't really from Odessa. "Well, don't worry, I told him not to leave the country for a few weeks."

"You what? Hold on." There was a brief conversation off-line, not very pleasant, from what I could tell. Han's voice came back on. "Listen carefully, Inspector, I'm not kidding around. You have nothing else to do with that Russian, or any Russian, until I tell you it's alright. Meantime, you figure out a way to get back to that stocking salesman and let him know that you've changed your mind. He can leave." Again, some shouting from off-line, nothing I could make out. "In fact, tell him it would be better if he left."

"I don't suppose you want to tell me what this is about?"

"You don't want to know, you don't need to ask."

"Difficult to stay clear, Han, if I don't know where my business ends and yours begins."

"For instance."

"The Russian. I don't need details. But he's part of my investigation. I just can't give him up on your say-so. Is he your body?" There was silence. "Look, I don't care if he's yours or not, but he's already in my report"—not true—"and if I just cut off contact with him, it will raise questions." Another silence, then again a conversation in the background. Not a conversation really, more like someone had lost a vital body part, then some very blunt words, though I couldn't catch everything; Han must have had his hand over the phone. When he came on the line again, it didn't sound like he was in the mood to chat.

"Inspector, this conversation is over. And keep your mobile phone on all the time. If I call, you'd better answer."

I put the phone down and looked at my thumbs. They had warning flags all over them.

Chapter Six

What makes us different, O?"

Rarely am I at my desk after midnight; rarely does the Sad Man say more than a word or two if we run into each other in the morning when the shifts change.

"Some of us stay out of other people's apartments unless they're asked in." My mood was not the best, all things considered.

Yang shrugged. "The chief told me to go, so I did. That's not what I meant."

"But you never went in, did you?"

"No. It wasn't my idea to snoop around your place without your permission. So why are you mad at me? Especially if I kept out."

"But you would have gone in if you could have."

"Meaning?"

"You didn't turn around on your own. It was the old lady kept you out, wasn't it?"

Yang frowned. "She's tough."

"Why didn't you just go to the side entrance?"

"I did. She was waiting for me."

"She moves pretty fast for someone her age. She's smart, too. What did she say?"

"She didn't say anything. When I opened the door, she was standing there with her arms crossed. I told her she could be cited for interfering with the work of an investigation. She snorted."

"So you just backed out. But if you could have sneaked past her, you would have gone in." I paused, thinking I'd calm down, but I didn't. "If you'd had some gumption."

Yang pretended not to hear my last remark, but I could see it had struck home. I wished I hadn't said it.

"She's an old lady, O, why should I hassle her? She did her job." Yang looked sadly around my room.

"And you? What was your job, Yang?"

"I went for a smoke and a walk around. But I saw something while I was leaving. Two guys."

Yang was uncomfortable. He looked over his shoulder, down the hall toward Min's office.

It was already the longest conversation I'd had with Yang in years. "Go on."

"Two guys, not SSD. They didn't dress like SSD, they didn't walk like SSD, not even when SSD is trying to pretend to be someone else. Clean shirts, nice cuffs."

"So, not SSD. So, what?"

He shrugged. "I don't know. Also not military intelligence. Something else, not like I'd ever seen. Maybe a new group that they haven't told us about. I walked."

"You followed them?"

"Nah, I was just walking behind, and they were walking in front. I happened to see the license plate on their car. It's a special series, I think."

"And this concerns me, my apartment, or the wallet?"

"Maybe none of them. There's probably someone else in your building it concerns. Some old war widow, or the high school teacher that lives below you. Sure, that's it, they sent two guys with nice cuffs out in a car with special series plates to play hide-and-seek with a high school teacher."

That Yang could be sarcastic was a revelation; maybe it was a good sign. That he had stumbled on an unidentified surveillance team was not such a good sign.

"Well," I said, "what if this teacher is up to something? Could be this teacher has a black-market radio; very likely, this teacher skipped a key lesson in the social studies section. I don't teach social studies." No sense avoiding the obvious question, so I asked it. "Why would I be of interest to anyone?"

Yang threw the wallet on my desk. "This."

"I thought you said you didn't make it to my apartment?"

"I didn't, not when Min sent me."

"You went there another time?"

Yang shrugged. "So, get mad. If someone saved me a lot of trouble, I might be grateful."

"What trouble?"

"When I got there, a man was just opening your door. I coughed, and he limped down the hall. Cool as could be, didn't miss a beat. Went a few doors down from yours and let himself in. He was a tall fellow, though a little stooped. Pretty good clothes for your neighborhood. Couldn't see his face. You might try putting at least one bulb in the hallway; I'll get you one. Maybe some locks, too. Doesn't your building believe in locks?"

"We don't fancy light in our building; it ruins our sense of sacrifice. Locks suggest a lack of trust. This man, maybe he mistook my room for his. It happens once in a while." Actually, I'd never heard of it happening before, in all the years I'd lived there. Even the drunks knew their own doors. "How'd you get past the old lady?"

Yang put his finger to his lips.

I put the wallet in the very back of the drawer, right next to a piece of persimmon wood that I had been keeping for a slow day, something to pass the time. "Alright, I owe you a favor. What is it?"

There weren't going to be any slow days; I took the persimmon out of the drawer and slipped it in my pocket.

"Answer my question. Just do that for me. Why are we different?"

"Different, meaning what?"

"Apart. Separate. You are you, I am not. Why?"

"Is something the matter with you being you?" Maybe after years of not talking to people, the man had lost the knack. He wasn't making sense.

Yang finally moved all the way into my office. "Mind if I sit?" He pointed to the chair but then walked slowly to the other side of the room, so we were talking across a space, however small. "I'm serious. What makes us different?"

"You ask a question I really hadn't thought about before." I was feeling my way along and watching Yang closely. "But now that you mention it, we are different. I'm older, I have more time in the Ministry. You're taller than I am—which is a point I never underestimate, height—and probably smarter. Your mind works better than mine; you observe things I can never see." Yang waited, motioned for me to continue, but I didn't want to continue. It was going to get painful in a minute. The only things left would be unpleasant. "That's about it, I'd say."

"You know better, O, there's more to it." He looked at the floor for a long time. "I'm sad, you're not." Already it had the makings of a mournful list. "I have bad luck, yours is good. You have shown bravery, I am a coward. Your grandfather was a hero, mine was a traitor who went south. What would you do if someone's life were in your hands, if by your sacrifice you might save them?"

"Depends."

"On what?"

"On the moment. Bravery is momentary, it doesn't stay with you. It's a wave, it comes out of nowhere and then recedes. It's not the same as goodness. That soaks into a person, never leaves them."

"Like sorrow."

"You've been through bad times, Yang. It's not easy. Bad things happen. Lots of families had someone who went south and have had to live with it. Give yourself a break."

"No, the others, my children, they went through bad times, I went through nothing. I was here. Just like I am now, talking, sipping tea. I probably had my feet up on the desk while they were suffocating. Nothing happened to me. But you know what? I have disappeared, O, by degrees. I don't exist anymore. That's what makes us different. You're here, I'm not."

I cleared my throat and started to respond, then just gave up. Whatever it was I was going to say, something appalling and hollow, decided not to get said. "I'm glad you came in to talk about something like this, Yang. Talking about these things . . ." The words dried up all of a sudden. There were only a few left, so I said them. "I wish I knew how to help. I wish I did, but I don't."

"Perhaps you can, O, you never know." He walked into the hallway, then turned and came back in front of my desk. "It's impossible to be anything but sad. I have nowhere else to go, nowhere."

This was becoming embarrassing. I needed to break it off. "Maybe we should get a drink somewhere, after work. It's easier to be philosophical with a shot of alcohol in your system."

He shook his head. "No, I do better with a clear head. I don't drink. And you stopped after Pak . . . died. Everyone knows that."

Something in his voice made me sit up. "What else does everyone know?"

Yang moved over to my window and looked at the dark street. "It's impossible to be happy here. You, of all people, know that."

"Is that what you think? Is that what you and Li talk about in the dead hours?" I could have bitten my tongue. Why did I say something like that?

Yang pointed at the night sky. "Even the moon goes through phases. Not like this. Nothing should be this way, O. It shouldn't stay like this, endlessly. Something's got to change. Even the dead rot away."

He turned around. There was nothing to say. We might have stared at each other until dawn, but my phone rang.

"I need to see you right away." It was a woman's voice, shaking, barely above a whisper. I remembered what I had said to Han about anonymous phone calls.

"Who is this?"

"You know who it is, Inspector." The voice found itself; it was the Gold Star Bank manager.

"Where?"

"Near the Potang-gang Hotel, there is a group of three benches just where the road turns into the hotel lot. I can be there in ten minutes."

"Not such a good place for a woman at this time of night. Pick somewhere else. Where are you now?"

"I'm on my cell phone, Inspector. How about your apartment?"

"My place? Are you crazy? I don't have any chairs. Give me a second." I looked up at Yang. "Where do you and Li go if you get hungry at this hour?"

"Nowhere. He brings in his own food; I never eat. But there's a place where the foreigners go near the Koryo, open all night. The Ministry used to have a watch on it, just lazy duty. We pulled our people because nothing ever happened."

"I heard, Inspector." The voice on the other end of the line was building back to its regular sharpness. "I know where it is. I'll be there in ten minutes."

"You seem well placed, ten minutes from everywhere."

"See you." The phone cut off. Yang had closed his eyes.

"I've got an errand to run, Yang. You alright here?"

"Don't worry about me, O." He didn't open his eyes. "I've got plenty to do. Plenty."

2

The place was small, with round tables lining the walls. It was filled with people, cigarette smoke, and the smell of beef cooking on gas grills. The customers were foreign, and they all looked at me carefully, on edge. A woman in a short silk dress walked over. "We don't have any room. Everything's booked."

"There's a table right behind you." I knew she wanted me out, but she didn't want any raised voices. Raised voices might be bad for foreign investment. Keeping the frogs out of sight and in the mud had to be done discreetly, with dulcet tones.

"It's taken," she said. "The party will be here in a moment."

"Pretty busy place."

The woman flushed slightly. "I'm sorry, but this is our busiest time." She looked around. "Most of the customers will stay for another hour or so. People come and they sit. We make it friendly."

"But not for Koreans."

"Of course"—she flushed more deeply—"you are always welcome. Maybe another night."

"Sure," I said.

The woman looked past me, and relief suddenly filled her face. "Madam, how nice to see you again."

I turned. The bank manager looked even taller in a smoky room.

"Inspector, I see you arrived first. You should have sat down and ordered a drink. Come, over there is my table. It has the best view." She laughed, which was a surprise to me. I hadn't realized she was capable of laughter. It was a beautiful sound. I knew I wanted to hear it again.

Miss Chon was given the chair with the view. I sat with my back to the door—so no one who walked in late would know a local was in the room, I supposed. When we were settled and had given our drink orders, she leaned across the table. "You've never been here, have you?"

"I don't go out to restaurants very much."

"Perhaps you should. You'll meet people, a lot of people. Isn't that what you do in your job? Meet people? I always thought police detectives were supposed to be social animals. Otherwise, how can they catch criminals?"

"No, criminals are antisocial. So that's what we have to be to catch them. I'm quite antisocial myself."

"I take it that is why you are such a good detective."

"Who told you that?"

"No one had to, Inspector. I'm a good judge of people; in my job I have to be. Everyone wants loans. I can't afford to be fooled."

"You called me, you sounded upset. I'm here." I looked at the table closest to ours. Two businessmen, drinking whiskey, bored. They spoke German, but neither had much to say.

The bank manager glanced at them. "They are louts. Jurgen and Dieter, inseparable. Some people think they are homosexuals, but I doubt it. Jurgen pawed me during a reception last month. The next morning he called to apologize, but he didn't mean it. I told him I'd kick him in the balls if he did it again." Jurgen winced; even if he didn't understand the whole sentence in Korean, he must have had enough vocabulary to get the general drift.

I craned my head around, aware of a rolling wave of nasty glances coming our way. "You don't mind being here with me?"

"No, not at all, Inspector. It will help my reputation if people see us together. Gives me some extra menace."

"That isn't why we're here, though. You wanted to meet me somewhere in the dark."

"Is your apartment dark?"

"I told you, no chairs." Either she really wanted to come to my apartment, or she was playing a crazy game. Or she was just crazy. Whoever heard of a foreign woman coming to a local's apartment? Maybe some big shot could get away with it, whisk her in while the guards looked the other way. I thought about it for a moment, then shook my head. Impossible. Anyway, we didn't know each other. She didn't even have a file. "I'm still investigating the robbery at your bank. You are still a witness. And I am still asking questions."

"Fine."

"Who are you?"

"My, my, that's pretty broad. Can't we start with something more specific?"

"You have a Scottish passport."

"No, I do not."

"I know you do."

"Scotland doesn't issue passports, Inspector. Scotland isn't even a country, not anymore."

I considered this for a moment. "Is that so? I met a Scotsman once, at the bar in the Koryo Hotel. Very firm in his beliefs, if I remember correctly. Very proud of his 'country,' and by that he was quite clear he meant Scotland."

"He'd probably been drinking." She cupped her chin in her hands and leaned slightly toward me, it gave her a deceptive air of submissiveness. "I carry a British passport," she said. "I went to school in Scotland."

The worst of all possible worlds. I was in a restaurant that was her territory, at a table that she claimed as her usual place, and she was lecturing me on geography. I knew Scotland didn't issue passports, didn't I? I kicked myself. "You went to school there. It doesn't explain how a Kazakh woman gets a UK passport." When in doubt, growl. Hell, it works for dogs.

"I married a British citizen, God love them all. He was a Scot, actually, a fair-skinned man with lovely shoulders and no brains." She pursed her lips. "He's dead, car accident on a slippery road in the Highlands." I was momentarily lost; it was hard to believe she was a widow. She looked into my eyes. "That's the wild part of Scotland, more or less."

Her voice brought me back. "Thank you for the geography lesson." We weren't going to get anywhere at this rate. Maybe I needed to keep it simple. "Why did you go to school in Scotland?"

"Banking, Inspector. Kazakhstan wants to become the banking hub of Central Asia. Those with ambition go abroad to study, and Scottish banking practices are deemed to be just what Kazakhstan needs, tight, well managed, solid. The Bank of Scotland has a glorious history, centuries old. After eight years in Scotland, the idea of returning home made me restless, I didn't think I could do it, so I tried to get a job with a bank in South Korea. Impossible, they are so sexist it makes you laugh. Does sexism make you laugh, Inspector?"

Up went a warning flag. I frowned. She smiled.

"A careful man." She smiled again. "I heard about an opening for a foreigner to manage Gold Star. In London I went to your embassy for an interview. Do you know how hard it is to find your embassy in London, Inspector? No, I suppose you don't. But I finally found it, and here I am."

"You don't have to be ashamed of being Korean, you know."

"I'm not Korean. I'm Kazakh, you said so yourself."

"That's your nationality. But you're Korean. Your blood is Korean. Your body is Korean." I was speaking symbolically, but it wasn't easy.

She pursed her lips and thought a moment. "No, Inspector, you don't know the first thing about my body, do you?" Her foot brushed against mine.

Some questions you don't touch. If we'd had our drinks, I would have taken a big swallow.

"I'm Kazakh from the tip of my toes to the top of my head." That included her waist, I thought, and saw the little warning flag again. When were they going to serve drinks? "My father, and my father's father before him, as they say in our village. All Kazakh."

"You look Korean, because that's what you are. There are plenty of Koreans in Kazakhstan." Her face was Korean, but why were her eyes from somewhere else?

"Don't be a fool, Inspector. I wouldn't be ashamed to be Korean." She cocked her head slightly. "Certainly not a South Korean." She let the blade stay in for a moment. I waited for her to twist it, but she knew enough not to. I never take these things personally. I don't forget them, either.

"Let's get to the point," I said. "You asked to meet, and you sounded upset. If you have something to say, say it. Otherwise, I have things to do."

She laughed, only this time there was no tinkle to it. "I was upset, just something personal. I needed a little company. Do you mind?"

"That's not why you called."

"Yes, yes it is, actually. I was scared, I don't know why. This robbery thing has put me on edge. And then I started thinking about what you asked me. The point is, I don't know what happened to that desk."

"Meaning?"

"I didn't ask for it to be removed."

"You told me it was part of a redecorating scheme."

"I just said that because I didn't like your partner. Why is SSD part of this, anyway?"

"That would be none of your business, Miss Chon. None of your business. What was in the desk?"

"Nothing was in the desk. It was empty."

"I don't think so. It was too heavy to be empty."

"Maybe it was just a heavy piece of furniture."

"It was made out of pine. It was cheap, light wood stained to make it look like something else. I may not know much, Miss Chon, but I know about wood. If it was your desk, you must have some idea what was in the drawers."

"I only used it when I had a client. It was more convenient than mine. But I never went into the drawers. It was already in the bank when I arrived. I tried to move it once, but it was too heavy."

"The janitor wouldn't help?"

"He said it was covering a switch plate in the floor and I should leave it be."

"The janitor said that? I assume he was already at the bank, too, like the furniture. You didn't hire him?"

"No, I hired a few staff, a couple of girls as tellers and an accountant part-time, but the janitor and the cleaners were assigned by some other office."

"They probably work for SSD. The Ministry used to have control of locals working for foreign businessmen, but we don't have the budget for that anymore. The only office with that sort of money is

SSD. They are especially keen on watching the banks and hotels. Their off-book funds probably make up ten percent of your assets."

"You think they have the desk."

I shrugged. "Don't know. It may have had equipment in it, maybe recorders. They'd want to know who was coming in for loans, how much you offered, whether you were cutting any deals that weren't reported. If you were, they could use it for—"

"I'm not worried, Inspector, nothing of the sort went on."

"That's good, because someone robbed the bank. Maybe SSD figures the robbers came in earlier and looked around, sat with you for a bit, asked a few questions. Maybe they figure you are part of the robbery; you knew how much foreign currency was in the safe. Tell me, just for the hell of it, why did you sound so upset when you called tonight? I still don't know. It wasn't anything to do with the desk."

"What do you think?"

"Have you ever been to the Club Blue?"

"No, that's the sort of place the German hogs wallow in."

"So, you know where it is?"

"Of course I do. The owner had an account at the bank."

"Did he borrow some money?"

"I'm not at liberty to discuss bank business."

"I think you are, but we'll let it pass for now. Do all your customers have access to that back room after hours?"

She leaned close to me. "You seem like a nice man, Inspector. A little lonely, maybe. You don't have anything in your apartment you want to show me?"

"Like what?"

"I don't know. Etchings, maybe."

I stared at her. I was about to fall into her eyes. "Etchings? I don't know what you mean."

She sat back. "Will there be anything else?"

"I think I haven't eaten in a while."

"Then maybe you should order." She stood up and said something to the two Germans. This time they both winced. Then, without giving me a second glance, she walked out of the room. Several tables of foreign businessmen raised their glasses and smirked; whether it was for Jurgen or for me, I wasn't sure.

3

Han phoned early the next morning. "I found a few files on the lady."

"Congratulations," I said. "Sourced to the janitor?" The monitoring machines at SSD always click in a funny way when the call starts, so everyone knows it's them even before they say anything. There had been no click before Han had spoken. He wasn't on a mobile phone; the connection was too good.

"The what?"

"The janitor. I assume he's one of yours. I assume the desk was, too."

"The file says she's from Kazakhstan." He waited, but I didn't respond. "Well, that's pretty interesting, Inspector. Especially because she has a Scottish passport."

I perked up. "Scotland doesn't issue passports, Han. Scotland isn't a country."

"Says who?"

"She was married to a Scot with big shoulders, but he died. It happens."

"How do you know so much all of a sudden? You told me people like her don't have files."

"How many pieces of paper are in this file you are holding?"

"I haven't counted."

"One, right? You can count that high."

Silence.

"All you've got is the cover sheet, last name, nationality, age, and residence. That's not a file. They're holding back on you, Han, there's more. The janitor was reporting something to someone in your organization, and you don't have it. Go look. Call me back. While you're at it, look to see what you've got on the manager of the Club Blue. And don't forget, you promised to tell me how to fix my cell phone."

"It's easy."

"Yeah, good. Then it won't take long." I hung up. A minute later the phone rang again.

"I'm sorry I left you so abruptly last night, Inspector, but a woman had just come in." I never expected to hear an apology from Miss Chon. It had a nice ring, but it didn't come close to her laughter. "She's been following me for weeks. She was at the bank party the other day, pretending to be one of the hostesses. Do you know her?"

"No." There was no response, so I dug myself in deeper. "I don't know her, but she thought she knew me. It turned out she didn't."

This time there was a slight pause, just enough to tell me the denial was a mistake, which I knew it would be. When she spoke, though, her voice didn't have any suspicion in it, as if she weren't surprised at what I'd said. "Have you thought about what I told you last night, Inspector?"

"People tell me things all the time. What did you say to Jurgen when you walked out to make his eyes tear up?"

"It was Dieter, and it wasn't polite."

"I think he likes you. He smacked his lips after you left."

"How much do you know about him?"

"Nothing. He's never done anything to get my attention. Han's people may have something on him, but I doubt if we do."

"You might want to check. Oh, and the desk is back, Inspector. The drawers are empty, but it is still heavy. The janitor said he wanted to put wheels on the legs so I could move it around."

"Very thoughtful. I'll be over after lunch. Someone has the office car. As soon as it's back, I'll knock on your door."

"Don't be long, Inspector. I don't like to wait for men." She hung up before I could reply.

Miss Chon, I thought to myself, you are going to get one of us in trouble. Then I wondered how much a couple of etchings would cost. Maybe Logonov would know, if he hadn't already left.

Min walked in with a couple of thin files. "How we got these, you are not to ask. We got them, that's enough." He put them on my desk and stood back. "All for you. Don't say I never did anything for you."

I opened the first one. It was an Interpol file, background on international bank robbery rings.

"Since when do we have access to Interpol?"

"Never mind. Read through it and tell me if you want more."

The original was in French, but there were flimsy sheets of Korean attached to each one. The translation seemed rough, but good enough to give me the flavor. It was mostly junk, all about people boring into vaults from adjoining sewer systems. "Fascinating, but not what we need." There weren't any sewers strong enough or big enough in Pyong-yang for that sort of operation, not in my sector, anyway. The city's plumbing had been put in hurriedly after the war; anyone trying to stand up in one of the sewers would put his foot through the bottom. And he couldn't stand up unless he was very short, someone like the ugly bartender.

As my eyes danced down the page, I noticed a section on Kazakh gangs. I tore out the paper and put it in my pocket. "Don't worry," I said to Min, "I'll never say you didn't do anything for me."

"Hey! You can't tear anything out of that file. It isn't ours. It has to go back where I got it."

"Oops."

Min scowled, not an expression he had mastered. "If we can't show some progress by tomorrow morning, I'll have to go to a lot of meetings and answer a lot of questions. You never go to those meetings. You don't realize how aggravating they are."

"Who knows about the Germans in town?"

"Am I supposed to be impressed with that question, Inspector?"

"No. I was just wondering. We don't have anything in our records. SSD might, but I don't want to check with them; they'll tromp around the bushes and scare the birds away."

Min took a deep breath. "Names." He held out his hand.

I wrote the names of the two Germans on a piece of paper and gave it to him. He scowled again, better this time. "These are only first names. I can't search on first names."

"Sure you can. There's an entire section marked 'last name unknown.' Besides, there aren't that many Germans in town."

"What are we looking for?"

"Not sure, exactly. Just put the files under my pillow and let me sleep on them."

Min shook his head. "No wonder I'm so cranky."

A few minutes after he went back to his office, my phone rang. "Make yourself busy, Inspector. It will be tomorrow before there's anything on these Germans."

There was nothing else I wanted to do at my desk, so I went for a stroll. I found myself back at the restaurant where the well-connected go to eat. If the man with all the relatives and the knife in his back had been there more than once, Miss Pyon, the lady with the noodles, might know something about him, maybe overheard a little table conversation. Anyway, it was going on dinnertime.

The restaurant was nearly empty. Miss Pyon walked over to my table. She didn't look happy to see me.

"You want something to eat?"

"Is this how you treat a regular customer?"

"You ain't regular. You've only been here a few times, and the last time you didn't keep things quiet. You also didn't pay, if you recall. After you left, there was nothing but trouble for days. I kept thinking you'd come back and help straighten things out, but no."

"What kind of trouble?"

"You know, the regular kind. Questions, warnings, threats, more questions, a table overturned to make the point."

"It wasn't my people."

"Who cares, your people, their people, what the hell difference does it make? Why? Am I supposed to be grateful you had nothing to do with it?"

"Never mind. Look, if you have a problem, I can go somewhere else to eat."

She shrugged. "Suit yourself. If you leave, then I guess you and me don't have anything to talk about."

I decided to stay. "Just bring out something that wasn't here since yesterday."

"You want a drink with that?"

"If you have a beer, that's fine."

"Of course we have beer. What kind of place you think this is? Don't go away, Inspector, I'll be right back."

When she'd brought a bowl of noodles and the beer, she sat down at the table.

I looked at her closely. Her teeth were crooked; her eyes were puffy from fatigue. And if you were being honest, you'd have to admit she had a face like a horse. Real long. But there was something in the way she carried herself. It appealed to me. I relaxed. "Pretty friendly, Miss Pyon. Won't you get in trouble, sitting with a customer?"

"This is mine, or did you forget? I sit with whoever I want, whenever I want."

I smiled. She owned the place.

"And I decided to sit with you. That okay, Inspector?"

"Fine. It's fine. I'm happy for company. You mind if I eat in front of you?"

"It's a restaurant, people eat in front of me all night long."

"Sometimes they fall off their chairs."

She smiled a crooked smile. "Only happened once. I'm sorry I started screaming like that. But I was all tensed up. Whenever he and his friend came in, there was trouble. It was like they picked it as a meeting place; of all the noodle places in the city, they had to choose this one." She shook her head. "Once they walked out without paying. I tried to report them, but I got my hands slapped, hard. They didn't belong here, acted like they were too good for the place. They did more drinking than eating. And the crowd they brought in was too rough, foreign types, I don't know."

"If I had some questions, I'd ask them now."

"You want another beer?"

"No. What do you mean by foreign types? Were they foreigners?"

"They were and they weren't. They were Koreans, but funny, if you know what I mean. Might have been Koreans from China, but they didn't have that know-it-all attitude. A couple of them spoke Russian, but they weren't Russians."

"Kazakhs."

She shuffled the little dishes of vegetables around the table. "A good guess."

"When were they here?"

"The foreigners came in twice. The first time was maybe a month ago, still dusty outside. All that grit in the noodles, even my regulars complained. Damned Chinese dust."

I patted her hand, mostly to get her attention again. She sighed. "Those foreigners," she said, "they drank too much. I told them not to come back. The last time was a week, maybe ten days before their friend fell dead off his chair. They sneered at me. One of them got too familiar, right here, in front of the customers. I told him if he did it again, I'd make sure he walked with a limp for the rest of his life."

"What'd he say?"

"He laughed and said when I was mad it got him excited."

I finished my noodles, picked up the bowl, and drank the soup. "Well, I guess that's what happens when you live around so many sheep."

"That's all you have to say?"

"Don't worry, I don't think they'll bother you anymore."

"Thanks for nothing."

"They've left town. A couple of them have even left the planet."

"Dead?"

"Maybe. What do you know about the man with the red shirt?" I didn't want to get Miss Pyon hysterical again; she didn't need to know the red shirt had a knife tear in the back.

She stood up and took the dirty dishes to the kitchen. As she disappeared in the back, two customers walked in, a man and a woman. They sat down at a table near the window on the front wall, looked at the menu, then got up and left just as Miss Pyon emerged from the kitchen. She watched them with a disapproving frown. "Why'd they come all the way up the stairs? The menu is posted on the front door. You say anything to scare them away?"

"Nope."

"Maybe they recognized you."

"In that case, they would have stayed. I don't have any enemies."

She threw back her head and laughed. "Everyone has enemies, Inspector."

I smiled. "Sure, everyone has enemies. The man with the red shirt, did he have enemies?"

She sat down and looked at her hands. Her fingers were short, the nails broken. The thumb on her left hand sat at an odd angle. She saw me looking at it. "Bent back until it broke. The sound was sickening. It never healed. The doctor said they must have twisted it to make sure it wouldn't set. It hurts sometimes, but only sometimes. One of these days, I'll kill the bastard who did it."

"Have you got any fruit?"

"You're loaded with sympathy, aren't you? Yeah, I have some apples, though they're scrawny."

"Never mind, I'll get one some other time. You don't want to talk about the man in the red shirt. Too bad. He seems to be a Mr. Big. Did he ever mention some drinking place called Club Blue?"

"I don't monitor conversations, it's not polite. I run a restaurant, Inspector; it gets busy sometimes."

"Yeah. Sometimes. Don't worry about the red shirt, he won't be here anymore." The imparted information hung between us for a moment, then floated away. She didn't try to stop it. "Well, back to the office for me. What time do you get off work?"

"My, my, Inspector, I didn't think you were interested."

"I'm not. I just wanted to know how late I could get noodles."
Nobody mentioned the bill.

4

Yang was on the phone when I stuck my head in his office. It was unusual; he didn't talk much on the phone. I backed up and listened
from out in the hall, but there was not much to hear. He said "yes"
once or twice, "no" once, then banged down the receiver.

"Sorry, Yang, didn't mean to interrupt."

"Nothing to interrupt, O." He looked sick.

"Anything the matter?"

"No." He paused, then said it again. "No."

"I was wondering if you would do me a favor."

"If I can."

"What did you find out from that fellow you questioned the other
night?"

"The red shirt? Very nasty, very assertive, very unhappy."

"Who was he?"

"That I didn't determine. He refused to give me his registration
card, wouldn't fill out any forms, threatened me with terrible punish-
ment."

"What did you say?"

"I told him his trousers were unzipped."

"True?"

"No, but it sort of broke through his resistance. It's hard to be
adamant when you're checking your fly. After that he calmed down a
little. Still wouldn't answer questions, though. I let him use the
phone. Twenty minutes later, a big black car pulled up outside. Two
toughs in long coats ran up the stairs into my office and told me they
had jurisdiction."

"And they were?"

Yang shrugged. "Didn't matter. One of them had a pistol on his hip. I couldn't keep the guy, anyway. He hadn't done anything, remember?"

"We don't know he had nothing to do with his dinner companion's murder."

"Murder, is it? I thought the doc said it was his heart."

"Maybe." I hadn't shared the autopsy results with Yang, and I doubt if Min had. Yang wasn't someone who rang up the morgue on a whim. I suppose the morgue might have called us late at night with some more information and he took the message, but I never got a message. Curious; maybe Yang did more than sit around in the quiet before dawn. Maybe he was coming out of his shell a little. "That's all?"

"No, but there's not much more. When they got downstairs, the two toughs shook hands with our nasty friend, then they all got in the car and drove away. The toughs in the front, him in the back. I got the license plate from the guard at the gate."

"And?"

"Special. No traces."

"You wouldn't kid me."

"No, I was surprised as hell. They didn't dress like anyone I ever saw from around here. Greasy shirts, though not like his. They had funny accents."

"I'll bet."

"The guy made a lot of threats, O."

"Scared you? I don't think I've ever seen you scared."

"He made me angry more than anything. That's what's wrong with—" Yang choked off the thought abruptly. He waited a moment until it was gone, or buried back where it had been. "Anyway, he left this, though he didn't know it at the time." Yang put a small identification wallet carefully onto the desk. "He may be looking for it by now. But maybe not."

"He left it?" If Yang didn't know the man in the red shirt was dead, I figured it wasn't my place to tell him.

"In a manner of speaking."

"You lifted it from him? And you don't think he'll miss it?" I opened the wallet and thumbed through the contents. "Why is that?"

"All phony. Pretty good, but phony. The residence address is given as Huichon."

"Swell." When I got to my office, I leaned back in my chair and stared at the ceiling. "Hey!" I went back to Yang's office. "Huichon. That's in Chagang."

Yang looked up. "You should get out of Pyongyang more often, O. Of course it's in Chagang. Where'd you think it was, Scotland?" He smiled at me. I should have felt good, to see him smile again after so long, but somehow it gave me a funny feeling.

5

The stairs down to Club Blue were dark, but the treads were supremely quiet. Concrete stairs don't make a lot of noise. There's no give to them, either. They crumble sooner or later and break off in ugly chunks, but for stealth, nothing is better. Metal stairs are probably the worst. They clang when you stumble, which happens in the dark. In absolute darkness, wooden stairs are best. They may creak a little, but if you know enough to walk where they have support, you can minimize the sound. And the stairs near the top and the bottom have a different feel to them. With concrete, you never know for sure where you are, which might be why I missed a step and grabbed for the handrail.

At the bottom of the stairs, I kept close to the wall, found the door to the club, and then, as I rounded the corner, could finally see from a thin streak on the floor that the light was turned on in the office. The office door was shut, but I could hear voices from the inside. One of them was the owner, anxious but still with a polish to it. The other, high-pitched, insistent, and full of fear, was the bartender. Nothing else; the place was silent, no clinking of glasses, no laughter, no customers.

I could have tried the handle, but if for some reason the door was locked, it would have given them time to react. So I just kicked it in. It was a cheap door, but the hinges were even cheaper, put in with screws that must have been made of tinfoil. The hinges came out of the frame, and the door sailed across the room.

"Anyone home?" I strolled in as if I were paying a friendly call. The bartender had been hit on the back by the door. It probably hurt a little, but from the look on his face, it scared him more than anything. The owner stood up, and as he did so he reached to open the top drawer.

"If that's a gun in there," I said, "leave it. Right now, you're not in any trouble, nothing you can't get out of, anyway. But if you pull a gun on me, I'll make sure you regret it." I don't know why I kept imagining the owner had a gun. He looked like someone who knew how to use one, or had used one.

"If you're still around." The bartender looked at me balefully.

"I'll be around, don't worry your ugly face about it. I've got news for you, if you're in the room when he pulls a gun on me, you're in it, too. Only you probably don't have the money to bribe the camp guards, so they'll work you until you drop, if they don't rape you first."

"What?"

"Don't listen to him." The club owner still had his hand on the drawer handle, but I could tell he had already decided not to open it. He just didn't want me to think I'd scared him. "No one's going anywhere, isn't that right, Inspector? This is just a friendly call to collect that drink I promised you. If you wait around a little, the girls will start showing up. Might be there's one that likes cops."

"Yeah." The bartender smiled, so that the scar across his jaw writhed like a snake. "She probably likes all sorts of barnyard animals."

I walked up close to him and bent down until my eyes were drilled into his. "Get out of my sight, now."

"Go get ready for the first customers." The club owner nodded his head toward the bar. "I'll handle this."

The bartender turned and walked into the dark barroom. He clicked a single light on and, from the sound of it, started sweeping.

"Inspector, what is this? Surely it's not the license causing you to break in here. That's not what you boys care about. But I can see I do need some protection—look at how that door came off the hinges. Let's say a hundred euros a week, and drinks anytime." He had his wallet out and was thumbing through some bills. "We can make the first payment a little higher, just to get things started on a good note."

"You always open up so late? Hard to make money, if you don't have any customers. Or are you running something else on the side?"

The manager counted out a few more bills. "You really are a bold one, aren't you, Inspector? A real shakedown artist."

"There was a body found in the alley next to your club."

"You don't say."

"Friend of yours?"

"Everyone is my friend, Inspector, but since I don't know what body you're talking about, I'm not prepared to say whether I knew him."

"Him?"

"What was this, er, body wearing? No identification papers? Now, that would be strange. In the alley next to the club, you said? There were no fights in here. Maybe it was a robbery." He held out the bills.

"Put away your wallet. Wait, on second thought, let me see it."

The club owner smiled. "Why settle for some when you can have it all, that's the game now?"

"Sit down and keep quiet, would you?" I flipped open the wallet and looked at the money. All small euro bills, all in order, from highest to lowest, back to front. "Pretty meticulous, aren't you?" I threw the wallet back at him. "The body had a knife in the back. I just thought I'd warn you. Maybe you want to get some extra security out front."

"You volunteering?"

"Me? No, I don't stand in front of rat holes."

PART II

Chapter One

Things went quiet for about a week. They do that sometimes. Like a sheet has been thrown over a whole case, and no one wants to lift up a corner to see if it's dead or just sleeping. More than ever, I wanted to get rid of the whole thing, if I could figure out how. Three murders. I didn't think it was coincidence that the bus had been there when the robber stepped into the street in front of the bank; I still didn't buy the finding of "heart failure" in the noodle restaurant; and a knife in the back is pretty conclusive. Three murders and a bank robbery, all in my sector. Three murders but one body missing. And SSD, or somebody, breathing down our necks before I'd even sharpened my pencil.

On top of this, a foreigner with a funny past and no file. It was possible, a Kazakh-Korean woman with a British passport getting a job in a bank in Pyongyang. Barely possible. And hers the bank that was robbed, not that we had so many banks. I couldn't picture it, her standing meekly while the robbers did what? Told everyone to lie on the floor? Went in the back room and cleaned out the euro bills? She hadn't volunteered any information, just seemed offended that I was asking questions. She'd probably told the robbers to keep their voices down.

I wandered around the office, wrote a few reports, watched the willow trees across the street soak up the afternoon sun, and then I got tired of waiting. Nobody answered the phone at the morgue, or maybe the line was out of order. I tried the Ministry, but they still claimed to have no reports on the murder of the man in the red shirt. Not a surprise; if you're well connected enough, a knife in the back can be kept pretty quiet. We hadn't even opened a case file and the incident had been yanked out of our jurisdiction. That was fine, I didn't want to know anything about the politics or the personalities, but I needed to find out a couple of details, enough to reset my operations if that's what had to be done. Maybe Han would have some information. When I called SSD, the phone clicked once, and then the operator said he was "out of range." I asked when he'd be back, and she said that was not for me to know. Okay, I said, have a nice day.

I picked up the Interpol notes on Kazakh bank robbery rings and read through them again, maybe for the fifth time. One sentence kept catching my eye. It said that some of the robberies had been aided by informants in the bank, usually women who were hired only a few months before, then disappeared. The rest of the report was mildly interesting. The list of countries where robberies had taken place included everywhere in Western Europe except Portugal and England. The only country where more than one bank had been robbed was Germany. The Germans had experienced three of these apparently related robberies, two at the same bank in Köln and one in Dresden, but that one—the latest—was more than four years ago. The overall spate of similar robberies had started in 1991; the pattern was one bank got hit every fourteen months. Two robbers had been caught but died mysteriously while undergoing questioning in a Berlin jail. Another, after the second robbery in Köln, got through the police roadblocks but was killed a day later when his stolen motorcycle went out of control and ended up in the Rhine. The most recent robbery had been in Sweden, five months ago, in the middle of a snowstorm.

That seemed like a pretty quick transition, from Sweden to Korea in only five months. I called SSD again. The operator said she would pass Han the message and he would call me back. The words were okay, but the tone of voice said not to call and bother her anymore. It took a few minutes, but finally the phone rang. When I answered, there were no clicks, just Han's voice, good and clear.

"You know anything about a body with a knife in the back?" I figured I'd get straight to the point, skip the pleasantries.

"No." A short silence, which can mean a lot of things. "What are knife handles made of, Inspector?" he asked, finally.

"I assume this is completely unrelated to my question."

"Simple query, isn't it? What kind of wood? I thought that was right up your alley, wood."

If I wanted to know where he was going with this, the easiest thing seemed to be to answer the question. "A knife handle could be anything. It might not be wood."

"Thank you for that. Your Ministry is known for offering alternative theories, Inspector. But let's say it was wood. Can we do that?"

"Like I said, could be anything."

"What if it were birch? Where would it have been made?"

"Birch? Probably not from around here. It could have been made in Russia, that's the obvious candidate."

"Recently?"

"Hard to tell. Besides, how would I know, over the phone? You'd have to look at the wood, maybe chew on it a little."

"You kidding me?"

"Just slightly."

"So, there is a way to tell how old it is. I mean, you're saying it's not impossible."

"Few things are impossible, Han."

"What if it wasn't really a knife?"

"More like a bayonet, you mean."

"What then?"

"Then it might depend on the marks on the blade. If the handle is birch, somewhere up north is a good guess. Like I said, Russia, maybe. Then you would want to look at the marks on the blade, to see if they point in the same direction."

"Birch trees don't grow in rich people's gardens where it's warm?"

"They do, but rich people don't cut down the birch trees in their gardens for lumber to make bayonet handles."

"Could it be Japanese?"

"No. Almost certainly not. No."

"You're sure?"

"Very."

"Then why is there Japanese on the blade?"

"Because it's Finnish."

"What?"

"The Finns bought Japanese rifles in the 1920s, along with the bayonets. If the handles broke, they were replaced with birch." I wasn't making this up; I just happened to read it somewhere and it stuck in my memory. "The Red Army probably made off with a few of them when they were running from angry Finns. Now one of them has ended up in someone's back. You want a guess, just idle speculation? It could have been put there by a Russian. Or someone who worked for the Russians. Someone born in Odessa, say." I didn't think Logonov was capable of murdering anyone, but I wanted Han to know I hadn't forgotten about the Russian just because I had been warned off seeing him again.

"That's the other thing your Ministry does, speculate on the basis of nothing. It's not very smart."

"Don't tell me, you think it's a sign of insecurity. If you're finished, I have another question for you. Do you still have the bank lady's file?"

"According to you, it's not a file, only a cover page."

"I changed my mind."

There was a long silence. This was not always a bad sign. Some people think when they aren't talking.

"Still with me, Han?"

"Inspector, if you need something, just ask, alright? I hate it the way you Ministry people tiptoe around."

"That's a wonderful image, the Minister on tiptoe. Nothing at all like you, asking straight out and flatfooted about knife handles. Tell me this. Does the file say when the lady entered the country?"

Another silence.

"You there?"

"I'm here."

"Well, when did she enter the country?"

"It doesn't say."

"Isn't there a copy of her entry visa?"

"Nope."

"Why not?"

"I guess it must not be a file. Good-bye, Inspector, I'm busy." The phone clicked twice, and the operator came on the line. The connection wasn't as good; Han must have been calling from somewhere else.

"Anything more we can help you with, Inspector?" Same tone of voice, edgy, maybe condescending, though with all the SSD buzzes and clicks this time of day you couldn't be sure.

"Yes, tell your technicians congratulations. They've almost fixed those clicks."

"That's it?"

"I don't suppose you know anything about cell phones."

"No."

"How about silk stockings?"

The line went dead. I went out to find some cold noodles in a quiet restaurant where people didn't fall over dead or end up with knives in their back, knives with birch-wood handles.

2

After lunch I strolled around a few back streets. For April, it was hot, but it was still better outside than sitting in the office staring at the ceiling and pretending not to be thinking about a case I couldn't even figure out if I was supposed to solve. If things were so quiet, something must be wrong. If no one was prepared to let me know which way to jump, then it was going to be a very long way down. I dodged a woman on a bicycle who pedaled as if she were daydreaming, and kept walking to nowhere in particular. Just as I turned a corner, I suddenly got that feeling—I was being watched. Someone had marked me, there was no doubt in my mind. Harmless glances, uninterested stares don't register with me. This was no longer little warning flags flapping in front of my eyes. This was a skin-prickling, hackle-raising klaxon that somewhere, relatively near and directed specifically at me, was a pair of eyes brimful of death and destruction.

I never made a careful study of it, but I've looked at a few books about survival behavior. At one point in my career, it seemed a wise thing to do. The theory is that an animal—or a person—marked as prey can sense an intense look that pierces the invisible force surrounding everything living. The heart jumps, chemicals pour into the bloodstream, muscles tense. If it's a deer, then the deer is ready to run, run for its life, crazy with fear, breathless to escape. I never altogether bought the theory; how could there be anything physical about looking? It sounded like death rays. Yet I knew the physical reaction was real enough. Theory or not, somehow when I was being watched, I sensed it.

With my heart pounding, I stopped to tie my shoe; it usually works better than bounding away like a frightened roe deer. When I stood up again, I walked slowly in the opposite direction. There was no one around who seemed to be paying attention, not even anyone who seemed conspicuously inattentive. I wandered aimlessly for about twenty minutes, long enough to be sure the lion, or the wolf, or whatever it was, had dropped away. Being followed doesn't bother me, but I never like knowing I'm someone's prey. At least now I knew where things stood. I was in someone's sights. Whether that was because I was getting too close or not close enough remained to be seen. It was becoming vital to know which, but I hadn't figured out yet exactly how to test the waters without getting swept away. I thought about it as I walked, but every conclusion suggested its opposite. Maybe it was the weather. It's hard to be decisive when the air is so clear that you can see the buds on an old tree's highest branches turning to the sun.

It could have been just coincidence, or a subconscious compass at work, but my wandering ended up at the top of the stairs leading to Club Blue. As long as I was there, I figured, I might as well go down and chat. The bartender was bound to know something useful. Whether he would volunteer it was another matter. Besides, it was hot and I was thirsty. The place was quiet when I sat down at the bar. No music playing. I looked around, then got up and poured myself a glass of beer.

"You shouldn't be stealing drinks, Inspector. It can be reported." I looked around and there was the bartender, holding something that looked like a crowbar.

"Funny thing for a bartender to use," I said. "You need that to open those little bottles of olives? I can do it for you with these." I wiggled my fingers.

He smacked the crowbar hard against his palm. "It comes in handy for lots of things."

"That's fine. Where's the manager, the guy with the sharp trousers?"

The bartender hit his palm again with the crowbar. "He's not around. I haven't seen him today at all. So I guess you'll be leaving."

"No, I think I'll have another glass of beer." I walked behind the bar. That put something between the crowbar and me. "Your manager on vacation, is he? He forgot to put up that license we talked about."

"Yeah, he forgot. Probably has a lot on his mind." He laughed. "You know what I mean?"

"How long has he been gone?"

The bartender shrugged. "He comes and goes. I don't keep track. That's the job of your people, isn't it, keeping track of us citizens?"

"You like it in those old apartments? The ones by the bank?"

"So, you been watching me? I'm flattered, Inspector, really I am."

"Good. Let me give you a piece of advice. Don't walk in front of buses."

"Are you threatening me?"

"Never."

"What do you want here?"

"Want?"

"You know what I mean. You brought in that stocking the other day. I got nothing to do with that stuff."

"You should have bought two pair, it would have been cheaper."

"Ease up, will you?"

"You tell me what I need to know, I'll think about it. And put down that crowbar before I stuff it down your throat." It clattered to the floor, which surprised the hell out of me. I thought at least we'd argue about it a little. "Now, walk over here, sit down on one of those bar stools, and put your hands on the bar, both of them. Everything nice and slow."

He did as I said. When he lifted one of his hands to scratch his cheek, I grabbed his wrist, just like I had the first time, and gave it a twist. He yelped. "Hey!"

"Hey, nothing. I told you to put your hands on the bar. I meant it. Once you answer my questions, you can pick your nose with all ten fingers for all I care. I'm asking you again, where is your manager, and don't tell me you don't know."

"He walked out of here with a couple of guys."

"Okay, he walked out of here. When?"

"Day before yesterday."

"What time?"

"Afternoon, I don't know, maybe four o'clock."

"You know what I'm going to ask next?"

"Who were the guys."

"Very good. Maybe you've been interrogated before. Maybe it's in your file. Maybe you don't want another report in your file because it would mean you'd have to leave Pyongyang and move out to the country. Very dull, out in the country."

"Say, why don't you let me answer the question?"

"Alright, who were the guys?"

"I don't know."

"Sure you do." I slapped him across the face, not very hard, but his head snapped back and for a moment he looked as if he might fall off the bar stool. He seemed surprised, but not half as surprised as I was. The pressure from the case must be getting to me even worse than it was getting to Min. I rarely get physical during an interrogation. A lot of inspectors do, but I don't. It isn't very effective; too many people just shut up after being hit, and then you either have to raise the ante or back off. I didn't know why I slapped him; I hoped it wasn't because he looked so scared. "And keep your hands on the bar."

"If I tell you who they are, they'll kill me."

"Tough luck for you," I said. "A couple of Kazakh boys, weren't they?"

"I'm not saying yes, I'm not saying no."

That made me mad, and I thought about it for half a second before I remembered reading somewhere that if you bottled up tension it was bad for you. I slapped him again, harder this time. A lot of tension drained off. But this time he was more ready, so he didn't lose his balance. "Did they threaten him?"

"No." He was grinning. He knew I wouldn't hit him again.

"So why'd he go with them?"

"You'll have to ask him, won't you?"

"Have it your own way." I patted him on the cheek. "From this afternoon, word will be out on the street that you talked to me and told me everything I needed to know about a couple of Kazakhs. I'll come by your apartment tomorrow to claim your corpse."

"You don't scare me, Inspector."

"That's good," I said and finished my beer. "I'd like your last memories of me to be pleasant ones."

Back in the office, I picked up the second Interpol file, which was mostly background on Kazakhstan. When I had first skipped through it, there didn't seem much of interest. There was a little history and a few economic statistics. But this time I noticed that attached to the second page was a list of prominent officials. The head of the security police was a fairly young man who had a degree in criminology. Whether that did him or the country any good was not made clear, but from the reporting on the crime rates, it did not seem to have made a major contribution. There were all sorts of crimes, crimes against persons, crimes against property, street crime, car theft, drugs. Bank robberies were not a special problem, apparently, except where they involved gangs of criminals who were armed and needed money for unspecified purposes. They shot the guards; the police shot the robbers. In one case, the robbers were caught in a cemetery. It sounded noisy and dangerous and not the sort of thing we needed in Pyongyang.

On the list of officials were a number of bankers, with an indication of their worth and addresses. Many of them were well-to-do. No reason they shouldn't be, working in such close quarters with all that money. Several of them had second or third residences abroad, expensive residences. Why did people need to live somewhere else other than home, among strangers? I made a mental note to ask Miss Chon if she knew any of these people the next time I saw her.

3

"I don't recognize any of them." She put the list down on the table and looked at me coolly, defying me to contradict her.

"Naturally, it's a big country, sixteen million people, maybe more. No one could be expected to know everyone, certainly not all the top bankers." I nodded and smiled. No sense pretending I believed her. "Especially not you, someone interested in banking, I mean. You were probably focusing on other things at the time."

She picked the list up again and studied it. "A few names, one or two may have been mentioned, I may have heard someone say something about them. What difference does it make?"

"Funny, I thought I had mentioned to you that this is an investigation. I get to ask you, and I don't have to tell you why. That's how it's done. It's a regular, accepted pattern in most places in the world, and we have adopted it."

"Why all the interest in Kazakhstan?"

"Ah, tut! I told you—the pattern."

"We'll have to continue some other time with your pattern, Inspector. The bank is being audited tomorrow, and I have many papers to prepare."

"Not unless you answer my questions, you don't have anything to prepare. You still can't seem to get it. We don't have a lot of bank robberies in this town. So we don't just shrug them off and say, oh, well, there goes another truckload of money. And we don't just run down suspects and blast them to kingdom come in gun battles in cemeteries." Her eyes flashed for an instant; it could have been a glint of sunlight off a passing car, but it wasn't. She'd heard about the shootout in her country, the one connected with the bank robbery, and she knew what I was getting at. Maybe now she would start to cooperate.

"Whom do you know from Kazakh banking circles with a residence outside of the country? I'm not asking you to betray anyone, Miss Chon. You don't have to tell me how they got the money. Actually, I don't care how they got the money. I'm just following a line of thought. Do you mind?"

"Not at all, Inspector. I just don't see the relevance, that's all." She fell silent, in a sullen sort of way.

I let her stew for a minute or so. While we waited, I found a piece of wood in my pocket, an old piece of Siberian elm I'd forgotten I had. Not very interesting wood, too needy, too eager to please; it took any shape you wanted to give it. It gives you a sense of being smart and in charge, not good on this case—and especially not good when dealing with Miss Chon. I put it back. "Let's make it simple. Has anyone on this list moved out of the country, taken a pile of cash and gone overseas?"

"I wouldn't know about piles of cash. A few of them have gone abroad, yes. One moved to New York, I heard somewhere."

"Somewhere you heard someone moved to New York. That's good, that's very helpful." I paused. "Expensive city, New York, that's what they say. Must cost a lot to live there."

She smiled. "Maybe for the working masses, Inspector, but not for a banker."

"You wouldn't know the name of this fellow who moved to New York?"

"I'll think about it."

"Do that, I'd be very grateful." I wasn't so interested in Kazakh bankers, but I wanted to get her in the habit of answering my questions. She wasn't there yet, and I didn't know much about her habits. I decided to change the subject. Maybe it would put her off balance. "You ever go out to clubs? Ever been to a place called Club Blue?"

"We already discussed this." The lady had a perfect center of gravity. She also had a better memory than I did.

"Is the owner there a friend of yours?" The image of the owner walking out of the bar with a couple of toughs and, so far as I knew, not returning didn't fill me with happy thoughts. The little bartender didn't seem worried, but he didn't seem the sort who worried about much more than his own skin. If looking the other way when his boss disappeared was required, he could obviously do it. Once his cheeks stopped smarting, I'd have to go back to talk to him again.

"No. I don't know the owner." She was a good liar, very natural, but this resonated in a funny way. I had to think maybe she knew him pretty well.

"You told me he had an account."

"He did. That doesn't mean I know him." This second time it almost came out more believable.

"The first time I asked you, when we were having drinks, you said he 'had' an account. Why 'had'?"

"I didn't realize you hung on my every word, Inspector."

"Why 'had'?"

"He closed it."

"Is that so?"

"Anything else we need to discuss before I get back to my work?"

"He's disappeared. Did you know that?"

She didn't pale or take a funny breath, but she may have swallowed a little strangely, sort of out of sequence. It was difficult to be sure, because she was Kazakh, and I didn't really know what Kazakh women did when they were surprised, or shaken. I shrugged. "Too bad. I'll bet he could have sliced bread with the creases on his trousers. He promised me a drink. I guess that's out now." I stood up. "Well, I'm sure we'll be running into each other again, Miss Chon. Call me if you remember the name of your friend in New York."

4

A pall hung over the city the next day, the whole day, a gray that would not go away, would not be scrubbed out of the sky, no matter what. A breeze came up around noon, but the pall didn't move. The wind rustled some trees and then stopped abruptly. The buildings were mute. They were resting, casting no shadows and finding no light. A few faded off in the distance, disappearing into the murk. Blurred at the edges, the city was silent in its center, the only noise the whistle of a traffic cop warning pedestrians out of the empty street.

After a day like that, the night came straight down, a deep black velvet blanket dropped from above. No sense of darkness creeping in from the east, street by street. The city, the buildings, the roads and alleys, even the river, all dissolved rapidly into a deeper gloom, the sky never touched with the final color that sometimes appears beneath the clouds on normal evenings. No sense of sunrise or sunset, no rhythm; the day simply disappeared. It went from gray to black in a heartbeat. Finally, a window twinkled, then a few more. Out of the gloom, building shapes emerged, like miners struggling from a coal mine that had collapsed, leaving them gasping for air.

I was on the street, walking in the darkness with no place to go and damned irritable about it. A few people clustered around a stall on the corner, one of those small stalls that sell little snacks, bread, fried cakes. The crowd fell silent when I walked up; one or two gave me ugly looks. The others moved away as if my presence were diseased. Inside the stall, lit by a row of candles, a woman was straightening the cakes on the shelf along the back. When she turned around and saw me, she made a low sound of disgust.

"It's supposed to be a day off, Inspector. Why can't you leave me alone?"

"I'm happy to see you, too. Close up shop. We have to talk."

"Now? It's my busiest time. It's a holiday, in case you've forgotten. People are in a good mood for a change, and they like standing around my place. If I have to close up, I'll lose money, and I can't afford that. Come back later, around eleven o'clock."

"I know the holiday calendar, thank you very much. I said now; I meant it." I blew out several candles.

She studied my face. "Why do you make my life so miserable? What have I ever done to you?"

Someone behind me spat. I looked to see who it was, but it was too dark. I turned back to the woman. "You complain a hell of a lot, you know that? Close up this crummy shop, or I'll throw your goods in the street and cite you for wasting the people's resources."

Without another word, she dropped the cloth curtain over the front and stormed out of the stall. "This is unfair, you'll ruin me!" Her voice was barely under control, strands of hair stuck to the sweat on her forehead. Her fists clenched in anger.

"Over there." I pushed her across the street and into an alley. When we were in complete darkness, hidden from view, I let go of her arm. "Overdid it, don't you think?"

"You have a problem?" She straightened her hair and smoothed her apron. "I'm the one who should be offering criticism. Every time we have a meeting, I end up black and blue."

"What have you got?"

"Plenty. But I don't want to tell you here."

"Where?"

"At the river. In an hour."

"Are you really making money?"

"None of your business." She walked back out to the street, rubbing her arm.

5

An hour later, I was sitting on a bench near the river, listening to the water go by. In a nearby tree, a bird was singing to itself against darkness broken only by the hesitant light of a half-hidden moon. The night breeze had swept the sky clear of all but a few clouds. Someone walked up behind me, slow, thoughtful steps that barely sounded on the pavement. "You want to meet here, in the open?"

"Just sit down, will you? Maybe you noticed, it's the dead of night. Even if anyone sees us, they'll think you're trying to bribe me to leave you alone."

"Shall I offer to sleep with you, to complete the picture?"

"Forget it. I don't sleep with street agents."

She sat down. We'd worked together for many years. Nice woman, very smart, excellent instincts, brave as a tiger. But the first time we met I thought something about her face was wrong, and that was the first thing I thought of every time we sat together. Her face was almost round, but not quite, and that sometimes seemed to me the root of the problem. If she had a perfectly round face, more like Chief Inspector Min's, you wouldn't have noticed her eyes were not on the same line; if you didn't notice her eyes, it wouldn't occur to you that her cheeks were too high; if her cheeks hadn't been so high, her lips wouldn't have looked so full, and with different lips, there is no way you would have noticed that her nose was a little too flat. And yet, altogether it fit, it was all perfect, somehow. My palms started to sweat every time I saw her.

"You want a report, or should we stare at the moon? It looks constipated tonight." That was normal for her, a hard edge, as if she had to get back at me for something.

"Romantic to the core, as always. Well, you called the meeting," I said. "Anytime you're ready." I noticed she wasn't looking at the moon; she was staring into the black water.

"A German man hurried by the stall three nights ago just before I closed. He ran back and asked for directions. There were drops of blood on his shirt cuff. When I reached for the pen in his breast pocket to draw a map, he nearly went berserk."

"Tall or short?" A German, how many could there be? Dieter was shorter. Or was it Jurgen? I hadn't looked closely at either one. Neither had been standing; what I remembered best was the way they winced.

"Short. Late middle aged. I'd say he was about your age, or maybe a little younger." She waited a fraction of a second, but she knew I wouldn't give her the satisfaction of reacting, so she resumed. "Atrocious accent, I could barely understand him. Actually, that was a good thing. He did a lot of gesturing to try to make me understand. So I got a good look at his sleeves. It was a white shirt. The collar was frayed. The right cuff had the blood. It hadn't been there long."

"What about the pen?"

"I don't know. I had the feeling it was special, almost life or death."

"Ever seen him before?"

"No."

"Ever heard of a place called Club Blue?"

"Once or twice. You want to take me there?"

"Not your style. Anyway, I'm too old for places like that." I stretched my arm along the back of the bench; someone looking might have thought I had my hand on her shoulder. "Good job, though a report a little earlier might have helped. Anything else?"

"Don't patronize me, Inspector." She stood up. "You know your trouble?"

"No, but I guess you're about to tell me."

"You want people to think you're April, but you're actually August."

The moon had come out from behind the lingering clouds, and I could see her face in profile. She was looking at the stars. My palms were sweating.

"I've got a few other tidbits, but they go to the highest bidder. And you"—she looked good in pale moonlight, I noticed—"don't even come close. Good night." The sound of her footsteps faded quickly. I listened to the river for a while, heard the murmur of a couple sitting nearby, gentle laughter, like music, then wondered what life would be like if I paid less attention to details.

6

In the morning, Min appeared at the door to my office. He wore the expression of a dog hoping for a kind word. "How is everything, Professor?" You could almost hear the sound of his tail thumping against the floor.

I was reading something complicated and didn't look up for fear of losing my place. "Everything's fine." It was the closest I could get to saying, "Go away," and that wouldn't have done any good.

"Progress?"

"Some." I picked the book off the desk and propped it up in front of me.

Silence, but not because he had left. "Dammit, Inspector, what is so important that you can't talk?"

I marked the page with a pencil check and put down the copy of the Criminal Code that I was trying to digest. "I'm doing background research. It's something insignificant, probably, but I thought I'd try to figure out exactly what law these bank robbers broke."

"Who cares? That's not our job. Leave the details to the procurators. Just find the bastards."

"You mean, keep going on the case?"

"Didn't I just say find the bastards?"

It wasn't the unambiguous set of orders I was looking for, but it would have to do for now. "Alright, here's my thought. If I can figure out what law they broke, maybe I can put some pressure on accomplices, or abettors—as they are referred to in this." I held up the book. "If you abet a crime, you're liable to several years of labor correction, unless you confess or repent or didn't know you were involved. But to prove you didn't know you were involved, you have to give some indication of what it was that was going on so you can indicate how it was you knew nothing about it."

"All true, Inspector, but given that we have a deadline staring us in the face, I don't think we have time for these subtleties."

"Just listen, it gets better. If I can find an abettor and put on a little heat, I can press him to prove why he shouldn't be charged with not acting to prevent the crime."

"He'll just say he didn't know about it until afterward."

"Then he should have reported it," I said. Min could have at least expressed appreciation for my effort.

"Inspector, I don't want to know who abetted in the crime, I want to know who committed it, who planned it, who led it, and where the hell he is now."

"What if the ringleader is the stiff who ended up in the morgue?"

"Tell me, Inspector O, that you don't really believe any such thing. Ringleaders don't step in front of buses. They tend to be survivors, and smarter than the people beneath them."

"They just might step in the street if they have no reason to believe a bus will be coming; if they have been watching the bank for weeks and never saw a bus on that street; if they have timed it so they will be picked up by a car at the very moment when a bus occupies the same spot in space and time."

"You're making this all up, aren't you? Or do you have something new from the traffic people?"

"They weren't going to give me anything. Nothing but a pat on the head and an invitation to leave. Li might get them to be more cooperative. But think about it, what are the odds a bus would have appeared just at that moment? Buses don't go that route; I did some checking with the people in the neighborhood. Once in a while army trucks use the street, but mostly as a place for the drivers to stop and smoke."

"So, you are making this up."

"No, it's not fantasy."

"What do you call it?"

"Surmise." I threw the Criminal Code onto a copy of the Ministry regulations. It slid onto the floor.

Min pulled at his ear, then walked away without comment. A few minutes later, the phone rang. I knew what it was. "Yeah?"

"Don't answer the phone that way, Inspector. What if it was somebody important?" He paused. "I mean . . ."

"Never mind, I know what you mean."

"Well, come in here, then. We need to talk."

I put down the phone and frowned. It sometimes occurred to me that Min's compulsion to call me into his office when he could just finish a conversation standing at my door wasn't voluntary behavior on his part. Maybe it was a defect that had crept into the Min clan at the dawn of time, when the first Min male grunted and sweated while his bride shut her eyes and considered suicide. Maybe it was a trait that wouldn't fall away, strengthened through intermarriage over the centuries until it was dominant in a whole layer of the population, like having a narrow nose or crooked teeth. Then again, maybe not. Maybe it was an idea, an impulse imparted from a childhood experience that just grew on Chief Inspector Min over the years like a wart. Who knew? I shrugged as I walked down the hall. At this late point in Min's evolution, it couldn't be helped.

As soon as I arrived at his doorway, he waved me in.

"A British official is coming to town, Inspector."

"Bully for us."

"We are assigned to security detail. The written orders will arrive tomorrow morning. The visitor will be here next week. We are in charge of presecurity checks of the schedule, and then we have to co-ordinate with the Traffic Bureau to keep the route clear from the airport to the hotel."

"Easy, we can do that with our eyes closed." Not really. I'd made a few enemies in the Traffic Bureau lately. "But it takes time, just filling out all the necessary forms. If I have to do that, I can't work on the bank robbery, too." Maybe I could get away from the robbery case after all. Visitors required a lot of effort, especially Westerners. "You could assign someone else to the security detail."

"Like who?"

"There are other people in this office." Not really. "How about Yang?" I knew Min would hate the idea.

"Don't be absurd, Inspector. The man wouldn't know how to behave. He'd have tears streaming from everyone's eyes before you knew it. This is supposed to be a goodwill visit. No, not Yang, and not his tall friend, either. We can't have someone on a security squad who walks like a circus bear."

"Most of SSD does."

"Forget SSD. This is Ministry business, and we're going to do it right."

"Implying what?"

"Implying nothing. I want a dignified, invisible security detail working this visit. That means you."

"Where will you be hiding?"

"I'll be here, coordinating, keeping the paperwork in order, that sort of thing. If necessary, we'll hold Yang in reserve should anything come up, but you are the most experienced in field operations. Besides, you've been abroad and understand how to deal with those people."

"What people?"

"You know"—he paused before saying the word—"foreigners. There is something about them, they are always so demanding, never satisfied. It's hard to grasp the problem, actually."

"What else?"

"What else, what?"

"What else do you want? This isn't just about a security detail. It's about the robbery, isn't it?"

"Let's go down to your office."

"Why?"

Min stood up and looked out the window at the Operations Building. "It's easier to talk in your office. I like the view better."

We walked down the hall in silence. I sat down at my desk. Min leaned against the wall. "As a matter of fact, the British ambassador was complaining at the Foreign Ministry yesterday that British businessmen who had accounts in the bank were being harassed by the police. It's not us, so it must be SSD. We need to show them that we do not harass people, and we certainly don't harass investors. You can do that, Inspector. People respond well to you, somehow. If this British official's trip goes well, it will be a plus for everyone." He cocked an eyebrow slightly, to indicate this included the two of us.

The phone rang in Min's office. It rang three times and stopped. Then it started ringing again. Min gave me a funny look. "That's not normal." He went down the hall, walking with an agitated gait. A minute later, he was back at my door. His color wasn't good.

"You want to sit down?" I pointed at the chair next to my desk.

Min shook his head. "Inspector, that was SSD."

"It can't be all that bad. Han and I haven't argued, not overly, and when we parted, we parted on good terms, I think."

"It's not the robbery. SSD has information." He stopped. He gave no indication that he intended to continue until I said my line.

"And what was the information?"

"An attempt will be made on the life of the British official, on our visitor, on the very man you are assigned to guard."

I considered the idea. "That I doubt," I said finally. "SSD is just having one of its crazy nightmares. It's a natural result of trying to digest too much bad information, like getting heartburn. Don't get yourself riled up."

"No, this is good information. It was picked up by another service, in a third country. It was passed to us recently, they said, in the past week. They've been checking it, checking the source, checking the channel. They think it's believable."

"They don't like working with the Chinese, so it's probably Russian. How good could it be? How come this information comes in at exactly the same time we learn about the visitor? Who could have planned an attempt on the life of someone we didn't even know was coming? Isn't it a little too convenient?"

Min shook his head. "Damnation, Inspector, every time I say something, you contradict me. I'm in no mood for that. This was from an SSD contact I trust, alright? If I say I trust him, then I trust him, and I don't need your observations to the contrary."

"Fine. So a trusted source told you about a plot. So your trusted source just found out about it himself. What if we simply accept the information and pronounce it good? Then what? Then we have to conclude that it lets us out of the game of the security detail. You want me to guess? Someone really didn't want us in the middle anyway, because we don't deal with assassinations, coups, or—"

"Who said anything about a coup, Inspector?" Min's voice was low and very controlled. He moved over to my desk and leaned down so his face was nearly level with mine. "You will never say anything like that again in my presence, never, ever. Ever." He straightened up slowly, his round eyes intensely black. "There's no stepping back from that line, Inspector. You went over it, now you live there. If the question ever comes up, if I'm ever asked, I didn't hear you say it. But I won't wave good-bye as the truck drives you to the mountains. Try and remember that."

I sat, stunned. Not at Min, at myself. I knew better than to talk about a coup. I knew better than even to think the word. It didn't only endanger me, it endangered everyone around me, anyone who even looked at me in the street. Min walked out the door like a ghost, without a sound.

I didn't leave the office that night. I wasn't hungry and I wasn't tired. I just sat at my desk, asking myself again and again, why had I mentioned a coup? The pressure must be at the breaking point. Or worse, my subconscious had spotted something and was screaming at me to pay attention. Min was right; at this rate, my subconscious was going to get me sent to away to a camp in the mountains, if not actually stood up against a wall. Yang came in once to ask if anything was wrong, but I only looked at him blankly. He shrugged and went down the hall. I heard his door close, and then it was quiet.

Chapter Two

The next morning, Min came up the stairs at seven o'clock. He walked by my office without looking in. I heard him open the file cabinets at the end of the hall and then the sound of him humming. A few minutes later, he walked back. This time he stopped at my door. "Good morning, Inspector." He smiled and pointed out the window. "Beautiful spring day, fresh air, not a cloud on the horizon." He smiled again. "Makes you glad to be alive. Had a good night?" There was no touch of irony in his voice. He sounded completely free of worry.

"Yes, great night." I raised my head and searched his face with bleary eyes.

"Good. Let's go over the bank robbery in about an hour, sort of put it in order. Then we can work on the security detail, nothing elaborate. Fine by you?" Min was practically bouncing on his toes, he was so full of good cheer.

"What do you know that you aren't sharing?"

"I know, Inspector, that gloom only leads to more of the same.

This morning I got up, put my feet down on the floor, and told myself that nothing can be as bad as it looks. We have troubles? Other people have more. This summer it may flood, the rivers may overflow their banks, and the glorious dams we read about every day in the newspapers may burst. But not today, and this is the day we are going to live in."

I groaned. "On second thought, don't share it with me. Just leave me alone for another hour."

Min shook his head. "Your problem is, you don't get enough exercise." He grinned and walked back to his office, humming.

A moment later the phone rang. "O, get in here." There was no lilt in his voice, just naked urgency. "Now."

Min was staring openmouthed at a single piece of pale blue paper when I walked in. Actually, not very blue, but very lightweight, the paper that the Ministry uses for Most Sensitive information. Sometimes it is even on regular white paper, because the blue stuff runs out. But we still call it a Blue Paper. If we need to see one of those reports, we go to the Ministry to read it. They never get out of a special area in the Ministry, and certainly never make it to our office. Never, except of course for the one that was in plain sight. Min looked up. "Shut the door."

"There's no one else here."

"Shut the fucking door, Inspector!"

I swung it shut. "You want it locked?"

Min rubbed his face with both hands. "Sit down. This"—he picked up the single sheet of paper between his thumb and forefinger and waved it limply like a flag of surrender—"this was in the daily mail I picked up before coming here. It isn't supposed to be in our mail. I think we aren't even supposed to know it exists."

"Bad?"

"Bad? Oh, no, not bad. Terrible, appalling, horrifying." He didn't even have to pause to find the triplet; I mentally braced myself. "It says SSD suspects Yang is part of the plot against the British VIP."

"Ridiculous," I heard my subconscious mutter.

"It also says that you and me and Li are to be put under special surveillance."

"Finally, a useful piece of information." I had the sensation of threads being pulled together. "That explains the squad Yang saw at my apartment house the other day."

"What? Surveillance? If he saw them, that means they saw him near your apartment. And they may have heard what you said yesterday."

"About what?"

"First, you suggested that Yang lead the security detail. The man is part of the plot, and you recommend him to get on the inside! We don't even have to guess how they'll interpret that." He looked at me strangely for a moment, then shook his head. "And then, you know, the other thing." Min got up from his desk and looked out the window. "They're probably over at the Operations Building right now watching us. I knew this was going to be a bad day, as soon as I woke up."

"What about Yang?" If that report was right, Yang was in danger. He was in danger even if it was wrong. Anything on paper was dangerous.

"What about him?"

"Do we let him know?"

"Are you crazy, Inspector? I want him out of this office, immediately."

"Why? Yang wouldn't hurt a fly. SSD is being fed a line by someone, and I have a feeling I know who it might be—a Russian who sells stockings." Logonov might not be capable of murder, but spreading disinformation was another story. The Russians liked to keep SSD jumpy, overload the circuits. Somehow a few years ago they got hold of a Ministry phone book, and they just went down the list. Someone's big Slav finger ended up on Yang's name, and it got cranked into the disinformation machinery. They probably hadn't even checked to see who he was. "That Russian's visa stamps are phony; Han was furious I had anything to do with him. I think he's mainly here as a spotter, but who knows what he passes in those stockings? Tell me, why would Yang get himself involved in a plot of any sort? The man can barely stumble down the stairs without feeling he has offended someone."

"I'm not interested in the drama of his inner life. We need to get him out of here before he takes us all to the coal mines. And you need to stay away from SSD's operations; I shouldn't have to tell you that. We have enough trouble of our own, without stepping on their flowers."

"You going to take that Blue Paper back to the Ministry?"

"How can I? If I take it back, they'll know I read it, and I'm not supposed to have done that."

"They'll know it's missing, not right away, but it's numbered. By the end of the week, when they count the copies, they'll see it's gone. Then they'll search. They'll question people. Nasty questions. Bad technique." I paused. "Wait a minute. How do we know they didn't plant that in your mail bundle? How do we know they just don't want us to think Yang is involved?"

Min glumly turned that idea over in his mind. "Sure, and how do we know this isn't a test of my honesty? They want to see what I'll do. What am I going to do?"

"But what if it's real?"

"You just said Yang wouldn't hurt a fly."

"Yes, but they don't know that. They may think the information is real, and they need to know if we can be trusted."

"Inspector, we can go on like this for hours. Anything is possible."

"Get rid of it. The Blue Paper. Get rid of it."

"But if they planted it . . ."

"Trust me, Min, I was just thinking out loud. They didn't plant it. It was a mistake, an unintentional security breach. If you report it, the clerks in the central mailroom will be put through hell. As soon as they realize it's missing, they'll fix their logs. No one else will know it's gone. It's happened before. But we have another problem."

"I don't want to know."

Min knew the problem, he just didn't want to hear it out loud. We had to do something about the case in order to bury these crazy reports that someone in our office—and by implication, all of us who dealt with that person—was involved in a plot against a foreign visitor. It was so ridiculous it could only be a cover for something else. I put a gag in my subconscious before it could say what I was thinking.

"You do what you have to do," Min said. "If it doesn't work, don't forget, I won't be there to wave when the truck drives away."

"Don't worry, if it doesn't work, we'll both be in the back of the truck."

2

Even a man with short legs will take long strides. He walks along the street, you tag along behind, simple as can be. A man can be followed at a reasonable distance, comfortably. I once followed someone we suspected of trafficking in bad medicine for two days. The weather was good. It was a pleasure to be outside. I almost bought him dinner afterward, he made it so easy. But women are different. They amble, they saunter, they stop for no particular reason to look at nothing at all. It is impossible to adjust your pace, to anticipate what they will do, and so you end up running up their backs if you aren't paying attention. It does no good to find yourself standing next to the woman you are tailing. She won't turn her head to look, but she'll notice you out of the corner of her eye, and then you might as well go home.

If I was going to get serious about the bank robbery case, I had to make up for lost time. Someone didn't want us to be on it, whoever was floating those stories about Yang and the British visitor. But someone else did want us on it. The only thing I had to go on was the weeklong silence, and the fact that people who seemed to be connected with the robbery, or to know something about it, were disappearing. Or turning up dead. Silence never meant quiet, not on these sorts of cases. It meant a frantic, ferocious struggle in offices I never visited, on phones I never called, in places I had no wish ever to see.

Getting Yang in the clear, and pulling everyone else in the office to a safe place, required our getting traction on the robbery case. Whether that meant actually solving it, I didn't yet know. Either way, we had to be seen pursuing it, and to do that, we had to start up the active investigation with something simple. Jumping too far ahead would suggest that we realized this was more than a robbery. The easiest, safest thing at this point was checking each one of the bank clerks. Little Li was too conspicuous. Yang didn't like crowds, and anyway I couldn't put Yang out on the street now; he'd be followed by a train of people from a special group whose purpose and place in the scheme of things we didn't know. It was unlikely there would be a move against him; it was too soon for that. But sometimes people get desperate out of sequence, and if they did, they might try something against Yang.

Luckily, the weather was good, and I liked walking at sunset this time of year. The light was pure, and the air was very soft. How bad could it be, following a young woman and watching the sun go down?

I picked up the first clerk as she left the bank at dusk. The files said she came from an unremarkable family, and there was nothing in her background to excite suspicion, except that her grandfather had gone south during the war. There was a vague note about tragedy on her mother's side, but no details. You'd have thought someone would have included a page on that; maybe it had fallen out. Tragedy was leverage, or weakness. Her school records seemed fine. She wasn't married, but she lived in her own apartment rather than with her parents. That was a little unusual; it probably meant that someone was keeping her. The one thing in the file that grabbed me was the entry under her employment. She had been hired at the bank about two months ago.

The clerk had long hair and wore a trench coat that went to her ankles. It was slit in the back. The tiny picture in her file showed her to be plain looking—small oval face, sharp chin, wide-set eyes, high forehead. I couldn't see her face very well as she came out of the bank, but I thought I recognized the chin. She had on dark brown high-heel shoes but couldn't walk in them very well, so it meant we would not be going too fast. It wouldn't be much trouble to keep her in sight, even as the light faded and the moon climbed into the night. I kept back about seven or eight meters. Once I dropped my keys and pretended to hunt for them while she stopped to talk to an older man. I didn't get a good look at him, but when he walked away, he moved slowly, as if his feet hurt.

From the route she was taking, I felt pretty sure that the clerk was headed for a bus stop near the train station. That was a guess, but it seemed a good one. If nothing else, it let me walk as if I really had a destination in mind in case she started noticing me. If I needed to, I could drop back a little. I didn't even have to look at her anymore; to anyone watching, it would appear we simply happened to be heading to the same place.

Getting too congratulatory over your own technique is never a good idea. Keeping back is smart, until it isn't. I lost her for a long minute in a crowd of people unloading onto the sidewalk from a broken-down tram, but I just kept walking toward the train station and finally picked her out of the gloom again about ten meters ahead.

When she went down the steps of an underpass, I gave her an extra twenty seconds. The underpass was dark, and you could lose someone in there. I wanted to see her come up the other side. A minute passed, then two. She didn't emerge. People were streaming up and down the steps, but she wasn't one of them. Finally, I went down. No one was stepping over a body; people weren't swerving to avoid someone standing still. She wasn't there, she hadn't climbed up the other side, she hadn't doubled back and come up the steps where I was waiting. She was gone.

3

As I walked back to the office, bad thoughts kept running through my mind. My skills might be getting rusty, but I would not lose a woman on high heels unless she was very well trained. And she wasn't alone, it seemed. What was it I'd heard at the bank party about Miss Chon, that she was good at slipping away? Away to where?

After losing the clerk in the underpass, I doubled back to make sure she hadn't ditched me and gone for a bowl of noodles somewhere. She hadn't, at least not along the route we'd covered. I might have missed her as she climbed the underpass steps; she might have come up the other side exactly at the moment I went down. There is such a thing as coincidence, but the Ministry doesn't favor it as an explanation. Frankly, I didn't, either, not in this instance. Who had trained her? Why would a bank clerk need to know how to lose a tail? Worst of all, was my technique getting so bad that she spotted me, even in the dark?

By the time I got up the stairs and into the hallway leading to Yang's office, I knew it would be impossible to solve this case by putting together a clue here and a clue there. There simply wasn't time, especially if everything was as complicated as it now appeared. The first thing I had to do was pin Yang up against the wall and make sure none of that crazy conversation we'd had the other night led anywhere. I wasn't worried that he was involved, though I made it a point never to be sure about anything until I was. The fact was, he was mentioned in a report where he shouldn't have been, and we needed to know why. Despite my first reaction, I knew it couldn't be the Russians who had floated his name. Someone in our unit appeared in a Blue Paper, in the middle of everything that was going on—coincidence? Not a chance. This wasn't from a foreign service. It was from the inside, people who knew something about Yang. They might have picked his name at random, but that would have been out of character. When they wanted to use someone, even for target practice, it was for a reason. If they put his name in a Blue Paper, they had thought about it, researched, weighed other options and other people. What was there about my melancholy colleague that rang bells for them, whoever they were?

I didn't bother to knock. "Yang, I'm going to phrase this as delicately as I can. Whatever you're up to, it's not courage. It's foolishness." Yang was at his desk, staring off into space with a sad look in his eyes.

He glanced up and acknowledged me standing in his doorway, but he didn't change expressions. "So, you figured out who was driving that car with the special plates," he said. He waited, but I didn't reply. Only then did he nod for me to sit down.

The visitor's chair had one leg shorter than the others. It had been that way for years. Sooner or later we'd fix it or get another chair. "Did I?" I said, trying to stay upright. "Did I figure it out?"

"They've been watching you in order to watch me. And once they spotted me at your apartment, they became doubly interested." Yang hunched over his side of the desk. He and Li shared an office; they sat on either side of a single worktable. Li was at the Traffic Bureau, checking reports on bus accidents. I hoped he might be able to shake something loose, where I had not.

"Alright, tell me. Why are they watching you?"

Yang shrugged, a minor movement of his shoulders. He blinked slowly while he took a breath. It was like a mask of death, his face when he closed his eyes. For a moment, I almost thought he had died right in front of me. Then he moved slightly and opened his eyes again. "You'd have to ask them."

"Look, Yang, if I had the time, I'd probably play this game with you for weeks. I raise a subject obliquely. You parry implicitly. I tiptoe to the side door. You slip out over the roof. Back and forth. We'd even begin to look forward to it. Every day, a new line of attack; every afternoon, a new line of defense. But we don't have time, and I just lost someone in a tunnel, which I always hate to do. So, I need to know why you are being followed. I need to know urgently, am I clear?" It made me uneasy to push him like this, but I didn't have much choice.

"I told you, O, I don't know. How would I? How would I know why anyone follows anyone else in this country?"

"'In this country,' Yang?" I smiled so broadly my cheeks hurt. "What would that mean?"

Yang stood up and took a half step toward me. "Nothing, O," he said. "It doesn't mean anything. Don't worry, I'm not afflicted with a sudden dose of courage. I can see. But I can't act. It's a sort of moral paralysis. Many people have it, I'm beginning to understand."

"My friend, nothing you've said in the past two minutes makes me feel better, put aside that most of it doesn't make any sense at all." There wasn't any decision to make. It had nothing to do with believing Yang or not. I wasn't going to throw him to the lions. "Alright, if you didn't do anything, and you aren't about to do anything, then how do we get this special squad off your neck?"

"Don't bother," Yang said. "It's not worth your time."

"I'm not bothering for your sake. The person I'm worried about is me. If they don't like something about you, then it rubs off on everyone nearby, and I'm pretty near. I have enough to worry about. Don't forget, the guy who was in here the other night said I stole his wallet. Min says the guy was well connected, and you told me he was pulled out of here by people with guns and funny plates on their car. He turns up dead, they go down a list of suspects."

"No one is going to touch you, O. You lead a charmed life."

I laughed.

4

"I'm only going to tell you this one more time. Sit up when I'm talking to you."

I sat up, not because I knew why, but because when I hear someone using that tone of voice and my hands are tied behind me, it is automatic.

A hand shot out and hit me across the face. "Not fast enough. When I say something, you do it, don't stop to think."

It was too dark for me to distinguish any details, though whoever had just hit me didn't seem to have the same trouble. I sat as straight as I could and tried to look intelligent. Sitting straight seemed to clear my head. A simple question bobbed up: Where were we? I took a breath, and the oxygen helped me decide it was the wrong time to ask. Whoever had just smacked me wasn't there to answer questions.

"Good, now at least you are with us." It was growled, the way people with big bones sound. Probably not someone I wanted to annoy.

A door opened off to the right, and then a lamp clicked on. The light was subdued. It was soothing in a way, though I would have liked to be able to see more. A tall man dressed in a brown suit took a step out of the darkness in front of me. He stopped just at the point where I would have been able to see him clearly. When he talked, he hung back a little in the half-shadow, so I couldn't watch his eyes. "I'm sorry we had to hit you like that, but you seemed to be dozing off." He spoke slowly, in a pleasant voice, low and flowing. You might think he was the host, carefully considering the needs of a guest. "Would you care for a drink of water?" Very amiable offer.

"Who are you?" I knew the technique. Start soft. Maybe the man in the shadows would give me an answer. He was moving like one of those interrogators who try to establish "trust" at the outset. For sure, things weren't going to get any better, so I might as well ask my question before they got worse. At least I'd know whose toe I'd stepped on.

"Now, Inspector, let's put a few simple rules on the table. Lay them out, get them straight between us, and then not have to concern ourselves with them anymore. I know who you are; you have no need to know who I am. I ask the questions, by and large. You answer what you can, as honestly as you can. If I think you are lying—well, you have a reputation for being straightforward, so I won't worry about it." All said pleasantly, as if these rules were well understood by every guest but needed to be reviewed anyway.

"A drink of water would be fine. But I need my hands free. I only drink when I hold the glass." I needed to set my own rule, if only a little one.

The man in the brown suit moved a millimeter into the light, just enough so I caught a glimpse of a smile. "That is exactly what I would say in your place, Inspector. I think we will get along quite well." He nodded to whoever was standing in the darkness beside me, and as he nodded, the shadows played on his face. The cuffs were removed from my hands, and I closed my eyes as my arms regained feeling. "There, you see, Inspector, already the situation has improved."

"I'll take that glass of water now." The glass appeared in front of me. I put it to my lips and drank enough to wet the inside of my mouth. I held the glass out, and it was taken away.

"When you want more, Inspector, you need only ask."

"I thought I was supposed only to give answers."

There was a low growl behind, but from in front of me I heard a faint laugh. "Fair enough. Let us say I give you blanket permission to ask for water. In fact, any creature comfort that is lacking, you need only ask. I can't promise to supply everything, but what I can get for you, I will. Shall we proceed?"

"Let me say something, if I may."

There was silence. The man in the brown suit was studying my face. I couldn't see him, but I knew what he was doing. Finally he said, "Of course you may, Inspector." He stepped back, completely into the shadow.

"You have the wrong person."

It was quiet for a moment, then an explosion of laughter echoed around the walls. "Really, Inspector," the man in the brown suit said when he got back his breath. He let me see that he was drying his eyes with a handkerchief. "That is what everyone says, but you say it so matter-of-factly. One could almost believe it."

"And you don't?"

"I don't have any basis for making a judgment. If you are completely the wrong person, we will establish that soon enough." I never disliked the word "completely" so thoroughly as when the man in the brown suit said it. "If you are the wrong person, but only because circumstances have not yet made you the right person, we will establish that as well. And if you are the wrong person, but have tendencies that impel you in the very direction you say you have not taken, well, then let's find out beforehand and save us both a great deal of trouble."

"In other words . . ."

The man in the brown suit leaned forward slightly, another millimeter, enough so I would feel the space between us had diminished. "There are no 'other words,' Inspector. Those words you just heard me speak are the words which convey what I need you to know.

Words are what we have, and we will use them with great respect, you and I, in our conversation. In particular, you will notice that I am precise in what I ask. A precise question deserves a precise answer."

"Not always. What if you ask the wrong question?"

Again, from behind, I heard a growl. The man in the brown suit moved his legs, a gesture of annoyance, though I could not tell if it was at me or at the mastiff in the rear. He took back the millimeter we had gained. "I have no doubt you will correct the question, Inspector. I'm in no hurry to proceed, incidentally. I have all day, and all of the next day, and the next. We can sit here until summer, and it gets quite hot in these rooms in summer, believe me. The sooner we get started, the sooner we will be done. But it is all up to you." He brushed something off his shoulder, perhaps a stray bit of unwanted light.

"I'll tell you the truth, I'm very tired, and I don't think clearly when my mind is clouded. Perhaps I can sleep for a few hours, and we can resume later." I half expected to be hit again.

"Sleep deprivation is not a technique I practice, Inspector. Some people think it works wonders. I have never been convinced. Please sleep, if you wish. Perhaps you'd like a pill to help you?"

"I think not."

The man in the brown suit sounded amused. "No, I didn't suppose you would. Never mind." He nodded his head. My arms were grabbed from behind and tied to the back of the chair. "Sleep well, Inspector."

"Here, sitting up?"

"My goodness, yes, this is not a hotel." I thought he moved into the light, but then the lamp clicked off, a fist came down on my neck, and if I dreamed anything while I was unconscious, I had forgotten it by the time I woke up.

5

The man in the brown suit was leaning against the wall when I opened my eyes. I couldn't see his face in the shadow, but his posture was one of patience. There was nothing aggressive about it, not a hint of tension. That might have been soothing, except I sensed he had been watching me for some time, and being under observation put me on edge whether I was walking on the street or tied up in a chair. "You slept well, Inspector?" he asked solicitously.

The word "bastard" rose up through the fog in my mind. "I've slept better."

"It isn't easy to sleep sitting up that way, I realize. But it can be done. I did it, others have done it, I knew you could, too. In any event, while you slept, I was busy working."

I looked down and was surprised to see my hands on my lap. They were completely numb.

"Feeling will return in the next few minutes, don't worry. But don't let them fall off your lap just yet, lest they detach themselves from your wrists and clatter to the floor. I don't think we have the means to put them back." He chuckled and let a few beams of light strike his lips. "I'm only joking." There must be marks on the floor; I never saw anyone who could judge distance so precisely.

"You were working while I slept, and what were the results, if I may ask a question."

"A good question, one I might ask if I were you. I discovered that you were right, you are the wrong person."

"So, it's good-bye, then." I started to get up, but a hand behind me pulled me back onto the chair.

"You are the wrong person, Inspector, but that still leaves a question."

"No, I don't know who the right person is."

"Ah. You don't know who the right person is. Good, then we are a team; we are on the same side of ignorance. In that case, why don't we establish some common perceptions? Maybe we can help each other."

"That's unlikely, but what did you have in mind?"

"First of all, I have a chart I'd like to show you." He took a paper from his jacket pocket and unfolded it. After studying it for a moment, he sighed. "It has a number of blanks, troubling blank spots. I'm not yet sure where to put you, for example." The chart came out of the darkness and was dropped on my lap. When I could move my arms and my fingers, I picked it up.

"You forgot my grandfather."

"No, Inspector, I know you are the grandson of a Hero of the Revolution, but he died a long time ago, and if I don't put a time limit on these charts, they get too big. That's why your parents don't appear, either. They died during the war; if I notated everyone connected to you who died during the war, we'd run short of paper. Let the dead rest in peace, Inspector; we have enough problems with the living."

"Fine." I glanced at the chart again. "It looks alright."

"Actually, it errs on the thin side, but that's deliberate. If I asked you to study it carefully, you might add one or two acquaintances and then think it was done. People have a tendency to feel they only know a few other people, but the interconnections over time are actually quite complex, especially for someone like you."

"Someone like me," I repeated. That did not have a good sound to it. My heart was starting to beat so loudly, I thought for sure both the man in the brown suit and the mastiff behind me could hear it. A bomb had been dropped; they were waiting for me to react. In so many words, I had been told that the shield my grandfather's status had provided all these years was suddenly worthless. "Let the dead rest in peace," the man in the brown suit had said. The only possible conclusion was that someone in the center had decided that my being raised by a Hero of the Revolution—and equally important, my knowledge of the old stories—had become a burden. But why now, all of a sudden? To most people, the appearance and disappearance of protection stemming from the Center seemed whimsical, shifting winds over an ocean of people treading water. But I knew that usually there was nothing whimsical about it. These shifts were almost always a reflection of something important, a failed policy or an unexpected event that the Center saw as a threat. Not a bank robbery, something bigger, much bigger.

"Your work brings you into contact with the sort of people who have, shall we say, threads reaching around the world." The man in the brown suit let the words cover me, like a net. "Russians, for example. You often have business with Russians?"

Yakob seemed to be on everyone's list. "Not really."

"You speak Russian."

"My grandfather spoke it sometimes." I wasn't going to let them discard my grandfather without a fight. "He learned it when he was working against the Japanese, and he taught me. He said if I was going to outsmart the Russians, I had to think like them, and if I was going to think like them, I had to know the language."

"So, do you think like them?"

"Only when it's necessary."

"And when would that be?"

"Let's stop dancing around the forest. I never met that stocking salesman before. I was looking for information that was germane to a case I'm investigating." The man in brown must know about the bank robbery, but I wasn't going to be the first to raise it. "I had a tip he might have what I needed."

"Did he?"

"Good question. Maybe, yes."

"Let me give you a piece of advice, Inspector. Stay away from that Russian."

"Everyone tells me that."

"Don't pay attention to everyone, Inspector, just pay attention to me."

I looked down at the chart and saw the name Chon Yu Mae, with the words "Gold Star" next to it. So, at least now I knew Miss Chon's full name. She must have had a file after all, even if SSD couldn't find it. Miss Chon's name was connected by a dotted line to someone named Pang.

"May I ask a question?"

"Please do, Inspector."

"Who is Pang?"

"The manager of the Club Blue."

"Why is he connected to Miss Chon?"

"You didn't know? They are very close. She spends a lot of time at his place, most nights, actually. It probably shouldn't be a dotted line."

No, I thought, it probably shouldn't be. Yang's name was on the chart, along with everyone else in the office, and even the chain of command up to the Minister. Also on the chart were my apartment neighbors, the man who fixed my bicycle tire, and my brother, whom I rarely saw. Off to the side, not connected to anyone, in a box drawn with red ink was Han Gun So—who, I supposed, was Lieutenant Han from SSD. Also, as the man said, there were a number of boxes left blank. One of them was labeled "Prague," in a different hand-writing.

"I need you to sign it, just so we know you looked at it carefully."

I flexed my shoulders and wiggled each of my fingers. "I don't think I can hold a pen yet. You realize, this might be easier if I knew what you were looking for."

The man in the brown suit pulled out a pack of cigarettes. "Yes, and it would certainly be even easier if I knew what I was looking for." He held out a cigarette. "Perhaps holding one of these will help your fingers, Inspector. Here, I can light it for you."

I shook my head.

"Well, as you wish. I'm told you prefer wood to cigarettes. Odd. Any reason?"

Something told me this was about to take off in the wrong direction. I wiggled my fingers again.

"Alas," he said, "we have no wood around here, nothing suitable, anyway. By the way, where do you get this wood you prefer, Inspector?" It was a curious question, but the man had not followed a particular line ever since he opened his mouth. Mostly he had been setting up, marking off our boundaries.

"Scrap wood; you run across it here and there if you are looking for it." I didn't think that would exhaust his interest in the subject.

"And you are, I assume, looking for scrap wood. All domestic wood, from our forests?"

"That I wouldn't know. I don't go out and chop things down, if that's what you mean."

"You never deal in foreign wood, of the Siberian variety, for example?"

"I'm not partial to Russian wood, no. In any case, forests don't pay attention to national boundaries. There's no such thing as Russian wood, or Chinese wood, or"—I paused a fraction while I considered whether this would get me on the wrong foot—"or Korean wood."

"Forests do not follow boundaries; trees are not particularly concerned with ethnicity or social systems—is that what you are saying, Inspector? I should note that for future reference."

"Do you want me to say whether I think some countries have better trees than we do?"

A low chuckle came out of the darkness. "What about ash, Inspector?" the man in the brown suit said after a moment. "I'm interested, how would you describe the wood from the ash tree?"

I ran through the possibilities. At least this was specific. Maybe he was getting at something, finally. "Strong, flexible, lots of uses. Very friendly tree, grows quickly. You can use it for furniture, veneer mostly." I felt a tapping on my shoulder; I didn't have to turn to know what it was. "It can be used for sticks and clubs of all sorts. You can beat someone with it. Most people will break before the stick does."

He lit a cigarette. "And the Sogdian ash?"

I watched his fingers as they cupped the flame, so it would not light up his face.

"Couldn't say. I never saw one."

"Is that so? The Sogdian ash grows in Central Asia, Inspector. One of the largest remaining forests of these lovely trees"—a puff of smoke drifted into the light—"is in Kazakhstan."

The hairs on the back of my neck prickled. So, we had arrived. "Is there a question in there for me, somewhere?" I could feel the club resting on my right shoulder. The man in the brown suit shook his head. The club moved to my left side.

"We don't get a lot of Sogdian ash in this country, would you think?"

"I have no way of knowing." The club bounced, not hard, but I could feel the effect down to my fingertips. I exhaled slowly. "I wouldn't think there would be a lot of anything from Kazakhstan in this country."

"No, you're probably right, not much. But perhaps more than one might expect. By the way, have you ever been to Prague, Inspector?"

Another question out of nowhere; it might have jolted me more, but I'd seen the box on the chart. And he knew I'd seen it. "It says so on the chart. I must have been there at some point."

The man in the brown suit clucked his tongue. "People forget many things," he said, "but they know when they have been abroad, when they have held in their hands a passport that permits them to cross the border. Passports, by the way, are stamped, Inspector. Shall we have a look?"

"I didn't say I'd forgotten." I thought of Yakob's passport stamps. Mine at least were real, even if they weren't accurate. "It isn't a mystery where I've been. It's all a matter of record; every won I spent is accounted for."

"No one doubts your financial probity, Inspector. Would you say there are thorough reports on everyone you met in Prague?"

"Of course."

"Of course." I didn't care for his tone. "So when word reaches us that in Prague several years ago you met with a member of British intelligence, and there is nothing about that in your trip report, we can assume . . . well, what can we assume, Inspector?"

I contemplated the situation. The mantle of my grandfather's protection was in grave doubt. Now they were suggesting I was a traitor. Only the British knew I had met a man who called himself Richie

Molloy in Prague, that we had talked for a few hours, that I had given him information on a colonel from the Military Security Command who had been responsible for many deaths and whom I was determined to destroy. If the man in the brown suit had heard even faint echoes about the meeting, it could only be because the British wanted him to hear it. And they must have wanted it because they knew that, when word got to the right people in Pyongyang, I would be squeezed. Then, they hoped in their European way, I would come running to them. They were wrong, of course. I wouldn't come over to them. But unless I convinced the man in the brown suit it was false information, I would probably never get a chance to tell the British to fuck themselves, which at the moment I fervently wanted to do. The ash club tapped me on the hip bone. The pain radiated down to my leg and up into my chest. I gasped for air.

"Prague, Inspector, that was my question."

"Well, there won't be any answers if that club touches me again."

The man in the brown suit waited.

"I need a drink of water."

He nodded from the shadows, and a glass was held in front of me. I took a swallow, shook my head to clear my thoughts. "I was in Prague on a courier run for my ministry. There are reports in the file describing everyone I met. The embassy had someone with me the whole time. You can probably check that in their logs. If I had disappeared for even a few minutes, it would have been noted." The embassy had lost track of me for half a night, but they didn't dare admit it. They didn't care; I was just another visitor, and they didn't want to use their funds to look after me. But I didn't have to tell that to the man in brown; either he already knew it, or he didn't.

"I think we are getting somewhere, wouldn't you say, Inspector? Perhaps it's time for a break. You must be fatigued."

Only an interrogator with bad things in mind would say "fatigued." I wanted to get this over and, if it was still possible, go home. "I'm wide-awake. There's no reason to take a break, though if there is a toilet nearby, I could use it." My hip ached; I needed to walk, maybe splash some water on my face, get out of the suffocating gloom of this room.

"Of course, of course." The man in the brown suit nodded.

6

When I got back and sat down, I couldn't tell if the man in the brown suit was in the room. It was completely silent; I couldn't even hear my own breathing. His voice came out of nowhere. "Well, we've established a few useful things, but there remain a few questions."

"I'm ready."

It was a long list, and they came at me from what seemed like every direction. He refused to stand in one spot. Maybe he thought it would disorient me; maybe he was agitated and felt the need to pace. Abruptly, he stopped. "At this point, Inspector, you should have something to eat, while I do some more checking."

I was exhausted and still in pain. Food was not on my mind. Prague hadn't come up again, not directly, not implicitly, not even in an echo or a reflection. It had seemingly dropped down a well, but I knew it was not going to be erased from that chart. Something like that is never erased. They would keep it in my file until I had been dead so long that there was no one who would remember my face.

"Since we're colleagues now"—I turned in the direction of his voice—"perhaps I could go to sleep. I mean, natural sleep, blissful, restful, restoring, lying down somewhere. You know, knitting the raveled sleeve."

"Good, Shakespeare. Good. And why not? Sleep will do you good. Consider this your room, and all that it contains at your disposal." The room, as far as I could tell, was bare except for the lamp and the chair I sat on. "The concrete is not so comfortable; we'll have to look for a pad. I know we have blankets, somewhere." He was suddenly fussy, the solicitous innkeeper, and judging from the way his voice moved, he had resumed pacing slowly back and forth in front of me. "We don't usually entertain guests overnight, you see." From out of the shadows to my left, the man in the brown suit walked toward me with his arm extended. First his hand, then all of him was in the light. He was tall, a little stooped; even in the lamplight, he had a sallow face. Brown was not a good color for him. We shook hands; he smiled in an odd way, then limped toward the door. Before he reached it, he turned. "Ah, one thing. What do you know about the clerks at the Gold Star Bank?"

"Nothing." If he thought I would let down my guard when I saw him about to leave, he was mistaken. Even as tired as I was, my guard would never get that far down.

"You were following one of them," he said. It was incredible to me, how much detail he had at his fingertips.

"Yes, but I lost her."

"Strange. An experienced person like yourself, you lost her? Pity." He put his hands in his pockets and walked outside. I heard the ash club tap on the floor behind me, then a footstep; the door in the back of the room opened, and I was alone.

7

After the interrogation, they let me sleep a few hours. When they woke me, the first thing they asked was if I was alright. My shoulder hurt; my hip hurt. "Fine," I said. They asked if I wanted a doctor to look at me. I told them no, and they had me sign a form that said I'd refused the offer. They said that I was free to go and that they would drop me off where I wanted. "Maybe a restaurant near my office." They said it was my choice; they helped me up, and we went to a car parked outside. It was night. I didn't know for sure how long I'd been there; I couldn't even remember where I had been when they picked me up. We drove for about thirty minutes, from somewhere out in the country. It was cloudy and very dark, and it wasn't until we finally got on a road I recognized that I realized we were coming into the city from the east. The car stopped; the man in the front seat beside the driver turned and said we were at the restaurant I'd requested. I could get whatever I wanted to eat. They'd pay for it, he said. He imparted this information morosely, as if he didn't agree with the practice but hadn't been consulted.

"Well, then," I said, "thanks again for everything." I got out with difficulty. I'd barely closed the door when the car pulled away.

The restaurant was half full. No one looked up when I dragged myself across the room. I took a table against the wall, so I could lean back and take some strain off my shoulder. After something to eat and a drink, I'd go home to sleep. In the morning, I'd start full bore on the case, no more half measures, no more wondering what its importance was, or to whom. It was vitally important, above all to me. I still didn't know whose toes I'd stepped on, or even if that was the right part of the anatomy. But it was clear I couldn't back off. If I solved it—and it was going to end up involving more than a bank robbery, that I knew—the odds were I wouldn't have to go back to that room with the ash club. Which would be good, because if I did have to go back, the next time they sat me in that chair, I might not stand up again. I closed my eyes, and when I opened them, the man in the brown suit was standing beside me.

"May I join you, Inspector?" What a silly question. Of course the man could join me. From here on out, he practically owned me. It was clear he could haul me back whenever it suited him, as long as he thought I knew something about whatever it was that was such a threat to someone at the center. I absolutely didn't want to sit in that darkness again. Better if he came to visit me, someplace I could see his eyes. "I was saving it for a beautiful woman, but she didn't show up. So, please." I nodded toward the chair opposite me.

The man smiled. There was nothing menacing in it. His face had taken on more color. This close, in the light, I could see he had an intelligent manner. "No hard feelings, I hope, Inspector. We checked, we double-checked, we decided you were not the man we were after. What can I say? You'll accept my apology, surely. Let me buy you a drink."

The last thing in the world I wanted was to let him buy me a drink. "Of course, I would be honored."

What shall we have for such an occasion? Something out of the ordinary, I think. They probably have something they shouldn't, hidden away in the rear. These places always do. Excuse me." He got up and limped to a door at the back of the room, knocked once, then turned the handle and walked in. A minute or so later, he emerged with a bottle in his hand. "This is good Scotch," he said. "Real Scotch. Not that colored water everyone drinks." The waitress brought over two glasses. "Better without ice." He poured some into my glass and then poured his own. After he held up his glass to the light, he looked at mine and laughed. "Here's to friendship, Inspector, wherever we find it."

The rest of the evening came out of the bottle. We drank until I couldn't sit up straight, but the more he drank, the more dignified he seemed to become. Some people get sloppy when they drink; not him. Eventually, he asked if I wanted to know why he limped. I shrugged. "Of course you do, Inspector. Something for you to think about. Learn a lesson."

He had been sentenced to a labor camp as a young man, a fifteen-year sentence for not reporting a conversation with a visiting Hungarian. "My elder sister had been sent to Budapest during the war; they thought she was an orphan, and the Hungarians took her in along with hundreds of others. She was there for several years, learned Hungarian, went to school, almost married a Hungarian man, but something happened and she finally came back to teach. She took ill one day and a week later was dead. It was a shock, let me tell you."

Though I was drunk, I watched his every move, one step removed, as if I were watching myself observing him. He wasn't the interrogator anymore, no trace of it. He sat across from me, dignified and composed, in contrast to my inability to keep my head upright. I sloshed my drink. He drank his with a careful flourish. Each time he raised the glass, it began a ritual, an elaborate code, a tribal ceremony that had a beginning, a middle, and an end. The glass went up to his mouth, he took a small sip, then lifted the glass slightly before it began a downward arc, his sleeve seemed to billow, his elbow ticked out an elegant degree or so, and as the glass settled onto the table, he smacked his lips, once.

He never gestured when he spoke, except when he was drinking. At first I assumed it was the alcohol, but then I realized it was the glass in his hand. He used the glass to point, to emphasize an argument, to indicate a joke was coming or had just been made. I could tell from the way he did this that the size of the glass made no difference, nor its shape. The glass didn't have to be full. But it couldn't be empty. He never gestured with an empty glass.

As an interrogator, the man in the brown suit was in complete control. He sent that message in a way that you understood, precisely, without any doubt. When he asked a question, you were forced to concentrate on his voice. That was why he stood in shadow. No distractions, no physical cues, no watching his hands or even the slightest play of emotion around the lips, unless that's what he wanted you to see. No eye contact, only his words. But what had begun as technique had taken over completely. He was left with this and this alone—only the glass in his hand freed him.

He took a sip, waved the glass in my direction, then started it again on its journey to the table. "After she died, I wanted to thank the Hungarians, but I didn't know how to do it, so I hung around outside their embassy. I saw someone at the corner, a Westerner. I walked over and asked him if he understood Korean. He said he did, that he was Hungarian and could carry on a conversation if I didn't speak too fast. I told him I was grateful to the Hungarian people for taking care of my sister, that she had spoken highly of them and their country, and that I hoped to be able to repay the debt. He smiled and said if I came back to this corner the next afternoon, at the same time, he would drive by and pick me up." The glass was empty; he pushed it aside and composed himself. Sitting very still, he continued, "The next day when I got to the corner, a security man emerged from behind a tree. He said I was to come with him. They said the foreigner I had talked to was a Hungarian spy, and that I had disgraced the country. I wrote a confession. I was shaken, believe me. They put me in the back of a truck with ten other young men, and a woman who was weeping, and we drove off to a camp in the mountains." He stopped talking, just stopped, as if he had run out of words.

"Bad luck," I said softly.

Anyone else might have laughed, or roared in protest, or sighed. He sat motionless. Finally he put his fingers around his glass and tipped it back and forth. "When I got out I was a little older, thinner, and had this limp. Ash, the guards carried clubs made of ash. Mostly they kept order by shouting at us and waving the clubs. But one of the guards took an instant dislike to me, no reason, he just did. He tried everything he could to kill me. One day he beat me so hard his club broke. I couldn't move for a month. I finally healed, all except for my leg. Six years into my sentence, a car drove up to the gate, a colonel got out, and they hustled me over to him. He asked if I was well, I said I was. He asked if I had been fed, I said I had. He told me I had been wrongly sentenced, that the vermin responsible had been punished, and that I was now free to serve the people. He shook my hand, looked around at the other prisoners, and led me out the gate to his car."

"Luck changes." I could hear I was mumbling, but it wasn't my main concern. By now I couldn't keep my eyes open.

"That's how things happened in the old days, Inspector. In the old days, you wouldn't be here right now."

In a sudden spurt of clarity, I sat up. "You been watching me long? I saw you on the train, you were watching me."

He moved back his chair. "Put your head on the table and sleep a little. I'm sure we'll meet again." I didn't see him leave, but I heard the irregular gait of his footsteps disappear into the long night.

8

"You're back." Min put down the newspaper he wasn't reading. He stood up and moved around his desk toward me. "Are you alright?"

"Fine."

"We were worried. You didn't show up for work, no one knew where you were. I called the Ministry, they called around. SSD said they had no idea where you were, that they didn't want you for anything. They said they'd check. A few hours later they got back in touch. They said you were out of the system." Min put his hands up, in a gesture of helplessness. He swallowed hard. " 'Out of the system'—what a term. It sounds like a piece of meat that dropped off the table." Min looked closely at me. "You sure you're alright?"

"I already told you, I'm fine. They finally figured out they had the wrong person. Made friends with me, took me out for a drink afterward."

"Sure, I know, you don't have to talk about it, probably shouldn't. But the Minister doesn't like it when they snatch his people like this. We'll have to send something in, a piece of paper or something saying you've reported back on duty. I'll call and tell them you're here." Min picked up the phone.

"Let's wait a while, okay? Give me a few minutes to get my head clear. Why don't we review things, just go over what we know. That Blue Paper on Yang, has there been any follow-up?"

"Inspector, you're in no shape to review anything, and frankly I'm not in the mood." He put the phone back down. "You shouldn't even be here. Go home, get some rest."

"There isn't time for that. Look, a new unit is out there. First Yang spots them nosing around my apartment, then I get the feeling I'm being watched out on the street, and then I get hauled in."

"Where? SSD wouldn't dare do it. Who?"

"I don't have any idea. I don't even remember being picked up."

"They beat you?"

"No, I drank too much."

"That's okay, you don't have to talk about it." Min started to pick up the phone again. "They hurt your shoulder, didn't they?"

"It's not so bad." He was right, this wasn't a good time to review. Lying down would be better.

"You look like a man who doesn't want to move his arm if he can avoid it, Inspector. And your left hand is odd. Like the blood isn't getting there in normal fashion. Maybe you should see the doctor at the Ministry. I'll call and tell him you're coming."

"No, he'll make a record of it. Just let this go. I know a doctor. Really, it wasn't so bad." I nodded toward a chair. "You mind if I sit for a minute?"

"Sure, sit. Let me get you some tea." Min hurried out of the room before I could stop him. I put my head against the wall and closed my eyes. My shoulder did hurt now, worse than last night. Maybe I'd go home for the rest of the day.

"Here, it's good tea. Yang brought in a package, said he got it somewhere. I don't know." Min held out the cup, changed his mind, and put it down on his desk. "Forget the damned tea, Inspector; get to a doctor, would you? You won't be a lot of use to me if you end up having only one arm." He took a quick step to his file cabinet, opened a drawer, and then slammed it shut. "Bastards." He stood with his back to me for a moment, then turned around. "They really did that? Apologized, then took you out for a drink, after doing that?" He nodded toward my shoulder. "Get it fixed, Inspector. Don't come back until you do."

9

The next day I stayed home and tried to sleep. The doctor at the morgue had given me four pain pills. "It's all I have," she said. "Cut them in half, in quarters if you can. Take as little as you need so they'll last. It's not dislocated, nothing's broken, though they could have shattered the collarbone or severed a nerve. It could have crippled you for life. It's bad enough that the bruise is so deep. You'll be in pain for a week, at least a week." She helped me back into my shirt. "Good thing you're right-handed."

"They knew it."

"Oh." She considered this. "Well, that's something, I suppose." Her voice faltered, and then she snapped it back where it belonged. "Sleep as much as you can. Don't move your shoulder around for a couple of days, then try to flex so it doesn't get stiff. If you can put some heat on it, that would be good. Maybe heat up a brick and wrap it in cloth, anything like that. When you're taking these pills, don't drink any alcohol. Not a drop. Come back in a week. And try to keep moving your fingers." She walked me to the door. "Do you have anyone who can help out for the next few days? Maybe cook a meal, or help you wash?"

"No. I can manage."

"I doubt it, but we'll see."

"Thanks. I was never here."

"No, you weren't." She gave me a half smile. "Maybe none of us are."

10

The pills made me jumpy, or maybe I was already jumpy because of how the man in the brown suit had sidestepped my question about why he had been watching me on the train. There could only be one reason he wouldn't answer the question—he wasn't finished with me. I worried with that through the haze of the pills, then the haze got deeper and the worry softened into a white cloud that drifted away. It was the best I'd felt in a long time, watching that cloud. I must have been dozing when there was a knock on the door. Getting up was difficult; I could only use one arm. "Just a minute."

When I opened the door, it was Miss Chon. I was surprised and irritated. "You shouldn't be here. One of us is going to get the other one in trouble. I already told you, you're a suspect. Now I'm a suspect, again."

"A fine welcome, Inspector. In Kazakhstan, we invite visitors in and offer them a piece of fruit. And if we're both suspects, wouldn't it be strange if we didn't get together?"

"I don't have any fruit."

She looked past me into the room. "You don't seem to have much of anything. I thought you were fooling when you said you didn't have any chairs. You live like a hermit!" Her fingers touched my arm. "I heard."

"You didn't hear anything, and you're about to go away." I backed up a few steps, sank down on my knees, and then rolled onto my side on my blanket. "How did you get past the old lady at the entrance?"

"I'm a bank manager, Inspector. My job is to talk people into things they don't think they want, and out of things they do. She didn't put up much of a fight, especially after I told her I was worried about you. She said people here have been wondering what's wrong." Miss Chon stepped tentatively into the room. She had on a long coat that was cinched around her waist. "I've been calling and calling you at your office. Whoever answered said you weren't there and that you don't have a phone at home, not in your room, anyway. That's all they'd say."

"Good, that's all they're supposed to say, and anyway it's true. Some people have phones. I don't want one. It would only ring at the wrong moment."

She laughed, and my shoulder stopped hurting for a few seconds. "Oh, and when would that be?"

"When I'm not here, when I'm here, anytime at all." Sometimes, they say, laughter stays in a room, but it didn't in mine. It faded quickly, as if it wanted to get out of there as soon as it could. "I told you the other night, I'm not a social creature, I'm antisocial. Right now, I'm particularly antisocial. When I throw a party, I'll send you an invitation. I need to sleep." I closed my eyes. The door slammed before I managed to say, "Thank you for coming."

11

Min put me outside for a few days, said I needed exercise and fresh air. "Stay away from the office," he said, "I mean it." He couldn't give me any leave, but this was nearly as good. I didn't want to be out of the office, but I still couldn't think straight because of the pills and the pain. The one thought that marched around in the haze in my head was Miss Chon. Every time I blinked my eyes, she was standing at my door, and I wondered why I didn't have any fruit. I tried to force myself to forget the fruit and concentrate on why she had come to my place. Foreigners didn't do that; they stayed in their hotel rooms, or somewhere. So what was she doing at my room?

I thought of an answer, but it disappeared in a burst of pain from my shoulder and I gave up thinking about anything. Midmorning, while I was sitting on some steps watching the sunlight as it came through the new leaves of the trees, an army guard marched over with an old man. "He's causing trouble." He handed me a piece of paper. "Get him out of my area." The guard was young; the collar on his shirt was too big. But he was serious about his job. He gave me a serious frown and walked away.

I stood up. "You heard the fellow. He said you're a troublemaker, Grandfather. Are you?"

The old man looked at the ground when he spoke. "You'll believe what you want."

We were standing on the sidewalk. Nobody stared directly at us as they walked by, but they all slowed, as if the thin, bent figure were a dead animal on the road. I skimmed the paper the guard had handed me. "Don't let's make this complicated. This is a list of complaints against you." I held it up for him to see. "It's a long list. You're lucky it got to me before it went to someone else."

He looked up at that. I thought he had the eyes of an old dragon, powerful eyes, smoldering for centuries with indignation. "I've not bothered anyone in this city," he said. "No one has cause to complain. I live my own life. I follow the rules. I speak the words. If this generates complaints, then the Leader himself is as guilty as I am."

"How about we lower our sights for the moment and just go over the list, shall we?" I looked around to make sure he hadn't been overheard. "Leave other people out of it, if you know what I mean. We'll make a few notations, maybe close the file and get on with our lives.

It might be that easy." I went down the list with my finger until I found something that could be dealt with in a simple word or two. "It says here you told a group of people at a restaurant that food prices were too high. True?"

"You have to ask me? Don't you buy food, or do they just give it away in this city?"

"I'll take that as a yes. And you reportedly said that prices are high because farmers can't plant what they want."

"There isn't a farmer doesn't know that, and half of them would tell you if you asked."

"I'm just going down the list, Grandfather. Why should I trust the farmers to plant the right thing? Why wouldn't they plant what is easiest to grow?"

"Country people ain't lazy." He held up his hands. "This is how we live, with these. Not a bunch of merchants reselling the sweat of someone else's labor."

"So that's it. A communist, are you?"

"Is that against the law nowadays?"

I folded up the list of complaints and put it in my pocket. "You're in the capital, my old friend. What farmers say in the fields among themselves can get taken the wrong way by people in a restaurant."

"That's not my concern."

"Well, it better become your concern, because the next time your name gets on a list, it won't be a pleasant conversation. Do I make myself clear?"

"Is that a threat? Maybe the last person you bullied crawled away, but you won't get that from me. I'm a simple man. I tell a simple truth."

"Listen to me, the truth is too far away for either of us. Don't go looking for it. I'm just giving you some advice. If you can't follow it, then keep your mouth shut."

"And if I don't?"

"Where are you from?"

"Close by Kyonghung. Over that way." He waved vaguely in the direction of the East Sea, a few hundred kilometers away.

"Who gave you permission to leave North Hamgyong and come all the way across the country?"

"I did."

I stared at him. "You? You gave yourself permission? You can't do that."

"And why can't I? General Yi did. Have you forgotten, or did you never know?"

"Six hundred years ago, they didn't have the same rules we do."

"And maybe there is a lesson in that." He looked at me calmly. It was a simple observation.

"Yi Song Gye was at the head of an army when he marched into town. I expect he had someone along to advise him on what to say in restaurants. Well, I'm looking, and I'm not seeing anyone but you. You can't do these things; you just can't give yourself permission to travel across the country. That much I know."

"But I did. I'm standing here, ain't I?" He gestured broadly at the scene around him. "Who fought for this during the war? Somewhere near this place, there were hardly any streets left, no buildings, trees all broken, the bombing was so bad you couldn't breathe the air. Dust and bones all mixed together. You wouldn't know that to look at things now. Did I or didn't I nearly die for this place?"

I said nothing.

"Well, did I or didn't I? How can anyone keep me from coming back here? Do I need permission to visit the place where I nearly died a hundred times? Do you think country people are simple? Do you think we don't understand?"

"We're going in circles, Grandfather. Someone is going to notice you are missing at home; some nosy neighbor will wonder where you have gone off to. Let's get you back where you belong."

"When I'm ready, if I'm ready, I'll say so. I'll go back the same way I came, and if anyone doesn't like it, they can kiss my hind end."

"Here's what I'm going to do." I took out my wallet and peeled off a few bills, euros and dollars. "This is money for the train back home. There's enough for a few overpriced meals, and since I'm paying, you don't get to comment on the cost of food. Frankly, I don't think you'll make it to Hoeryong without running into someone who has no tolerance for people without papers. But that is your business, not mine. Get out of town. And try to remember, you're not General Yi." I studied the old dragon's eyes. "Though I'm sure he would have wanted you on his side."

Chapter Three

The office was deserted when I returned a few days later. My shoulder still bothered me, and I couldn't sit very well because of my hip. Min had left a note on my chair: Do not answer the phone, no matter how many times it rings. I glanced at the file on the bank robbery case. No one had touched it in my absence. We were bumping against the deadline the Ministry had set, but I didn't see any notes attached complaining about the lack of progress. I looked for reports on the disappearance of the nightclub owner, rumors picked up on the street, anything. Nothing. No one was willing to talk about it. Or rather, no one was willing to talk to us.

On the top of my cabinet was another note from Min, saying I was to look at a new file in his absence. He didn't bother to say what it was about or, more important, where it was. I looked in my file drawers, but there was nothing that hadn't been there for a long time. I walked down to Min's office and checked on his desk. The phone rang, and I nearly picked it up without thinking. It rang six times, went halfway through a seventh, and then stopped. I don't like not answering the phone. It seems untidy, vaguely impolite, even if it obviously isn't for me. The phone started ringing again but this time only rang twice. This was easier to deal with. If someone hangs up that quickly, they might not be so serious about the call. A quick check of Min's desk drawers didn't uncover anything. His file cabinet was locked, and though I knew where the key was, I decided to leave well enough alone.

I went back to my office and retrieved my copy of the Criminal Code from the pile of books on the floor. When I stood up again to stretch, I glanced out the window. A man was standing across the street, gazing up at our building. People rarely hang around Ministry offices; they usually think it bad luck even to walk nearby. The man pretended he was simply gawking, but he wasn't doing a good job. It was definitely surveillance; whether it was hamhanded or provocative I couldn't tell. Well, if he wasn't going to pretend he was just standing around, neither was I. When he saw me wave from the window, the man threw his cigarette into the gutter and walked slowly away. His face was hidden by the brim of a cloth cap, but he had a strange gait that was as good as a photograph. The heel on each of his shoes was worn so much that his ankles stuck out. It made his white socks look like small dogs nipping at his feet the whole way down the street. I made a mental note to check the logs. If the guards had seen him standing around before, they would have made an entry.

Min's car drove up. It stopped for an overly long time as the guard poked his head in the driver's side window. I could hear an angry exchange before the guard finally backed away and waved the car through without much enthusiasm. Min emerged from the driver's side. He never drove if he could help it, but the duty driver had gone missing a week ago; no one knew where he was, and we couldn't get a replacement until he was accounted for. From the passenger's side unfolded a tall, solid-looking Westerner with sandy hair. Min looked up to my window and nodded, before saying something to the Westerner. Then the two of them disappeared.

I contemplated going out the back way, but Min had already seen me. There was nothing to do but wait. I sat down and rearranged the piles of paper on my desk. A piece of chestnut wood fell out of one of the stacks. I like chestnut, though there isn't enough of it around. Very self-possessed wood, knows exactly what it is doing all the time. Besides which, when I have it in my hand, it reminds me of the smell of roasting chestnuts in autumn. Finally, something good, I was thinking, when my phone rang. It stopped. It rang. It stopped. It rang again. Then I heard footsteps, and Min landed heavily at my door. "Dammit, Inspector," he said in an angry whisper, "don't you answer your phone?"

"You told me not to."

"Never mind that. Come to my office. Let me do the talking."

The Westerner was examining a security patrol map of Pyongyang that was hanging on the wall next to Min's desk. This is not a map foreigners are supposed to see. Min blanched and coughed. The foreigner turned around. He looked even taller and more broad-shouldered up close. "Detective, er, Boswell, was it?" Min said. "This is Inspector O."

"Superintendent James Boswell, Inspector, delighted to meet you." This was in fair Korean, though he sounded much like the Scotsman I'd met at the Koryo, with an accent that made some of the words sound like they were wrapped in fog. The man held out his hand, which was huge. We shook. I was relieved he did not feel obliged to demonstrate his strength by crushing my fingers. "I understand we will be working together." The visitor sized me up solemnly as he spoke and, despite his greeting, did not seem delighted to meet me. Even pleased would have been stretching the point.

I glanced at Min, who frowned at having used the wrong title for Boswell. Min thought protocol was important—it was one of those rituals that helped make the world turn more smoothly—and he did not like to make protocol mistakes. He moved behind his desk, and for a moment, I was afraid he was going to sit down and lean back in his chair. "Detective, er, Superintendent James has been sent by London to work with us on the security for next week's visit. Actually"— Min turned to the foreigner—"we thought the visit was going to take place this week, but I was just informed it has been postponed—scheduling, aircraft clearances, something. The usual reasons. This was all only recently decided at high levels." Min was lamely trying to defend the Ministry's sloppiness in not informing us sooner. "In fact, I only learned of the superintendent's arrival this morning when I was instructed to meet him at the airport. No arrangements have been made for his accommodations, I'm afraid." He laughed at this, as if it were an amusing oversight on the Ministry's part. "Inspector, you'll see to that detail, I'm sure."

"I'm sure."

Boswell gave me a look that suggested he could detect barely disguised sarcasm as well as the next man, no matter the language. I smiled at him. This broke no ice.

Min supplied a few more details of why an English—Scottish, I thought to myself—policeman had been dumped on our doorstep, and then he sent the two of us out to establish our own working hierarchy. Min indicated that Boswell was the visitor and thus was expected to follow my lead. This seemed unlikely to me. The visitor was twice my size. I imagined if an oak tree could walk, it would have his tread. We didn't speak until we were down at the duty car, which had been sitting unused since I returned from Beijing. Besides being dirty, it wasn't very reliable.

"It's not new, but it runs and it gets us around," I said when we were both inside. I had to hope it would start. The seats were worn, the dashboard was cracked, and the knobs were covered with a film of nicotine, so, no, it was not new. Normally I didn't care what people thought of the duty car, but if we had known we were going to entertain a visitor, I might have cleaned the knobs. I turned the ignition key. There was a click, then nothing. We sat in silence as I turned the key twice more and got two more clicks, the second somewhat fainter than the first.

Boswell put his paws on the dashboard and looked out the window on his side. "It won't dewwww," he said in something that resembled English.

"I'm sorry?" I said. "What won't?"

"So, you understand English, Inspector. Good." He switched to his accented Korean. "You've no gas. Or your battery's gone. Or your starter motor is shot. We'll have to walk, wherever it is we're going."

"Could be," I said. "Wait for a minute. I'll check something." Car engines I don't understand, but I opened the hood and looked inside. I jiggled a few wires, thumped a dirty piece of machinery. I spat on what I knew was the air filter, which looked clogged, probably with that damned Chinese dust. I slammed the hood, got back in, and turned the key. A wheeze, then the motor caught.

The visitor sat back in his seat and crossed his arms. "We're off," he said.

Damned right we're off, I thought. "First, we'll stop at the hotel and get you a room. After that, we'll review the procedures."

"Forget the hotel. I need a drive around the city, get the feel of the place, look at the roads, gauge the shadows."

"You must be tired after your flight." I didn't have a single approval to go with this fellow anywhere but to the hotel and then back to the office. I certainly wasn't going to drive him around the city without filing the paperwork. The last thing I wanted was another session with the man in the brown suit, asking me about the time a foreign police official spied on the city as I motored him around. "We can take a drive later, perhaps."

"Sorry, we don't have time for later, Inspector. I have my orders, and my orders are to make sure the permanent undersecretary gets in and out of here in one piece, the same piece."

"You're not suggesting there is anything wrong with security in my capital, surely." It sometimes puts foreigners off balance to use the possessive—"my" capital.

"I wouldn't be here if the porridge didn't smell bad." Maybe Scots didn't respond to the possessive. He put his hand up to his mouth and yawned, a particularly delicate gesture for a tree, I thought. He stretched his legs as best he could. "Incidentally, Molloy sends his regards." He pretended it was an afterthought.

My shoulder screamed; I swerved slightly and shook my head. He waited until I looked over to flash me a sardonic grin. Then he leaned against the side window and closed his eyes. The only sound the rest of the way to the Koryo Hotel was the engine coughing, from the dust.

2

When we got to the Koryo, Boswell said he wanted to see the hotel store, maybe buy some gifts. That was fine with me. I wanted some distance between us. Sitting down and having a drink by myself would have been even better, but there was nowhere to get a drink, so I just sat. Prague. Molloy. I took a deep breath and looked around. No one was interested, no one was paying attention; no one except the man in the brown suit and his friend with the ash club. They were somewhere else, going over what I'd told them and whatever else they knew, or thought they knew. The question was, what did they know? What had they heard about me from the British and, equally important, how? Of course my meeting with Molloy had gone into the files in London; that wasn't a surprise. And anything that is put in a file runs a risk of coming out again. A file gets pulled on a slow day, and someone gets a bright idea. Alright, it had happened; a slow day and my file had fallen onto someone's desk. I'd been waiting for the British to make a move; sometimes I forgot about it, but mostly it was just below the surface. I thought it would be something subtle; I hadn't expected it like this. Not so directly, not in Pyongyang. There was no reason to do it here; it was not only dangerous, it was incredibly inept. If they had wafted word of my meeting with Molloy onto the winds that blew over Pyongyang, why send someone so soon afterward? Or had Pyongyang known about this for a long time? Had they been waiting, too? I imagined what the report looked like in the file that the man in brown had on his desk. Probably neatly typed. Maybe with a photo taken of me as I walked out the door that night in Prague.

I stood up and strolled around the lobby. If Boswell had any other moves, he'd have to make them soon. I wasn't going to give him any encouragement; in fact, I was going to get as far away as I could from him. Anything I did in his presence would be misinterpreted, by both him and the man in brown. Tonight I'd tell Min to assign someone else to this escort duty, that I couldn't do it. Then I'd go home and wait for a knock on the door.

I walked over to the front desk. "I need a room for a visitor." I showed the clerk my ID.

"I'm sure you do. But we don't have any."

"All I need is a simple room for that man." I pointed at Boswell, who was examining the lobby. "I'm not asking for the royal suite." I showed the clerk my ID again. "Someone must have a record of the reservation." I knew there wasn't one, Min had already made clear the Ministry had botched this, but I might as well put the clerk on the defensive. "If you have misplaced it, just assign a room. I don't have all day to stand and argue with you. The hotel isn't full."

"I saw your ID the first time, Inspector. And tonight, I'd suggest the roving patrols should be doubled on the river between midnight and 5:00 A.M."

"What?"

"You an expert on hotel occupancy? Let's make a deal. I'll stick to my business, you stick to yours. I happen to know there was never a reservation, nothing was misplaced. But we'll let that pass, alright? How long does your big friend intend to stay?"

I lowered my voice. "The man is a guest of our government, and he happens to speak Korean."

The clerk didn't seem to care. "I asked how long he intends to stay."

"What difference does it make? The room will be paid for."

"You bet it will be paid for. We have a big group arriving tomorrow, two big groups, actually, who will be here all week. I'm not about to give away rooms to strays who wander in and then discover we need the space for people with reservations."

I looked around for Boswell, but he was walking down the steps into the hotel store. There was no sense indicating to the clerk that I didn't know how long he was staying. "He'll be here until Saturday. Stop wasting my time."

"Passport."

"I just showed you my ID."

"Yeah, but I need the tall man's passport. He can't check in without it, even the police know that, Inspector."

"Give me a room key, would you? The man is tired and he needs to rest. I'll get you his passport before we leave."

"Not possible. You want me to read you the regulations?"

When I told Boswell that he would have to give his passport to the clerk, he shrugged. "As long as I have it back in order to leave this happy land," he said. In the elevator going up to the room, I worried he would say something stupid, but he was quiet. When we stepped into his room, he suddenly found his voice. In big, booming English, he said, "I assume, Inspector, that all unnecessary devices have been disconnected or removed. I hope so. If not, I'll do it myself."

I stayed in the open doorway and replied with as much crispness as I could muster, in simple Korean so no one could miss my words, "I don't understand what you are talking about, Superintendent."

"Of course you wouldn't." He laughed loudly, went over to the phone, and held it up. "If there is anything in, on, or around this damned thing that doesn't belong, I'll throw it in the toilet. Dewww I make myself understood?" He walked into the bathroom, turned on the bathwater, and let it run a minute. "I'll have a bath when there's some hot water. Let's go for our city tour now. What we don't get done today, we can do tomorrow. I want to see some of the route in the morning sun, check the shadows."

"Tomorrow isn't possible. It's a holiday, the anniversary of the army, lots of people dancing in the streets. I don't dance, so I won't be there."

"You're kidding."

"No. If you want, maybe we can arrange for you to take part in the dancing. It's very chaste, but people have a good time."

"Is there a parade?"

"You mean a military parade? No, not this year."

"Speeches? I don't want to go and listen to speeches. Maybe I'll just stay in my room and sleep tomorrow. Let's cover as much ground as we can today."

3

When we returned to the hotel later that afternoon, Boswell told me he could find his way to his room, thanked me for my cooperation to this point, and disappeared through the glass doors. The doorman bent back slightly, pretending to look up as the visitor strolled by, then grinned at me. I started the car so violently it frightened a woman walking up the drive, and she fled back onto the sidewalk. What was the man talking about, cooperation "to this point"? My shoulder hurt and my fingers were tingling. It made me think of the man in the brown suit, and the uses of ash wood. That was just as they'd intended.

Min was at his desk, reading a magazine, his face serene, like an October moon coming up over the hills. "Our Englishman all settled in? Where have you been?"

I'd calmed down on the ride to the office, but only slightly. Min could tell I was riled about something. I could see his ears trying to tune themselves to catch my tone. "He insisted on seeing the 'lay of the land,' as he put it. We drove around the city."

"Unwise." Min was instantly sorry he had offered any criticism and strained to pull back the word before it reached me.

"Don't worry." It was something I always said when I was worried. "I was followed by two SSD cars and someone I didn't recognize the whole way, so no one can say we did anything untoward. The only time we stopped was in the square."

"Did he like it?"

"He said the man with the beard didn't look Korean."

"What did you say?"

"I said he was probably right."

"You didn't tell him who it was?"

"I didn't have the heart. If he doesn't recognize Lenin, I'm not going to rub his nose in it."

We both laughed, Min a little harder than necessary.

"So, where is he now?" Min asked in what he meant to be an off-hand manner.

"Safely in his room, I hope. He's probably going through the lamps and the outlets. He will take it as a personal affront if he finds anything, or maybe if he doesn't. Give this duty to someone else, Min." I paused. "Please, I don't have time for it. You know as well as I do that they didn't beat me up for practice."

Min started to respond, then thought better of it. He tapped his pencil on the desk. "Did you check the security route? Let's handle one thing at a time." He looked out the window at the Operations Building.

I could feel my shoulder getting stiff, and I only had part of one pain pill left. "We did, in a manner of speaking. Mr. Oaktree said he needed to drive the same route again tomorrow, at exactly the same time of day the visitor will, so he can check the shadows and the sun angles. He wasn't very happy to hear about the holiday; he kept asking why I can't get a pass or something to allow us to drive around tomorrow. Don't ask me why or what he expects to discover or why he seems to be in such a hurry. He wasn't talkative, spent a lot of time drumming those big fingers of his on the dashboard."

"Mr. Oaktree?"

"He's very big, Min."

Min put his hand over his eyes and slumped in his chair. "Can we not bring foliage into this, Inspector? It's complicated enough for me to keep track of everything that is going on."

"We could use it as a code name, on the radio," I said, "if we still used radios."

I kicked myself for raising the subject of devices. It would lead us onto cameras, and I didn't want the topic to come up. Photography was a painful area for Min. A visiting public security delegation from Syria once refused to attend a banquet he was obliged to throw them. In the hotel lobby, they informed us with a lot of shouting and rude gestures that we had insulted them by confiscating their delegation leader's camera. The delegation leader hopped up and down, bellowing that the trainload of army tanks was in plain view, none of them was covered with a tarp. This was true, but it was still against regulations to take any pictures of military equipment. In the middle of this, Min got called away to the Ministry. On his return, somewhat paler around the gills than when he left, he told me to give them the camera back.

"Please tell me he didn't take pictures during your drive." The chief inspector didn't have to spell out what he was thinking. He looked queasy.

"Not many." The Scotsman did not seem the type who would listen to even a short lecture on rules for taking photographs. And it was obvious he wouldn't hand over his camera without a fight, probably a protest, and a lot of irritation. "Maybe a few more day after tomorrow. But not with me. I need off of this duty."

Min groaned and went another shade more pale. "He understands he isn't to step out on his own this evening?"

"Who cares? He'll be obvious wherever he goes. There are plenty of checkpoints for the holiday already set up. He can't get into trouble."

"No, he can't. But we can, if he gets lost, or trips on a curb in the dark and breaks his leg. Slip over to the hotel later and sit around the lobby, just to keep your eye on him, would you?"

"I really don't want this duty. Don't ask me why. Send someone else, someone his size."

"You mean Li? Forget it."

"Why? Maybe they'll get along. Besides, my shoulder hurts. It hurts more at night. And, if you need another reason, I've got a lot of work to do on this whole mess before every single lead goes cold. People keep dying or disappearing. I think the robbery has something to do with it, though I don't think the robbery means a damned thing by itself. No one gives a shit about the money."

Again, Min put his hand over his eyes. He looked like he was getting a headache. "The leads are already frozen solid, Inspector, and you know it. Let's don't get ourselves tangled up in murder cases." He paused a moment, then glanced up at me. "By the way, when am I going to get the report on your surveillance of the first bank clerk?"

"When I type it up, which will have to be when I find her again. I lost her in an underpass."

"You lost her? That was a week ago. Why wasn't I told?"

"She disappeared in the dark. I was going to tell you"—the pain flared in my shoulder—"but I was preoccupied."

"You'll have to get back to her as soon as we get rid of this Englishman."

"He's not English. He's Scottish."

"He doesn't have a Scottish passport." Min rummaged through a pile of papers on his desk.

"Don't they teach geography in the schools anymore? Scotland doesn't issue passports. It's barely a country."

"Calmly, Inspector, speak calmly. You're giving me a headache. Yes, here. He's connected with the Scottish police. It's mentioned in the message we received from our man in Beijing this afternoon."

"All I know is what he told me. He said the Scottish police are a separate branch. To hear him describe things, they do their own farming; he says they have their own yard. It wouldn't hurt us to grow some vegetables, maybe out in the courtyard." Min didn't look like he wanted to discuss cabbage, so I dropped it. "The main thing is, he's a superintendent, which means he outranks me. Not to be too blunt about it, he also outranks you. The Ministry should have assigned a higher-level escort. It was embarrassing when he asked how many people I supervise. I can't escort someone of his rank."

Min considered that news, gloom gathering above his eyebrows. "He might take it as an insult. How was I supposed to know a superintendent outranks a chief inspector?"

I was silent, in what I hoped would seem a gesture of commiseration. "Never mind." Min waved a hand. "We're stuck with him. No one in the Ministry cares what the Scottish police think, or the English police, or the Germans. We're only babysitting to please the Foreign Ministry." Min looked where the calendar should have been on his wall. "He's out of here in three days, Inspector. Surely you can keep him busy for three days. Show him the sights. Get him drunk at night. Maybe we'll get lucky and he'll have an upset stomach for a day."

"What if he doesn't drink?"

"Trust me, Inspector. I may not know about passports, but I know someone who drinks when I see him. This Superintendent James likes to drink."

4

I needed to calm down. As I walked back to my office, it felt like my feet were barely touching the floor. Some people float when they're happy; I do it when my blood pressure goes up. A piece of wood would soothe my nerves, but not just any piece. I drifted up to my desk and grabbed the chair to keep myself from floating higher. Where was it? I opened the desk and rummaged around, but it wasn't there and that annoyed me so I slammed the drawer shut. Min shouted, "Hey," from down the hall, and I thought, to hell with "Hey." I remembered I had put it somewhere, but where? A piece of Burmese rosewood; someone had brought it back from a trip a few years ago, and I'd hidden it away for a serious emergency. Burmese rosewood is hardwood, extremely hard. It looks exotic. It feels exotic. It made me think of jungles and elephants just to touch it. And that was what I needed right now, to think about jungles and elephants, not oaks and giant Scotsmen and Prague. It was in my file cabinet, under a couple of empty envelopes. I looked at it for a few seconds, rolled it around in my hand, and wondered if that explained why visitors from Southeast

Asia always seemed so low-key. Why did they smuggle drugs, I wondered, when they had all that Burmese rosewood?

Just as I sat down and started to relax, Little Li poked his head in the room. "You want to hear something funny?" He was smiling, and he wasn't going to go away until I let him tell me why.

"Sure, at least once a day, everyone should hear something funny."

Just then my cell phone rang. It was in my desk, but the sound poured into the room, bounced against the walls and out the window into the street. The guards at the front gate started laughing, I could hear it.

"Li," I said, when the fairies stopped dancing, "you're a smart guy." Well, I thought, actually bigger than you are smart, but smart enough. "A sharp guy like you—you went through the tech class, am I right?"

Li shook his head. His face was carefully composed. That much he had down pat, keeping his face under control. "I heard about your phone, O. It never rang around me, but I heard about it. Some people in the Ministry dial you just so it will ring. They think it's hilarious."

"Is it?" If my blood pressure got any higher, I would float to the ceiling. Li would watch with that serious expression on his big face as I bobbed up and down. "You alright, O? Maybe you want to go get a glass of beer?" he'd ask after a minute or two, looking up at me. "I can always come back later."

I gripped the armrests on my chair. Li watched me do it, watched carefully, and then he measured his words. "No," he said slowly, very calmly, "I don't think it's funny." He waited. He watched as my grip on the armrests loosened a little before he went on. "But I don't know the first thing about those phones. And I hope they never assign one to me. What good are they, anyway?"

That did me good, hearing Li say that. I took a deep breath and let go of the armrests. "Before the phone rang, you were about to tell me something."

He smiled. "Yeah, those construction boys, they put in another order for my transfer. And they attached a threat. If I don't come along,

they'll fix it so I'm moved into one of those units up in the mountains."
The smile disappeared. "You know what I mean? Those guards."

"You don't want that duty, Li."

"I know that, O. You think I don't know that?" We stared at each
other, then the smile crept back on his face. "This transfer order is going to get routed clear across the country." He held it up for me to see.
"They'll never be able to trace it. But the signature sheet will show that
it's still in process." He laughed. "They don't know who they're dealing with, do they, O?" He laughed again and walked down the hall.

Well, I thought, they're not the only ones who don't know who
they're dealing with. Who the hell am I dealing with? I put the little
piece of rosewood within reach and started a new sketch for the
bookshelves. There wouldn't be much room left in the office if I ever
built them, but the plans didn't take up much space. After a few minutes, I felt myself about to start floating again. I put down the pencil,
picked up the piece of rosewood, and closed my eyes. I couldn't work
on the plans because other things were racing around my brain. Like
the bank robbery. Like the missing owner from Club Blue. Like
Yakob, the phony stocking salesman. Yakob, who was working for a
Russian service, I stopped to think about that. Lots of people worked
for the Russian service; we had long lists of suspects. Apparently, he
was being watched by SSD. Or just as likely, he was working for SSD.
And he was in contact with Club Blue. Funny connection: Han,
Yakob, and the missing owner from Club Blue.

My shoulder started to ache. New list. Stockings, a bank robbery,
and an ash club that nearly crippled me. I get knocked around with
an ash club, and a few days later, out of nowhere, a Scottish policeman shows up, unannounced. That doesn't happen. It never happens.
Visitors don't just show up. The Ministry has an entire wing of people whose job it is to screen visitors, slow them down, think up reasons they can't be admitted: not yet, not now, not ever. You have a
question? The answer is no. But I didn't ask the question. Doesn't
matter, the answer is still no. They get paid for that. And they don't
get paid to let visitors suddenly appear on our doorstep.

I thought that over. No, the Ministry wouldn't make that mistake. But what if the Ministry didn't have any choice in the matter? What if the Ministry got a yellow envelope with a black seal on it, on Saturday, early in the morning, early when it was still dark? "You will direct Office 826 to be at the airport to meet the Air Koryo flight in order to receive a British police official. More to follow." Something like that. Another list. Bank robbery—ash club—Scotsman. My shoulder was throbbing.

What else? The disappearing bank clerk. She'd stopped to talk to an old man with bad feet. Maybe he was a lookout. I shook my head and put the piece of rosewood down. The stuff was making me hallucinate.

5

"I found something in my room, Inspector."

"Congratulations. There's no extra charge."

"This isn't a joking matter. I told you if I found something, I would rip it out."

"So you did."

"It is infuriating that you treat guests this way."

"My apologies, Superintendent. Of course, no other security service in the world would do such a thing. We are the only ones."

Boswell rubbed his boulder-sized chin. "I'm not saying we do, I'm not saying we don't. But *if* we ever did, it would only be after going through strict, formal approval procedures."

"And what would those be?"

"One must go to a magistrate."

I slapped my forehead. "Yes, I see now. If only we had someone in a powdered wig give his okay, then that would make us part of the civilized world! Let me put that in the next set of recommendations for the Central Committee."

"Don't get sarcastic with me, Inspector. The question is one of limits. A political system without limits is a menace to its people. And magistrates don't wear wigs."

"More ignorance on my part. Ah, Superintendent, how difficult this must be for you, being amongst such savages."

"You're not helping your cause, Inspector."

By now I had forgotten I was standing in the hotel room assigned to a foreign police official, with the door closed, something that had certainly already been observed by the floor-watcher. "You think we don't have limits?"

"Do you? And what would those be?"

"How many of these devices do you actually think we can afford? You've just eaten a hole in someone's budget. You didn't have to step on it, you know. You might at least have removed it gently and wrapped it in toilet paper for them to claim later."

That broke a piece off the iceberg. Boswell laughed so hard he nearly choked; he dissolved in laughter; he danced around the room laughing, bumping into furniture, slapping his hands on the wall, and then, in what was probably meant as a gesture of fellowship, he clapped me on my left shoulder. Pain was instantaneous; I could hear it as it roared down my body. I almost cried but sat down instead on his bed and put my head between my legs, which only made my shoulder hurt more. Boswell stopped laughing at once and, in a practiced gesture, opened a bottle of whiskey he'd put on his side table and poured some into a glass. "Drink this," he said. "My God, man, what's the matter with you?" I looked up lamely. "Drink it, man," he shouted at me. "Hav ya gone deef?"

I had no idea what he said, but I took the whiskey with my right hand and downed it in a gulp. It burned my throat; my ears went numb, then my cheeks, then, thankfully, my neck and shoulders and my arms above my elbows. If I could have curled up on the bed and slept, I would have, but even in my benumbed state, I realized that sleeping on the bed of a foreign police official would get me another session with the man in the brown suit. I stood up, with effort. "Let's go," I croaked, "downstairs." I pointed in the direction of the door and walked out of the room. The floor-watcher had the good sense to keep out of sight, though I knew she was there, at the end of the hall around the corner, watching.

6

A Japanese businessman was on the stage, singing karaoke along with one of the bar girls, who was doing her best to look happy and attentive. The man was sweating; his voice wouldn't have been quite so grating if he had been a little more sober. He couldn't hit the high notes, but it was apparent that, in his state, he didn't care.

Boswell watched the stage for a moment. "Make sure no one asks me to go up there and sing, Inspector. I only know songs that aren't on your machine."

"You never know. Ever heard of Willie Nelson? A Pakistani scientist did Willie Nelson one night. Everyone clapped."

"Well, I don't seek applause. But will you have a drink? We may as well get better acquainted, seeing that you're stuck with me for the next few days."

There was a tall, thin girl tending the bar. She said hello quietly and asked if we wanted anything. I shook my head, and she went back to writing in a notebook she had open on the counter, next to the bottles of liquor. She knew enough not to stare at Boswell.

"No, not stuck," I said. "You're a guest. What's more, you're here on a mission, apparently important to your government, and to mine. If I don't make your visit comfortable or help it succeed, I will not have done either of us any good." Just saying that made my shoulder start to throb.

"I'll make you a deal." Boswell leaned against the bar and looked around the room. The Japanese businessman had finished singing and stumbled to a table in the corner, where he sat alone, swaying gently from side to side. Otherwise, the place was deserted. "The deal is this. I won't cause you trouble, and you help me get through this assignment without incident."

"That's it?"

"Too simple? You want me to add some complicating factors?"

"No, I like it just the way you said it. Alright, it's a deal, let's have a drink."

I called the bar girl over. "How about some brandy?" I asked Boswell.

"Brandy is for French touts. We'll have Scotch. And none of that Japanese stuff." He reached into his pocket and pulled out a flask. "This is real Scotch whiskey, tastes like Scotland on a wet spring evening. You'll like it." He switched to his odd Korean. "Give us two glasses, young woman, maybe three if you'd like a sip yourself." He turned to me and was back to English. "No harm in that, is there, Inspector? She seems a fine fresh lass, as the other James Boswell would say."

"Just a drop for her," I said. "Her name is Miss Kwon, and she doesn't drink much. To you, she may look like a kind and gentle maid, but she rules this bar with an iron hand. I wouldn't underestimate her." Miss Kwon smiled sweetly at me and brought the glasses.

"We had a man from Scotland here last year," she said. "He sang in a sad voice, pretty but sad. The songs were all mournful. I tried to get him to sing something happy, but he wouldn't, insisted he didn't know any. We talked about it afterward, when he'd gone. The other girls said they never heard anything so depressing. On his last night here, he said he would come back soon, but we never saw him again." She looked at Boswell for a moment. "Will you do the same, disappear forever?"

Boswell poured the liquor into her glass, then into mine, and finally into his own. "I don't sing, and I can't promise to return to your happy land." He raised his glass and gave Miss Kwon his full attention; she held his gaze, and though he probably didn't see it, I noticed a touch of defiance in her face. "But I'll drink to your happiness," he said, "and that of your loved ones, as well."

Miss Kwon flushed, the defiance melted away, and she hesitated before she spoke. "Come back tomorrow night," she said at last. "I'll sing you a good song. Maybe you'll want to join in." She raised her glass. "To Scottish friends."

They both turned to me. "To hell with sentiment," I said. "The two of you are putting a damper on the evening, and we haven't even started." I picked up my glass the same way the man in the brown suit had done, made a flourish with it. "I'll drink to our deal, and to songs with happy endings."

"Let's get comfortable, Inspector." Boswell pointed to a dark corner, where there was a table by itself, as far away from the stage as possible. He turned to Miss Kwon. "Maybe we can encourage that Japanese chap not to sing anymore. Why doesn't someone sit on his lap?"

Miss Kwon laughed. "Unless you want to be the one, we don't do that sort of thing here, do we, Inspector?"

"Probably against the law, in both cases, whether it's you or me," I said, "though I'd have to check for sure which one is considered worse."

We sat without talking very much for twenty minutes, or rather, I didn't talk. Boswell went on at length about the history of Scotland. I was still sipping my first drink; Boswell was on his second. "Oh, yes." His knees barely fit under the table, and whenever he shifted position, the table tipped. "We Scots have been everywhere, and if I may say so, everywhere we've been we've improved things."

"A shame you didn't make it here sooner."

He pinned me with a glare, then softened his expression and bowed slightly. "From what I have seen so far, it would have done no good."

"True, perhaps, but one never knows. We might have been apt pupils, once."

"Oh, no, you misunderstand, Inspector. I don't doubt that even this place could have used a good dose of Scottish influence."

"You make it sound like the clap," I said.

"What I mean is, the Chinese were here first, and if you got the clap, I should think you got it from the T'ung, or the Ling, or what-ever they are."

"T'ang. But not the T'ang. More likely it was delivered by the Khitan or Jurcen or some nameless barbarian tribe that favored rape and pillage. Of course Westerners don't know it, but we had our own kingdoms, our own greatness before the Chinese. Now all we do is catch their dust. Hard to fathom what went wrong." I looked around the dark room. "I'd say, when Scots still painted themselves blue, we already had a very civilized court life."

"For the love of Mike, Scots never painted themselves blue. Picts, maybe, but not Scots." He sighed and put down his glass. He peered into the flask, then shook it sorrowfully. "That's the last of it. What will I do for the next two days?"

"You don't have any more in your room?"

"I do not, and your little friends who are even now going through my bags won't find any."

"No one is going through your bags, Superintendent. And even if they did, if you had any extra Scotch, it would be quite safe."

"I suppose all you have down here is that Japanese whiskey. I don't favor it. It's not real."

"It's expensive enough to be real."

"You'll never taste the peat in Japanese whiskey, Inspector. You know why?"

"I don't."

"Artificial. Imitation. Copied."

"If we had anything in our glasses, we could drink to that."

"Aye, but we can't."

"I have a question for you, Superintendent, if you don't mind. What is a 'cowering beastie'?"

He cocked his head and blinked slowly. "A what?"

"A 'cowering beastie.' I read it somewhere, a poem, seems to me it was Scottish. I can't remember anything else, but those words stuck with me."

Boswell sat in contemplation. "You are full of surprises, Inspector.

It is from a poem by Robert Burns. How did you ever get hold of it? I wouldn't think he made it into your required reading."

"You'd be surprised what we read in our spare time, Boswell." I waited to see how he would react to my using his name.

He showed no emotion. Then he waved to Miss Kwon. "Bring some of your best local whiskey over here, my fair, iron-fisted lass. The Inspector and I have some serious conversation ahead of us." He sat back in his chair and, in a sonorous voice, recited:

> "Wee, sleekit, cow'rin, tim'rous beastie,
>   O, what a panic's in thy breastie!"

I nodded. "So, what is it, this cowering, timorous beastie?"

"The title of the poem, Inspector." He gave me an odd look. " 'To a Mouse.' "

"Ah, now I remember. Yes, a mouse. That's why I paid so much attention to the poem in the first place. Why is it, Boswell, that people think mice are afraid, that they cower?"

"James. If we're to discuss Robert Burns, call me James. Did you prepare for my visit? Tell me, Inspector, just as one cop to another. Did they give you books, background files to read up?"

"I didn't know you were going to visit. You were a bolt from the blue. But we were speaking of mice. Why are they always portrayed as afraid?"

Boswell shrugged, wary. "Dunno. In my house, if you turn on the kitchen light and catch one at midnight, it scoots across the floor, nose twitching in terror. Perhaps you have a different species."

"Mice are small, Superintendent."

"How about if we use our names instead of titles? More friendly, like."

"Small. Size is equated with cowardice; see something small, assume it is afraid." The mountainous Scotsman looked at me thoughtfully, waiting for me to complete the thought. I did. "But they don't correlate. We never make that mistake. I suggest you don't, either."

Boswell rose from his chair slowly, and when he was at his full height, he looked down on me. For a moment, I could tell he was weighing whether to pound me into the floor like a stake, to prove that size meant something after all. Then he exhaled mightily. "We'll try this again tomorrow night, Inspector. You might do some more reading, if you've a mind." He went over to the bar and whispered something to Miss Kwon, who was pouring our drinks, downed his in a gulp, then grimaced and walked out the door, singing a melancholy tune.

7

"I need to see a list of all UK passport holders in the country, and any Irishmen to boot."

"I'm not sure I can do that." Irishmen, he said. In the distance, I heard a warning flag snapping in the stiff spring wind.

"Inspector, you must have records you can access, shouldn't take but half a second. In this of all countries, you must know where people are."

"Of course." I snapped my fingers, then looked around the office. "Funny, last time I did that, things appeared instantly." The superintendent was sitting in my office, his long legs stretched to the edge of my desk. "Perhaps you don't understand, James, my friend." I kicked myself, hard. A sarcastic reference to Boswell as "my friend" would go down on a transcript as just that—"my friend." I never knew a transcriber with an ear for humor. "'Access' is not a word that has any particular meaning to me. The records at the border are kept by the immigration section. They consist of scraps of paper that tend to tear or otherwise fall apart. The Foreign Ministry has records of visa applications, but these are kept separate, and are available only to the immigration people, who ask for them at the last minute, when they realize their own forms have gone missing or been trashed. The police, in whose offices you sit, have 'access,' as you put it, to exactly nothing. I couldn't even squeeze out the license number of a bus the other day without a fight."

"And did you get it?"

"No, I didn't."

"So you can't get me a list of UK citizens in your country. Your government has no way of contacting them in an emergency."

"Ah, that's different. Pose a different issue, open different windows. If needed, we could ask the provincial police to help. People have to register with the local authorities. But that would take longer than you have, perhaps. Surely your embassy has its own records. It urges your citizens to keep in touch when they are here, am I right?"

"I don't want the embassy to know I am doing this check. I don't want anyone, other than you, Inspector, to know."

"Wonderful, now I am conspiring with a British policeman against his own government. It might work." I paused to consider, then shook my head. "No, too many angles. Anyhow, even if I did have a list, how would I justify giving you the names of Irish citizens, though I doubt there are any in my country. Ireland is a sovereign state, or am I wrong in my geography?" It was dancing with death to raise the subject of Ireland, I knew it. I opened my desk drawer and began feeling around for the Burmese rosewood, anything to tranquilize me.

"Inspector, we agreed that you would help me and I would help you."

"So we did. But nowhere in our agreement was there anything about lists, or access to records. Let's go at this another way. You don't really care about all UK citizens. You have a particular few individuals in mind, though you would rather I not know who they are."

The long legs shifted and the Scottish mouth set itself in a slight frown.

"Actually, I don't care who you meet, James. Meet whoever you please, if you can find them and think you are invisible so that no one will see you doing it. Invite them all to your room for a drink and throw the phones in the toilet to be safe, if that is what you want to do. But I'm not going into any records. I have enough trouble getting access to them for my own cases; I can't be doing it on behalf of Her Majesty's Government."

"How about Germans?"

Somehow, it wasn't a surprise; he wanted the Germans, so of course he started out asking me about something else. "Who do you want to see, Dieter or Jurgen?"

The Scotsman leaned back and smiled. "I'll be damned."

"Never mind, you don't have to tell me which. Both of them are staying in the Sosung Hotel, near the golf driving range. They sit on the balcony and drink the day away while they watch young women chase golf balls." Ever since I put them on twenty-four-hour surveillance, they had done nothing, gone nowhere. Neither of them had a shirt with blood on it, either.

"You've met them?"

"In a manner of speaking." There was someone else he wanted to see; I could tell from the way he sat, trying to frame the question so it would seem innocent. "Perhaps you need to go the bank?"

His eyes never flickered. "You are a son of a bitch, you know that?"

On the drive to the Gold Star Bank, Boswell seemed preoccupied. When I pulled over and parked under the big trees, he sat still for a moment before turning toward me. "I have a favor to ask, Inspector. Let me out here. You go back to your office. I know the way to the hotel, and I need some time to think. I'll call you when I get back, in about an hour or two, you have my word. Then we can drive the route again; the shadows should be right by that time."

"Shadows." I shrugged and looked out my window. "Wrong shadows. Right shadows. I think you are obsessed with these shadows." I turned to him. "I could wait out here, if money dealings embarrass you."

"Thanks, but not necessary." He spoke carefully and nodded toward the bank. "Let's let it lie, shall we?"

"Be sure and count your change, that's all I've got to say. And don't get lost on the way back to the hotel, or I'll have to explain how you happened to be on your own." I watched him cross the street, just to make sure no buses suddenly appeared.

8

It wasn't until the shadows were too long to do us any good that the phone rang.

It was a deep voice speaking in accented but unmistakably angry Korean. "I'm back. More precisely, I'm at your front gate. The guards won't let me in."

"Good." I looked out the window and saw Boswell on the gate phone. I waved.

He made a rude gesture. "We have work to do, Inspector," he said.

"Maybe we did an hour ago. Now we have nothing. And I'm plenty busy with my own business, you might consider that."

"I bring greetings from Kazakhstan."

"I'll bet you do." I was smoothing the scrap of chestnut with my fingers. It was dark, like my thoughts. I laughed at myself. "Alright, put the guard on, I'll tell him not to shoot you."

When Boswell got upstairs, I was standing by the window. "What do you know about chaos theory?" I asked as I heard him step into the room and sit down on the chair against the wall.

"Why?"

"Interested, that's all."

"Not much. Something along the lines that events happen according to no particular plan and in no particular order, that a minor event in one place can set off ripples that cause major developments somewhere else. The usual example is a butterfly flapping its wings."

"Yes, and what happens after that?"

"I don't know, a vast storm halfway around the world. Air currents,

I guess. I don't much care for chaos. Certainly not in our line of work."

"Still, chaos is interesting, don't you think?"

"No, I've seen it happen on soccer fields too many times. It's messy."

I smiled and turned around to face him. "You know what I would like to do someday? I'd like to bathe in chaos, stand under it like you would under a waterfall and have it cascade over my body. Maybe drown myself in it and be swept into a vast nothingness."

"Whew. Heavy thinking, Inspector. Had a wee nip of the barley after lunch?"

I turned back to the window and waved my arms.

"What was that, if I may ask?" Boswell was peering at the files on my desk; I could see his reflection in the window.

"Check the weather in England in a few days."

"Aye, I will."

"Did you get your money laundered?" He sat back as I turned around again.

"Something bothering us, Inspector?"

"I could get in a lot of trouble, leaving you at the bank like that. That bank was robbed a while ago."

"Robbed? In this city?"

"You know it was. And you know who the manager is. Don't toy with me, Superintendent. Many things I can endure, but don't toy with me."

"Right, I'll rephrase the question. What makes you say I already know?"

"Your people at the embassy will have told you something about life 'in this city,' as you put it. Certainly the events at the bank will have come up, among other things. How long have you known her?"

I thought he would dodge the question, or pause. He did neither. "Long time ago, when we were all much younger, Inspector. I didn't know she was here, until the embassy told me. I'm glad I went over there. She knows the Germans."

"One of them pinched her fanny."

"Yes, well, that makes it easy. Shouldn't be too hard to find a German who sings castrato."

"Tell me about the Germans."

"Tell me about the bank robbery first."

"What does that have to do with your mission? And unless you tell me so that it's believable, there's nothing I can share about the robbery—nothing beyond what the lady with the tiny waist has probably already told you."

Boswell crossed his arms and regarded me thoughtfully. Finally, he slapped his hands on his knees. "Alright. I'm going to regret this, but alright. There have been a number of bank robberies over the past several years across Europe, by one gang operating always from the inside."

"A number. Any special number? Never mind, go on."

"Some time ago, two banks were hit in Germany."

"There were two Germanys. One for each." This was a small lie on my part, seeing that I had read something about the case. But the Scotsman was supposed to be supplying me with information; our deal had not specified that I tell him anything that I knew. More to the point, everything and anything he told me was suspect. He would tell me exactly what he wanted me to hear and no more. He would tell me because that's what they needed me to know. Or think. Or imagine. It was probably part of his mission, to feed me something. Okay, I wasn't learning anything from him; he sure as hell wasn't going to learn anything from me.

"No, this was after unification." He looked at me with a hint of suspicion. "Although now that you mention it, one of the banks was in the former East, the other in the West."

"I continue to listen, Superintendent, but I've yet to hear anything relevant to me."

"Patience, laddie." He grinned. "That's a term of endearment."

"Or condescension."

"For heaven's sake, man, give me a break, can't you? Don't be such a . . ." He hesitated.

"Cowering beastie," I finished his thought. "Never mind, we'll deal with the insults in due course. Just get on with it, the Germans." This I wanted to hear. Maybe it would give me a clue why one of them had been racing through the streets a week ago with blood on his shirt.

"Well, your two Germans were working in those banks, Jurgen in the West and Dieter in the East. They're old radicals, from the days when people were still moved by ideas and killed capitalists for reasons no one understood. Them together, here. And you just having had a robbery. A curious coincidence, one might say."

"But they didn't work in our bank."

"No, but they did business at your bank. They were inside it many times, I'm told. According to the manager"—he coughed—"they hung around and made sheep's eyes at her."

"I still see no relevance."

"You don't? We need to get them off the street. They're dangerous. You must be blind, man. I would have thought law and order were right up your alley."

"No, not blind. Cautious, maybe. I need something more. You say 'we' need to get them off the street, but it isn't your street, Superintendent, it's mine. Perhaps in Scotland you could roll up a couple of Germans on suspicion and the German government would politely applaud. I can't do that here. It will cause nothing but grief. We will be accused by foreign governments of abuse of power, extrajudicial proceedings, violation of human rights. Where's the proof, we'll be asked. The German ambassador will be phoning and knocking on doors, sending notes here, there, and everywhere. Where's the proof, I'll be asked. And my answer is, well, I can't answer that—because you don't want me to quote you, am I right?"

The Scotsman sat quiet, composed, resigned.

"Thank you for not giving me an argument." I reached down and picked up the Criminal Code. "What do you suppose would happen if I cited the relevant articles in this? More international protest, calls for diplomatic pressure, Europeans roaring about our lack of due process. The best I can do is put them under surveillance. But these Germans are guilty, that's what you think."

"A fine point of law, Inspector. I think they could be guilty of something, or at least of planning to participate in something that would make them guilty. The facts at least raise a reasonable suspicion. Surely your procedures allow detention on the basis of reasonable suspicion. I mean, this is Pyongyang." He paused, held up his hand to ward off any objection, closed his eyes, and nodded his head. "Forget I said that. But there is more, one more thing I want you to know."

I studied the molding on the ceiling. "Proceed as you wish, Superintendent. I'm afraid there isn't much more for us to discuss."

"As near as we can tell, all of the bank robberies are connected, in some way or another, with political motives. These are not thieves who want to buy gold neck chains and sun themselves in Majorca." He paused again. "That's an island."

"I have seen globes, Superintendent. Even ours suggest the world is round." The world is round, bank robberies have political motives, and I suddenly had no idea what game this man was playing. None. Next he would ask me if I wanted to invest in a joint venture harvesting a forest of Sogdian ash. Or if I would like a new hip. Maybe he could get me one made in Spain. I always wanted to move like a Spaniard.

"The point is, Inspector, these two Germans may be here for something else, something political."

My color must have gone bad. The Scotsman blinked at me. "You alright?"

I sat down. "Now it's my turn to share something. Your undersecretary may be in danger."

The Scottish neck muscles tightened; a deep breath filled the chest. The voice took on a rock-bound hardness. "Explain that."

"It's all I know. Information I've never seen, from a source unknown."

"Where was it, written on the walls of the jakes, for crying out loud!"

"The what?"

"Never mind. It's Shakespeare. Fuck Shakespeare."

That shook me a little. I thought English people only spoke in awe of Shakespeare. Maybe the Scots didn't. Boswell lowered his voice. "If you have information that a British official is in imminent danger in your country, why didn't you let me know immediately?"

"Frankly, I didn't believe it. I still don't. There have never been threats to visitors to this country, official or otherwise. You've had some problems, I seem to recall. Us, never."

"Oh, really, what did you have in mind?"

"Bulgarians. Libyans. Irishmen. Maybe Palestinians, though I may be wrong."

"You never had a bank robbery before, either, I'm guessing."

"True."

Neither of us spoke. The Scotsman flexed the fingers on one hand to let off the tension. He seemed to grow more agitated by the minute, like a large tree whose branches sway and fight the wind. I had thought he was supremely calm; I thought height gave a perspective that gave way to a steadiness those of us closer to the ground cannot afford. For myself, I was not so much agitated as glum, wondering whether things were heading toward a shootout in a cemetery. I wondered which one it would be. The Martyrs' Cemetery outside of town would be an interesting place, the busts of honored revolutionaries shattering as bullets whizzed around.

"That's it, then, Inspector." Boswell stood up slowly, unfolding toward the ceiling. "We cancel the visit."

"On what basis?"

"Basis? The threat, what else do we need? I don't plan to be covered by the undersecretary's bloody brains before I make up my mind."

I shrugged. "You are assuming the threat is to his person."

"Ah, well, then, perhaps in your country you have different grada-
tions of threat than we do. Let me see, there could be a threat to his
moral dignity, to his reputation, to his financial probity, maybe to his
family escutcheon. Yes, of course, Inspector, someone is coming here
to smear his family name! Don't be idiotic. I'm canceling the visit,
and then I'm leaving."

"You don't care who might be threatening one of your officials, or
why?"

"This is your country, it is your problem," he grumbled.

"How do you know these people won't try again, in another country? Maybe even in yours?"

Boswell paused in midgrumble. He cocked his head and looked at
me through what were for him unusually narrowed eyes. "What are
you suggesting?"

"Nothing in particular. You can't leave until Tuesday anyway,
when the next flight takes off. The visitor doesn't arrive until several
days after that. We still have plenty of time to think about this. You
can cancel his visit as late as next Tuesday, even Wednesday if you
want to spend a few extra days here. Meantime, I can figure out if
there is something more to do about the two Germans. And we can
go over the security details as many times as you like."

Boswell sat down. "Right. I apologize if I seem rattled. Jet lag,
maybe. Something about this place—" He paused. "Let it go."

"No, what about this place?"

"Now, don't be getting angry on me. But the stress levels go up,
something in the air, maybe not for you, but there it is. Since I arrived, I've had a sense that people are holding their breath—no, not
people, but the place, the whole place. It is holding its breath."

I took the scrap of chestnut out of my pocket and smoothed it
with my fingers for a long moment. "Let me tell you something, Superintendent. People breathe perfectly normally here." I opened the
desk drawer and put the piece of wood carefully to one side, lining it
up so the thick end was against a brown pencil. Then I closed the

drawer and took a deep breath. "But the butterflies"—I smiled—"they don't flap their wings."

The Scotsman hesitated, looked out the window, then settled back in his chair and nodded.

9

"We'll assign Inspector Yang to the security squad. He hasn't been on the street in a long time; no one even knows what he looks like."

"You trust him?"

A very odd question, from a foreigner. "I do." Why would he think I might not have confidence in Yang? "Of course I trust him." We were driving toward the river, and Boswell, as usual, was drumming his fingers on the dashboard.

"Stop the car!" Boswell's order was so loud and so unexpected I hit the brakes and we skidded, careened, across two lines until I got control again. A traffic policeman began jogging toward us from the nearest intersection. A van behind me honked its horn, paused a moment to see if we were alright, then sped away.

"What the hell?" I don't like to skid, it makes me nervous, and I don't like people shouting at me.

Boswell ignored my question. "Right here. This is the spot. If something is going to happen, this is it. Look at the shadows."

I groaned. "You and your damned shadows. Where? It's a normal street; they'll be speeding down the center lane; the road will be blocked, and there won't be any traffic. You think someone is going to shoot from a window from one of these buildings? Most of them can't even be opened, they're so badly out of alignment."

Boswell stuck his head out of the car and surveyed the rooftops. He paused at one, pulled out a pencil, and wrote himself a note. "Let's walk a bit. I want to get a better sense of this stretch. I still don't like it."

"Fine, just don't shout when I'm driving."

"Inspector, I had no idea you were so sensitive." The huge Scottish hand rested on my shoulder. "Accept my apologies. Let me take you to dinner tonight. You pick the restaurant."

"Get out and walk around if you want. There's nothing here. Incidentally, a long-standing request of the Germans to visit the east coast will be suddenly accepted, much to their surprise. They leave tomorrow morning and won't be back until next week."

Boswell hesitated, confused. Then he laughed. "Very efficient, by God. There's something to be said for your style."

"I'm listening."

"Yes, I'm sure you are, but I'm not finishing the sentence. Pick out a decent restaurant, someplace they might have some liquor we can drink, would you?"

The traffic policeman, out of breath, puffed up to the car. He looked twice at my license plate, then straightened his hat, walked around to the driver's side, and leaned into my window. His eyes took in the Scotsman beside me, but his face showed no emotion. "What's with the brakes?" It was a traffic cop voice, sort of nasty, as if he owned the street.

"I use them to stop the car. It's routine. You have regulations against that?"

"Look, I know who you are, Inspector. I have a friend."

I whistled. "Miracle of miracles."

"A friend who doesn't particularly like you."

"A fine citizen."

"A friend who doesn't like it when someone puts their paws on his arm."

A light went on in my head. The traffic patrolman's hands were resting on the open window. I gripped his wrist. "Tell your friend to be more polite next time someone visits your bureau. You'll do that, won't you?" He was pulling away violently just as I let go, so he fell backward a step.

"Get this car out of here, you and your gorilla friend with it," he said. He adjusted his hat again, then in a quick motion kicked the side of my door. "Too bad about that." He looked at me. "You've got a dent. Must have been that hard braking." He smiled coldly and walked up the street.

Boswell had been watching the whole time. The exchange had taken place in short bursts more like gunfire than conversation, but from his face I could see he had followed most of it. "Did I hear what I thought I heard?" he said.

"Just a light discussion between brother security officials." I shrugged. "That's how Koreans make love, Superintendent."

"I figured it was something like that." He nodded toward the traffic policeman, who by now had resumed his place on the side of the intersection ahead and was reaching for the white gloves tucked in his belt. "Do you know that greasy, stringy, bad-tempered son of a bitch?"

I laughed and started the car. "For a dour breed, you Scotsmen sure can talk. Let's get out of here." I pulled into traffic, did an illegal U-turn in front of an old Toyota, and squealed the tires. I looked in the rearview mirror, but the traffic cop wasn't paying attention. "Never mind him," I said. "Let's get a drink."

"What about the route?"

"Screw the route. Nothing ever happens here, anyway, Superintendent. We spin our wheels endlessly chasing shadows and listening to echoes. You ever been so tired of the same thing you could punch someone?"

"Pick on someone your own size, Inspector."

I gave him a sharp look and accelerated around a corner.

"Christ, that was a joke!" Boswell held on to the dashboard with both hands. "Not a dig at your . . ."

"My what?"

"Let's just get that drink, okay? A man could go crazy around here."

"You said it, Superintendent, I didn't."

The silence in the front seat was heavy for the next several minutes, while I drove through a neighborhood where I knew no traffic police lurked on corners. Finally, my protocol juices began flowing again. I put a smile on my face. "I've got a treat for you. I'm going to take you to someplace that's part of an investigation. Look out for ground glass in the drinks, though. The bartender's a tough bastard. I don't think he likes me."

The visitor narrowed his eyes. "Does anyone like you, Inspector?" He paused. "Besides me, I mean."

"Good, you almost missed that one, but you came back fine. By the time you leave here, Boswell, you'll be ready for the real world."

"God help us all."

PART III

Chapter One

I arrived at the Koryo twenty minutes early. The place was deserted except for a few security types and the doorman, so I stood around minding my own business. On the second-floor balcony, a waitress leaned against the railing, looking down into the lobby. At first I thought she might be waiting for someone, but there wasn't any concentration in the way she stood or idly scanned the room. It wasn't as if she was relaxed; it was more like she was longing for something but wasn't sure what. When her eye finally caught mine, she looked away quickly, but I knew her glance would sweep back. I didn't recognize her as part of the normal staff; probably she was new. Sweet looking, even from a distance, she had an innocent air, a country girl who could tell a joke and mean nothing by it. I smiled when she looked my way again. She smiled back; then someone must have said something, because she covered her mouth and retreated into the shadows. In her place, a tall hotel security man appeared. He gave me a sour look, but it wasn't anything personal, just his normal expression. I winked at him and moved off to one of the benches so I could wait for Boswell. We were supposed to meet at six o'clock for dinner, though I wasn't hungry.

A group of well-dressed Europeans made their way past the doorman. They looked around the lobby, the women with amused smiles, the men with a touch of contempt. One of the men said something to the others, and they all laughed unpleasantly. If they walked over and sat down near me, I would have to move. I didn't want to have to listen to snide observations, and I especially didn't want to have to answer any questions. Foreigners usually asked about the crops, as if I followed that sort of thing. It was Monday, the wrong day for anyone to be arriving by plane, and none of them were wearing travel clothes. I figured they had already been here for a few days; maybe that was why their guide was nowhere in sight, probably suffering from nervous exhaustion.

The man who had made the others laugh was thin. He looked even thinner because of the way his suit was cut. The jacket was over his shoulders, like a gray cape; a pair of glasses hung on a chain around his neck, where they bumped against his chest as he strolled toward the front desk, then toward the restaurant in the back, shaking his head slightly, calling to the others. You might have thought he was in a zoo, the way he pointed. I could see the girl behind the money-changing counter look down and pretend to concentrate on something else when he approached. It did no good; the man stopped and pulled out his wallet. He put several euro bills on the counter and summoned her, in bad Chinese. She looked at him blankly, though she knew perfectly well what he'd said. I checked my watch. These people were gawking as if they hadn't seen the lobby before. They must be staying at one of the other hotels, maybe the Potang-gang, and were just crawling around the Koryo for laughs. If Boswell didn't show up in the next thirty seconds, I was going to get up and leave. He could have dinner by himself, or with the cape-man and his friends.

After the run-in with the traffic cop, I had taken Boswell to Club Blue. I told him it was so we could have a drink together, but really I needed to see the tough bartender again. I wasn't happy about having Boswell along, but there was no way to get rid of him. The tough bartender wasn't there anymore. And the old owner had already been replaced, which was a surprise. I thought he might be roughed up a little but then crawl back, not that he'd vanish. The new bartender wasn't talkative. The new owner wouldn't stop. He pretended to be glad to see us and shook Boswell's hand four or five times, until Boswell put it in his coat pocket and kept it there until we got back to the car. I didn't think Miss Chon would be attracted to the new owner. His shoulders weren't much to look at.

As we were climbing the stairs, Boswell asked me if there was much trouble at these sorts of clubs. I said no, nothing besides a stabbing not long ago. He pretended not to be interested. "Happens all the time, Inspector," he said. "Drunken patrons in a scuffle, am I right?" Out of the corner of my eye, I thought I saw a warning flag.

The wait at the hotel was getting long. Just as I decided to leave, Boswell came out of the elevator on the second floor, waved curtly to me from the balcony, and rode down the escalator to the lobby.

"Evening, Inspector. Shall we dine?" He looked at the cape-man with distaste. "That fellow should either put on his damned jacket or take it off."

This startled me. "I thought you would be glad to see your countrymen."

"They're not my countrymen, they're Italians. What do you suppose they want here?"

I ignored the question; how could I know what they wanted? It was like asking me about crops. "Where would you like to go to dinner, Superintendent?"

We were speaking in English, and the cape-man turned to observe us. He adjusted his coat and perched his glasses on his long nose. He glared at Boswell, as if our having a normal conversation broke some sort of unwritten rule. Their guide probably went to her room and drank every night.

Boswell took my arm and started leading me away. "What's wrong with this place for dinner? They have a dining room here."

"Here?" I knew the hotel had a dining room, I had eaten in it. But the Ministry didn't like us to use it for entertaining guests, foreign or domestic.

"A problem? What's the matter, doesn't it fit with your Ministry's guidelines?"

"I just thought you'd like to go out somewhere, that's all. There are a few new places that visitors seem to enjoy." I wouldn't have minded ending up at the all-night foreigners' restaurant, just to see the look on the lady in the silk dress as she walked us to our table. This time, I wouldn't sit with my back to the door.

"I'm tired." Boswell was slouching, as if to emphasize the point. It wasn't a posture that fit him very well; it made him look like an oak tree in love with a dandelion. "I don't want anything with singing or dancing. Let's just eat here, Inspector. At breakfast, I peeked at the dinner menu. They have pot roast, can you believe it?" If the menu said so, I believed it, though I didn't know how good it would be. Beef was tough; unless it was in a soup or grilled in little chunks, I couldn't see why foreigners thought so much of it. "Anyway"— Boswell had dropped my arm and was walking ahead of me, his posture much restored by the chance to be sarcastic—"I can't resist restaurants with mirrored ceilings."

At dinner, our waitress was the same girl I'd spotted on the balcony. She pretended not to remember me. And from the way she moved, I could see she was nervous, just out of training and worried because she knew every step she took was being observed by her supervisor, an older woman who stood off to the side. Her hand shook when she filled the small glasses in front of us with liquor. A tiny bit overflowed, spilling onto the tablecloth. It was nothing, no one could have noticed, but it was not what she meant to do, not what she wanted. Her eyes were so pained that for a moment I thought she might faint. Boswell paid no attention. He downed the glass in a gulp, then sat and chewed in silence. I asked him how the food was; he only nodded. Once or twice he appeared to gather his thoughts, and I thought he was about to say something but nothing came of it.

"Maybe we should have gone somewhere else," I said at last. He said nothing. "Something the matter?" I asked. It was fine with me not to carry on a conversation about nothing, but this was getting awkward. "If something is wrong with the food, we can tell the waitress." It passed through my mind that the girl might be transfixed, actually physically incapacitated, if we complained to her about the food. "I don't know pot roast, but my soup is not bad. Maybe you should try some. Here." I pushed the bowl toward him.

Boswell put his fork down, then his knife. He looked at them intently for a moment, then at his plate, and finally, as if it cost him to do so, at me. "Have you never sat in silence, Inspector? It is not a mean thing to do. How can I think if someone is talking all the time?"

When the meal was over, he folded his napkin and left the table without a word. I sat for a while by myself, half expecting the man in the brown suit to show up, but no one else came into the dining room, so I finished my soup and went home. Something was eating Boswell, and it wasn't the pot roast.

2

The next morning after I checked in at the office, I went for a walk. Min wouldn't be in until late. This was his regular day for meetings at the Ministry. Boswell could sit alone in his room for a few hours in silence and think; for all I cared, he could sit there the whole day. The whole damned day. I had some thinking to do, too. I looked through my desk drawer for a piece of wood to keep me company. I found a piece of acacia and put it in my pocket. Acacia knew how to mind its own business and let a person think.

Boswell's moodiness at dinner still irked me. I hadn't ever dined with a Scotsman, but as far as I knew, there was a level of politeness that civilized peoples maintain while eating together. Boswell was concerned about something, pressured. More pressure, first Min, then me, now Boswell. Everyone was feeling it. Something about Club Blue had set him off, especially the stabbing.

Club Blue seemed to set a lot of people off, even Miss Chon. I had formed a strong impression of her the first time I went into the bank—apart from her waist, she struck me as haughty, someone used to ordering people around, and yet there was this odd gap. Yes, she was a very competent woman, about as self-assured as I'd ever seen. In that case, why wouldn't she admit she was close to the owner of Club Blue? You'd have thought she'd want to wave it in front of my nose, how she had bagged those big shoulders. I doubted if banking practice forbade sleeping with the customers. She must know by now he was missing and be worried, unless she knew where he was. Then it came to me, the one thing that stood out now that I thought about it—and it was as if a big bell was booming next to my ear. Why I hadn't heard it before, I couldn't say. She didn't seem off balance. She hadn't once complained to me about how things were done here. The janitor moved the desk, he didn't move the desk, the desk suddenly disappeared, all fine by her. The fussing that night at the restaurant about the desk, it was an act. She wasn't worried, because she wasn't surprised. I stopped. She even knew that the name of my ministry had been changed from Public Security to People's Security. That was more than ten years ago. How the hell would she have known that?

I walked a little farther, trying to tickle my subconscious into action, but it seemed otherwise occupied and silent. It must have been preoccupied with the group of Italians, because when I looked up, I found myself heading toward the Potang-gang Hotel. A woman was waiting at the entrance to the park that sits beside the Potang River. The trees in the park were in leaf, fresh green, delicate in the sunlight. The shadows were still dainty, not like the ponderous shade that trees manufacture late in the summer. I thought I'd sit in the park for a while and let my thoughts roam, but something about the woman caught my attention. She was standing perfectly still. You might have thought she was a statue except that her ponytail stirred slightly in the breeze. So did the belt on her coat, where it hung down in front. Unlike the waitress at the Koryo Hotel, this woman was waiting for someone. You could tell she wasn't looking forward to the meeting. If the way she had set her feet meant anything, she was becoming more impatient by the minute. Finally, she glanced at her watch, looked back up along the street, and then walked down the path to the river. Something about the way she moved made me follow. It took a moment to realize this was the bank clerk I'd lost in the underpass. In the dark, I never had a good look at her face, and now, with a ponytail, her chin wasn't so sharp. Faces sometimes fool me. But I never mistake the way someone looks from behind, the way someone walks. If you follow enough people, pretty soon you stop looking at faces anyway. Hips and heels, those are the signatures.

The bank clerk walked along the river. Without her high heels, she took longer, more confident steps. This time I wasn't going to let her out of my sight. A few blocks later, she turned into a building with empty stores at ground level. I relaxed, waiting across the street until she came out. There were no entrances in the back. This was my section of town, I knew it inside out, and I had made a study of buildings that had rear entrances that couldn't be seen from the street. This wasn't one of them.

An elderly man appeared in the same doorway where the clerk had entered. Just for a moment he stepped outside and seemed to enjoy the air. Then he glanced in my direction and disappeared back inside, but not before I noticed that his feet turned out. I took another look at the building. There was nothing unusual, except maybe that the curtains on the second floor drew back slightly for a moment and then closed again. That and the fact it was one of the buildings in the block Boswell had insisted we stop and look at more closely. He had said he didn't like the shadows. Maybe he didn't, or maybe he had just wanted to make sure he saw the building.

My phone rang; that ridiculous tune I couldn't get rid of blasted from my back pocket down the entire block. Perfect, absolutely perfect, I thought. "Yeah?"

"Fine greeting, Inspector. Good communication skills. Let's work on that, can we?"

"Come on, Min, I'm in the middle of surveillance, or at least I was until this phone alerted everyone in the neighborhood to my presence. I'm not in a chatty mood."

"Good, good, no need to chat. Remember your friend the nightclub owner? The one with the silk stockings? His body is floating in a river up in the hills. Communications with the patrol on the scene aren't good, but through the static it sounded like maybe his head was bashed in. Apparently, there was plenty of identification in his pocket, so whoever did it must have wanted to make sure he was identified. According to the leader of the patrol, it looks like he's been in the water for two days, maybe longer."

"Maybe he just slipped and fell. Accidents do happen, Min." The man had been missing for two weeks, and he wasn't on vacation, hiking around the countryside. Ending up in a river was no accident, but there was no sense in saying so to Min. He'd only complain that I hadn't told him sooner.

"No, Inspector, these country patrols may not be very smart, but they can usually tell an accident from a homicide. They said it was murder."

"Well, if it's murder, it's murder, but it's not in my territory."

"It's your case, and he was one of your suspects, wasn't he?"

"He wasn't a suspect." I thought of Miss Chon. When was the last time she saw him? "His bar might have been mixed up in it somehow, but he didn't seem the type to rob a bank. His connections were too good for anything rough like that."

"No time to argue, Inspector. Come on back here, pick up the initial scene report that was phoned in, get the superintendent from the hotel, then go take a look. Whatever you do, keep the Scotsman out of town for a few hours. SSD called just after we got the news; they must have heard almost the same time we did. They told me they wanted the Scotsman out of the way. They were clear on that."

"Who did you talk to?"

"Han."

"Did his phone click?"

There was a prolonged silence.

"Never mind," I said, "forget I asked. Why don't we just ignore him?"

"Not this time." The strain was back in Min's voice. "When I was at the Ministry this morning, I got severe looks, a lot of them. Something is up, and I'm not going to be under it when it comes back down. I also checked with some people I know. Han is a comer; he's under someone's wing, they said, though that's all they would say. I got the feeling that if we get on his bad side today, he'll eat our livers tomorrow."

"He'll choke on a feather long before that, Min. You worry too much."

"You want to stand there and argue, or will you do as I ask?" Min wasn't giving me an order, he was pleading. "One more thing. Little Li dropped off a report he'd been working on all night."

"Yeah, so?"

"It's about the bus."

Min wasn't sure how to tell me this; it was obvious from how he was dancing around what he wanted to say. "What about the bus?"

"Little Li found the driver. They had a long conversation, once the guy felt good enough to talk."

"Something happened to him?"

"He fell down or something. Li says once he regained consciousness, he was fine. His story is that his brother was the regular driver but got sick all of a sudden. This guy volunteered to help out, though he'd never driven a bus before. He got lost, went up the wrong street, and then panicked when he saw someone in a strange costume in the road in front of him. He hit the gas instead of the brake."

"Pretty convenient."

"Maybe, but it checks out. The regular driver really was sick, and this guy really couldn't steer a bus."

"Good, we can eliminate the bus." I put my hand over my eyes. "All right, now what do you want me to do?"

"Han said it was important to make sure the Scotsman is with someone. Don't drop him off somewhere, like you did at the bank. They weren't happy with that, not a bit. Han said to stop for lunch along the way if you need to stretch it out."

"Is he going to pay out of his big budget? I don't know of any restaurant en route, do you?"

"Must be something around there; people have to eat, don't they?"

"Maybe we'll steal a goat and roast it over an open fire."

"What! Did you say steal a goat?"

"You're fading, Min. I'll see you later." I clicked off the phone. Maybe banning these things wasn't such a bad idea. Who invented them? And why was it so complicated to change the ringer?

3

Boswell was still moody and said he wanted to stay in his room, but I told him about the body in the river and he perked up a little. We drove for about two hours off the main highway, along dirt roads past fields that had been newly ploughed, between rows of acacia trees that didn't yet have the leaves of the trees in the city but showed new branches that were limber in the breeze. We crossed a bridge without side rails that went over a riverbed with only a trickle of water. Amidst a pile of rocks in the center was an old steam shovel, its bucket resting on the cab of a dump truck that had no tires. "What was that?" asked the Scotsman. "Wait, I want to take a picture of it."

"No need," I said. "It's just some construction equipment."

"No, really, it's perfect. I want to get a picture. Stop the car, back up."

"Impossible, can't go backwards on a bridge without side rails. It's against traffic regulations. Anyway, you can't take pictures of construction equipment."

"Inspector, there isn't anyone around here worrying about traffic rules, and who is going to know I took the picture except you?"

I accelerated and hit the bump at the end of the bridge hard enough to cause the Scotsman to bounce against the car's roof.

"Hey, watch out."

"Nearly there, just past those trees."

When we got to the end of the road, there was a black car parked, one uniformed Ministry of People's Security officer standing in the road, hands behind his back, looking up into the nearby hills. The driver and a second man were squatting in the middle of the road, in the shade of the car, smoking, not talking, not looking at anything in particular. When Boswell and I pulled over and walked up to them, none of them said anything. Boswell looked at me, sort of questioning, and cleared his throat. I shook my head and pointed up the path. I didn't recognize the MPS officer, and he didn't indicate he knew who I was, or cared.

Boswell walked ahead of me for about fifteen minutes up a steep slope, slippery with pine needles. At a place where the trail widened, we passed two more MPS officers slouched against a tree. We didn't stop to chat. The path became steeper, and Boswell was starting to breathe hard when we came to a fast stream. We crossed on a line of boulders that barely served as a bridge. The far bank was more thickly wooded, and the path disappeared.

"Good and lost, what else could go wrong? So typical of this place, I have to laugh." Boswell was swearing under his breath, thinking I couldn't hear him. "A path leading nowhere, then dissolving into nothing, what a fucking country." He swatted a bug on the back of his neck. "Let's get out of here. I don't need to be mucking about in these hills. There's nothing for me to see."

"No, we're not lost. The path is around here somewhere." It had to be. Paths didn't just give out like that. Maybe in Scotland, but not in these hills. I took a few steps off to one side. "Here! You see?" I started up the narrow track and in a minute or so emerged into a clearing with a small, oddly shaped temple. Next to it was a ramshackle watchman's hut. An old man shuffled from around the back, a thin brown dog at his heels. The dog trembled and wagged its tail until the old man muttered something and the dog dropped to the ground. It was quiet all of a sudden. Not a sound. Even the deep voice of the water rushing over the rocks disappeared.

"Nice dog." I smiled and raised my hand to scratch the dog's head.

As soon as I did, the dog cowered and crawled behind the old man. "I'm not going to hit him, just give him a pat."

"Dog doesn't know that, now does it? People come by here, do all sorts of things to the dog. Never hurt nobody, young pup like this, but people don't care." The old man gave me a sly smile. "He likes the sound of money in the shrine box, though, makes him sit up and bark."

"I'll bet it does." I walked over and stuffed a few small bills into the slit in the box sitting on the raised wooden platform. The dog sat up and barked twice. "Must have good hearing; those bills don't make a lot of noise."

"Dogs can hear a lot more than most people. Good judges of character, too." Boswell emerged from the trees. The old man turned slowly in his direction. "Welcome, friend. The dog likes you."

Boswell whistled, and the dog walked over. "Pretty thin, but good, alert eyes," he said. "Might learn some commands, if you give him a chance. Not a lot of sheep around here, I take it. But any dog likes to work for his keep."

The old man cocked his head, unsure whether he was hearing Korean or not. Then he nodded. "Scraps mostly. Dog here eats what I eat." He pulled the waist of his trousers to show he didn't eat much. "No harm in being thin, for either of us. As for work"—he laughed—"the dog and I have an agreement. As little as possible, and then rarely."

"Good location for a shrine. You must be from around here." I wanted to move the conversation beyond dogs, which I had the feeling Boswell would happily spend the rest of the day discussing.

"Nope." Then a long silence from the old man. As we stood there, the sound of the stream returned, along with the drone of a bee moving in and out of the blossoms of a cherry tree that grew beside the shrine.

Boswell looked up at the sky. I nodded at the old man. "You're not from around here?"

"I am."

"Ah. Then, by 'nope' you mean a bad location for a shrine."

"Very bad. Not far enough from the water, not set right with its back to the mountain. Nothing very good about it. But here it sits. You'd think someone would have changed its alignment, falls down often enough so it would be easy to do. But no, every time, it's put back together just the way it was." The old man shook his head. "Last time it was rebuilt was maybe sixty or seventy years ago." After a moment, he shrugged and sighed. "That's how things get to be like they are."

"Yes," I said. The old man sounded like Yang. It made me uneasy. Something else was making me uneasy, too, though I couldn't figure out what. Boswell had moved over and was pretending to watch the bee, but I could tell he wanted to follow the conversation, if it ever got anywhere. "You pretty much see everyone who goes up this trail, I'd assume." Sometimes a new tack helps with these old fellows.

"Hard to miss them, unless you're blind," he said.

I looked at the man's eyes. "You're blind, aren't you?"

"It depends," he said, "on your definition."

"We're going up the trail." I started to point in the direction we were heading but it seemed foolish. "Did a patrol pass this way?"

"They did."

"You know where they went?"

"I do. It will take you five, maybe ten minutes to get there."

I nodded at Boswell, who fell in behind me. "We'll be back."

"Yes, you will, unless you plan to swim down. Only one path. I'll be here whenever you get tired of looking around. Right here," said the old man, "same as always."

4

The stream went around a sharp bend and formed a series of deep pools, backed up behind piles of rocks. It was hard to tell if they had fallen naturally from the hills above, or if a few hundred years ago someone had rolled them down. The pools were mostly protected from the water's flow. It was a quiet place; the shadow of the hills kept it out of the sun. A few small trees grew all the way down the bank to the water's edge.

The body had been pulled up onto the rocks. I wished it had been left alone, but there was no sense complaining at this point. The two-man patrol sat on the farthest pile of rocks, beyond the shade in the sunlight. They had their shoes off and were dangling their feet in the water. They stood up when they saw me. One of them straightened his belt, which told me he was new. The other one stared at Boswell, said something to his companion, and looked away. He wasn't so new; he'd probably sold his belt. If he'd had boots, he would have sold those, too.

I looked around the path for a moment, not expecting to find much. Boswell stood off to the side. "If you need me, Inspector, I'm here. But I don't want to get in your way."

"Let's go down and take a look, Superintendent. Maybe you'll see something that I miss."

The body had been in the water awhile, but it didn't look to me like it had been two days. Min must have misheard the report, or maybe the patrolmen had said they had been sleeping on the rocks for two days with their toes in the water. I knelt down. It was the Club Blue's owner; his features weren't damaged, though the flies were pretty thick. His head had been bruised on the side, but nothing you would have thought would kill him.

"He looks to me like he was plenty strong." Boswell stood a little way off with a handkerchief to his nose. "Big shoulders. He could have slipped and fallen into the stream, I suppose. Maybe he hit his head on the way down, knocked himself out and drowned."

"We'll see. If he drowned, they must have drugged him first."

Boswell dropped the handkerchief for a moment. "What makes you say that?" He took a breath, then gagged and put the handkerchief back in place. Looking at him, you wouldn't have guessed he was so delicate.

"He wasn't shot. The old man at the temple would have heard it. A shot in these hills would echo, even a pistol."

"They could have knifed him. Who can tell at this point from that soggy mess?"

"Maybe, it looks like there are plenty of wounds on the body. Look at his hands." He was missing two fingers on his left hand. And his left ear had been nearly torn off. Flies didn't do that, and there were no animals in these hills that would have chewed on a body. "Getting him down from here will be a chore. It would be good if someone could check it at the scene, but that won't happen. Anyway, the patrol already moved him."

"Who is he?"

"Not exactly sure. I met him at that club we were at yesterday."

"The one who kept shaking my hand? No, this is a different guy."

The patrolmen had put on their socks and shoes and were making their way over to where we were standing. I motioned to them to wait. "This is the previous manager. I didn't think he was involved in anything serious, but it looks like I was wrong."

"Your bank robbery?"

"What would make you say that, Superintendent?"

"I don't know, just a guess."

I thought a moment. "Could be you're right. Maybe somebody thought he was going to talk when he was supposed to stay quiet, or maybe they thought he was keeping something they thought was theirs. In those clothes, he didn't come up here for a picnic or a day of hiking in the hills. That soggy mess is his work clothes. I guess the crease in those trousers is gone for good."

Boswell looked away and gagged again. "Sorry, I don't do well with this sort of thing." He took a moment to regain his composure. "There, well, that's better. Just a body, after all. Sounds like you already knew a lot about him." He was still a little pale.

"This is my case, Superintendent." I walked over to the patrol. The new officer was uneasy; he kept his eyes averted.

"I thought we should leave the body where it was," the new man muttered, "but then we remembered the regulations said to preserve the evidence, so we figured we'd move it out of the water. I remembered the regulation." He looked at me for a moment but decided it wasn't going to get him anything.

"Well, by moving the body you ruined the evidence. Remember that next time. Just go back to the rock and stay out of the way. I'll call someone to come up from Pyongyang to take care of what's left. They'll want a statement from both of you. And it better be accurate to the last stone. I don't know how you're going to explain that your shoes were off when I arrived, but you'll think of something."

5

"Come, let's talk, my friend." I started to take the old man's hand, but he was already moving toward the step that ran along the front of his hut. He sat and patted the place beside him. Just from that, I knew he would tell me the truth.

"You're a security man, I can tell. But who is your friend over there?" He nodded at the tree, where Boswell was standing. "He talks funny. Nice man, I can tell, but who the hell taught him to speak Korean?"

"Foreigner." I paused. "From Scotland."

The old man nodded. "I know Scotland, I fought a company of Scots not far from here during the war." He lifted his face toward the sun. "That's when I lost my sight, in that battle. If you can call it a battle. It wasn't much, no big thing. Didn't turn no tide. Just a tiny shootout, me and them. They found me lying in a hole. My face was covered with blood and I couldn't see. I heard their voices. One of them jumped down and turned me over. I heard the safety click of a pistol up top the hole. But that one, he washed my face with a wet cloth, left me a biscuit, put it in my hand is what he did. Then they went away. The next night I ate the biscuit and crawled toward the sound of voices. I could hear Chinese, but I didn't want them to find me. They would have left me to die. But it was just a Chinese officer talking on the radio. This shrine was being used as a command post for a company of our boys, with a Chinese advisor attached. Our troops were nervous, they almost shot up the bushes when they heard me crawling toward them, but then I shouted who I was and they came for me. They said they didn't have any medicine or anything, but they gave me some food, and got me some water from the river. It was cold, tasted good, just like it does now. They told me to stay at the shrine. I've been here ever since. So I know Scotland, that's what brought me here, you might say."

Boswell had moved closer. He was pale and his eyes were closed. We listened to the river for a moment, and the wind in the trees. Then I stood up. "Don't let it bother you," I said to him. "The country's littered with these stories. Your countrymen came over, shot up the mountains, then went home to your peaceful valleys and trout streams. We were left here." I looked around the hills that surrounded the spot.

The old man got to his feet and faced Boswell. "Never mind," he said in a strong, clear voice and then again, but softer this time, "Never mind."

"I need to ask you a question or two. Alright?" He knew a lot, and he was only going to tell me a little. That's how he survived out here. I'd take what he gave me. People think the truth is bulky, like a big package. More often, it comes in small drops, like rain from the eaves. You can listen to it all night long, but in the morning when you go outside, there might not be anything there.

"Go on." The old man turned his face to me. "You want to know about the body in the river."

"I do. What do you know about it?"

"Nothing. The dog was awfully upset. She howled a little. It was two nights ago, maybe more." He could have lost track of time, but I didn't think so. Maybe that's why the report the barefoot patrol had phoned in mentioned "two days," because they heard the same story from the old man. "She took me over to that group of rocks upstream, slippery at night with the mist, so we took our time. I nearly stumbled over the body, but I heard the flies and stopped. The dog froze, she doesn't like dead things. I think death confuses her." He scratched the dog behind the ears. "A group of strangers walked by here earlier that day. Not very friendly."

How could he stumble on the body if it was floating in one of those pools? I looked over at Boswell; he was wondering the same thing.

"Besides their not being friendly," I said, "what did you notice?" I'd have to come back, without Boswell, to question the old man again.

"Talked sort of strange, but they were Korean, not like your friend here." He turned toward Boswell. "No offense." He turned back to me. "One of them asked if the path went very far upstream, and how deep the water was."

"How many of them were there?"

"Three went up. One of them walked funny, like he was dragging his leg. He was taking short breaths, sort of painful. Only two of them were talking. They were saying something about snakes. I pretended not to notice."

"How many came back?"

"Guess."

6

We walked down the path in silence; the car with the security men was gone but there was a note on my windshield. I crumpled it up and threw it away. That bastard didn't even acknowledge my presence, and he's leaving me notes?

Boswell looked at me over the top of the car before he got in. "Whew." He shook his head. "Warn me next time, would you?"

"You mean the war story? That was nothing," I said. "You should see the ones without legs."

He pointed at the wad of paper I'd thrown on the ground. "Aren't you going to read that note?"

"Why bother? It's from that guy who was standing in the road. He didn't look very busy. What do you think he was doing?"

"Keeping an eye on us?"

It occurred to me that Boswell might have hit on something. Han might just have been keeping track of where the two of us were. Well, if SSD—or whoever he worked for—had enough manpower to toss around like that, let them choke on it.

"Me, most probably," I said. "I think I've seen him around. He's from a different section altogether. The paperwork will never get to our office. He won't file it, anyway. Too much trouble."

"What about those two uniformed guys up the path?"

I shrugged. "They were probably sent to watch the one in the road."

"You're kidding."

I grinned. "Yeah. Get in. Let's not stand here all the dooh-da day."

Boswell looked surprised. "Where the hell did you learn that, Inspector? Did you know it's from an old American song?"

"I know where it's from. I have a degree from the University of Karaoke. You ever heard 'Red River Valley'? Very sad song, some people tear up, especially when they've had a lot to drink. I can sing it on the way back."

The superintendent shook his head. "Perhaps another time, Inspector. I'm not in the mood for a sad tune right now."

7

I took another route, not too much out of the way, but I didn't want to go by the steam shovel again. Partway back into the city, we passed through a village. It was covered with coal dust from a factory set behind the fields, and even in the bright sunshine the houses and the inhabitants carried a grimness that made me wish Boswell had stayed in his hotel room. His eyes were closed, and I thought he might be asleep, but then he opened them and said, "Looks like an old town I used to patrol at home. Not even the rain could make it clean."

"What did your embassy say?" I asked casually.

"About what?" He turned to look out the window.

"About the threat. You've told them already, so they could send an alert back, I assume."

"No, Inspector, I told no one, least of all the embassy. I don't want anyone to know, not yet." He rolled down the window and put his hand on top of the car. "I'm the person on the scene. That's how it's done."

"Sure," I said. "Makes sense." It didn't make sense. Unless he had his own communication system, how was he going to get the information back to his capital? Carrier pigeon? The embassy was the only place he had for secure communications, unless he had something in his luggage that was exceptionally well concealed. News like this couldn't go back over an open phone line. I thought about it. Maybe his security service didn't trust the embassy people. No reason it should; I'd never heard of a security service anywhere that didn't consider its foreign ministry personnel as anything but a running wound.

As the road turned north, we drove toward a clump of forsythia bushes, a brilliant explosion of yellow, next to a group of three or four plum trees in blossom. "Now that," Boswell said, "is what I like to see in the spring, don't you, Inspector? Some signs of life. Very thoughtful how they plant these things, to give some color this time of year. Wait, it looks like a monument just up that hill. Let's see what it is. Maybe I can take a picture."

"I know what it is. You don't need a picture of that."

"It's a park or something."

"No, it's a marker. It commemorates a visit."

"Historical?"

"I suppose, if you care to count the past fifty years as history." I sped up to get past so he wouldn't ask to stop.

"Well, it's nice anyway, the trees and all."

I pressed down harder on the accelerator. The car jumped.

"What's the matter?" Boswell reached for the dashboard to steady himself. "You don't like a bit of color in April for these poor folk?"

"I do. I just don't think it should be all banged together this way. People should appreciate nature for itself." I stared straight ahead. "Not connect it with . . . other things."

Boswell looked at me, then turned back to concentrate on the scenery. Finally, he shook his head. "Did you say something?" he said quietly. "I didn't hear a word."

"No, nothing." My eyes never left the road. "Must have been the wind."

Chapter Two

My head was heavy, but I lifted it anyway. The darkness of the room made me instantly alert. Somewhere, just beyond where I could see, the man in the brown suit was watching.

"Welcome back, Inspector. I saw a movie once in the West; the actress said, 'We've got to stop meeting like this,' and everyone in the theater laughed. I didn't find it funny then, but I think I see the point." He took one of his measured steps forward and clicked on the lamp. The tips of his shoes shone. "In all the world, you and I must meet to talk again. Here. I find that depressing, actually." He jangled some coins in his pocket. "Let's begin."

"What if you and I have nothing to say to each other?"

The club nuzzled against my neck, pressing my head to the side.

"Last time was only a warning, Inspector. This time you might be crippled."

I tried a more positive tack. "You said you had decided I was the wrong man."

"That was then."

"Does my ministry know I'm here?"

"Why should it matter?"

"So, they don't know."

"No, actually, we don't ring up employers, although I know of a few instances where next of kin were notified. Or lovers."

"Why am I here?"

"Good, straight to the point. I was getting there myself. What is this with you and the British? First in Prague, now here, in your own capital?"

"I already told you about Prague. Check the files; that's why people keep them, isn't it? The Scotsman was dropped in my lap by the Ministry. I never saw him before, I had nothing to do with his showing up, and I'll be happier than anyone when he leaves."

"Perhaps, Inspector. That isn't what this file says, however." A paper appeared out of the gloom, then disappeared again.

"It could be wrong; some files are less reliable than others. I should know."

"We'll see." He paused, and I heard pages being ruffled. I would have thought that he had the file marked exactly where he wanted the questioning to go, but he must have lost his place. "Let's spend a moment on your professional life." Another page or two turned; they sounded like dry leaves.

I thought of Yang and licked my lips. "How about another glass of water?" I needed a moment to lock all the doors to my memory.

"No, no water, Inspector, until we finish. Then you can have as much as you want." I didn't like the way he said that. There was a low laugh from behind me. I didn't like that, either.

"Alright, what do you want to know?"

"The file says you come from a troubled office. Your former chief inspector was a good friend of yours. He died under suspicious circumstances, is that right?"

"You know exactly how he died, but I wasn't there, so I can't add anything."

"He was shot by Military Security. Not a deserving end for a loyal Ministry of People's Security official, would you say?"

"I told you, I wasn't there." I didn't want to talk about Pak.

"It must have made you bitter. Thoughts of revenge ever cross your mind?"

"You want me to say yes? Will that make it easier?"

The club tapped on the floor a couple of times behind me, but otherwise it was quiet.

Finally, the man in brown crumpled a piece of paper and threw it between us. "We'll leave Pak alone for a moment, Inspector. Let's start with a clean sheet. Your new chief inspector, Min. Just between us, would you say he is competent at what he does?"

"I don't rate his competence. He rates mine. We get along pretty well; he gives orders, I follow them."

"Much of the time I suppose you do, though some might disagree. But I'm not really interested in the particulars of your ministry's operations. I'm interested in people. Do people interest you, Inspector?"

Here we go, I thought. I knew what was coming next.

"Your colleague, Yang. He is an interesting case, I'd say. The sort of person who attracts the attention of anyone concerned about security. The poor man was practically paralyzed with grief when he lost his family. Yet he was kept on in the capital. His transfer orders out to the countryside were revised; by whom and for what reason was a mystery. Who do you think did that?"

"I was as surprised as everyone else. But he's getting better." I remembered what I had told Min. "It just takes a little time, that's all." That was the extent of my wiggle; if the subject of the Blue Paper came up, I had no idea what I was going to say.

"You often entertain women in your apartment?"

"Entertain who?" Having the subject changed so abruptly was a surprise. I thought for sure he would want to dig some more about Yang. "No. The old lady who guards the building would find out, and then I'd be in trouble. Everyone would talk."

"Even foreign women?"

"None, of no description. Who is peddling this stuff?"

"Not even from Kazakhstan?"

I sat back in the chair and closed my eyes. "This is a waste of time, you realize that."

The club hit my right arm, just below the shoulder. It made my fingers ache, then my wrist, then the pain shot up the back of my head. I took a breath and exhaled slowly.

The man in the brown suit moved forward into the light so I could almost see his face. His mouth was contorted. "Damn you, Inspector, just answer my questions, just do that." He worked to gain his composure, shook his head, then stepped back into the darkness.

"What did you discover up at the shrine?" His voice had returned to normal, but there was an edge to it that hadn't been there before. He was interested in the shrine.

"Not much. You spend your days following me around?"

The club tapped the floor, but the man in the brown suit held up his hand. "How old is that shrine?"

"How should I know?"

"Let me put it another way. When was it last reconstructed?"

"Not long ago." That was what had been bothering me about the place. It was too new.

"When?"

"Recently."

"What makes you think so?"

"The lumber."

"Go on."

"The boards were warped, they weren't dried long enough, and they weren't milled. The Japanese had mills, older lumber came from better trees, and there was time to season it."

"Conclusion."

"I'm going to say this carefully, because I haven't had a chance to think about it. Alright with you?"

"Go ahead."

"There aren't a lot of mills around these days, for whatever reason. And most lumber isn't seasoned; the logs are cut up and the wood is used before anyone has a chance to give it a look."

"Conclusion."

"Could have been a few years ago, but I'd say more recently."

There was a silence. The man in the brown suit shifted his feet, a sign that the questioning was going to take a new direction.

"What do you know about Kazakhstan, Inspector?"

"Nothing. No, really, nothing. I hadn't even thought about it until a few weeks ago. Of course, you mentioned those trees."

"Did you know that Trotsky was exiled there?"

"Is that a fact?"

I didn't even feel the club, not then. Maybe I heard the swish it made, but probably not. That might just be part of a broken memory. I couldn't tell. I don't remember any more questions. Or how I got back to my own room.

2

Min was there when I woke up. His round face was creased with worry, and I saw a twitch at the corner of his mouth. He stared at me with dull eyes.

"Did you miss me?" I started to sit up, but Min pushed me back down. I didn't have the strength to resist. I didn't want to sit up anyway.

"No, certainly not. I hadn't realized you were gone for another two days, Inspector." There was only a feeble irony in Min's voice. "Were you gone that long? I just figured, what the hell, O has probably gone on a vacation and neglected to mention it. So I came over to your place, and you were here, not in very good shape, actually. Did you know that you moan in a rich baritone, Inspector? You should take up singing, once your jaw heals, I mean." Min's twitch had moved from the corner of his mouth up to his cheek. He looked like he was in a gray pain. "What have you gotten into? What have we gotten into? Don't answer; don't say anything, just rest. Do me a favor, rest. I'm going out to find you something to eat. Don't go anywhere. Tell me you won't get up. No, on second thought, don't say anything. Just nod. You won't get up, am I right?"

I nodded, and the motion moved something in my head against something else, so I didn't want to go anywhere or say anything. Maybe some water would be good, a drink of water. But there was none. When Min had closed the door behind him, I blinked against the darkness and fell through a loose board in my consciousness.

3

Boswell was frowning when I woke up. To hell with him, I thought. What does he have to frown about?

"Well, at least you're alive."

I couldn't tell if this was supposed to be an expression of sympathy. But he stopped frowning after he said it.

"How long have you been here?"

"A day." He started to put out a cigarette. "You want a puff?" I shook my head, nothing vigorous. "Less, it just seems like a day. Min was hanging around, biting his nails, but he said he had to check something. He asked me to stay. You want something to eat?"

"Even if I did, there isn't anything."

There was the rustle of paper. "Don't be so sure of everything, Inspector. I have here rice, soup, no longer piping hot, alas, and some vegetables. Roots maybe. I can't tell."

"Soup. Just a sip. Help me sit up."

Boswell did as he was asked for once. "Jesus, Inspector, you looked like death when I got here. Min was in shock, sitting here looking at you. So was the restaurant lady."

"What restaurant lady?"

"Where do you think the soup came from? I didn't cook it myself. There's no stove, no hot plate, nothing in here. You live like a caveman."

"It's my home, Boswell, don't be so critical. What is it, " 'Home is the hunter, home from the hill . . .' "

"'And the sailor home from the sea.'" Boswell sat back and laughed. "Sweet Sisters of the Glen, Inspector, you are something. Finish your soup before it gets cold."

"It is cold. Who let Miss Pyon in here? Keep her away, or she'll get herself in trouble."

"Pyon? Is that the restaurant lady? I don't think you have to worry about her, Inspector. She seems to know her way around."

I put the soup aside. "Any other visitors?"

"Now who could you be thinking of?"

My head hurt like hell. It made no sense fencing with him, I didn't have the strength. The only thing left was to ask the question straight out. "What do you know about Miss Chon?"

There was a soft knock, and a piece of paper appeared under the door. Boswell sprang up and wrenched open the door, but the hallway was empty. He went out and walked from one end to the other; I heard him cursing under his breath about the lack of light. "Gone, never here, what a place!" He reached down and scooped up the paper. "Here, it's in Korean."

"You speak the language, I believe."

"I do. That I do. But I don't read it. Speaking isn't so difficult, but reading takes effort. Especially if you have to learn a whole new alphabet. I never had time to memorize strange alphabets. What the hell difference does it make? The note's for you, anyway."

"Maybe, maybe not. Everyone knows you're here, Superintendent. From the moment you got out of the car, everyone knew. They listened to you climb the stairs. Maybe it's a love note; maybe some heartsick lass wants to be swept away to some loch or another, to sit over the fire and boil your oatmeal while you're out in the damp fog."

"Very amusing, Inspector. I like that in a man who has just had the piss beaten out of him by his own authorities." He dropped the paper on my chest. "Read it and then try standing up. I'll be downstairs, if I can find the stairs in the gloom."

The note was typed. It said, "Native to Korea is one venomous snake, whose bite is lethal but which is not aggressive. The tigers left long ago. New bears have been seen." Snakes. I had to get back to the temple to see the old man.

4

Across the table, she lit another cigarette, puffed nervously, put it down, then picked it up again, just held it. It quivered as her fingers shook for an instant, then was still. "I have a child. A son."

Just like that. It was a plea for forgiveness. She looked at me as if she had made a horrible admission, as if she had broken a favorite vase of mine. I never knew a more painful silence. It didn't last more than a second, but I thought it had swallowed me up and left me in some other place on the other side of the world, so I didn't know who she was or what language she was speaking. It wasn't the fact that shook me, not that she had a child, but the anguish it caused her to say the thing out loud. I couldn't see what there was to forgive.

We were sitting in her apartment. It made mine look like a closet. She had said she needed to talk to me, only this time I could tell she meant it. That was good, because I needed to talk to her. I was still wobbly from my last meeting with the man in the brown suit, but I couldn't lie in bed forever. She came over to my apartment house to pick me up just past noon. A group from the apartment was sitting on the ground near the bushes, arguing about whose fault it was that the garden plot hadn't been weeded. They pretended to ignore me when I passed them, but as I climbed into her car, a lot of necks were craning. She drove fast, with a nervous foot on the gas and not much attention to lanes. I closed my eyes and relaxed; after what I'd been through, there wasn't any sense in worrying about my fate. When we got to her apartment, she pulled around the back. A guard checked her license plate, flicked his eyes at me, then waved her into a space reserved for six or seven cars. There was another guard at the door, but unlike the old lady in my apartment house, he didn't say anything as we passed by.

The apartment was on the tenth floor. The elevator worked, which I was glad of because I didn't want to climb stairs. There were lights in the hallway, and the gray-white paint on the walls was only just beginning to peel from the moisture. She had a few framed photographs on a low table in the main room; they looked like they might be family. One had her posed in front of a mountain that came down to a rough and foggy beach. She wasn't smiling in the picture.

"I can see it in your eyes, Inspector. You've already begun to look at me differently. You are one of those who can't forget anything, aren't you? Forgetting is a coin you can spend anytime you want, but you are a miser. You have no memories." She wasn't speaking to me now, not exactly, but off into the distance at someone else I couldn't see. "An inability to forget is not memory. It's a form of cowardice. Like pulling yourself back from sleep at the last moment. You remember too much, you forget too little. You know why? Because you are afraid if you forget often enough, it will become an addiction."

I knew she wasn't expecting me to say anything, not yet. My silence seemed to bring her back from wherever she had been. Her voice was calmer. "Is there something here"—she gestured not around the room but as if we were on a hill and she was pointing out the city and the fields and the solitude beyond—"something here you would choose to remember? Better forget it, or is there nothing else for you to hold?"

She was wrong. I had forgotten something; why had I come, what did I want to ask her? It was as if she had taken an eraser to my memory. I couldn't remember anything except her face, and how close it was to mine. "That's fine," I said finally, but hearing the words I knew they were wrong, wrong words, wrong voice. I sat back. "What I mean is, it's a fine thing, bringing children into the world." I paused. What was that supposed to mean?

"He's with my relatives in our village in Kazakhstan." The cast of her features became impassive, like ancient rock, but her eyes were filled with fury. "No, he isn't part Scottish. He's all Kazakh." Her voice trailed off. She turned away, so I took a breath, nothing too deep because I was afraid it would sound like a sigh.

"A son is a good thing." Not what I meant to say, not at all what I meant. My voice sounded strange in my ears. "All children, they're good." That sounded worse. She turned back and looked at me with such ferocity that I began to squint.

"Shut up! You bastard, can't you hear me? I told you I have a son, Kazakh, he's fifteen, do you know what that means?"

I started running through the list of possibilities in my head. That put her at least at thirty, maybe a little younger, but I was doubtful. It meant she'd been with a Kazakh man when she was just a girl. I sighed without thinking. Maybe an arranged marriage. I could feel the pulse pounding in my temples.

"You have nothing to say? You don't care? You despise me?" At this rate, the volcano inside her would explode just as the headache broke across the top of my skull. I looked at her dumbly, more dumbly than I intended.

I shook myself into speech. "No, why should I despise you? You have a child. I'm glad of it." I brightened at the sound of that thought. "Yes, I am, I'm glad of it. It makes you, I don't know"—I held up my hands in hopes that the gesture would release me, but it only made me look like I was holding a watermelon—"it makes you fuller, more complete, even more beautiful." Was that what I meant to say? It was, I think it was, or close to it. But it wasn't why I had come over, or was it? I couldn't remember. Such a horrible moment, when everything hung in the balance, maybe this was like being in front of a firing squad. I'd seen a prisoner shot, once. He had held his breath, waiting. I decided to breathe, chanced another breath, a small one. Unless she was listening closely, she wouldn't know it was a sigh. She put her head down on the table and began to sob. "Yes," I said, not knowing what to do, "a son is good, and I know he must be a fine boy." This was an impossible conversation. I had never had a conversation like this, sat so close to a beautiful woman, a woman who was sobbing, her body convulsed with sobs, and I didn't understand why, I couldn't have told anyone why. It escaped me utterly, what I was to do. I felt diminished, unequal, drowning. It was a relief when the sobbing stopped, when she lifted her head and looked at me, straight into my eyes, and I shivered at knowing, in that instant, who I was.

5

The next day, as soon as my head cleared, I went into the office. If I stayed in my place, I'd only think about Miss Chon, and I didn't want to do that. If she knocked on my door again, this time I might not ask her to leave. And I still didn't have any chairs. Even worse, letting another day go by without any progress in figuring out a rational way to arrange the pieces of this case simply increased the chances of another session with the ash club. Case? What case? I didn't even know what this was about anymore. Or maybe I did. Maybe the man in the brown suit was trying to motivate me to find out what he couldn't discover on his own. If so, it was effective technique, up to a point. Other than avoiding Miss Chon, there was nothing else on my mind except not seeing him again, either. I needed to solve the problem, but I couldn't do that unless I defined it first.

"This is a simple bookshelf problem," I said to Boswell.

"Textbook case, you mean." Boswell's eyes were closed. He was resting his head against the wall, the far wall where the bookshelf belonged.

"No, Superintendent, I mean bookshelf. As in, building a shelf to hold books. A box, basically, four ninety-degree angles. A plain board in the middle, maybe two, depending on your sense of symmetry and the number of books you own."

Boswell opened his eyes. "We are not amused, as royalty used to say. What is the point, exactly?"

"Every problem is reducible to essential elements. Pull off the finials, the decoration, the brass fittings. There has to be a basic structure, something that holds the problem upright, keeps it unified."

"And this structure, this problem we are dealing with, this is a bookshelf?"

"Apparently. It seems to have four ninety-degree angles."

"Such as."

"The two Germans did not enter the country legally. Neither did the robbers from Kazakhstan. Ninety degrees. Clear and crisp."

"What does it mean?"

"It doesn't mean anything, necessarily. I'm just describing what is; in carpentry, you have to start with reality. Ninety degrees is just an angle, after all."

"Well, what if the Germans had come in legally, but not the Kazakhs?" An interesting question. The answer might not be important, but the question was.

"Forty-five degrees," I said.

"You can't build a bookshelf with that angle?"

"No. Not even Scandinavians do that."

"Go on, Inspector."

"The Germans have both been associated with, or at least in close proximity to, banks that were robbed in the past in various countries. The man hit by the bus, one of the robbers, was Kazakh."

"How do you know?"

"I know."

"That's ninety degrees?"

"It is."

"Pretty thin gruel."

"You're thinking oatmeal, Superintendent. Don't."

"What if you're wrong, Inspector?"

"It wouldn't be the first time. It's no different with a bookshelf. If the angles aren't right, you'll know it soon enough. No use trying to force anything. It won't work. You can't force boards together any more than you can hammer facts into fitting."

"But you shave boards, don't you?"

"No, you plane them. But only to get at the truth. You can't plane a board to do something it won't. If you have a twisted board, that's all there is. It's twisted."

"I suppose."

"You're a skeptic, that's good. But in the end, you still need somewhere to put your books. I'm going to build you a shelf."

"Life isn't like carpentry, Inspector."

"Says you. Look, German radicals, a bank robbery, and a threat to a foreign dignitary."

"Coincidence."

"Maybe somewhere else on the planet. Not here. Here, it's a ninety-degree coincidence."

"What's left?"

"I don't know."

"You only have three corners."

"That's right."

"So you don't have anything, really. The thing wouldn't stand by itself."

"Correct."

"You need another angle."

"Ninety degrees more, Superintendent, and we're in business. Without that, we have a pile of lumber."

"What do you think you're missing?" He had been uninterested in the first part of the conversation, but I could tell he was suddenly paying attention.

"You are a foreigner, Superintendent, no offense. You work for a foreign service, in a country hostile to mine. Your government is allied with a government that is seeking the downfall of my own."

Boswell said nothing. His fingers tapped on his knee. Then he pointed at me. "Politics. Don't mix politics with police work, Inspector."

I smiled. "Strange thing to say." I turned to the window. "Pretty day. It's the first of May, wonderful month to be alive, don't you think?"

"Already the first of May? Time slips by in your country, doesn't it, Inspector." He was on the verge of saying more but pulled back.

"Have I showed you the trees along the riverside, Superintendent?"

Boswell stood up and stretched his arms over his head. "Do those trees have anything to do with bookshelves?"

"Unlikely, Superintendent, they're mulberries."

"So?"

"No good for shelves. A wood with too much of a mind of its own."

"I'm surprised such trees grow here." He paused and waited half a beat. "I mean, cold weather and all."

Neither of us spoke on the walk to the park. It was hard to ignore the SSD checkpoints along the way. A woman with a black bag over her shoulder loitered on the corner at the end of the block. She moved away as we passed, walking in the other direction. A car drove up and parked across the street when we stood for a moment in the shade. Two old men waited, smoking cigarettes under a tree fifteen meters away, not talking to each other. These were just static posts. It would take a few minutes for the mobile team to arrive. Before that happened, I needed to get things clear with Boswell. We sat on a bench facing the river. The sun was hot and the breeze was cool; the sky was brilliantly clear in all directions except for two small clouds drifting side by side. In a few weeks, on this sort of day all the new leaves would dance gently, in complete silence, still too young to give off the rustling that sits on the edge of summer, or that dry chorus six months away that sings of winter and death. I remembered the man in the brown suit asking me about Prague and felt my shoulder ache.

"You and the Irishman work together, do you?" I asked.

Boswell turned to me with a quizzical look. "Here? Now? You ready?"

"Ready?" I couldn't arrest him; my meeting in Prague would be confirmed. I couldn't smash his face or roar at him or break his thumbs. "No, I'm not interested in taking that road. I told Molloy I'm not working for your damned queen, and I'm not." My shoulder flared again. "I don't like you people setting me up. You'll tell Molloy that, won't you? Tell him my shoulder is not good anymore, and it's his fault. Is that why they sent you, to see if I'm ready to bolt? Or is there something more? Why are you here, Boswell? And don't tell me it's on a security detail for your visitor. You don't know the first thing about security." I glanced around. The mobile team was taking its time moving into place. Boswell shifted uncomfortably. "Just listen," I said.

He looked down at the grass. "If I can hear you, so can others out here."

"No, not yet. Another few minutes, maybe." I reached into my pocket and pulled out the small piece of persimmon I had been carrying around. "See this wood? It's very complicated. Difficult to understand. You have to look at it for a while; even then you might not be able to figure out what it's trying to say. That's why furniture made out of persimmon can go wrong so easily."

"Now you've lost me, Inspector."

"Whatever this is, this German-Kazakh-British connection, it isn't what it seems. It's internal. I'm convinced of it. Someone on the inside has set it up. The body of the bank robber disappeared from the morgue, and they have orders not to talk."

"Could be coincidence."

"Again, you opt for coincidence. Is that a Scottish trait? Things just happen? Not here, Superintendent. Nothing just happens here. Not even close. The man in the restaurant, the dead one, his friend was sprung by people with influence. Then he falls over with a knife in his back. Not coincidence; a knife in the back is not a coincidence, especially when it happens outside Club Blue." Boswell frowned. I continued. "The owner of Club Blue was sleeping with Miss Chon." Boswell had stopped frowning; the blood had drained from his face. "Not important," I said. "Anyway, he drowned, but a big man like him wouldn't drown in a shallow pool of water without some help and, apparently, several days of torture. Just to add the final touch, I was hauled into a room with a man who is trying to find out something from me I don't know. No coincidence. For the rest of my life, if it threatens rain, my left shoulder stops working. What do we call that?"

Boswell said nothing. I didn't think he was paying attention anymore; his thoughts were somewhere off in the distance. Finally, he shook his head. "Rotten luck. Rotten all around." He stood up and looked both ways down the path. "This man who was trying to find out something from you, do you know who he was?"

"What do you care? He won't touch a foreigner, don't worry."

Boswell sat down again. "Are we getting any closer to your final ninety degrees?"

"A lot," I said. "Someone on the inside set up the robbery. They used outsiders. Why? Do they want the foreign currency so badly? Not a chance. They could get it without stocking masks. All they have to do is to dip their hands into the cash bag. Easy to do. No, this has nothing to do with a bundle of small euro notes." Something occurred to me, out of nowhere. "Funny, the person spreading the stories about the bank robbery was an Englishman."

"So?"

"Next, someone wants to stage the assassination of a visiting dignitary. *Who* isn't the issue, I suppose, it's *where*. They want it here."

"Why?"

"A pretense. An excuse. Doesn't matter if they kill him or not. Just the event, just a whiff of the event is enough."

Boswell took an uneasy look around the horizon. "For what?"

"A coup, Superintendent." This time the word didn't just slip out. I had thought about it ahead of time, and that's the word I wanted. "If there is such loss of control that a foreign visitor is threatened, that's enough to galvanize support for a move by those who want to yank back hard on the reins, stop this foolishness with ideas about economic loosening. Moral laxness, that's what they'll say."

"Can they do it?" He tried as hard as he could to make it an idle question. He did everything but yawn. It was almost funny. With that one question, it was obvious he had never done this before.

"Reassert control?" I waited half a beat. He half turned to me, then realized how anxious that seemed so turned away again and sat back. "Maybe. Probably. But there are winners and losers in that sort of crackdown. Unhappiness, grudges, egos."

"So, who is on our side? Who helps us protect my man? You may not like my security technique, but he is my man."

I saw the mobile team turn the corner and amble down the path toward us. A man and a woman. Terrible choice, typical of SSD. No one in his right mind would think this couple had anything in common. Couples who belong together walk in a kind of a rhyme, even if they're mad at each other. There was nothing between these two; they probably didn't even share the same office building. Probably only met five minutes ago. Hopeless, SSD was hopeless. No wonder the British sent such an amateur; they didn't think we were much of a target. I'd mention something to Min, if I ever saw him again.

I turned back to Boswell. "Those trees"—I pointed at a line of gingko trees along the path—"they were planted soon after the war. Not many trees were left. What the bombs didn't blast apart was used for fuel. Someone decided to plant replacements. They've grown to full height now. They make a kind of statement. Very calm place, right here, wouldn't you say?"

Boswell stood up and walked a few steps. "I don't know what I'd say, Inspector, not here, not now." The woman on the mobile team moved her head slightly when he passed. Her companion looked up at the treetops and tried to adjust the microphone wire that was under his coat.

6

Boswell didn't appear back at the office, so I sat at my desk and sketched a bookcase with three shelves. I put a door on it. I put on brass fittings. It didn't matter what I did. The thought was stuck in my mind, and it wouldn't shake loose. Boswell should have canceled the visit; as soon as I gave him my crazy theory, he should have demanded to be driven to the British embassy to have the whole thing shut down. He didn't do that. Yesterday, he'd been adamant that he was going to call off the trip. Today, he didn't even mention it. But

why would he want it to happen? I must be wrong about the assassination attempt. Nothing fit. Or everything did. In that case, I'd cancel the visit myself. I'd just call the Ministry and say the bank robbery
had raised enough questions to make it a bad time for us to entertain
a foreign guest. If there were complaints, I'd say the visit would inter-
fere with the investigation. I'd call the Ministry directly; I wouldn't
even tell Min.

There was a knock on the door. It was Min.

"We have to talk."

"Shall we go to your office?"

"No, here."

I stood up. Min gestured. "Sit, Inspector."

"Something I did wrong?"

"What did you discover about the site where the Club Blue manager was found?"

"Funny place. Whoever did it must have scouted it beforehand."

"The club manager was a former special service officer. I just found
out."

"What? Well, that explains the shoulders." It explained the long
gap between when he disappeared and when he showed up dead.
They had to take their time squeezing as much information out of
him as they could and, when they thought they had it all, go back and
squeeze some more, every drop. Make him reveal who was under surveillance, who had been turned around, which plans had been com-
promised.

"He was called back and put on assignment."

"Oh." Threads began tightening. Even before we had been given
the robbery case, someone had been on the inside.

"Something happened to his cover. It cracked."

"He had me fooled." Me, but not everyone.

"You really didn't know?"

"No one tells me anything; sometimes I think it's better that way."

"Well, like I said, I just found out. They were thinking you might
have done something to finger him."

"Tell them to go somewhere else, will you? My shoulder won't ever be the same."

"What do you know about Boswell?"

"Meaning what?"

"A question, Inspector, nothing more. Question-answer, a good sequence, wouldn't you agree? Otherwise, a conversation would have no end." He sounded like the man in the brown suit. My hip flared up. I gaped in pain and grabbed the desk. I should stop complaining just about my shoulder.

"You alright?"

"Fine," I said. "Boswell says he is here to check security for a British dignitary. He has an inordinate interest in shadows."

"You believe him?"

I was silent.

"I take it you don't believe him."

"What has prompted this, Min? If it's a big secret, don't tell me. Just let me drift in the normal fog of ignorance that covers my days."

"I realize, Inspector, to you it sometimes seems that I am not paying attention. I know you don't think I measure up to all of your expectations. And perhaps sometimes I don't. Other things crowd in on me. My mind becomes occupied, overoccupied you might say. But this case, this robbery, has captured my attention as nothing else has for a long time. You don't think it's just a robbery. I agree. I think about it day and night. Nothing like it has troubled me to this extent. It is taking us someplace very bad; I feel it, and you do, too."

"You think the robbery and the appearance of a tall, broad Scotsman is not a coincidence. Well, neither do I. I think he's here for something else. If I had to guess, I'd guess he's not here to cooperate. I'd say he's up to no good. Worse than no good."

"Thank you, Inspector, for that." Min reached down and unplugged my phone from the wall. "A Ministry team was here last night to sweep the building. I'm led to believe that all is well, but I'm also reliably informed that they left these in place." He twirled the phone line in the air and then let it drop to the floor.

I looked at the wire for a moment. "I'm going to recommend that the visit by the British VIP not take place. As soon as we're done, I'm going over to the Ministry and personally putting in the recommendation."

"Too late. Too late. Too ever fucking late, Inspector."

"Why?"

"He's already here. Special aircraft. Arrived yesterday evening."

"That can't be. Why would they allow him in early?"

"How should I know? Do I look like an airline reservation clerk? He's here. Though exactly where he is right now I couldn't say." He held up his hand. "No, I'm not keeping it from you, Inspector. No one has told me. I'm in charge of security for this delegation, but I have no idea where the visitor is at the moment. And if something happens to him in the meantime, you know who gets blamed, don't you?"

I jumped out of my chair. "Where's Boswell?"

"He's your responsibility, not mine. You're supposed to be babysitting."

"Where are the Germans?"

"Probably at their hotel."

"They're supposed to be on the east coast. It was arranged."

"Countermanded. Little Li complained all morning long that he thought he was finally going to get a vacation, trailing after them."

"This is a disaster. It's a setup. Boswell and those Germans are in this together, but they're not leading the parade. We're being led to slaughter, Min. But by whom? Who is going to cut our throats?"

"Let me tell you what I think, Inspector. I think that I am being carried in the jaws of death. Lightly, gently, like a lioness carries her cub. But she will not drop me this time."

"Lovely imagery."

"Coming from you, Inspector, that could be funny. We both know what is going on. From the moment they assigned us that bank robbery, something wasn't right."

"That's what I said weeks ago."

"Then you disappeared."

"Twice."

"Twice." Min spoke the word carefully, as if he were stepping over a hole in time. He pulled on his ear and looked at nothing. "Fate, I suppose. The whole road, leading to this."

"Well, you may be ready to bow your head and accept what comes. I am not, not yet, anyway. We didn't do anything wrong, and we're not going to be anyone's excuse. That's for sure."

"Better to go limp, Inspector. It might not hurt as much when the blow comes."

"Don't talk to me about blows, I know all about blows. Want to see my bruises?"

"Some other time."

"Give me the keys to your car. I'm going up to that old man's hut again. There's something there. Why would they set so many dogs to watch my behind if someone wasn't worried I'd find something?"

"You just figured that out?" Min tossed me the keys. "There's enough gas in the tank of the duty car for you to go and get back. If the gauge is to be trusted. Are you going to take the Scots bear?"

"You want me to?"

Min smiled, so that I knew fate had slipped a tiny bit in his calculations.

"Okay, then." I fished in my pockets for some wood and came up with a piece of walnut. I held it up with what must have been a look of surprise on my face.

"Something wrong, Inspector?"

"This is walnut."

"If you say so."

"I don't know why I'm even carrying it around. There's a certain smugness to walnut that you can feel."

"I hadn't realized."

"My grandfather used to look at a piece of walnut and say, 'Ugly.' He claimed walnut needed discipline. Too many people say, 'Oh, how beautiful,' every time they see walnut burl, and they ended up spoiling the wood, that's what he thought." It was clear Min didn't know what to say, so I put the wood in my pocket and stepped out the door. "If Boswell calls looking for me"—I turned back to Min—"you heard me say I was going toward Sinuiju to collect on a bet."

"I did hear you say that." The phone rang. Min let it ring twice, then waved for me to get going. As I went down the stairs, I heard him say in convincing tones, "Superintendent, I don't put bells on my people. How should I know where he is at this moment?"

Chapter Three

The first thing that registered was how quiet it was. I walked around the back of the hut with a bad feeling coming over me. The old man was sitting in the dirt, with the dog in his lap. The dog was dead. It had been shot. The old man cocked his head at the sound of my footsteps. "You've come back, Inspector, but too late. Look, here, my dog is dead, has been murdered by the bastards. I wish they had killed me, too."

"Are you alright?" I couldn't tell if we were being watched. The dog had been shot with a rifle from point-blank range. The shell casing was a few feet away. "Maybe we should go inside."

"No, I won't leave the dog, not till she's buried. There's a shovel beside the door. If you bring it around, I'll dig the grave myself." He put the dog's carcass gently on the ground and stood up. There was blood on his shirt, a lot of it. "This dog was all I had, Inspector. They knew that."

"I'll get the shovel."

After the dog was buried, the old man stood over the grave, his mouth moving but no sound coming out. I didn't say anything, just waited. After a while he stopped and turned to me. "There was an old monk that lived at the temple right after the war. No one bothered him. A couple of political types came up that first September and asked him a few questions. When they were leaving, they told me it was my job to watch him. It was funny and we all laughed. Setting a blind man to watch a monk. The monk died a few years later. He must have known it was coming. A few days before, he sat beside me and told me something I haven't forgotten. He was a small man, tiny hands, a light voice, like the wind in high trees."

I took the old man by the arm and led him to the steps of the temple. "I'm listening."

"The monk, he said the world is finite, and everything in it is limited. They all say that, but then he went on. Everything is rationed, you might say. Even pain. Endlessly recycled. Like atoms, and parts of atoms. The same atoms are here as were here when the world began, isn't that right? Might be some changes because of those atomic bombs, fusion or fission or something. But by and large, same atoms. Life comes and goes, but same atoms. This is not cycle-of-life fantasy, 'oh, we are all part of a Great Wheel.' Life isn't everything. Life isn't at the center of creation. No. No, it isn't. What are the elements of the universe but the parts of life, color, and sound, and taste, and so forth. Emotions, goodness, evil, melancholy, sadness. Love. All of it, limited, rationed, finite. Only so much of everything. These elements come in, how can I say, packets. You don't create red, red is outside of you, but then it strikes your eyes and goes inside, and you remember red. Same with blue, and so forth. Same with the smell of the mountains at dawn, and the wind against your skin in autumn, and the sound of the stars. Only so much of it out there, and it becomes you, over time, you absorb these and they are you and you are them. Emotions, too, you don't pull them out of nowhere, from nothing. They are part of creation, maybe that first instance in creation, all created, all formed, once and for all. Love and melancholy and hate and happiness. So when people were new, when the earth was new, there was a lot of it around. The sky was vivid blue, the wind was fresh, the meadows would knock you over with the smell of the grass and the flowers. Pools of sadness hung in the air, and if you walked through one of them, you could be sad for a week, but no matter because it was a pure sadness, pure white, sadly white if you know what I mean. And hatred was pure, and maybe it floated and maybe it didn't. I don't know. But I'll tell you this. The more people there are, the less of this there is for everyone. The world is duller and duller. Colors are dull. The seasons are dull. Pretty soon you can't tell one from another, pretty soon sadness and evil and melancholy and love are all gray, pounding gray lumps that enter you and sit in confused silence inside your heart so you don't know anymore what you are. But when you die, these things, they separate out again, they go back into the world in their pure form, little splinters and fragments of them, and some-one else gets them, and if they bathe in goodness, why, we rejoice and smile at the luck, but goodness is light and usually floats on the wind so no one gets much of it, less that than love, which dances across the empty spaces and so you only run into it by mistake, or by surprise."

2

After the old man finished, we sat side by side and didn't feel the need to say anything. A breeze blew against me, and I wondered if it was goodness, or love, or just the wind. Finally I stood up. I had a job to do, and I might as well get it done. "This temple, it's brand-new, isn't it? All reconstructed. You have a good reason you didn't tell me? I trusted you to tell me the truth."

"I told you what I could." The old man's fingers lightly touched the blood on his shirt. "I didn't want to say much with the foreigner hanging around. I told you it was rebuilt several times."

"You also told me you stumbled on the body, but how could you do that if it was floating in one of those pools?"

"I needed you to come back. The only way to be sure you would was to make up something that you knew couldn't be right. The truth waits, sometimes."

"When was the temple rebuilt?"

"Three months ago. It was in the dead of winter. They moved me out of here, told me to shut up, that it was some special decision and that if I said anything they'd send me off to a camp in the mountains. They said they'd send the dog to Pyongyang for foreigners to eat."

"When did they let you move back?"

"Two, three weeks ago. They said they'd put everything back and nobody would ever know the difference."

"Who's been here since then?"

The old man rubbed his chin. "They'll kill me if I tell you."

"If I can get to them, they won't be back. It's up to you."

"Just a minute." The old man stood up and went into his hut. When he came out, he was wearing a different shirt. "I'll have to burn the other one. Otherwise that dog's ghost will come back, looking for its blood. You ever heard a ghost howl in the dark, Inspector?"

"I can't say that I have. The living cause me enough trouble."

The old man laughed, bitterly. "Are you going to take notes? Or can you just remember?"

Chapter Four

The four-car caravan turned off the paved road onto a dirt track. The first car, a Mercedes with bad springs, carried the British visitor with his Foreign Ministry escort. In the next car, a fairly new Toyota with a right-hand drive, sat the two aides, an older woman who brayed when she laughed and a young man with a haunted expression and a long nose. The third car was mine. Boswell sat in angry silence beside me. He kept curling his right hand into a fist. Yang was in the backseat, staring out the window. The final car, a van, had the luggage and two extra MPS guards.

We came to a stop. Boswell brought his fist down on the dashboard. "This is the craziest security I've ever seen. The craziest. The target is in the lead car, unprotected. Are you trying to get him killed?"

"Your visitor was briefed about the plot this morning. He said he didn't believe it. His aides yawned; the woman said it looked like an effort to discredit him. We can't tell him to go home; the Foreign Ministry says it would cause an incident. So just in case, we've redoubled the guard at every site he's to visit. Anyway, who says he is unprotected? For all you know, the lead car has bulletproof glass. Just relax."

"Mary and Joseph in a stewpot, how can I relax?"

"We got past your buildings with the shadows, didn't we?"

"Where next?"

"I don't know."

Boswell snorted. "Don't be ridiculous. There are only so many places this dirt road can go. Don't tell me you don't know where that is."

The caravan started again, the lead car speeding ahead. Yang leaned forward. "There's a secure guesthouse up in the hills, about a fifteen-minute drive from here."

Boswell turned around and stared, as if information coming from the rear seat was unwelcome. "You mean he's not going to stay at the Koryo?"

"Would seem that way." Yang sat back in his seat again and looked out the window, ending the conversation. From his tone of voice, you'd think he was bored, but looking in the rearview mirror, I didn't think he was.

We hit a bump; Boswell bounced and hit his head against the roof. "Christ, every time we go anywhere that happens. Can't you people build roads? I thought this led to a VIP guesthouse."

"Who said it was for VIPs? All Yang said was it's secure, well protected."

"You can't bring a visitor someplace in the middle of nowhere, out of the blue." Boswell's Korean was starting to deteriorate. "You can't just dump a foreign official wherever you choose. No one does that. I haven't checked out this place."

The dirt road became paved again; we roared past one guard post, then another. Abruptly, the road became barely one lane. It climbed a steep hill in a series of switchbacks; there were no guardrails, not even any rocks painted white along the side, which dropped down a few hundred meters. "Slow down a bit." Boswell spoke carefully, not to jar my concentration.

"Relax, would you? I've driven roads like this much faster, at night, in the fog." I took my eyes off the road for a moment and looked at Boswell; he was gripping the dashboard. "You'll like it. We never build guesthouses where there are shadows."

Yang coughed. "Mind if I open my window?"

We went around another sharp bend, then the road became straight and broad. It passed through an open gate with sentries on either side. They weren't slouching. At the end of a long drive was a one-story building, surrounded on three sides by a high concrete fence, with broken glass cemented along the top, and barbed wire on top of that.

The first two cars were already parked and the visitor was walking with the driver and the Foreign Ministry escort to the front door when gunfire broke out. The driver dropped the two suitcases he was carrying and hit the ground, fumbling for the holster under his coat. Three more shots; one kicked up dust near the lead car's front tire, the other two shattered its windows on the driver's side. I braked and steered off the road onto the dirt. The Foreign Ministry official dropped to the ground and covered his head with his arms. Boswell cursed and fumbled with his door handle. He half fell out and scrambled toward the house. "Get fucking down, you idiots," he bellowed and looked wildly around to pinpoint the source of the shots.

The two aides started to get out of their car, but Boswell ran over and shoved them back inside. "Stay there, stay there, don't move, don't move a muscle." He crouched behind the second car, took a deep breath, then ran toward the house.

I turned to tell Yang to follow him while I circled around the back. He had a pistol in his hand. "What the hell is that?" It was the first thing that came to my mind, though I already knew the answer. It was a Russian Makarov.

Yang stopped, clicked off the safety, then looked at me. "Stay out of the way, O. Please." Another shot rang out, just as Boswell reached the visitor and pushed him onto the ground. I had no time to think. I threw myself at Yang, caught him on the shoulder, and we both fell off balance. His gun hand swung around and hit me on the side of the head. If I hadn't been so much off balance, maybe I could have kicked him in the chest. Instead, I fell down.

Two men stood over me. Jurgen and Dieter, or maybe the other way around. One of them said, "Oh, shit," in German and loaded a shell into a hunting rifle he held easily, the way some people hold a familiar book. He had a pen in his breast pocket. Yang put a hand on his shoulder. "Don't bother," he said. I didn't know the man could speak German; first the waitresses at the guesthouse, then Yang. Maybe he taught himself during all those night shifts. He switched to Korean. "I'll take care of him," he said, pointing at me. "Get the others and finish the job here."

The German with the rifle looked disappointed but nodded. "We'll see you later," he said curtly, in Korean that was better than Boswell's.

As I stood up, two men with their shirttails flapping hurried across the road toward the back of the guesthouse. Two others emerged from the luggage van and strolled into the woods without looking in my direction.

I turned to Yang. "Go on, get it over with."

"Nothing left to do, O. I've finished my part."

"You can't get very far, you realize that. They know all about it now."

"So what?"

"I'm disappointed."

"Don't be, O." There was an exchange of shots and then a shrill scream. Yang stiffened. "That's it, then. Time to go." He nodded to me and jogged off into the woods.

The two guards from the entry gate and another enlisted man came running up, waving their arms. "We heard shots and then saw people running." The first one pointed his pistol at the trees. "What is going on? We've radioed in an alert, but they said they need more details."

"Who told you to leave your post? One of you has to get back to the radio." They stared at each other dumbly. "Never mind, come with me. Just don't shoot at anything unless I tell you to." We edged up toward the guesthouse. The front door was open. When I eased myself inside, the two aides were crouched, white-faced and panting with fear, in the corner. Boswell was standing over the visitor, who was bleeding slightly from the upper arm. "He's been shot," Boswell said and turned away.

"Where's the driver? I'll tell him to get help." I looked around.

"Don't bother, he's dead."

The visitor raised his head and said tonelessly, "My arm."

Boswell motioned to me to walk outside with him. "Flesh wound. He'll be fine."

One of the aides, the woman, stood up. "We've got to get out of here. They may come back."

"You stick to arranging tea parties, I'll do security. No one is coming back. Sit down and don't say anything." Boswell didn't even try to hide his contempt.

I shouted at the guards to watch over the visitor, then followed Boswell out the door.

Boswell took in the scene in front of the guesthouse, then asked neutrally, "Where's your friend Yang?"

"With the others, I suppose."

"You suppose. Inspector, the man is rotten to the core."

"Maybe." I was thinking how he had stopped one of the Germans from blowing my head off.

"Can you call in and get help, or do you have to drive all the way back down to find a phone?"

"My phone is in the car. Who knows if it will work up here in the hills. The gate guards already issued an alert, but I doubt their communications unit will pass the word to someone who can do us any good. Maybe the lead car has a radio in it." The radio, under the seat, was so new that I knew the car wasn't one of the Ministry's. Probably SSD. That explained why I didn't recognize the dead driver. I didn't know any of the call signs or even who I was going to be talking to on the other end when a voice came up. "Identify yourself." There was a series of clicks.

"This is Inspector O, Ministry of People's Security."

"What the hell are you doing on this communications net?"

"Forget that. I need you to pass a message direct to MPS headquarters."

"Passing MPS messages is not my job. You have your own communications."

"Listen to me, you idiot. I'm on the security team for a British VIP who arrived yesterday. We're at Koko Two. Do you know where that is? There's been a shooting. One dead. One wounded."

"A shooting? Who is this?"

"I told you who it was. We need emergency medical help. We also need a big squad of reinforcements. Is this a State Security radio?"

"None of your business. I still don't know for sure who you are. Put on Lieutenant An."

I looked at the dead driver. "Does An have a mole on his lip?"

"Yeah. Put him on."

"He can't talk right now."

"Don't screw with me. Let me talk to An."

"Not easy to do. He's dead."

There was a crackle as the voice on the other end breathed into the microphone. "You killed An?"

"I'm telling you one more time. We need medical assistance and heavy reinforcements fast. Cordon off the Martyrs' Cemetery, that's where they're headed. You better move fast. I think the Capital Command may already have been notified. If they have, they'll lock down the city and you'll never get anyone up here."

A new voice came on. "O, is that you?"

"Han?"

"Where are you?"

"Koko Two. There's been an assassination attempt here, the British VIP is wounded, and your Lieutenant An is dead."

"How about your boy, Yang? Seen him around?"

I ignored him. "There are at least six of them. The two Germans are part of it."

"Hang on a second." He shouted at someone, then came back on. "Alright. There are sketchy reports of gunfire at the cemetery just coming in, I don't know from where. We already have people on the way to that temple up in the hills. Reports say there might be weapons there."

"There were. They're gone."

"Well." He paused. "What about the old man?"

"There's a group of assassins loose and you're worried about an old blind man? He's blind, Han. He's pathetic."

"Politics and blindness, Inspector." Han's voice was fading in and out. "I'm not qualified to judge. Wait, hang on again." There was more shouting, then Han came back on the radio. "Listen, the army has sent out patrols in your direction. I'll bet the soldiers are nervous as hell. Don't look at them cross-eyed, that's my advice. They're not supposed to go into the cemetery, though, just cordon it off. So get over there as quick as you can."

"What about the situation here at the VIP quarters?"

"What about it? Have someone close it off. Where are the other guards?"

"I think the term is 'melted away.' The gate sentries seem loyal."

"They better be. Leave them there. A truck with one of our squads should get there in about twenty minutes, if they can make it up that hill. You better get moving. You're closest to the cemetery. Get there."

"Front gate or back?"

"Show some initiative, Inspector. It's your call."

"What about Boswell?" The radio clicked and went silent.

2

By the time we got to the cemetery, there were already three SSD cars scattered on the grass and another car, with plates I didn't recognize, parked neatly behind a fence. A conference was going on under a tall, straight plane tree down the slope, next to the path that led toward busts of revolutionary martyrs. When Boswell and I ran over, the man in the brown suit was just folding a piece of paper into his coat pocket.

"We don't need either of you here, Inspector. You've caused enough trouble already."

Boswell broke in. "This was an assassination attempt against an official of Her Majesty's Government. A guest of yours, I might add. I'm not leaving until those involved are in custody and we can question them. That's firm, and that's final."

The man in the brown suit turned to Boswell and smiled patiently. There was nothing friendly in his face, however. Simply patience, the sort of patience that a skilled interrogator has in abundance, a bottomless pit of patience. "Her Majesty's Government has no authority, no writ, no nothing for as far as the eye can see, Mr. Boswell. Certainly not this side of Suez. You have even less standing, I would add." In a dark room, he would have paused to let the point sink in. "Go back to your hotel and stay there; do not stick your nose outside of your room. A car will come by to pick you up the morning of the flight. You don't want to miss that airplane, Mr. Boswell, believe me."

"I'll do no such thing."

The man in the brown suit shrugged. As he turned to one of the SSD officers, a shot rang out. All of us flattened ourselves on the grass, except for the man in the brown suit. He looked around calmly. "It came from over there"—he pointed to a slight hill to our left—"but it wasn't aimed our way." The sound of a machine pistol interrupted; two of the busts of martyrs fell to the ground fifteen meters away and rolled across the path into an azalea bush. "Whereas," said the man in the brown suit, "that was more or less in our neighborhood." He sat down heavily and stretched out his bad leg. "Splendid, they want to make a stand here." He took out a cigarette, put it to his lips, and let it dangle there. "Dumb bastards."

Boswell pulled his ample chin off the ground. "I need a weapon. Give me a revolver, anything."

"You need to get back to your hotel, Superintendent." The man in the brown suit was brushing the twigs off his jacket. "This isn't your fight. This isn't even your country. Stay the hell out of it." The SSD officers had drawn their service pistols and were hunched behind a stone marker. "You," the man in brown called to them, "don't sit around like goats. Spread out and get us some idea where those shots came from." He looked over at me. "Inspector, circle around back and see if you can figure out how many there are."

"There are six."

"Oh, really? And what are they wearing?"

"Blue trousers and tan shirts. Two of them have their shirttails flapping; those are the Kazakhs, I'd say. Two others were posing as MSS guards, looked like Koreans but I don't know. Their shirts are creased on the back, like they're brand-new. Good shoes, very smart dressers for assassins."

"The last two?"

Boswell broke in. "Those are the Germans. They're as slippery as you'll ever find. They'll get away if you don't close every exit, and I mean every possible exit." He reached over and lit the dangling cigarette.

Another machine pistol burst, and three more martyrs' busts rolled down the hill. The man in the brown suit sighed. "Arrogant bastard." It was not clear whether he meant Boswell or the shooter. "Not very far away, maybe two hundred meters," he said. "Okay, Superintendent, I'm giving you a weapon, and if you move one whisker off course, I'll have you shot, is that clear? The inspector will put three bullets in your back." He took a puff on the cigarette and exhaled carefully, not like a man in a national cemetery where a gunfight would get him nothing but a bad report in his file, no matter how it ended. "Stay close behind him, Inspector."

A single shot and the lead SSD officer fell to the ground. He didn't move. The other two sniffed at him like dogs who had found the moldy carcass of a cat. They looked back at us, fear on their faces. The man in the brown suit pointed at the body. "Leave him there.

Get on with it before they pick us all off one by one." He scanned the terrain. "That was not a handgun, not a machine pistol. One of them has a rifle and knows how to shoot. A hunter, maybe. Well, we'll see about that." Another single shot, a sharp crack, then a burst from the machine pistol that shredded the leaves on the tree and brought down a shower of twigs.

Boswell and I crawled off toward a little cover. "You go first, Superintendent, I'll watch."

He looked at me without expression. "You won't shoot me in the back?"

"Let's have this conversation another time." I gestured toward a statue that sat at the base of a small rise about twenty-five meters away. "Get to that and plop down. I'll be close behind." Without another word, he rolled over twice to the left, got onto his knees and looked around quickly, then sprinted to the statue. A shot rang out, and he fell forward just as he made it. I cursed, fired twice, then ran like hell.

Boswell was moaning when I flung myself behind the statue. "I'm not hit, but I think I broke my leg when I fell. I hate this fucking country, do you know that, Inspector?"

"You mentioned it once before."

"No, really, I hate it, this fucking country."

"Anything else?"

"My leg, I can't walk. What should we do?"

"It's your leg."

"I need a doctor."

"That could take days."

"Days? Why, in God's name?"

"Getting a visa, flying from England, that sort of thing."

"England? England? You have doctors here, surely."

"In this fucking country, you mean? We couldn't have you submit to our backwardness. It wouldn't do."

"Don't be getting droll on me, Inspector, not at a time like this. Call someone. You do have a phone on you?"

"I don't." That was true. The phone was still in the car. "Tell me, Boswell, what would the British Empire have done? In the old days, I mean. Gloriously wounded on the field of battle, the superintendent looks around for his subaltern, that is the word, isn't it? Out in the field, surrounded by wogs, that's what you called them. All those wogs, and one of your sturdy Scots legs, broken."

By now I could see Boswell was in pain. "I can't go back to the car just yet," I said. "There are still too many people roaming around with guns. You seem to be a target, why I can't imagine. Must be your size." Boswell looked like he might snarl but then uncurled his lip and turned his face away. I wasn't in a charitable mood at the moment. "Personally, I think there are more people out here than we imagine, and none of them are sure who they can trust. What about you, Superintendent, who do you trust?"

When Boswell turned back to me, he was sweating with pain. He moaned softly, took a breath, and turned pale. "I think I might be bleeding internally. Maybe the bone punctured an artery." He moaned again. "Did I tell you I hate this fucking country?"

"Yes."

"I do."

"I get your point." I crawled closer beside him and took his pulse. "It's racing, but it's plenty strong."

"All of a sudden, you're a doctor?"

"As long as we have nothing else to do, why don't you tell me what you know about all of this? Your visiting official, what's his name? I have a feeling you don't care that he was shot. In fact, I think you actually wanted him killed."

Boswell grimaced. It might have been a smile in other circumstances, though not a nice one. "Why would you say that?"

"You didn't want to cancel the visit."

"He's a bad man, Inspector, a very evil man. Immoral to the core of his soul." Boswell's face was getting gray; his skin looked clammy. "It actually wasn't in the planning, but at least if he was killed here, his death would accomplish something good."

"And that would be, what?"

"You already know what his death will trigger. You told me yourself."

"No, it won't happen here. Not on my watch. Not in my territory."

"It almost did, and that might have been enough. This isn't about you, Inspector, it's about something bigger. The future of your country. Your people's future."

"You have no idea what you're talking about, do you? You're just reciting some crap they handed you at a briefing. My country's future? Forgive me, Superintendent, I don't know anything that flourishes when it's watered with blood. Let's not float away on visions of the future. Your man, whoever he is and whatever he's done, is not my problem. Am I clear? If you have a bone to pick with him, take care of it yourself, on your own turf. What happens here is not yours to worry about. It's for us, it's our business, our future, our fate."

"Surely you don't believe that."

"Don't tell me what I believe. I live here, you don't."

"Thank God."

"Let me guess, Superintendent, this whole thing involves a sort of Western calculus, moral weights and measures. The sacrifice of one evil man is worthwhile if it is for the greater good, is that it?"

"You don't know this man, Inspector. He is disgusting. Everything he touches takes on a stench."

"Oh, bravo! I congratulate you on being so sensitive. You have the ability to separate the moral wheat from the immoral chaff. Who in your system makes this decision? Who decides how to add it all up? One evil man, led to his death, set up to be murdered in order to trigger the deaths of others—how many we cannot guess—in the expectation that it will lead to something good. Someday. Maybe."

"No one decided to have him killed, Inspector. If it were up to me, I'd say it was immaterial whether he died or not, what we call collateral damage. If he happened to step in front of a bullet—some of us thought that would be a bonus, but it wasn't crucial. All he got was a flesh wound anyway. It might be enough." Boswell stared at his leg.

"That bastard only gets a flesh wound, and I break my fucking leg in the middle of a fucking cemetery." He closed his eyes. "I may be out of options, Inspector, but so are you. This operation is already under way. You don't dare try to stop it. You don't have any idea who your friends are."

"Friends?" I laughed at the thought. "Under the circumstances, I think I still have one or two, and that's a hell of a lot more than you can be sure of. In fact, I'm the only friend you have in this place, at this moment, and I have orders to shoot you if the need arises. Look around. Believe me, you are completely naked, not to mention lame. Do you think you're going to hang around here for a few weeks while your leg heals? Let's say by mistake I tell one of your so-called friends about recent events, thinking by mistake he is actually a friend of mine. How will he react? Will he do anything to me? Not likely. Instead, he'll figure it is necessary to eliminate you, because you're the risk. Are you sure the plans ever really called for you to get out of here in one piece?"

"A bluff, Inspector, but unconvincing. I know enough to get me out of here safely, whereas you still don't even know the extent of what is going on."

"And you do? In my country? You think you know the difference between shadow and substance? Between bears and tigers and snakes?" I laughed again. Laugher was better at relieving tension than hitting someone, though I wanted to hit Boswell. "Tell me one thing, then I'll go for the phone."

Boswell propped himself up, with his back to the base of the statue. I could tell the effort cost him plenty. "What?"

"Scotch egg."

"Say that again?"

"Scotch egg, what is it?"

"Where did you hear that term?"

"If my face were as gray as yours right now, I wouldn't ask questions. I'd answer them. Don't you know?"

"Of course I know. You don't think I'm from Scotland, is that it?"

"One thing's for sure, you're not a member of the Scottish police, not the regular police, anyway."

"A Scotch egg is an egg covered with pork sausage."

"Disgusting."

Boswell smiled briefly. "There, Inspector, we agree." He winced suddenly, then moaned, and his head fell forward. When he looked up, his eyes weren't focusing. "Now find a phone, will you? This leg is bad. It isn't a simple fracture or I'd hobble out of here all the way back home."

"How did you plan it?"

"You said you'd get the phone if I answered your question. Do I have to beg for medical help? Is that how things work around here?" He closed his eyes. "I don't know anything about the plan, not in detail. I came in late. They gave me the hurry-up treatment, sort of like training someone for only one parachute jump—just enough to get out of the plane and onto the ground in one piece. One of my jobs was to keep you occupied. We heard from somewhere that you were involved, and Molloy said you'd be trouble, that you had to be neutralized. Nearly succeeded, didn't I?" His breathing was becoming labored.

"If you think so, Superintendent. Tell me, though. You must know something, even a scrap about the planning."

"Christ almighty. No, I don't. Not a thing. I can speculate, anyone can speculate. If I speculate, will that get me a doctor?" He licked his lips. "We needed help on the inside. Only two ways to get that. Commitment and money. The first came with the Germans. Old diehard revolutionaries; they convinced someone here, someone big in your leadership, that they opposed the changes in your system and would help to snuff them out. The incident with the British official would bring down the roof on change, that was their sales pitch."

"And money?"

"Easier. There are always people willing to supply money, especially if they think it will save souls."

"Good Christians?"

"In the name of the goodness, they will do plenty, Inspector."

"Why did you put me onto the Germans?"

"I didn't."

No, he was right, Miss Chon did. "But you wanted to make sure we could get them."

"They're half crazy, Inspector, too rabid for my taste. I see their type at home—different era, same lethal focus on the ideal. We all agreed, once the Germans did their job, they were expendable. They'll probably never leave this cemetery. That's the plan. I wanted them out of the way earlier. We could have avoided this sort of a blowup at the end."

"Maybe that's why they're shooting at you, they just caught on." I got up on one knee and looked around. No one shot at me. "The old man at the temple showed me how the place had been rebuilt over an underground room for a meeting place. Three rifles still packed in shipping crates. A bag of euros, small bills, mostly. And two pairs of stockings. He said a young woman had been there."

Boswell groaned and grabbed his leg. "None of that interests me, Inspector."

"I couldn't tell whether it was the bank clerk or Miss Chon. He said she was speaking in a foreign language. It might have been German, but the old man didn't know for sure."

"Miss Chon doesn't know German, I'm sure of that."

"Well, what does she know?"

"You haven't figured her out, have you? She's working for the Russians, as far as I can tell. Very simple work. Make sure loans get funneled to Koreans who want to do business with Russian companies. Try to keep up with the Chinese. Establish some contacts for later."

"Why would she work for them?"

Boswell licked his lips. "Why do you think, Inspector? They went to the Kazakh government and told them to find out what would make her sign on. It wasn't hard."

"Her son."

He shrugged. "She told you? That means she wants you to help her."

"Do what?"

Boswell shook his head. "There seems to be a lull in the action. Why don't you do something besides sit and talk?"

"Alright, I'll go for the phone. If there's no more shooting, I'll be back in around five minutes, maybe ten."

"Stay down. Dieter is a good shot with that hunting rifle."

"Well, we know he can hit a dog at point-blank range. What's the pen in his pocket?"

"Don't try to write with it. It's explosive, so he won't be captured. Pulls the cap and bang! It's supposed to blow his head off."

"Hell of an operation," I said. "Sounds like one of ours."

3

I ran back, keeping as low as I could. "Found the phone, Superintendent." Boswell was sitting up, facing the statue. He started wheezing just as he pitched forward. I turned him over. His right hand was shattered where he'd tried to block a bullet. There was a hole in his throat, and another in his cheek, just under the eye. He blinked at me and moved his good hand, so I thought he might have a chance, but then he shuddered and was still. None of the wounds was big; they were from a small-caliber pistol. There was the pop of a shot off to my left. It seemed far away, but in these hills, you couldn't be sure.

I moved off in the direction of the sound, rested against a stunted tree for a moment while the sweat poured off my face, then scrambled across an open area to the top of a small rise covered with azalea bushes. I poked my head around the side. At the bottom of the opposite slope, I could see someone sunning himself, his shirt off. It seemed odd, under the circumstances.

I stood up and walked slowly down the hill, a stupid target, a stupid way to come down a hill on this spring day, the sky too high, the light too crisp, a breeze so slight that it barely rustled Yang's hair. He lay on his back, one arm stretched away from his body, the other flung across his chest. He had shot himself in the heart, not an easy thing to do, but I had no doubt it was important for him, to aim at what he thought he had long ago lost. He had held the pistol close, there were powder marks, but still visible was the small tattoo over his heart, an aiming point he'd paid to have burned into his skin so he would not miss when the time came.

I knew that whatever had been in him, all color, all experience, everything from a lifetime of pain, was drifting out, bit by bit, even through that tiny hole in his chest. If there was any laughter, it had left long ago. I picked up the pistol he had dropped and put it in my belt. The sound of children's voices floated upward. He'd held those until the end, and now they were free.

4

When I walked back to the top of the hill, the man in the brown suit was waiting, looking down at Yang's body. "Let him be," he said. "He did us a favor, killing the Scotsman. I knew you wouldn't do it. Though you should have, Inspector, it was your job."

"My job? My job was solving the robbery. I almost did it, too."

"Forget the robbery, Inspector. In fact, forget this whole thing."

"Sure, forgetting is good." I thought of Miss Chon. "A good habit, forgetting. But first I need to know a few details. Gives me more to forget, if that makes any sense. I think it does to you."

"I owe you nothing, Inspector. But go ahead."

"Who does Han work for?"

This made the man in brown smile. "Believe it or not, Inspector, I don't really know. He doesn't work for me. Beyond that, it was something I had on my list of things to find out. That's why no one else is going to know about Yang's death, or Boswell's, no one but us for a couple of days. I want to see who scrambles around, trying to find them. No one is to know, not even SSD."

"Han is SSD?"

"Very unlikely. He's too clever, in his own way. He's just attached to them for the moment."

I nodded. "What about the special group, the ones with new shirts?"

"Might be connected to the army, might not. This much I know, they did a better job dressing them than training them. The group wasn't as efficient as someone hoped. Apparently, it was formed to support the overall operation, and to tag people that needed to be eliminated at some point."

"You know who's on the list?"

"Better not to know, Inspector. Those sorts of lists are always upsetting."

"Can I give you a theory? The bank robbery was just a diversion."

"Nice theory, but wrong. They were serious about the robbery; at first they thought it would be enough, but then they got worried and decided to add a layer. Layers are always bad. They knew someone on the outside was playing, but they thought they had control of the whole operation. You, as it turned out, were a complicating factor."

"Not by choice."

"They knew you'd hang on, even if you said you wanted to dump the case. You are one hell of a problem, Inspector, for everyone."

"I'm the one who tipped you off, remember?"

"We must have been at different sessions. You weren't very helpful at all. You spent most of the time sparring with me, although the information you passed on about the temple having been rebuilt recently turned out to be useful. My people suspected you were in the middle of it. No one could believe you kept drifting into our sights like you did."

I remembered that afternoon when I had the sense that I was someone's prey. "You had people on me all the time?"

"Now and then. After you drove the Scotsman around the city, the concern spiked. And when the door to his room at the Koryo closed with you inside, it was almost decided to pack you off to the mountains."

"But someone objected."

"Someone did."

There wasn't much sense in saying thank you again, so I didn't.

"Now I have a question, Inspector. He mentioned Prague to you?"

"I don't think he said anything, no." On the hilltop, looking at Yang's body, it didn't seem like a good idea, discussing Prague.

The man in the brown suit nodded. "If you say so." Not that he believed me for a moment.

"You knew Boswell?"

"Me?" He smiled. "Until he showed up here, I never met the man. He wasn't a policeman, though I know you eventually realized that. Based on how he went about his business, it looks like he had other connections. He acted more like an internal operative than he did someone who was used to being overseas. Of course, I'll never know for sure." The man in the brown suit laughed. "I rarely know anything for sure. You impress me as someone who doesn't suffer from that same fate, Inspector."

"That's a relief."

"Let me rephrase my question. Did Boswell say anything to you before he died?"

"No."

The man in the brown suit looked at me. "You two were up there for quite a few minutes. You must have talked about something."

"We did. Scotch eggs."

He thought about this for a moment. "You realize, they decided to neutralize you. That's why they let it be known you'd been talking to someone named Molloy, thinking you'd run into their arms."

I figured it was time to change the subject. "Why were you on the train, staring at me that day?"

"I wasn't staring, Inspector. I was just observing, quietly."

"That's not what I asked."

"No, it isn't, is it? Let's just say, I'd already heard something about Prague, and I needed to get a sense of who you were. The question was starting to gnaw at me, what would happen when those same rumors reached you. I wasn't sure; after I raised it during our"—he paused—"our session, either you would get mad at me, or you would get mad at them. I bet on the latter."

"Am I so predictable?" The breeze had died, and the sun was hot. It occurred to me that spring never lasted as long as I hoped. "I'm just an insect in one of those webs?"

"Even insects fly off in strange directions. No, that's why it was a bet, and all I could bet was that your grandfather's blood runs in your veins."

"My grandfather?" I looked over at the rows of graves on the hillside. "I thought you said we should let the dead rest in peace."

"We've just had a shootout in a cemetery, Inspector. I don't think anyone is sleeping soundly."

"One or two more questions. Do you mind?"

"We're on the top of a hill with no one around, no one that can still hear us, anyway. We both live by asking questions, Inspector, go ahead."

"What if I ask you about silk stockings?"

"The Russian." There was no hesitation. "He works part-time for SSD; the rest of the time he works against them. I don't worry much about him, as long as I know where he is. I've never heard a single piece of information that came from him that could be trusted."

I looked down at Yang. The man in the brown suit took off his jacket and hung it neatly over his arm. "What about Pang?"

The man in brown paused. "He didn't want to come back in. He said he'd done enough already. But he couldn't resist women with small waists." So, Pang worked for him, and he didn't care if I drew the conclusion about who had broken Pang's cover.

"And Miss Chon? She seems to be in the center of a lot of this. If you drew one of your spiderwebs, she'd be the spider in the center. Though that wasn't the way it was on the chart you showed me." I didn't believe Boswell's story about her working for the Russians, channeling money. She was too complicated for something that simple. No one would waste her talents on that.

The man in brown turned abruptly and led the way back to the cars. When we got there, he put his hand on my right shoulder. "I'd say that it's over, Inspector, except it never happened."

5

The next morning, Han was sitting in the office; Min was looking out the window. Neither spoke, and from the way the air was not moving, they hadn't said much in the last several minutes. Han looked exhausted, like he had been up all night. When Min turned around, he had a bandage on his forehead.

"What happened to you?" I waited at the door.

"Don't stand there, Inspector. Come in and sit down." Min put his hand to his head. "No one believes it, but I fainted. About three o'clock this morning, I finally got home and opened the door. Next thing I knew, I was on the floor. Not fainted, exactly. I'd say it was more like I collapsed, keeled over." He paused and waited.

"Swooned." Han shrugged. "In the middle of the biggest damned incident of the century, your chief inspector fell over. Don't worry, I won't tell anyone." He stood up and straightened his cuffs. His shirt was clean, fresher than he was. "Someone might think you did good work on this one, Inspector. I don't. So I'll tell you what. Say something nice about me in your report, I'll do likewise. Of course, they're going to come down hard on you about Yang, but that will be for your ministry to deal with. There are enough problems to go around."

I wasn't in the mood to be threatened, not by Han. "What report? I'm not writing anything. You were in the lead, Han. That means you get to explain all the shot-up trees in the cemetery, and why nobody can find two Germans, one of whom has a hunting rifle and is an excellent shot. You took over the investigation, you deal with it. I suppose your report will include something on the bank manager. Like who she really is. Or did she work for you?"

Han shook his head slowly. "That woman came out of nowhere.

And she's protected, I don't know by whom. You were right, she doesn't have a file, or if she does, whoever has it is keeping it out of sight."

"No one comes out of nowhere, Han. What about the clerk, for example? She came from somewhere. Who approved her for the bank? She didn't just walk in the front door and ask for a job. Something's missing from her file, incidentally. She was inside for the bank robbery, wasn't she?"

"Her?" Han put on his sunglasses. "No, she was working for us the whole time. At least we got that much right."

"That's what you'll put in your report, I suppose. Actually, did you know she was working for Boswell?"

"For Boswell? Very unlikely. In fact, impossible." Though he didn't seem completely sure. "What makes you think that?"

I hadn't liked Han from the beginning, and I didn't like him now, especially because I still didn't know who he was working for. "Boswell was part of whoever it was on the outside that planned the bank robbery, which you probably knew. He was well acquainted with the Germans, which you might have known. And he was here to supervise the assassination attempt, at least make sure the final steps came off smoothly, which you may have guessed. You were supposed to disrupt the plan, watch it as it developed, and then disrupt it at the end, the very end. I was just along to give you an excuse to stay close. Yang was the bait; he was supposed to get as many wolves after him as possible. The man was so confused, he was willing to do it. You must have made sure Yang was at the scene, at the guesthouse, because Boswell didn't. In fact, Boswell was unhappy Yang was in the car; he was suspicious about who Yang was working for."

Han sat down and took off his glasses. "What does that have to do with the bank clerk?"

"The clerk was seen with the Germans in the hills, at that temple. I don't think she was there to make a donation."

"The old man has disappeared. We need to talk to him."

"You need to talk to a lot of people, especially Boswell, but he's dead, and so is Yang." The man in brown wouldn't be happy I told Han. Not that I cared.

Han seemed to relax. "Well, well." He stood up again and walked to the door. "Remember that desk, the one in the bank? You were right, it was pine on the outside. But inside it was something else."

"Like what?"

"Something hard, sort of pretty. Rare, maybe. The desk was rebuilt so it could handle special equipment. All new."

"SSD?"

"Don't make me laugh. Since when does SSD know how to handle special equipment? They can't even deal with their own phones."

"What about the wood? You mind if I take a look?"

"I don't mind, but I don't think it will do you any good. After we took the desk apart, I told them to burn it." He smiled, then turned to go. "I never fixed your cell phone, did I, Inspector. Sorry, it looks like you're stuck with it." He fluttered his hands delicately. "Oh, and one more thing. Yang and the bank clerk were related, did you know that? She was his niece. Her aunt died in that fire."

Min put his head in his hands.

6

I overslept and had to drive fast to the airport. Whether she was in the middle of everything that had happened or just wandered in, I still didn't know. Pang, the man with the shoulders, might have figured it out; maybe that's why he ended up floating in the river. Dead men didn't seem to upset her; she hadn't seemed upset when I told her that Boswell had died in the cemetery.

"It may seem cruel, Inspector, but I discovered a long time ago that he was evil, in his own way. I vowed I would never forgive him, and I never will. Anyway, that's what cemeteries are for, isn't it, dead bodies?" She was tidying up papers at the bank, shredding some documents, putting others in stacks on a desk. "They took away that other desk again. I can't work when the furniture keeps disappearing, but that's not the point. You see, Inspector, I've decided this banking business isn't what I want to do." She gave me a rueful smile, only I could tell it wasn't rue that was driving her thoughts.

"You need any help, tidying up?"

"Thank you, I can handle it." She gave me another smile, this one a little more positive, but she still didn't put everything she had into it. She was concentrating on the shredding. "I've realized this isn't my future, not here."

"You're leaving?"

"On tomorrow's plane."

I considered this. "You need a ride to the airport? I could swing by and pick you up."

"That's kind of you, but it's all arranged. Too bad we didn't have a chance to get to know each other better, Inspector." This time there was no smile. "I was hoping we would. I had the feeling you were interesting, somehow. When you agreed to come to my apartment, I thought we would comfort each other." She looked away.

"Me?" I felt combustible all of a sudden. Then the image of Pang's body floated into my mind. She was down to one pile of papers. I didn't think she should be shredding anything; on the other hand, Min had told me that we had been ordered to stay away from the bank, which meant I had no jurisdiction here.

7

"SSD has completely taken over the case, Inspector," Min had said before I drove to the bank to see Miss Chon. "What's left of it. The good part is that the whole thing is such a mess, the Minister was glad to let it go." He got up and started to pace. I'd never seen him do that in his own office.

"There's a bad part?" I thought that on the truck up to the mountains, I'd prefer to stand and have the wind on my face, if that was possible. Min wouldn't care; he probably wouldn't speak for the whole trip.

"The bad part is, this goes on SSD's tally for cases solved."

"I thought there wouldn't be any record at all. They didn't solve anything."

"Neither did you."

I looked out the window at the gingko trees. Their branches were brushing against the side of the Operations Building in the breeze. Then again, perhaps it would be better to sit in the back of the truck.

"Okay, I stay away from the bank," I said to be agreeable. Nothing ever changed. This had been a case we never should have touched; now the only trace of it would be an inflated number in SSD's annual report. The details wouldn't be in the files, except on some piece of paper with a vaguely worded entry justifying extra expenses to clean up the cemetery. Not my problem. I turned to walk out the door. "I've got other places to visit. There's a new club in my sector, I'm told."

When I came through the entrance of the terminal building, I heard the announcement for passengers to proceed to immigration. I ran up the stairs into the waiting hall. She wasn't there, not in the restaurant, not at the counter buying a last-minute souvenir. I forced myself to relax and began a careful survey, sweeping the room degree by degree. I spotted her talking to a foreigner, a tall man, laughing and resting his hand lightly on her arm. They moved easily into the line to go through the final document check. At the last minute, she turned and looked straight at me, as if she knew where I had been the whole time. She didn't change expression; she may have nodded slightly, unless that was my imagination.

I wanted to walk over to her, to say good-bye; instead, I turned away. Standing across the room, in front of the big window overlooking the tarmac, was a man wearing a brown cloth cap. Somehow, it wasn't a surprise. The man ignored me but watched Miss Chon closely, with a faraway smile on his lips. A burst of laughter rose above announcements and the talking and the farewells. The Italian group was going through the line. The cape-man hung back; he hugged a Korean woman and kissed her on both cheeks. It must have been their guide. She waved sadly until they were out of sight. Nothing to do with her or them, just an ancient bond between the traveler and the one left behind. I wondered why Miss Chon hadn't waved, or was I the one who should have? When I looked back at the window, the man in the brown cap was gone.

I waited until all the passengers were loaded onto the bus, then showed my ID to a girl in a blue uniform and pushed my way past to the door that led out to the planes. The bus had just pulled up to the only aircraft with any activity around it—a fuel truck, a black sedan, a few officials standing under the wings with big hats and walkie-talkies. The passengers climbed the stairs; two or three turned for a last look before disappearing inside. The doors closed; the plane rolled slowly down the long taxiway, turned the corner, and was out of sight. A minute later, there was a far-off rumble of the engines. As it rose above the trees, I spotted the plane in the distance, climbing into the sky. It banked away to the west; the sun flashed against the wings. I stood and watched for a long time, longer than necessary, long past the point there was anything left to see.